Zara Stoneley is the *USA Today*-bestselling author of *The Wedding Date*.

She lives in a Cheshire village with her family, a lively cockapoo called Harry, and a very bossy (and slightly evil) cat called Saffron.

Zara's bestselling novels include *The First Date*, *Four Christmases and a Secret*, *No One Cancels Christmas*, *The Wedding Date*, *The Holiday Swap*, *Summer with the Country Village Vet* and the popular Tippermere series.

www.zarastoneley.com

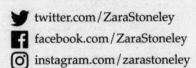

twitter.com/ZaraStoneley
facebook.com/ZaraStoneley
instagram.com/zarastoneley

THE DOG SITTER

ZARA STONELEY

One More Chapter
a division of HarperCollins*Publishers*
1 London Bridge Street
London SE1 9GF
www.harpercollins.co.uk

HarperCollins*Publishers*
1st Floor, Watermarque Building, Ringsend Road
Dublin 4, Ireland

This paperback edition 2021

2

First published in Great Britain in ebook format
by HarperCollins*Publishers* 2020

A catalogue record of this book is available from the British Library

ISBN: 978-0-00-843624-7

Printed and bound in Great Britain by
CPI Group (UK) Ltd, Croydon CR0 4YY

For Heather, every dog's best friend!

Chapter One

'Where on earth are you?' Georgina sounds stressed; she's got that high-pitched edge to her voice that suggests the next stop is hysteria. It's nothing compared to how I feel. If she thinks waiting for me is stressful, then she should be in this bloody car. 'It's after 2 p.m.!'

Yeah, right. Don't I know it. I'm hot, bothered, tired, sweaty and need a wee. I should have arrived at Georgina's place hours ago, not still be stuck in an over-heated, stuffy and smelly car.

This has to be my worst nightmare. Well, next to worst. I can't ignore the Teddy incident.

It's amazing what crazy ideas you come up with when you're stressed, depressed and feel like your life is crap, isn't it?

I must have completely lost my marbles, why did I think this would be a good idea? Relaxing? Inspiring? Hahaha!

Also, why did I believe my satnav and think I'd have a chilled drive and arrive with *bags* of time to spare?

In my dreams I should now be sitting on the terrace, sipping a gin and tonic as I look out at the magnificent view that my temporary home has to offer, and considering myself very lucky.

'I know, I know, I'm really sorry, I'm nearly there. I think.' I mutter the last two words under my breath and hope she doesn't hear.

For the last fifteen or so minutes (it feels more like hours) I have been following a dirty old cattle lorry, which is spurting liquid out every time it goes around a bend in the road. There have been lots of bends. I have a horrible feeling it is liquid manure. I have been behind it for miles. Lots of miles.

'Well, I've got t—'

'Oh my God! Shit, shit, shit!'

'Becky, Becky? What's happened?'

I can't answer. I'm too busy waving my arms around, hanging on to the steering wheel and trying to get rid of whatever has just come through the open window.

Something disgusting has landed on my face, on my lips. I think some of it has gone in my open mouth. I mustn't swallow, I must not close my mouth. I need to stop talking.

'Becky! Are you still there?'

Oh hell, I'm going to dribble, my mouth is full of saliva. I mustn't dribble down my brand-new jeans.

I need to stop or spit out of the window.

Oh bugger. I need to do something quick! I brush the back of my hand over my open mouth, then swipe it across my cheek. 'Yes, sure. Still here.' Oh my God. I stare at my hand in horror, then try not to. I need to watch the road. But my hand is green, it's slimy. I'm going to retch. 'Oh my God, this is disgusting. It's cow shit.' Don't wipe it down your leg Becky, do NOT wipe it on your jeans.

I'd been doing fine until Georgina distracted me and made me forget about keeping my distance. Bloody hell, the countryside is stinky. Never have I needed wet wipes more. Or the loo. I really need the loo. Why didn't I stop at the last services on the motorway?

'Cow shit? Where?' She sounds confused.

'On my hand, my…' eurgh, this is stomach-churning, '… face.' Nightmare. I need a pee and I need disinfectant.

There is a long silence. She's probably wondering exactly what kind of weirdo she's entrusted her home and dog to.

'Came through the window.'

'What?'

'Wi—ow.' I'm talking awkwardly through a slightly open mouth with my tongue out. I daren't shut it properly, who knows what lingers in there? I lick the palm (shit-free side) of my hand. It looks clean. Phew. I take a sniff. It smells clean. I do another lick to be sure.

This is good. Maybe it's not as bad as…

Oh Christ, it's on my steering wheel! And my dashboard!

There's a honk of a horn which makes me realise it's not a good idea to let go of the wheel. I swerve back into my lane, then glance into my rear-view mirror ready to give an apologetic wave.

Eurgh, it's on my nose. I'm sure I can see some on my

nose. I lean in as close as I dare to the mirror and nearly run into the back of the lorry. 'I've got to stop.' I stick my tongue out as far as it will go and try to look at it in the rear-view mirror while still keeping an eye on the road.

I think it's clean, but I daren't swallow, just in case.

This is worse than spotting a giant spider in the car when you're driving at seventy miles an hour on the motorway and can't just bale out. 'Oh no, it's on my T-shirt, this is one of my best, oh bugger,' I say through the bubbles of saliva in my mouth. I feel like crying. 'Does it stain?' Of course it stains. I'm sure it stains. Horribly. And never comes out.

'You can't stop, Becky! You've got to get here. You promised you'd be here before I have to leave for the airport! Shut your window!' Georgina shouts as though this will solve everything.

'I will be there!' Oh FFS, if she'd shut up things would be a lot easier.

I have to calm down, she has to calm down. Deep breaths. But not the type where you inhale the stinky air. Or swallow anything unmentionable that might still be in your mouth.

Okay, I will be calm, I will explain. 'I had to open my window, my aircon is blowing out hot air!' I try blowing out like they tell you to when you're giving birth. Not that I've ever given birth, but it's on TV a lot. It works. Always.

It is not working. I'm going to scream at her in a minute.

'Well, if you're not here soon I'll have to leave the key next door,' Georgina hisses, which doesn't help my calmness. 'I've got a bloody plane to catch!'

4

Smile. If you smile when you talk you sound happy. Unless your teeth are clenched. 'Fine.' I don't think I sound happy. There is silence on the other end. I think she's hung up. This house-sitting lark has not got off to a good start. Maybe the Lake District isn't the answer to my problems.

The phone rings again, and I reluctantly answer. 'Sorry about that, I'm stressed.' Her voice is tight. 'I wanted to show you stuff, there's things I wanted to explain, right?' There is a distinct whine to her voice that I didn't notice when I spoke to her the other day. Then, she sounded completely confident about everything.

Maybe she's scared of flying and the thought is stressing her out. Or she's just worried about her house and pet sitter. Totally understandable.

'Sure.' I try to stop looking at the sludge-coloured stains and sound understanding. 'I should be there soon; my satnav says twenty minutes?' Hah, my satnav has proved to be *way* too optimistic about this journey.

She can't change her mind though? Surely it's too late?

I think this is half the problem: right now, we're both wondering if we've done the right thing, but neither of us really have a choice.

It is too late.

My own house-sitter will already be rifling through my cupboards saying, 'WTF do you do with this?' (I like kitchen gadgets – you know those bits of plastic you see advertised that you can't resist, then two weeks later can't remember what they do?) then be settling down in front of my TV – so I don't have a home to go back to. And Georgina has a plane to catch. She needs somebody to look after her house and her dog. She can't pull out. Neither of us can. 'I'm so sorry, but I'm honestly going as fast as I can.'

She sighs. 'This is so bloody inconvenient; I'll have to write a note for you in case you don't get here in time!'

'I'm sure I will, I did set off ages ago, I've been up since 5 a.m.' I have. There just weren't enough hours in the day yesterday to do everything (including work) plus to clean and tidy my flat, and pack, so I was up early.

'Really?' Georgina sounds disinterested.

Drinking at this time might be something some people would disapprove of, but boy could I do with a stiff gin and tonic right now. Why didn't I pack a cooler box?

Except I am driving, so that would be totally unacceptable.

Honestly though, when Georgina had said she needed a house-sitter 'urgently' she'd meant it. Within a couple of hours of my saying I was interested, she'd checked over the references that are on the house-sitting website, sent me the postcode and told me which route to ignore on the satnav. Not only that, but she'd demanded I be there by 3 p.m. the day after tomorrow as she'd got a plane to catch, or the deal was off. She didn't mention any hazardous bio-waste that I might encounter en route.

Anyway, I wanted the deal to be on. I really wanted it to be on. I needed it to be on. This was the first thing I'd done just for me, without having to ask anybody else's opinion – for ages. It had to be right, I had to believe it would be.

I had to believe that this would 'fill my creative well' and make me feel better about life.

I needed to escape from my current reality for a while.

So, I said 'great'.

———————————

Things have not been going well for a while.

You know when you finally think 'hey, I've got life sussed', then find out you've been kidding yourself completely? That.

Just before Christmas I had a reality check. I found out that my life wasn't the life I thought it was.

Like you do when your bastard boyfriend sacks you then dumps you.

Or was it the other way around?

Anyway, unimportant, I mean, what the actual fuck?

Being sacked would have been a big enough slap in the face at any time, but when it's your boyfriend doing it, and then he follows up with 'and I don't think our relationship is working either', it's a double whammy. Apparently, demanding explanations is completely unsexy. A turn-off. Talk about kicking a girl when she's down.

What kind of boyfriend tells you your work sucks after you've spent the last six months compromising and not doing the type of stuff you really want to do because he says full-on supportive shit like *this is where it's at* and *trust me, I know exactly what you need to do* and *you might not be top-notch yet, but I can help even a novice like you get some brilliant commissions*?

The kind of boyfriend that your family try to warn you off. That's what kind.

The sort that you know your sister Abby calls a

dickhead under her breath when she thinks you can't hear, the sort that makes your mate ask you why you listen to him, and the sort that your mum tells you to get away from.

I knew better. They just didn't understand him. I knew that they'd warm to him. I told them he was lovely.

I took his side because I knew he was trying to help me. He knew what he was talking about and they didn't. When he told me that the work I was doing wasn't brilliant he wasn't being nasty or unsupportive, he was being the opposite. It was constructive criticism. He was helping me.

I mean, I knew him, didn't I? I loved him. I knew he was not at all self-centred, egotistical or controlling. Definitely.

Arghhh. Why does your mother always have to be right?

Anyway, the whole Teddy fiasco hit back in December. What is worse was that January, February, March and April have passed me by and nothing has changed for the better. I have been stuck in a rut. A deep, dirty, unproductive, self-destructive rut.

So, when Mum rang the other day and said yet again, 'You do sound a bit out of sorts, darling. You need a break!', my automatic response might have been, 'I've got a deadline, I can't just drop everything!' but I realised she had a point. It was nearly the end of May and I needed to get a grip.

I'd woken up that morning with this feeling of dread. You know, this hollow, empty feeling inside where you don't want to get up and face *yet another day*. Then I'd dragged myself to my desk with a coffee and just stared into space for a while with absolutely no sense of excitement. Which isn't the normal me at all, I've always loved my job as a book cover designer and illustrator – that's why I do it.

I also used to quite enjoy life.

Until Teddy burst my bubble and told me that my work had moved from 'mediocre' to 'lost cause'.

'Nonsense, Becky.' Mum could be persistent. 'Nobody is indispensable. I mean, even Abby has time off!' Even Abby, fancy that.

I'd been avoiding talking to Mum a bit, if I'm honest. And Abby. And Dad, and my brother Daniel. Well, we'd stopped chatting as much because I just knew they didn't approve of Teddy. Then when we split, it was just added pressure.

I mean, how could I compete with my brother and sister, who never put a foot wrong and were all sorted – like you should be at my age.

'Did you know Abby and Ed came around at the weekend to celebrate going out together for three years? Three years! Goodness, doesn't time fly?'

I didn't know. I'd stopped joining in with the family Sunday lunches after Teddy was rude about the 'supermarket wine' and Dad called the 'experimental and innovative' cover design Teddy wanted me to do, 'a bit weird' and asked why I wasn't painting animals anymore like I always said I wanted to. I tried to explain I'd grown up, and needed to be more commercial, Teddy kept saying 'Really? How chocolate box!' and laughing (he likes 'cutting edge' not cuddly), and it all became so bloody awkward and embarrassing that it was easier to take a step back.

Anyhow, back to that conversation with my mother.

'Wow, really Mum? Three years?'

'Yes, three years! Oops, sorry darling, didn't mean to sound insensitive. No new man on your horizon yet?' There was a hopeful lift of her voice at the end of the sentence.

'I told you, I'm not looking, Mum. I don't need a man to make me complete.' Maybe to put up a few shelves because I don't own an electric drill and would rather spend the money on practically anything else, but that's it. And maybe to scratch that itch between my shoulder blades, but that's what chopsticks are for isn't it?

'Ah, never mind, you'll find somebody! You're not seeing Teddy again?'

'No, Mum.'

'Oh.' There was a long pause. 'Good, as long as you're not just hanging on to see if he comes back.'

'Mum!' Oh my God, had she any idea what he did to me? Oh, no, she hadn't. I haven't told anybody that bit yet. Just the 'we split up' line. Which is acceptable, and way less embarrassing than in effect sticking an 'I'm a complete failure' banner across my forehead.

'I just don't want you to waste your life, Becky. Isn't it time you got another boyfriend then? I mean, it's been ages! How long is it now? Three months, four months? You shouldn't let a silly man like Teddy undermine your confidence.'

Easier said than done.

'I'm quite happy on my own, thanks. I think I'll get a dog.' I said it tongue in cheek. I'd actually love a dog, but there's a strict 'no pets' clause in my letting contract and the landlord is such a stickler I'm pretty sure he'd throw me out if I had a goldfish, let alone a dog. And right now, I can't exactly afford the deposit on a better flat, let alone buy a place.

'You should, much less trouble. Until they die of course, that bit is horrible. And they do, do you remember when we lost Dash?' We took a moment. I had to take a day off school when our Labrador died of old age. I'd insisted we had a full burial service in the garden. Dad did his back in digging the hole (you have no idea how big a hole was needed – though it could have been worse, it could have been a Great Dane), spent three days in bed, and never let us forget it. 'I always wonder how different life would have been if I'd had a dog at the start instead of your dad!'

There was no short answer to that.

It stumped us both conversation wise, so we settled for 'talk soon, love you, bye'.

I put my mobile down and stared at it. Then it flashed, with a text.

Write a list, that might help. You always liked your lists!
Mum xx

Mum was right. She usually is. Not about the Dad bit, though thinking about it, my life would have been quite a bit different if I'd gone for a puppy instead of Teddy, wouldn't it?

She was right about the other things though: needing a break and needing a list. And maybe about the dog thing as well. Dogs don't answer back, ask awkward questions or judge.

The whole thing was doing my head in. It was all wearing me down and sapping my creativity. This having-people-worry and having to put on my bright and sunny 'I'm fine, don't worry about me' smile.

So I wrote a list.

1. I need to escape from everybody. Including Teddy because seeing Teddy makes me feel that everything I'm doing is a bit shit, which isn't much of a motivator.
2. I need a distraction and inspiration, because otherwise all I can think about is Teddy saying my stuff is shit.
3. I do still have lots of (non-Teddy) work lined up, but I don't have to be here, in this flat, to do it. I can work from anywhere with a good internet connection. And if I'm not here it might be easier to concentrate.
4. I have some work that is urgent, but it's bloody hard when you are so angry you keep accidentally drawing fangs on the cute bunnies, and shading things in black. Very black.
5. I want a dog, not a man.
6. I currently hate being here in my lovely flat because it reminds me of the work I did for Teddy. I just can't concentrate.
7. I need to not be here (see all points above).

So, basically what I really needed was some space, some peace and quiet, some distance, no Teddy, and possibly a dog.

Simples.

I sat back and stared at my list. Actually, it *was* simple. I had been a moron. It was bloody obvious, wasn't it? I needed to do what I used to do before I met Teddy – house-sit. I mean, wasn't that part of the reason I'd gone freelance? So I had the freedom to work when I wanted, *where* I wanted?

Until I'd hooked up with Teddy, an editor with a major publisher, who'd become my main client. And all of a sudden, I'd been drawn into doing what he had decided was best for me and I'd forgotten all about flexibility. It was almost like being an employee. But without the benefits of sick leave and paid holiday.

When I'd been in a bit of a rut in the past (pre-Teddy), I'd got off my bum and gone out looking for inspiration. Not wallowed in self-pity.

I needed to live in somebody else's house. I always used to absolutely love living in other people's houses for a couple of weeks, living their life, getting a sneaky peek at their hopes, their dreams, their family – and it was even better if they had a pet.

If I went somewhere to house-sit I could totally chill.

With a dog. Well, providing they wanted a dog-sitter, not just a house-sitter.

Talking to Mum about Dash had made me suddenly realise just how much I'd missed the non-judgemental company of animals (as long as we're not talking cats here –

they can really give you the look if they don't approve) that I grew up around. They're soothing, you can talk to them, they're models for my pictures. (Dad was right when he told Teddy I always loved painting animals. Win, win.) I might not be able to have my own dog right now, but I could look after somebody else's.

A change of scene was just what I needed. It could be inspirational, and let's face it, even my doodles had been a bit lacklustre lately. I'd kind of felt Teddy looking over my shoulder, tutting. Now I come to think of it, he tutted a lot, even before he dumped me.

I grabbed my laptop and brought up my favourite site.

Where? Within commuting distance of London? Nope, this time that wasn't important. I'd not got Teddy demanding I attend meetings where face-to-face is non-negotiable. Bonus! The world is my oyster, well anywhere within a day's driving distance is.

Cumbria? Why not? I could feel the start of a smile. We used to have family holidays in our caravan in the Lake District quite a lot when I was a kid. It was fun.

I'm not sure if nostalgia for more innocent times was to blame, or if it was because:

1. It's a long, long way away from London.
2. It's exceptionally peaceful and quiet and beautiful.
3. It makes you feel like you've escaped from the real world and are in some kind of 'Five Go Glamping' alternative reality.

Either way, I was sure that was where I needed to go.

Must tick the 'pets' box.

How long for? Okay, I was thinking a couple of weeks, but I'm flexible, aren't I? Sure, fewer filters, more choice. Go!

There was something like a three-second delay, then…

Oh. My. God.

There it was. Top of the list. This was THE PLACE. Lake View Cottage.

There was a gurgle of anticipation in my tummy that was a cross between butterflies and hope as I hit 'more details'. It was gorgeous, amazing, out of this world. Totally different to all the places I'd stayed before – which, let's face it, had all been pretty ordinary.

I realised I was holding my breath, expecting something hugely disappointing to pop up, like 'no single people' or 'hidden motorway in the back garden' or 'eco warriors only'.

It didn't. Instead it said 'remote' – perfect, somewhere quiet to work where I could concentrate – and 'cute dog' – even more perfect.

I hit the submit button before I could change my mind. I wondered if I should check out more properties, but then before I could decide, the owner, Georgina, had forwarded a link to her Instagram account so that I could see what it was *really* like.

Was I serious about this? Ten seconds later when I clicked on her link, I was even more seriously serious.

Wow, just wow.

Everything was so photogenic. Most of the pics were

actually of the dog – she was even cheek-to-cheek with her in the profile pic. Bella the dog seemed to be some kind of influencer in the canine world. She was incredibly popular, even if she did just look like a cute, fluffy dog to me. I had never seen so many 'likes' for a dog posing in a fleece.

There was Bella balanced on a fallen tree trunk with her new harness (gorgeous leafy backdrop), Bella mid-dive into the amazing sun-sparkled lake after her new floating toys, Bella wolfing down Woofa-Woof food, Bella perched on a rock up a mountain sporting a bandana with the wind blowing her ears back, Bella curled up in front of the Aga on her new designer doggie bed. Get my drift?

She was the queen of canine brands, a marketeer's dream.

The stunning background helped as well.

I have to admit, she was cute though. It was the big eyes and the happy face, and the little splodge of white on her shiny black chest. And so was Georgina – cute, I mean, not shiny – who sneaked into quite a few pictures. And oh, he-llo!

Woah there! I had been scrolling down on autopilot, admiring the scenery and fluffy ears and went straight past… I scrolled back up.

My God, forget wet noses and waggy tails. This was a different kind of branding altogether.

There was this seriously hot guy posing in a white, sleeveless T-shirt, big boots, and camouflage trousers that would make most men look like jerks – but on him made your throat go dry. You know, army-style, like he was up for some serious action. He was in profile, gazing out over the lake, legs astride, hands on hips, all moody and sexy as hell.

Think modern-day Poldark and you'd get my drift.

There can only be one thing that can beat a buff man in uniform, and that's one who's taken half of it off.

Oh my giddy aunt, as Mum would say. Or just cor! Okay, call me shallow, sexist and guilty of stereotyping. I don't care. I'm allowed. He looked like he was in the SAS, but with a better haircut. Not that I'm dissing the SAS, they don't have time to shave, wash or do anything but crawl semi-naked through mud, dangle from helicopters and save the world.

Oops, I'd nearly missed it, the bloody dog had even got in on this pic as well. She was sat at his side, gazing up adoringly, her tongue hanging out. Like I'd probably be doing if I was in Bella's place.

Not that I was studying that particular photo in detail or anything. But bloody hell, look at the muscles on those arms! My God, who was this guy? If this was her boyfriend, then I was seriously jealous. The house, the setting, the whole perfect life in all these photos was one thing. This Georgina was everything I'm not: sophisticated, well-off, totally successful – and she'd got a guy like that? The full package.

Unless (I could be fantasising here) he was just there to chop the wood for her log-burning stove? Or maybe he was the gardener and he would be there when I was! An added extra. Now that would be some kind of bonus. That is my type of inspiration, and the perfect distraction. I reckoned if he sauntered into view once a day, I wouldn't even be able to remember who Teddy was, let alone what he did.

Or he could be her bodyguard. She had got zillions of Insta-followers after all. And so he'd be going wherever she did.

But he was probably her boyfriend, and he'd be off abroad with her for a month.

Which would be sad. But, whatever, I still *needed* to go to this place.

I emailed her back, and because I was trying very, very hard to not sound like I was begging, ended up saying things like 'it's splendid' and sounding a bit of a divvy.

At least I managed to resist the urge to ask if the gardener-cum-woodchopper-cum-army-guy was part of the package, or an optional extra.

Then I put my flat up as 'available' on the house-sitting site, and within two hours I had three enquiries.

It seemed like this was meant to be.

Anyway, after saying 'great' to Georgina I did some running around in circles hugging myself and grinning like a loon. Then I came to my senses and started to run around the flat like a headless chicken, wondering where to start, what to pack, and generally throwing random stuff into suitcases and holdalls.

I packed lots of socks and knickers, and the sexy undies went in and out of the case several times – I'm sure neither the dog nor the sheep (there's *bound* to be sheep, every shop in Cumbria sells sheepskin rugs) will be interested. But there again, you just never know what can happen in a month. And there is the woodchopper. I'd be totally devastated if he was actually there and I wasn't prepared.

Then I rang Mum to explain I'd be away for a while. (More trouble than it was worth – 'No, I don't want to move back home, I've just decided I need to be somewhere that isn't round the corner from Teddy right now. Must rush. Bye. Of course I'll stay in touch. I'm not going to Outer Mongolia!') And stayed up until after midnight to finish some work I'd promised I'd sub for agreement.

Then I got up at the crack of dawn and tried to jam everything else I might possibly need into the boot of my car.

And I cleared the fridge and cupboards. And cleaned the bathroom. And rushed to the shops to buy a 'welcome tray' for my house-sitter. Finally, I showered, defuzzed and applied emergency nail varnish.

All this took time. It was bloody exhausting and not at all cathartic and left me hot and sweaty and wondering if I'd completely lost my marbles.

But I ran around like a blue-arsed fly and got it all done, and it is now 2.24 p.m. and I am nearly there. Plenty of time. Ish.

Chapter Two

I'd quite like to stop and regroup a bit – just five minutes to calm down, clean up and make sure I look presentable. But these roads are incredibly narrow and I've already been jammed so tight against a stone wall (by a bus driver who doesn't seem to have noticed the width of the roads) that my paintwork squeaked and the wing-mirrors folded themselves in. There's a reason the Lake District makes for the perfect escape – it's a bloody long way and the roads suddenly shrink when you are oh so nearly there.

Oh, thank heavens, a layby! I pull in and practise breathing. Then look at my reflection in the rear-view mirror. It is worse than I thought. I definitely have a greenish-brown stain on my eyebrow and nose. And, yuk, there is definitely something stuck in my hair.

'What the hell?' I'm hit by a mini-typhoon and it is like a giant ashtray has been emptied through the window. My knees are covered in… straw! There's a roar, and a whiff of fumes, and I realise that a tractor towing a trailer full of bales has just shot past and showered me with yellow shards. At least it smells sweeter than the green stuff.

I splutter as the dust hits my lungs.

'Becky?' Oh Christ, I'd forgotten Georgina was still on speakerphone.

'I'll call you back. I won't be long. Honest. I won't let you down.' I am all gritty between my thighs. There is a prickle between my boobs.

I pull the straw out from my cleavage and wriggle about a bit on the seat.

The bonnet of my car looks disgusting, as does the windscreen. Like something you'd see in the Tate Modern entitled 'Country Life, straw on shit'. I'll have to scrape it off.

Oh my God, I'm sweating like a pig. I must not sweat, if I let out any more moisture it might mix with the poo and set like concrete. They make houses out of straw and muck, don't they? I'm sure I saw one on *Grand Designs*. It might never come off.

I have to get it off my face. Except I can't. I can't find any wet wipes! How did I not pack wet wipes? I've packed everything else!

And I do mean everything. Every spare inch of my tiny car is packed full of stuff. This is because a month is a long time and I don't reckon the clothes shopping will be that good. Unless I want to buy wellingtons, Barbour jackets or baggy walking shorts for middle-aged hikers that come down to mid-calf. And it's not just the month, it's the not knowing what you wear for wandering lonely as a cloud. I'm more used to city life.

It's also not knowing how entertaining it will all be, so as well as all my work stuff (which there is a lot of) I had to pack lots of books and crisps, and wine, and a frozen pizza or two. I mean, it's remote, which I guess means no dial-a-pizza or corner shop.

It doesn't look like there was a space left big enough for wet wipes, though.

The dry tissue (even with spit) just makes it worse. And I can't even put my window up now to stop any more crap getting in, because it will smell. I will smell. Especially in this heat. I am a mobile muck heap.

I have learned a valuable lesson – don't drive too close to livestock lorries.

Or stop at the side of the road with your window open.

'You have arrived at your destination,' announces my satnav proudly. Smug woman. I'm not talking to her, not only did she not foresee the livestock lorry, she did not foresee the sheep on the road. A word of warning: never try to herd sheep, unless you are a sheepdog. There's a knack to it, which I think involves an ability to skulk along and stare hard.

Anyway, phew, I am here – slightly smeared in excrement – but otherwise safe. Never have I been so pleased to get out of a car. And check me out, I've made it with five minutes to spare!

I also didn't need the snotty satnav woman to tell me I had arrived at the right place, because the gates swung open before I'd even stopped, then clunked shut behind me as soon as I was clear. Well, I hope I've arrived in the right place, because if I've not then I'm locked into a stranger's home and don't fancy trying to climb over that bloody big gate.

It seemed a bit OTT when Georgina asked for my car registration so that she could 'programme the main gate'; let's face it, we're in a cottage in the depths of Cumbria, not some high-security site. She muttered about keeping the dog safe (people leave gates open, you know, yah), and not liking unexpected visitors. Especially now she's so high-profile, her followers on Insta think they *'own me, you know?'*

I am a bit dubious. I mean, who wants to 'own' a woman who posts nice pics of her dog wearing the latest bling? Though I wouldn't mind gaining access to her gardener-cum-woodchopper. Now *he* would be worth climbing over the fence for.

It is more than a little annoying that the front door doesn't open in the same way the gates did. There is a note pinned to the door, with the opening line: 'Had to leave – you are **very** late, can't wait any longer'.

I am not *very* late. I am just in time. Even if I had planned on being *very* early and failed miserably.

I peel it off. Georgina, it appears, isn't here. She'd waited as long as she dared, then cracked as her self-imposed deadline approached.

Have sent you text with location of key to back door (the number 1 has a big circle round it).

I check my phone; she has indeed texted me. Many times. I'm not quite sure why she left the note as well, it must have been a fail-safe.

Key is under the third plant pot to the left of the bin at the side of the house.

I glance around. My God, this woman is paranoid. Seems a bit extreme as far as key hiding goes, especially when you're so far off the beaten track and you have automatic gates. But she does seem a bit extreme. There is nobody in sight, there isn't a road or any other house as far as you can see.

How can you be a paranoid recluse and an Instagram hit? Seems a bit contradictory, doesn't it?

This isn't my main concern at the moment though. I still desperately need the loo – I totally resisted the urge to pee in a bottle or squat in a field. I head off to find the key so I can get inside as quickly as possible. I carry on reading the note as I go.

Full instructions on table in kitchen.

This is good. I can relieve my aching bladder then carry on reading with a glass of wine in my hand. I'm sure I can find a glass without the aid of any more instructions. And yay!!! I have found the key!

SKYPE ME THE SECOND YOU ARRIVE BEFORE YOU EVEN OPEN THE DOOR (this is in big shouty capitals and underlined several times).

That must be important, I think as I open the door. Oops! Surely she's just being dramatic again, why wouldn't I open the door first? And why wasn't it the first thing she listed if it was that important?

Sugar, my phone's ringing now! I pause, one hand still on the door handle. It's Skype. I push the door ajar a bit. It is Georgina. Bugger, what do I do? How did she know I was here? Can she tell I've opened the door? Has it got some kind of alarm system that reports straight to her phone?

I hit 'answer with video' in a panic and she's there, all lit up brightly in the airport.

'Hi! Sorry, just got here.'

Fuuuuck, something black and hairy has just shot out like a bullet and launched itself at me. I guess this is Bella, and probably why she told me not to open the door!

If I hadn't been juggling the phone and door though, this wouldn't have happened.

'Are you alright, Becky? You sound strange.'

'Oomph.' Bella lands two chunky paws slap bang in the centre of my stomach and winds me. Then before I think to grab her, she spins round and takes off. 'Fine!' This is my new favourite word, and when it comes to Georgina means anything but. Bugger, I hope I don't sound borderline hysterical, like I've already lost her dog. Shit, I really need to go and find it. 'Bad signal!'

'Cool.' I am beginning to get the measure of Georgina. She looks totally immaculate, even though she lives in the middle of nowhere with only sheep and ducks to admire her. Which is exactly how she looked when we had our 'interview' before she agreed to me house- and pet-sitting. And not at all how she sounded when she was in panic mode an hour ago.

It is all about outward appearances. Like her Instagram account. Georgina certainly wants the rest of the world to think she's living her best, glamorous, life.

Which is fine. She probably is. I am a bit in awe of her. And, I admit it, I use filters and cropping copiously before posting a photograph anywhere (even to my mate Kate on WhatsApp, and definitely to my parents, and absolutely any pictures that my ex might possibly see). Who doesn't?

'You read my note? Found the key?'

'Sure yes, opened the door!'

'Oh.' There's a long pause. She hesitates, mid-stride. 'Where's Bella?'

That is a very good question.

'Bella!' she screeches at the top of her voice, which carries amazingly well considering we're chatting on my mobile.

Luckily this has the desired effect. The dog reappears. At top speed.

'Oh look, look, here comes my lovely Bella girl!'

I hardly hear, I'm too busy trying to dodge the black missile that has just hurtled into view and is heading straight for me and her mummy.

'Down Bella! Bella, stop it!' A picture might paint a thousand words, but they don't convey energy very well.

This dog is hyper. It's doing kangaroo leaps in the air, as I dance around like a boxer warming up for a big match trying to dodge the mucky paws, and holding the phone up high out of reach while Georgina shouts at her to 'calm down'.

'She's not usually like this.'

I stagger backwards, unsure whether to believe her. Maybe she'll calm down when Georgina's gone?

'She's just excited because she saw my suitcase and was upset, she probably thinks I'm coming back and taking her somewhere exciting now. Oh God, Bella!'

Bella has scored a direct boob hit with one very hairy, very muddy paw and nearly knocked my phone out of my hand, but Georgina's outraged bellow stops her in her tracks.

She sits down. I reckon if Georgina was here in person (and I wasn't), then cutie-wootie Bella might be getting a bollocking.

Her tail is wagging so hard it's polishing the floor she's sitting on, and her backend is wiggling. She is honestly even prettier and more endearing in real life than in her Insta pictures. Well, when she's sat and not pogo-ing.

There's something just *loveable* about her, with her black curly coat and the biggest brown eyes imaginable framed by luscious eyelashes. No touching up needed here.

She shakes her curly head, still grinning at Georgina, and one of her big ears flops inside out. I can't help but grin too; it's fair enough to laugh at a comical dog, I reckon.

Georgina sighs, which Bella seems to take as a cue that she's forgiven. She stands up, gives one bark and is off again. She spins round and whizzes past me and out into the garden.

'Where's she gone?' screeches Georgina as her dog disappears from sight.

I chase after Bella, worried I'll have lost my job before I even make it into the house. Luckily, I haven't. Yet. The dog gallops back into view. She's a bit of a whirlwind, and now she's dashing round at top speed with her tail between her legs.

'Haha. Doodle dash!' Georgina pulls a face as flower heads scatter in all directions. 'Cockapoos are a bit crazy, zoomies are their thing.' She frowns. 'Now what else do I have to tell you?' Bella starts to bark. 'Bella, shush!' Bella ignores her.

Zoomies seem to involve running around at full pelt in no particular direction and flattening anything in your path. Like plants. Or people.

She hurdles a lavender bush and gallops over to me, before flopping over on her side on the lawn and rolling madly, her tongue lolling out of her mouth comically. Then she's gone again.

Disappeared from view. Bugger. 'Er, should I? She's…'

'Promise me you'll read the list.' For somebody devoted to their dog she doesn't seem that bothered I might have already lost it – she's more bothered about her flaming lists. And maybe she totally trusts Bella to come back. I suppose she's got a lot on her mind. It's not easy going away for a month and leaving your pet and home in the care of somebody you've never met before.

And this place is pretty secure. I'm not sure *I'll* be able to get out, let alone a dog.

'Sure. Bella? Bella?' I yell. She doesn't reappear.

'Make sure you always lock up.'

We're in the middle of nowhere, but I'd lock up anyway; where I live it's second nature – if you didn't lock up while you took a two-minute walk up the road you'd come back to find the place stripped bare of everything but the dirty washing. Well, actually, the dirty washing would probably go as well. 'I will.' Christ, where is that dog? I'm back round the front, by my car, and there's no sign of her.

'Always?'

'Yes, yes, I'll definitely lock up.' Maybe she went all the way round the house and is in the back? I'm sure I can hear barking. I break out of my casual stroll and speed up.

'Even if you're just wandering round the garden.'

This girl is sounding more unhinged by the second. A tiny bit psycho, if I'm honest. Maybe she's a bit of a recluse since hitting fame with her Instagram account? Maybe there are stalkers! 'Sure.' I'll have to google her again later, but right now I have more urgent things on my mind. Where's the bloody dog gone now?

'It's a big garden.' She adds that as though she's realised she is sounding a bit batty. 'You might not hear if somebody comes.'

'Okay, I promise I'll lock the door, every time.' Maybe Bella's gone back in the (unlocked) house and is hiding?

'And the front gate?'

'Oh, definitely the gate.' I'll have to work out how to open it first, though I'm sure that's on a list.

'Oh shit, they've called my flight. Right, I had three rules! I've told you about locking up…' She ticks one off on her fingers. 'Oh yeah, the second one was don't let Bella out of your sight. You won't, will you? And don't let anybody else touch her!'

Number two has been well and truly broken. I don't know about touching her, I have no idea where Bella is, she has already disappeared, vamoosed, gone. Which for some strange reason her owner doesn't seem bothered about. Maybe she knows Bella will always come back to her, but how does she know she'll come back to me? 'Never, ever, yah? If I lost her or she got hurt, it would be a total disaster.' She frowns at me and leans forward a bit as though she doesn't want any passers-by to hear. 'My whole life would be ruined.' Strange choice of words.

Worrying choice of words as well, considering I haven't a clue where the priceless pooch is.

'And there's one more thing.'

I'm not sure I need her rules.

'Hang on. I think I'd better try and find Bella, she's disappeared again! Maybe you could call her again?' I jog round to the back once more and take a couple of steps into the house, hoping she's curled up by the Aga, or sat on the table or something.

She is not.

Chapter Three

'Looking for something?'

The deep voice sends my heart shooting into my mouth and my mobile phone clattering to the floor. Bloody hell, I put my hand on my chest, my heart is hammering. I'm in the middle of nowhere, I thought I was alone! All alone, with nobody to help me…

I spin round, fists raised in self-protection mode. 'Oh.' My throat is dry. I'm not sure they'll have much effect, faced with *this*.

Or rather him. There is a man standing in the doorway, holding a wriggling Bella, who is wagging her tail, squirming and trying to lick his face all at once.

I should be scared. But Bella clearly knows him, so he can't be too dangerous. Unless she does this to everybody? Heck. But he doesn't look like a murderer or rapist. Bloody hell though, he must eat his Weetabix.

He is big. Very big. I can't stop staring at him. How the hell did somebody that size manage to creep up without me hearing him? If my heart pounds any harder, it's going to explode out of my chest.

I think I might be gawping. Okay, I know I am. I'm taking in every inch of him in a very obvious way, and to hell with the danger, I can't help myself. He's wearing a black T-shirt which shows off tanned, muscled biceps to perfection, and I bet he has pecs to match, except Bella is blocking my view of them. She's also stopping me seeing most of his face, but the bits I can see are pretty jaw-droppingly good.

He's got messy hair, not that different to Bella's (except his is brown not black), kind of cropped but dishevelled enough to make you want to touch it; large, capable, strong-looking hands are holding the happy dog firmly enough to stop her leaping out of them. Trousers that barely do anything to disguise his muscled thighs and... OMG! Big boots.

Those boots. It's the boyfriend-stroke-gardener-stroke-SAS-stroke-woodchopping-man who was on Georgina's Insta account.

Flipping heck, he can special service me any time he likes.

I was so distracted by shock and the sheer maleness of him, and the fact that he looks *even bigger* in real life than in a photo, that I didn't recognise him at first. But those dirty boots have made me realise why he looks vaguely familiar.

He's studying me intently, probably because I just squeaked with recognition. Then he flips his sunglasses off, and I think I've come over all swoony. Those eyes. Piercing blue eyes which are serious and unflinching, and a little bit scarily interrogatory, but his dimples have got to mean he does smile sometimes, and the lines etched into his suntanned face around his eyes can't have come just from squinting, he has to be a man who laughs as well. Bloody hell, talk about 'all man', you can forget your Netflix action-man binges, I've got the real deal. On my doorstep! Holding my dog! Well, Georgina's doorstep and dog, but let's not be picky.

And he can't be her boyfriend, can he? Or he wouldn't be here!

Nobody would forget to pack a plus-one this hunky.

I've come over all hot and bothered and breathless. And speechless.

Too much testosterone in the air, I reckon.

Bugger, it's made me brain dead as well. He's holding the dog! The dog that must not be touched by anybody but me.

'Hey!' His voice really is sexy. Goose-bumpingly deep if you get my drift, like all the erogenous zones of my body seem to have done.

'Hi!' My voice is, in contrast, all breathy and pathetic. I want to lick him.

No! I don't!

'Sorry.' The corner of his mouth quirks up, 'I didn't mean to make you jump.'

'You didn't!' I squeak again. That voice is more than just deep, it's a velvety rumbling that, if I was semi-drunk and not in responsible house-sitting mode, would make me go even wobblier at the knees. As it is, I just feel weak from relief that he's caught Bella, and shock. Because he scared me. I didn't see him coming.

'What's that?' He leans forward – oh my God, he is close and he smells as good as he looks – and plucks something out of my hair. Holding it closer to his face, he pulls a very strange expression.

He holds his hand out and I look in horror as it dawns on me.

'Shit.' Cow shit. I still have cow shit in my hair. Or I did have, until…

He raises an eyebrow and my face scorches. I've just been touched by the hottest man I've seen in ages, scratch that, ever – and it was to take cow poo out of my hair.

He was staring at that, not gazing in admiration at the rest of me.

'Sorry, er, incident on the drive over,' I croak. Please ground, swallow me up. Let this be like *Groundhog Day* where I get a chance to start again.

He raises an eyebrow. 'Shit? Real country girl, are you?' Humour is lurking in his eyes; he's not actually laughing or properly smiling, but he's on the verge of it. How can a nearly-smile be so bloody sexy and make me so jittery?

'That probably sounds worse than it is.' How can anything be worse than cow poo in your hair? Must change the conversation. 'I didn't recognise you without your clothes on.' Maybe not quite that way.

'Isn't the line "with your clothes on"?' The corner of his mouth is twitching again.

'I mean your uniform, your combats, whatever.' It's

definitely the guy in Georgina's Instagram photo. So the fact he has Bella can't be *that* bad. It's not like he's a stranger.

He stares at me as though I've got two heads. 'My uniform?'

This is embarrassing. 'Your SAS gear!' Did I just actually say the words 'SAS gear'? 'Georgina had a photo of you…'

'Ah.' I'm not sure what 'ah' means. 'So, you are?'

Awestruck, unable to think properly. 'Sorry?'

'Cleaner?'

'No, I'm not!'

'Guess you're a bit too, er, windswept and sexy for a cleaner!' He grins.

Sexy. He just called me sexy. I'm all hot and bothered again. It doesn't matter that he used 'windswept' as another word for 'look like you've been pulled through a hedge backwards and showered in muck', he said sexy.

'Friend of Georgie?'

I shake my head. He called me sexy.

'Bodyguard?' The dimples that have just deepened at the sides of his mouth suggest that is not a serious suggestion. They are also very distracting.

'House-sitter,' I squeak lamely. 'I'm Becky, I'm Georgina's house-sitter and—' I look pointedly at the dog, '—dog-sitter.'

'Well, no need for the second bit, I came to pick Bella up.' He kisses the top of her head and she goes back to wriggling and trying to stick her tongue down his throat, which (let's face it) is what I'd probably do, to be fair, if he was clutching me to his chest. Except I'd melt against him, not wriggle. 'Okay? Don't worry about a leash, I've got one.'

'Pick up?' I am confused.

'Take her, er, out?'

Aha! 'Oh wow, you're a dog-walker.' He doesn't look like a dog-walker, and the way he's lifted an eyebrow suggests he thinks the idea's as weird as I do. 'As well as a gardener and er… soldier!' I drop those in to cover all bases. This might be easier though if he'd actually confirm or deny one or more of the options.

The other eyebrow has gone up, and he looks a bit taken aback, though to give him his due, he's not started laughing yet. I reckon he's about to any second, though, if I don't shut up.

'Give me a sec to change my shoes and I'll come with you.' The woodchopping gardener walks the dog. That means he will be a frequent visitor!

I grin. Then stop. Good heavens, what am I saying? I'm the one that's supposed to walk the dog! 'Er, Georgina never mentioned…' She did mention not letting Bella out of my sight. And not letting *anybody* else touch her. She must have forgotten to tell the dog-walking woodchopper that I was taking care of business. 'Sorry, I'll just, er, check with her. We were talking when you arrived.' I wave my hand in the direction of my mobile. 'I think she still is actually.' From the noises emanating from my phone, I'd guess she's still shouting out instructions about what I must and must not do. 'She's stressed,' I add apologetically as I stoop down and grope around to try and pick up my phone without taking my eyes off him. 'I was late.' I swear he looks a bit edgy; his hands have tightened around Bella, and he takes one step back. 'It's been a long day.' For both of us.

The noises coming from the mobile get louder as I pick it up. Then nearly drop it again.

'What the actual fuck!' yells Georgina at full volume, leaning in so close we're almost eyeball to eyeball. 'Don't you fucking dare, Ash James!' She drops her suitcase with a clatter and moves back so I can see her again. She is hopping mad. Literally, moving from side to side as though trying to see past me. 'I knew it was you, you... you... you wanker! You promised you wouldn't!' I flinch, but she's not paying much attention. She's wagging a finger wildly. I think that's aimed at the gardener, not me. 'Get my dog off him!' If I thought she was slightly hysterical before, it was nothing compared to this. 'For fuck's sake Becky. Get her! What am I bloody paying you for!'

Er, I didn't think dog-protection was my brief. And I'm not actually getting paid. I don't think now is the time to correct her on that though, so instead I just mouth at the gardener.

'She's not paying me.'

He takes a step back. Shit, if he tucks the dog under his arm and makes a run for it there will be no competition, he'll be miles away up a mountain, before I'm out of the starting gate.

I lunge forward and grab a paw. Bella squeaks.

'Let go!' It's a warning growl. From the gardener, not the dog. I think he's used to being obeyed.

'No way!' I tighten my grip, counting on the fact that he won't be prepared to leave a paw behind. For a second, I'm a bit worried he might do (army types are probably used to limbs being dismembered and can apply tourniquets) as we have a bit of a tug, with Georgina screeching in the background.

'I'll kill you if you let him take Bella, I'll write a crap review!' Second part hardly relevant if first part applied. Though not a good obituary. 'I'm not even out of the fucking country, you underhand wanker.'

'I'm only taking what's mine.' He is talking through gritted teeth, and there is absolutely no hint of a smile on that granite face at all. It should be scary, but it's actually quite sexy. I think the pure air out here must be affecting my brain, or it's all the stress. 'You never said you were getting a house-sitter!'

'It's none of your business what I do! We agreed! Get your hands off her. You total tosser.'

'Or what? You'll call the police?' His voice is even lower than it was before, but it is even and measured. A shocking contrast to Georgina's hysteria. Except to be fair, he's here, holding on to the dog, and she's stuck in an airport relying on a total stranger. Me. 'Georgina, be fair, you didn't tell me you were going—'

It's Georgina's turn to growl. 'Shithead.'

His gaze shifts up to my head, and there's a hint of a smile curling the corner of his mouth when my hand goes to check there's no more left up there. For a second, I think we're both going to break into hysterical laughter (well, mine would be hysterical, his would be deep and manly) which would send Georgina off the deep end.

'Wanker!' This girl has quite a turn of phrase. But for

heaven's sake, I need to put a stop to this. I came here for peace and tranquillity, a break from drama and stress and flaming exes, and my head is already about to explode with pent-up frustration.

Enough of being nice, no way is my job to be peacekeeper. My job is to look after the house. And Bella.

Though it looks like Georgina's had some kind of altercation with the gardener, and he won't be a part of the landscape. Shame.

'Let go yourself. Now!' I bellow, surprising the dog, the gardener and even myself.

'Oh, for Christ's sake. This is ridiculous, you're upsetting her. Have her.' He shoves Bella at me. 'But I'll be back!' It's not even remotely *Terminator*-style, but I giggle with relief and clutch the dog, as he marches off. Bella whines and looks dejected. I think she wants to run after him. I sympathise.

I really do need a stiff drink now.

'What's he said to you?' Georgina is still bleating as I go in the house, put Bella on the floor and firmly close the door. And lock it. 'He's a lying toad, what's he said?'

'Nothing, he didn't say anything apart from what you heard.' I feel drained. My sparring with absolutely anybody pales into insignificance compared to this pair.

'I'll die if he gets Bella. He's already ruined my life enough! What did he tell you? It's all lies!'

Ruined her life? Did he dig up a shrub he shouldn't have? Chop up too many logs? I am mystified.

'He won't, and he hasn't said anything you didn't hear,'

I repeat, trying to reassure her in a soft voice. 'And I've locked the door.'

'Good.' She calms down instantly. Picks up the handle of her wheelie case and straightens her hair. 'He's the third thing on the list.' She pauses. 'That's my ex.'

'That's your ex?' I think my tone has gone up a pitch. I struggle to dampen it down and sound normal. 'He's your ex?' Ex. I roll the idea round in my head. I suppose the reaction was a bit extreme if he'd just been the hired help. Landscape gardening doesn't normally cause ructions like that.

Why didn't I realise earlier? I blame being exhausted from the early start and crap drive over. And stress. Most of which came over the phone from Georgina. She is not a chilled person.

'Yes.' Her voice is tight. 'Whatever you do, don't let him in the house.'

'What?' Don't let him in the house? But yay! He's her ex. Not her current. But boo, he's persona non grata. Not allowed in the house. That's a bit of a bummer.

I might have to shag him in the bushes, haha. No, no why am I even thinking that? Definitely not. Be sensible and act responsibly, Becky.

'He might come back, he's been really kind of...' She pauses. 'Weird.' I raise an eyebrow. 'And nasty.'

'Oh.' Gawd, I've come here to escape bloody drama, not to fend off angry ex-boyfriends.

'You saw what he was just like! He might try and steal Bella.'

'Why?' I am puzzled. Why would an ex-boyfriend steal a dog?

'Oh, you know.' She waves a hand. 'To get at me because I'm happy.' She spits the last word out. Not much happiness there then. 'She's not his, whatever he just said. She's mine. And he's a loser. He won't leave me alone, you know?'

I don't know. Nope. Never had a problem with exes not leaving me alone.

'He's power-crazy.' I have had a problem with that. 'He's been coming out with all this shit about Bella being his just because he knows how important she is to me. So don't let him near her again, will you, whatever he says. Right? He was always playing bloody favourites, playing rough and tumble with her and giving her food. God.' She rolls her eyes. 'Some people have to be so competitive about everything, y'know? So fucking childish. In fact, don't talk to him at all, that's probably best. And don't tell him where I am or anything.'

As I don't have a clue where she is, this won't be a problem. 'Er fine, yes.'

'Ignore him if he gets arsey.' Arsey, arsey? What does she mean, arsey? How will I stop him doing anything if he gets... arsey? 'It's all a big act.' Easy for her to say when she's about to jet off, maybe this is why she's gone? 'He's a dick, what can I say?' She shrugs. I've tried that 'nonchalant, I don't care' shrug myself. Never comes off.

Trying too hard to pretend she doesn't care. I feel a sudden twinge of sympathy.

'Look, I need to go, I'm going to be right at the back of

the bloody queue now because of all this.' My sympathy fades slightly. 'And I need to know I can rely on you.'

'Sure,' I straighten up and try to look like a person that can be relied on. 'Of course you can.'

I put the phone down and sink into a seat. Then I remember I need the loo, desperately, and I don't even know where the bathroom is yet.

I search it out, sit down and take a deep breath. I've always found the bathroom a good place to think.

So, the gardener has a name. And he's not a gardener. He's her ex.

Ash.

I roll the name round, and then say it out loud. Bella cocks her head on one side. She followed me here and I hadn't got the heart to shoo her downstairs. As long as she doesn't come in too close and rest her nose in my knicker gusset then I'm cool with it.

'You like Ash?' She wags her tail, staying at a polite distance. Cool.

Am I really not allowed to even talk to him? That's a bit over the top, something really big must have gone off between the two of them. Oh my God, this is so not fair though, I want to meet him again. Just to have a proper look, to see if he's been Photoshopped to death, or somebody can actually look like that in real life. I mean, tussling over Bella's body didn't give me the opportunity to have a *proper* look.

I could barely see his chest, or his stomach, which in the photo was toned and flat.

And why am I not allowed to even talk to him, or let

him talk to the dog? That must have been one hell of a nasty breakup.

Unless he actually is a bit of a psycho stalker, like Georgina said.

I mean, I don't exactly have a good track record when it comes to judging men, do I?

'What do you think, Bella? You like him, don't you? I bet you could tell a few secrets. No?' Bella, who seems to have accepted me quite easily as dog-sitter and guardian, observes from the doorway as I sit on the loo.

Dogs are normally good judges of character.

It's a bit weird. This whole situation is a bit weird. Including the bit where I'm talking to a dog.

But whatever Georgina said, he did say he'd be back, so it's not my fault if I have to talk to him, is it? Even if it's only to tell him I can't talk to him.

Although it is all a bit worrying, having a possibly psycho, arsey ex (who looks like he could shoot people for a living) threatening to return. Maybe I should concentrate on *that* bit, not the fact that he's arse-clenchingly gorgeous. And I should think about the danger in a bad way, not find it exciting in a way that is making my stomach tip over with anticipation.

Though that could be hunger, or the fact I've not dated since before Christmas.

Not that Teddy ever made me feel like this.

Maybe I need a drink to calm my nerves.

And a lie-down. I'm overtired. Obviously.

Bella edges nearer, and I wag a finger at her then look her in the eye. 'And we need some rules, don't we?' She makes a low rumble, then barks. 'Bloody hell, and I've got a dog that talks back too. I get the last word, not you, right?'

She barks again.

I'm not sure I've got the upper hand here.

Bladder relieved, I sit down at the kitchen table to read the note that Georgina has left. Not that I can really be bothered. I've had enough of her instructions for one day. But I do have a duty of care, a responsibility. And I do need to know what I should and shouldn't do.

Points 1, 2 and 3 have been covered by her in some depth (and volume). Lock up, don't lose the dog, don't let the sexy ex in the house. Got it.

There is more. But it's all a bit less interesting.

Details about the heating (which I won't need – it's early June and the weather is gorgeous) and the internet router (which is erratic), the hot water (also erratic), what time Bella goes to bed, where I can walk her and where I can order groceries. Apparently, there is a spare key hung in the utility, a front-door key in the inside of the front door (presumably left there to stop anybody with lock-picking capabilities) and a button to open the front gate.

A quick poke around reveals that the fridge has been filled up with wine and other essentials (for me – maybe she's not so bad after all), the utility room has been stocked up with dog food (for Bella – 'she only eats this one, she's an ambassador for the brand') and there's a folder that has emergency numbers and a list of favourite dog walks. There is also a hell of a lot of dog paraphernalia – coats, leashes, one very, very long lead, harnesses, collars, towels, cushions, toys – how much stuff does one little dog need? When I was a kid, our dogs had a collar, leash, bowl and bed.

I pour myself a glass of the wine Georgina has left in the fridge for me – it would be rude not to – then have a proper snoop around the house. Bella follows my every step.

It's quite nice actually, her constant presence. I don't feel like I'm alone, in the middle of nowhere. I feel fine.

The place is as fantastic as it looked from the outside, and on all the Instagram posts. The perfect retreat – if you ignore points 1, 2 and 3 on Georgina's list, and try not to get in a panic that her irate ex is going to climb through the window and do something to get his own back. Wine helps calm the panic.

The kitchen is the real deal. The polished Aga that Bella curls up by in the photos, a fantastic chunky oak dresser complete with a pretty jug of country flowers, stone floor and big wooden beams. Oh yes, there are wonderful chunky beams throughout the whole place.

The woodburning stove in the living room has a pile of artistically arranged logs, there's a cosy window seat where you can sit and read or stare out across the lawn at the wonderful view, stacks of books everywhere and oak floorboards that look the genuine article.

There's even a little study, complete with large desk and light streaming in – the perfect spot to doodle.

I can already feel the tension ease its way from my body and a calmness take over in my head, stilling the clamour of voices and doubts. This is better than any massage or hot-stones treatment ever. And did I say? It is peaceful. Not a sound except for the gentle waffling snores of Bella (who has now decided she doesn't need to keep an eye on me and can settle down for a doze). But I know she's there, and even out here in the middle of the countryside I've just realised I feel comfortable, at home. Not at all lonely.

The best bit, when I climb up the narrow, steep staircase (ducking to avoid the low beam), has to be the bedroom.

I have to sit on the bed to look out of the low window, but boy, is it worth it. The views really are something else. Waking up in the morning is going to be amazing – I'm going to go and have another look in a minute. Once I've finished unpacking.

I also want another look at something else.

Don't judge me. I settle down with my drink and scroll through Georgina's Insta to see if there's more than one guy on there, and to check out those photos of her ex again.

Just to be on the safe side and recognise him immediately if he comes back. Haha. And nothing to do with the fact that I now know he's an *ex*, not current.

I mean, I might have forgotten what he looks like, yes? I don't want to cosh the wrong man over the head now, do I?

While I'm thinking about coshing, it suddenly dawns on me. How did he get in? There's a bloody big gate at the end of the driveway. Which closed behind me – locking me in.

Maybe he snuck in, commando-style, behind my car? Hitched a lift on the roof of it, while I was busy messing with my satnav? Or he put a brick in the way so that the gate couldn't close completely?

I must double check that it's shut. And mention this to Georgina. When I've finished this drink. 'What do you think, Bella?' Bella stands up and barks, wagging her tail, and then makes a beeline for the back door.

'You need a wee?' She barks again. 'A play?' Her tail starts to wag so fast I can feel a breeze. I smile. I can't help myself. It looks like it is time to have a wander round the amazing garden.

Chapter Four

I think this is what exhausted but happy means. I might be having the most stressful, knackering day ever but this view changes everything. I know I have made the best decision of my whole, bloody life!

A few days ago, I was close to packing in work, murdering my ex-boyfriend and his frigging newly discovered, *absolutely amazing* (unlike me) cover designer and drowning myself in pink gin. But today I reckon I've found the right place to discover my inner zen. I *will* be calm; I will have inner peace and learn to love my work again. Probably.

This landscape is incredible. Way, way more stunning than I remember as a kid. Well, kids don't tend to list 'stunning' as a bonus, do they? It's more about 'exciting', 'brill ice-cream', 'great hideouts'.

But now I reckon I can see why Mum and Dad brought us here.

It feels like this place is pulling me in and wrapping

itself around me. I mean, wow, just wow. And I can handle hugs from nature, which don't make me feel like bursting into tears of self-pity or hitting somebody.

I sit down and curl my fingertips into the lush grass of the emerald lawn, which gently meanders its way to the lake below. The lake is something else. Really. I reckon I could sit here for hours, transfixed by that blank canvas of water which mirrors the clouds and the yellow, brown, green and silver-grey of the mountains that wrap around it.

'Oh Bella, aren't you a lucky little dog, living here?' She is lying down at my feet but looks up at the sound of her name, head cocked slightly on one side and brown eyes fixed questioningly on my face.

There's a strange, floating, ever-changing feel about the view – a softness of blended colours which should be at odds with the harsh stone of the mountains, a subtleness in the way the clouds form changing shadows that lift out some features and mellow others, as though the landscape is a watercolour that is still being painted.

A work in progress.

Like me.

I've never seen anything quite as stunning in my life before, though. It is fluid, gentle and awe-inspiringly wonderful.

On a bright sunny day with a cloud-free sky, the landscape probably sharpens, but this afternoon the soft golden rays of the June sun leave it muted and hauntingly beautiful.

Below my feet is a soft cushion of mossy lawn, above me is open sky. Fresh air. Head space.

And this is exactly why I came here. I know I've done the right thing.

This is a place I'll feel safe to sit and ponder in. This is a place that my fingers are itching to get down on canvas. It might not be inspiring me towards Teddy-style creations, but that's not what I'm here for, is it? I need to rediscover what I want to do, find out if I can still paint at least some things after all.

It really is bloody gorgeous. I can't think of anywhere that's ever made me want to stop and just 'be' before. Anywhere that has made me want to paint so desperately in a long, long time.

I take in a deep breath and close my eyes; I am now breathing in pure, unpolluted air (as opposed to city-centre smog) and all I can hear is water, insects and birds (as opposed to city-centre traffic and piss-heads on their way home). And a dog panting.

I sink back onto the cool grass and can't help but smile as Bella crawls closer and tentatively licks my nose. I open one eye and reach out to fondle her ears.

If it hadn't been for Bella, I would have missed this magic moment right now. I'd have unpacked, curled up on the sofa and messed around with my phone, checking out my social media streams. I'd have brooded about Teddy and my lost commission, felt sorry for myself and wallowed in self-pity.

Instead I'm in this perfect place, and okay, I'm still thinking a bit about how shit everything is in my life right now, but for a second or two there I wasn't.

Bella won't let me, for a start. She paws at my hand,

reminding me that I've stopped stroking her and she needs attention. 'Alright, Miss Bossy.' Actually, it's going to be impossible to just think about *me* while I'm here, this little dog isn't going to allow it. 'You're a right little attention seeker, aren't you?' She licks my chin, then groans and tilts her head so that I'll rub behind her ear properly.

It is kind of nice, feeling the cool grass under one hand, and the warmth of her silky coat with the other.

But when I close my eyes again, all I can see is the man she was kissing with total over-enthusiasm just moments after I got here. Boy, talk about puppy-love. If anybody ever falls for me that hard, my life is complete.

Though, to be honest I totally get it. I wouldn't mind a sloppy snog with him myself. Big, sexy, totally hot Ash James.

A bolder lick, that also involves nibbling teeth, breaks the spell. 'Hey, stop it.' I open one eye and she's peering down her nose at me, her warm, doggy breath fanning my face. 'Have you never heard of personal space?' She wags her tail and leans in closer so that I have to put a hand on her chest to keep her from sticking her tongue in my mouth. I laugh at her. 'And French kissing is a no-no, okay?' She wags her tail harder and puts her full weight against my hand. Bella has to be the happiest dog I've ever met.

Mmm, French kissing. If that man tastes as good as he looks…

Shit. I must stop fantasising. And I must keep my mouth closed. 'Bella, stop it, before I get cross!' She barks. She knows I'm not going to get cross. I don't. Instead I run my hand over her velvet-soft ears.

I'm here to chill, and work, and think about just me for a change and what I want.

I am not here to kiss men. Definitely not. Even if it is hard not to want somebody that looks that fit. And when I say fit, I mean in every way imaginable. Where does a man get muscles like that? Seriously, he has got to be SAS, or at the very least some kind of personal trainer. And eyes, I mean, how can somebody glance at you and you feel like they see *everything*? I don't know whether it's scary or exciting.

Well, I do. I'm getting goose bumps just thinking about it.

Teddy, my git of an ex, never made me feel like that. Sharing a glance with Teddy was like, well, like sharing a glance with my brother. Or my dad.

Except my dad would never be that horrible to me.

'Oh, bloody hell Bella, why am I even thinking about the evil sod?' I must NOT think about Teddy. I'm here to get away from him.

If I think about him, then I won't be able to work. And he will have won.

Bella stops trying to stick her tongue down my throat, and instead collapses against me, snuggling in closer. She rests her head on my chest, cold wet nose only inches from my own. It's kind of soothing, stroking a dog. Feeling their warm body pressed against yours, the sound of gentle breathing as lulling as waves lapping a beach. 'You get it, don't you?' I sigh. She snuffles and stretches her legs out to make herself more comfortable, then with a gentle groan rolls onto her back so I can stroke her tummy.

Dogs are so trusting. I'm a stranger in her home, somebody she has never met before that she has to rely on to feed and look after her. And just like that, within hours, she's decided I'm okay.

I think I need to be 'more dog'.

Bella *does* get it. She's more in tune with me than Teddy ever was. In fact, I think she knows how to *be* what I need right now even more than my family does. I can also tell her anything and have absolute confidence that it will not go any further. And she won't judge me or tell me I'm crap at what I do and should consider a career change.

I can't believe Teddy actually said that. The total git.

Argh, I'm thinking about him again!

Bella kicks me as my fingers tighten in her fur, and I make a conscious effort to relax. She doesn't approve of stress.

But I can't let go, just like that.

Not when he tipped my whole life upside down.

Even if Dad's only comment on the whole thing has been 'Don't let him win, you're stronger than that.' Sometimes I don't feel strong.

Bella nudges me with her nose and I glance down at her. I need to think about Bella, walks and chilling.

Chapter Five

Okay, I might have arrived here with slightly unrealistic expectations. I'd thought that getting away to a beautiful place like this would inspire my work. It has relaxed me, it is fabulous and it is inspiring, but I'm not getting much work done.

In reality, the work aspect has hit snags because of:

1. My mother.
2. The mad cockapoo that is adorable but totally inexhaustible. The longest she sits still is seven minutes and forty-six seconds (I timed her).
3. The dread (or should that be anticipation?) of people knocking on the door despite the fact *I am miles from anywhere*. Honestly, at the slightest sound, Bella leaps up and barks which makes my heart skip into my mouth and sends me running to the window after her. I'm turning into a nervous wreck, because believe me, if a

bird farts Bella will hear it and get excited. We both peer out all tense and expectant, which is ridiculous.

Okay, to be fair, the third point is strictly speaking only about one person. Ash. And as far as Bella goes, I think it's more about the chance there will be a squirrel, rabbit, a big bird or even a small bird, or anything that moves really, in the garden.

Number three haunted me most of the night. My mind was a jumbled mess of I'll-be-back Arnie Schwarzenegger striding towards me, Bella under one arm, an axe in his other hand (I think my subconscious is still saying woodchopper and gardener, not ex). Then he whips off his shades and it is Ash.

I woke up in a sweat several times, just as he started to whip off his uniform in the style of *Magic Mike*. I think I've been watching too many movies with hot men in.

Anyway, in my waking moments I kept hearing strange noises. Not even SAS men can climb brick walls and break into your bedroom, can they? Okay, that's just me fantasising. I'm sure he's not *actually* SAS, he's just a normal man.

Bella (who was sleeping on the bed, not in her own room as specified on the list) snored throughout all my nightmares. So, maybe the noises were just the normal sounds of the house, and nature outside. Or maybe she's a very heavy sleeper, because I must have kicked her at least once as I thrashed about.

I did eventually drift off into a proper sleep, only to be

woken up when number one on my list of snags kicked in at what felt like about thirty seconds later.

'Becky, why does it say on Facebook that you're in the Lake District?'

Bloody hell, I really do need to block her. 'Because I am, Mum.' Okay, being in the middle of nowhere doesn't solve all my problems. I might have to add 'don't answer the phone' to my to-do (or to-don't) list. Except then she'd send out a search party. Or just worry. Neither of which would be fair. 'Stop it!'

'What?'

'Not you, Mum. It's Bella, she's licking my nose.'

'Bella?'

'It's the dog.' I fondle her ears. It was quite nice to cuddle up to somebody in bed last night, instead of being home alone.

She pauses. I hate long pauses; it means she's about to say something that I might not want to hear. 'Teddy has announced his new cover designer.'

Where on earth has she seen that? 'I thought you'd blocked him on Facebook?'

'I have. This was on Instagram. Oh, why didn't you tell us, darling? That's horrible of him, and you work so hard.'

'It's nothing.'

'Of course it isn't nothing. That's why you were so upset wasn't it? I just knew there was more to it than you two splitting up. Oh Becky, you should have said something.'

Bella stands up as though she senses I need a distraction, and shakes herself, then jumps off the bed and barks. I guess this is dog-speak for 'Let me out in the garden, I need a wee.' She's good at making her requirements known, and I've got a feeling one of them is going to be getting out of bed early. Which is good, it means I get a full day's work, something I've found difficult lately. It's the whole, *what's the point if all I produce is crap*, scenario. Bella doesn't care about that though.

'I think you are so much better off without him, darling. I didn't like to say, but I wasn't that keen on—' meaning *I hated* '—the pictures he got you to do. Your other paintings are so much nicer, more you.'

'He was building my career, Mum.'

She makes a harrumph sound. 'If you say so. I mean, what do I know? But did you really have to go so far away? I mean, we could have gone out for afternoon tea, or shopping. I could have taken you to that spa you like and…'

I get out of bed and head down the stairs as she talks. It's impossible to tell her, because I know she loves me, and I know she means well, but the last thing I want right now is a girly session in the spa, discussing my ex with my mother. There's a little lump in my throat, and I almost feel on the verge of welling up, but I stop myself. I'm here to get away from all the sympathy. To have some space. Get my act together. Work.

'I know, Mum. Maybe when I get back? It would be nice then, and I'm only here for a month, and I've got a sh—' I stop myself on the verge of saying 'shitload'. 'Shedload of work to do. It's just easier here, completely on my own. In the middle of nowhere. Here you go Bella, go wee!' I open the back door, and the dog bounds out.

'You're all on your own? Miles from anywhere?'

Probably better not to mention SAS men. 'Well, not miles, I can see a house.' If I stand on my tiptoes, on a large box, at the bottom of the garden. 'It just feels like I am. It's quiet.'

'Ahh. Won't you be lonely?'

'I can chat to you and other people on the phone, I've got Skype and Zoom and stuff for work, and I've got Bella!' Speaking of which, Bella is now barking wildly. 'Look Mum, I'd better go and see what's up with her.' I stand by the open door. I'm sure I can hear squeaking. Maybe she's just playing with a toy? Better to be safe than sorry though. 'I'll call you later, okay?'

'That's fine, Becky. As long as you're okay. So, what are you going to do with yourself today?'

'Dog walk, then work.'

'You can always bake if you're bored when you've done that.'

'I'm not bored.' See? She thinks my work is a little sideline, ten minutes' scribbling a day. 'I've got plenty of work to do, three commissions!' I have. They're only small, not very well-paid jobs, compared to what I was doing for Teddy. But I got them on merit, and the encouraging noises over the past couple of weeks have started to make me think that maybe, just maybe, I can still do this job.

'Did I tell you they've given Abby an office on the first floor?' Oh God, here we go. Abby, my perfect, younger sister. She's so frigging perfect it should make me hate her, but I don't. That's the other annoying thing. She's nice. Abby has a proper job – she's a solicitor, like Dad.

When I first finished college, and work was a bit thin on the ground, Mum did say (just the once), 'Why don't you retrain as a solicitor? Abby just got a pay rise, and you'll never believe how much it was!' This was followed up by 'This flat really is a bit cosy isn't it? Wouldn't you like one where you have to get off the sofa to open the door?' Yes, I would. 'A dog or cat would be company, you really should move somewhere they allow pets. And maybe somewhere with a garden?' It might have been easier.

'Wow! The first floor!' I jiggle about, I really should check on Bella.

'It's a move up.'

'Well, down actually, she was on the fourth.'

'You know exactly what I mean, Becky!'

Sadly, I do. There is a hierarchy. A desk on the first floor means you are one step closer to the fifth floor – which is where the seniors have offices. I know. It's complicated.

'It isn't too late, you know. You could always re-train.'

'Mum!' I am the black sheep of the family. We were all supposed to come out as fully formed solicitors. My brother, Daniel, went a bit bananas and decided he wanted to be a barrister, but that kind of bananas is fine. My kind isn't. My family deal in facts, not inspiration and creativity (well, sometimes creativity, but more along the same lines as creative accounting but with facts about people, not money).

'Well, as long as you're happy, love. I know this Teddy business has dented your confidence.'

With a sledgehammer.

'Sorry, Mum, I'm going to have to find the dog, I'm not supposed to let her out of my sight.'

We say our goodbyes before she has a chance to say anything else and I dash outside.

Bella is very excited. She is not doing a wee, she is doing zoomies around the garden, barking wildly and lunging at the shrubbery. Strangely, she keeps launching herself at one particular shrub. Maybe there's a squirrel or rabbit in it?

I would shout at her to shut up, but I know I'd be wasting my breath. I tried that last night when she decided to bark at a hedgehog that had wandered up to the patio windows.

She bounces onto the soil again, dives through the undergrowth and I'm sure I hear a yell. Unless it's a bird? Then she emerges further along the border looking very pleased with herself, her long ears adorned with grass, a single daisy dangling from her mouth.

Then I hear the squeaking again, and it isn't Bella playing with a toy, even though it's made her ears prick and she's stalking the bush again, cat-style.

I try not to laugh at her, and instead I skirt around the edge of the grass on the opposite side and creep up towards the border from behind.

The shrub is definitely squeaking, and not in an 'I'm a rabbit trying to stay alive' kind of way. More in an 'I'm a squeaky toy that somebody is squeezing' fashion.

Bella can't resist a second longer; she zooms in at top speed, wagging her tail and jumping about at the same time, and the bush makes an 'oomph' sound before she dashes off again and starts spinning around in circles.

There are a pair of large feet, or rather boots, sticking out from the shrub.

I take a tentative step forward, holding my breath as though it's going to make me quieter. I am so close I could hit whoever it is over the head, if I'd thought to bring a weapon with me. Surely there must be a branch handy?

It's gone strangely quiet. Because Bella has stopped barking. She has stopped moving. She is staring directly at me with an inquiring look on her face. The word 'shit' is still forming in my head when it happens.

'Eurgh.' I was about to say 'what?', but it's too late. I know the answer. I'm flat on my back and Bella is bouncing about with glee. 'Please don't jump on my stomach, please don't...' Too late. 'Argh.'

What the hell happened? I peer past her. My ankle is being held firmly by one very large hand (result! This makes my ankles look positively sylphlike). I glance to my side, half knowing what I'm going to see; a pair of startlingly blue eyes stop me dead.

Oh my God, those eyes are blue. The bluest of blue.

'You!' we say simultaneously. He props himself up on one elbow, so that his bicep flexes, and grins.

I try to copy, and grimace before flopping back down. 'Ouch.'

I'm side by side with the terrible Ash, like lovers in an herbaceous border, and all I can do is rub my elbow. He didn't clamber up my walls, he wriggled his way through the undergrowth.

'How long have you been here?' is the first thing that comes into my head. Better than 'Come here often?' I guess.

I'd noticed he had blue eyes yesterday, but up this close they take on a whole new intensity.

Must stop staring into them.

'Are you okay?' He looks slightly worried.

'Sure.' I stop rubbing and try and look chilled. As though I'm used to being flipped onto the floor, in a judo-throw kind of way, not a sexy way if you know what I mean. Though I'm not used to that either. Teddy wasn't the type to throw you on the bed and have his wicked way. He offered an invitation, turned back the duvet then straightened the sheets.

'Good.' His frown disappears. 'Couldn't sleep.' He winks, not looking at all uncomfortable at being found loitering in somebody else's garden. 'You?' His gaze never drifts from my face, but I am suddenly very aware of the fact that I am still in pyjamas and have bedhead hair.

This is not good. It makes me feel as squirmy as the dog, who, upset at being ignored, launches herself at him, using my chest as a stepping-stone. She nearly gives him a black eye in the process, and sends him flat on his back. He tries to hold her at arm's length, to stop her licking his mouth. She seems to have a thing about kissing on the lips. I just get the foot in the face.

He starts laughing and I can't help it. I join in. Which seems to egg Bella on, and she launches herself at him again, this time trying to get the squeaky toy that I've just spotted in his hand – which he flings across the lawn for her.

'Come here often?' I say it in the end, just for something

to fill the awkward gap, and stop myself from staring. I'm still lying on my back.

'I used to.' He nods without breaking eye contact, a hint of humour teasing the corner of his mouth. He's got lovely big dimples. They make his angular, chiselled features softer. Appealing. I could imagine kissing a man like him. Well, I did. Last night. In bed. Firm lips, firm hands, firm body. 'You are sure you're okay? I didn't mean to hurt you.'

I realise I'm rubbing my elbow again and stop, because I probably look like a complete wimp. Then I gulp to dismiss all those thoughts of firmness. 'You weren't planning on upsetting Georgina?'

'Would I?' He lifts an eyebrow. I suspect this man has a wicked sense of humour hidden underneath that strong exterior, although that could be me fantasising again. He's got his boots on again, as well as his combat trousers and olive-green T-shirt. Camouflage. He's also now holding the squeaky toy that Bella has retrieved. And then I notice something on the ground beside him and forget all about his sexiness.

Wire cutters!

I look at them pointedly. 'Really?'

'Bit of DIY to start the day!'

I can't let him charm me. I cannot. Georgina told me not to talk to him, because she must have known this would happen. And whether he is a sneaky bastard or not, it is not my place to judge. Only to look after Bella. 'You'd better not have made a bloody hole in the fence!'

He doesn't admit or deny anything. He just gives me his steady gaze which I try and hold. Then he blinks. Bugger, that makes me squirm and blush. Annoying – I do not categorise myself as the type of girl who blushes just because somebody looks at me. Never happened before. Not with Teddy, or any past boyfriend.

Ash is the only man I've ever come across who can make me feel wobbly by not moving, or saying anything, or doing absolutely anything at all apart from look at me. And wink.

Oh my God, he's grinning again now. I need to get away from him.

It must be a special SAS skill. Charming the enemy. Not that I'm his enemy, he is mine. Or rather Georgina's.

Bella bounces back, the toy in her mouth looking slightly chewed up and now just wheezing out air rather than squeaking properly. I know how it feels. Exhausted.

'Bella, come here.' This time I manage to grab her collar. 'I will be so cross if I have to check all the fences!' I'm going to have to. I'll never forgive myself if she manages to get out of the garden.

He rolls on his side, props himself up on one elbow and shakes his head slowly, a lazy smile playing across his firm mouth.

Must not let my head get back onto that topic of firmness.

'I was mending them, not breaking them.' He waves the wire cutters. 'Pliers, not cutters, for twisting it back together. Look.'

I look, but to be honest wouldn't know one from the other. They're just pointy tools. 'You don't even live here! Why would you…'

'I don't want Bella getting out, do I?'

'You don't?' I'm a bit confused.

'I don't want her getting hurt, or lost, but I do want her back.'

He sits up, his forearms resting on his knees. His voice is still at the same pitch, even, but there's a kind of non-negotiable edge to it that makes me feel uneasy. Like I'm being issued with some kind of warning.

I gulp down my reaction. I have a job to do. For Georgina. 'She's not yours to have, she's Georgina's.'

'Nope, she's more mine than Georgie's. I picked her, I fed her, I trained her, I walked her. All Georgie did was take photos and use her to get freebies. It would be easier if you'd just hand her over, let me have her.'

Oh. This is awkward. I blink at him while I take this in. He *looks* like he's telling the truth. And Bella *acts* like he's a pretty important part of her life. But I haven't seen her with Georgina, have I? She might want to snog everybody. She could be one of those dogs who loves anybody that is nice to her.

I am confused.

'Come on.' He gestures at me to hand her over.

'No way.' Even if he's telling the truth, she's still Georgina's, isn't she? I've still got an agreement to dog-sit, I promised to take care of her. I hang on tighter and Bella coughs. Flipping heck, I mustn't strangle her. I soften my grip on her collar a bit.

'Please yourself.' Phew, that was easier than I thought. 'You don't leave me much option then, do you?' Oops.

'I don't?' I have gone really squeaky now and there's a

flutter of anticipation in my stomach. What's he going to do? Murder me in my bed?

'I'm going to have to come and get her. I'm going to get her back, whatever it takes.' He folds his arms. 'And whatever Georgina has told you, I'm not the gardener, and I'm not the dog walker, I'm her ex.'

'I know.' If he murders me, everybody will know it was him. He's not going to be that daft, is he?

Unless he's planning on skipping the country. Can you skip the country with a dog? Has Bella got a passport?

'Well, if you know so much, then you'll know I don't need to cut down fences to get in here.'

'Will I?'

'I just open the gate, like anybody else who lives here would do.'

Ahh. Georgina hasn't changed the code on the gate. Bit of a slip-up for such a paranoid, security-conscious person. All this is her flaming fault. Which makes me angry and stops me worrying about being suffocated in my bed. 'Right.' I struggle into a sitting position and wince. I think I've got friction burns down my side, and probably nasty grass stains. And my elbow still hurts.

'Are you sure you're okay?' There's a look of concern on his face which takes me by surprise.

'I think you two are going to kill me! All this running up hills.' He raises an eyebrow. 'Well, maybe not running, but all the walks, and games. And being thrown on the floor!'

'This terrain is rough, if you're not used to it.' He used the word terrain, definitely SAS. 'Sounds like you need a workout, a bit of toning up!' It's my turn to pull a face, and he adds hastily, 'Not that you look like you need toning, I meant a bit of stamina-building exercise, you know.' He does a bit of mock weight-lifting, which lifts his top and shows a hint of... oh my God, I feel faint, that sliver of skin is so brown, so fat-free, so... I need to see more. And maybe he's right, I need to be a bit more fat-free myself. 'Tell you what.' He smiles, and it is a very appealing, gentle smile. 'Ash's bootcamp could be the answer!'

Chapter Six

'What?' Ash runs a bootcamp?

'Go for the burn!' I don't like the sound of that. 'You'll find running up the fells after Bella a piece of cake after a couple of sessions!'

'I will?'

'Yup! Five days to fitness!' His eyes are twinkling. It is very appealing, and distracting. Five days. Five opportunities to ogle Ash's body.

'With you?' Just to be sure.

'With me.'

'And how much would this cost me?'

'Nothing, it's for Bella!' He grins at the dog. 'Have to give you a sporting chance to chase me if I run off with her!'

'Very funny.'

'And I've got some spare time, I'd be doing the exercises on my own anyway.' He shrugs. 'Nothing wrong with a bit of company. And—' he waves a hand to encompass the surroundings, '—it's a great place to do it, fresh air, sun...'

I am tempted, very tempted. I did promise myself I'd do things differently here. Try new things. And I am out of condition. And… oh, who am I trying to kid? I have an SAS man at my disposal. I want to see more of that body, I might get bored stuck out in the sticks with only Netflix and a naughty dog for company. He's right. Company is good, and I'm still not sure how serious he is about trying to run off with Bella, but if she's in the house and he's putting me through my paces then at least she's safe.

Okay, I just want to see his body.

'I know some good moves.' I bet he does. 'If you're up to the challenge, that is?' He flexes his bicep. 'Quite understand if you're not.'

'Of course, I am!' I can't say no. I am not the kind of girl who will admit defeat.

'You're up for it?' He is grinning.

'Sure!' Sure? Did I just say sure? 'Sorry, must go, Bella wants her breakfast!' This time I manage to get to my feet without yelping, and without letting go of the dog.

I drag Bella a couple of steps and realise it isn't going to work, so give up and pick her up. Bloody hell, she's heavy… and wriggly.

She keeps glancing back longingly over my shoulder as I stagger across the lawn hanging on to her. I know how she feels, but I. Must. Not. Look. Back.

'Let's do this then!' His voice carries clearly across the large lawn.

I stop. 'What?'

'Bootcamp!'

'Now?' I spin around. Who said anything about now? I

need to think about this, plan, find something to wear that shows off my good bits and hides the wobbly bits. A top that will soak up sweat and hide damp patches.

'You've not had breakfast, have you?'

Breakfast? Does he know what time it is? I'd still be in bed if I was back at home, still be debating whether it was worth the effort to haul myself up and sit at my desk waiting for inspiration. I'm only up because of Bella!

'Er, no.'

'Perfect, you don't want to do it on a full stomach! No time like the present then. Feed Bella and get some trainers on and we'll go for it.' He claps his hands together.

Go for it? I feel faint. I spin back round and take a step towards the house.

'Nice PJs, by the way!'

I glance down. Bugger! I'd forgotten about them.

Not turning round though. Definitely not. Partly because my face is now completely burning up.

'Crap camouflage!' I yell back. 'You need to skip the squeaks next time!' Which is a bit of a silly thing to say really. Because firstly, I'm suggesting he should do it again, and secondly, I'm giving him hints on how to do a better job.

But bloody hell, not only have I been fraternising with the enemy, I've been lying on the ground with him in my skimpy sausage-dog nightwear and slippers! And I have agreed to get hot and sweaty with him on the lawn.

'I'll give you five minutes; we can do it here!'

'Never a dull moment round here, is there? You'd better not tell Georgina about this.' I wave a finger at Bella as I close the door firmly and let go of her collar, then turn the key in the lock.

Bella pads off to the kitchen, wagging her tail as she goes, then sits down next to her bowl and waits for her breakfast.

Squeaky toys and food are obviously the way to this girl's heart. We'll get on fine. Or maybe not. I glance at the toy she's dropped at her feet. She's managed to bite a hole out of it, which explains the wheezing. It is now a lobotomised squirrel.

'You don't tell her about us talking to him, and I won't tell her you ruined your toy. Deal?'

She barks.

'Did he really pick you?'

She wags her tail, then whines and looks at her bowl pointedly.

One bonus about dog-sitting, I guess, is that she adds structure to the day. No way is this bundle of fluff going to let me mope about the house in my PJs all morning.

'I guess I'd better get dressed then?' Bella doesn't answer, she's busy licking her bowl. 'I do have to do this? No way out?' He is SAS, how can I say no to such an opportunity? I've been meaning to get fit for ages, I just haven't had time. But now I have.

This will kickstart the new healthy Becky. Healthy body, healthy mind and all that. And quite a nice body to admire while I'm sorting my own one out.

I might even cut down on the wine and fill the fruit bowl.

Maybe. I think I'll see how it goes first.

The only question is, with all the walking, playing, fence-checking, tidying up and cuddling, not forgetting impromptu workouts – am I actually going to have time to do any work?

I have not come equipped for bootcamp. I do have running shoes, which I actually brought for walking as they are comfy. I had no plans to run anywhere. I do not have any go-faster Lycra, just some leggings. Nothing else is stretchy enough. And a strappy T-shirt. If I'd been at home and knew this was going to happen, I'd have gone shopping and invested in the latest 'bootcamp wear' like you do. I mean, nobody just throws on old clothes, do they?

'Great!' Ash is jogging on the spot. I wish he'd stop; he's making me feel tired already. 'Come on, let's get started!' He claps his hands together and sets off across the lawn at a jog. 'We'll start off slow.' He calls that slow? I was thinking more power walking. But this is bootcamp, and I do want to get a bit fitter, don't I?

I set off after him.

Actually, this is easy. And I've never seen such a toned bum in real life, no wobbling there. And that *is* inspiring.

'Let's step it up a bit, get you properly warmed up!' Ash has turned to face me. He is currently jogging backwards up the slope of the lawn. It's deceptive, it looked like a gentle incline but now I'm expected to run up it I realise that it is in fact a proper hill, a *very steep* hill.

Properly warmed up, what does he mean properly? I am

already more than warm: I am past the simmering stage, I am boiling hot. This is it, isn't it? We're working out, or rather I am.

What's wrong with staying on level ground? Oh my God, my legs are feeling heavier by the second. 'Three more laps then we'll get down to the serious stuff!'

'Three?' I pant out. Serious? What does he mean, serious?

'Want to do more?' He's grinning, as though this is a walk in the park.

'No.' I grit my teeth. I am not going to give up. I can do three laps. It's only a garden. On a hill.

Oh my God. I am going to die. My legs have gone all wobbly. My face is burning up and I'm literally dripping with sweat. You know that 'challenge'? Well, I have just realised I am not up to it. Not at all.

'You can do it!'

He's mad. I'm mad. I haven't even got the energy to ogle his body any longer, I'm concentrating too hard on staying alive.

'I can't!' I stagger. I can't even go in a straight line.

'You can, come on.' He's in front, facing me, urging me on, his large, strong hands tantalisingly close. 'Nearly, nearly there, and… rest! That was brilliant, well done!'

I need oxygen! I sink down onto the grass on my hands and knees.

'Breathe – in, out, you got this!' I think he wants a high five. No way. 'Right, on your back.' This is more like it. 'A few crunches.'

'Crunchie?' My voice might be weak, but something

inside me has perked up. He's offering chocolate – I can do this. If I get chocolate, I can do it.

'Crunches.' He chuckles, puts his hands behind his head and dips backwards and forwards.

Shit, he means sit-ups.

'Let's give your legs a break and think about your core!'

What does he mean, my core? I can't think about my core or anything, apart from chocolate. I need food.

'Knees up!'

'Now?' The word 'rest' to me means at least ten minutes, and a drink. I think I need wine actually, not water.

He has his hands on my legs. I'd kick him if I had the energy. He is not sexy, he is evil.

'Hands by your ears, and I'll count. We'll start off small, say ten? Concentrate on me and it'll be easy.'

I look into his eyes. Okay, he is sexy. When I'm lying on my back and not trying to move. Oh heck, his warm palm on my calf is definitely sexy. He strokes it down and parts of me tingle. Rests it on my ankle.

'I've got you, let's do this! Ready?'

'Yup.' I grit my teeth. I can do ten. I used to be able to do fifty when me and Dad had competitions. Okay, I was about ten years old, but it can't be that difficult.

Isn't ten a massive number? Five is good, but ten? I am never, ever going to try and do ten crunches again in my life.

'Lunges, then we'll do more crunches. You're doing great, three sessions a week and you'll soon be ready to kick ass.' I don't want to kick ass, I want to sleep. And what the hell does he mean, three times a week? I'd already abandoned the whole 'five days to fitness' idea and was thinking of this as a one-off! 'On your feet, lunges!'

I don't think I can get on my feet. He grabs my hand and before I know it, I'm up.

'Lunges?'

'Nice and straight.' I'm still gripping on to him. He's only inches away, his other warm hand on my stomach. It's a bit of a turn-on actually. He gently extracts himself from my grip. I was holding on quite hard, I'm worried I'll fall over if I'm left to my own devices.

'Hands on hips.' His finger is under my chin, lifting it gently so that I can't help but stare into his eyes. 'Look forward, focus on that tree.' Tree, what tree? His soft voice is silky smooth, so close to my ear it sends a shiver through me. 'Now step forward and back, other leg, forward and back.' No, it's not. It isn't a turn-on at all. I wish he'd go away.

He steps away, and I wish he'd come back closer. This is agony. In more ways than one.

'Over we go, let's get those upper arms working with a few press-ups. Legs straight, up on your toes.'

I can't keep my legs straight; I have gone all floppy. Even my feet are floppy.

I don't know how long he tortures me – sorry, 'puts me through my paces' – for.

When I have collapsed on my back, gasping for breath like a stranded goldfish, he straddles my body and grasps my hands in his.

They're firm and dry, not all sweaty like mine are.

'I think I'll just stay here for a while, if that's okay.'

He chuckles. 'You're funny!'

'I'm not funny, I am wrecked. I wish I'd kept my pyjamas on!'

'Can't disagree with that! I quite like you out of uniform!'

If I wasn't already burning up from over-exertion, I would be now. As it is, I think I'm as hot and red-faced as is possible.

'Same again in a couple of days?'

Any other suggestion would be tempting. I'd quite like to be manhandled by Ash again. They do say no gain without pain, but…

'Sorry, I've got a lot of work on, I'll let you know,' I say weakly. Never. I am never doing this again. Five days, ha! There are easier ways of getting fit. Swimming. I'll try swimming. That involves floating and not having to move much.

'See you soon then!' He waves a hand as he backs off, still grinning.

He is hardly sweating. Obviously, I have done more work, but he joined in a little.

It is so unfair.

'Sure. Thanks.' It's only polite to thank people, isn't it? It's not his fault he has actually no comprehension of the level of fitness of a person who hasn't been to a gym for over five years (though I have joined many, and even had an induction to find out how all the scary equipment works) and spends the majority of their day sat at a desk, moving only when they have to go to the loo or eat and drink.

I wait until he has gone and then roll over and crawl

back towards the house on my hands and knees. I need coffee, a long soak in the bath and a lie-down. A long lie-down.

I think I have a love–hate relationship with Ash. Much as I would love to get my hands on his fit body, I'd rather sit back eating pizza and admire it, than go through the agony of trying to tone up bits of myself that are quite happy wobbling about on their own.

Chapter Seven

Yesterday was a good day. On balance.

Ash did not come crawling through the undergrowth. Which was good because I did not have to worry about guarding Bella, also good because I could sit still and move very little – every time I moved it hurt. How can you ache *all* over? I didn't even do anything with some parts of my body that are complaining. And as for my calves, the muscles seem to have curled up into tight bundles that make it agony to even straighten my legs. I can't walk! How can that be right? Ash helpfully told me at the end of the session that the next day I might be uncomfortable, but the day after would be worse. Ha. How can it be worse?

Remind me never to take on any challenge set by an SAS man.

However, it was bad because, well, he did not come crawling through the undergrowth. Even though I did regularly glance that way. He's good company, when he's not trying to improve my cardiovascular health (his words, not mine); he's fun. A bit like Bella.

Bella lay quite peacefully stretched out on her back, legs akimbo, warming her belly in the shaft of sunlight by the window (very good).

And Mum didn't call.

This meant I got lots of work done.

It started off with a doodle of Bella, a daisy dangling from her mouth, it was only a rough sketch, but it made me smile and reminded me of her delighted frenzy when she spotted Ash. She might be a bit loopy, but she's also very loveable. I guess I'm beginning to understand why Georgina and her ex are having a tug of war over her. But if she's Georgina's then she's Georgina's – and possession is nine tenths of the law, isn't it? I'll check with Abby, but I'm pretty sure. And when I googled daisies I got the perfect quote to add underneath the sketch:

> *The daisy is a happy flower,*
> *And comes at early spring,*
> *And brings with it the sunny hour*
> *When bees are on the wing.*

> John Clare

How perfect is that? Bella's a pretty little dog, and it suited her. 'You're a happy flower yourself, aren't you?' I showed her the picture. She wasn't impressed. She'll be comparing it to the filtered Instagram photos that Georgina posts.

I liked it though, and I actually enjoyed doing it – which makes me realise how much I've had to compromise when I've worked with Teddy. Sure, I want success. But when I went to art school it was to follow my heart, and maybe recently I've forgotten about that.

She nudged my leg, so I let her jump up onto my knee. 'Well you're certainly inspirational, aren't you?' She licked my nose. 'I'll do a better one, then we'll send it to your mum, yes?' Who'd have thought that all I really needed was a dog – to force me to get up early each day, take some exercise, and act as a muse? Not that drawing pictures of a cockapoo is going to make me rich, Teddy made that crystal clear. I try and stop myself sighing inwardly. Bloody Teddy. I've got to stop thinking about what he said I should be doing.

As I doodled, I have to admit I did think of Ash in passing, but then before I knew it I'd had a brilliant idea for the cover of *Mischief the Magic Pony*, one of my non-Teddy pieces of work. Definitely not something he would approve of. But thinking about Ash made me *not* think about Teddy which kind of gave my imagination permission to take flight (along with Mischief). It was almost like I'd told myself I was allowed to follow my heart and not feel guilty. To actually immerse myself in my work and believe in myself, like I used to do. How weird is that? I also forgot all about muscled-up men ravaging me in my sleep (or making me do press-ups), and was transported into the world inside my head – where pretty fell ponies with manes down to their toes flew over the mountain tops and tiptoed their way over the deep water of the lakes, saving stricken squirrels and rabbits as they went. Yeah, I know that's a bit strange, but it's how my mind works. The imaginary world of a book wins over imaginary hot sex any day. Once my creative juices get flowing. Once I manage to forget my failures.

I didn't stop working until my back had totally seized up and it felt like somebody was stabbing me every time I moved, and Bella was nudging my knee again. 'Oh bugger, you need a walk.' She whined. 'We'll have a play in the garden, then I promise I'll take you for a proper walk tomorrow, okay?' If I can walk again by then.

Oh my God, every time I changed position, I felt new pain.

Not only had my back seized up, so had the rest of me. I staggered, stiff-legged and robot style into the kitchen for a drink of water, then hauled myself up the stairs by the banister and lowered myself gingerly onto the toilet.

By the time I got back downstairs everything was miraculously starting to loosen up. I could walk, I could bend over and do my shoelaces!

We had a long play in the garden with her favourite squeaky toys, which meant it was too late to open a bottle of wine by the time we finished. But at least it meant I didn't feel as guilty. And I didn't have time to think about all the shit things in my life. Because to be honest, if I've not got the Magic Pony right, then I'm a bit screwed. Where do I go from here? Designing business cards?

So, I was able to report quite truthfully to Georgina yesterday that all was well, and that today I would be taking Bella for the long walk I promised her.

I also sent her a photo of Bella lying on her back (to show how chilled she was), then sent a message:

I'm sure she's missing you like crazy, but she seems happy to accept me as substitute mummy!

Aww isn't she a babe, tell her I'll Zoom her tomorrow!

This was followed up ten seconds later with:

You won't post that photo of her anywhere, will you?

Oh no, just took it for you!

She's a bit weird. I mean, Bella isn't exactly going to care if people see funny or unflattering pics of her, is she? She's a dog! I think you can carry this whole caring-about-your-pet's-feelings thing a bit too far.

Despite Georgina being a bit of a pain in some ways though, she's thorough. In her file of information there are several walks with notes beside them on necessary footwear (*flip flops fine/I do it in my Converses or sneakers/proper boot territory unless you want to break your ankle!*). I do wonder if Georgina has ever walked the final category as I just can't see her in full hiking gear, but maybe Ash has advised on those routes. And I suspect I'd need a year's worth of his bootcamp sessions before I'd be up to that particular challenge. Which I am not going to do. I do not have time. It is nothing to do with the fact that at one stage during our session I seriously thought I was going to expire and be buried in my sweaty workout gear. It is all to do with work, and what I need to do while I'm here, and how busy I am walking Bella – who will not benefit at all from crunches and jogging on the spot. Honestly.

Ash is definitely a mountain gear type of guy. He probably carries emergency rations and a tent, just in case.

Anyway, there are also notes on the scenery and best weather to experience each walk in – so as it is a lovely sunny morning I'm very tempted by the one that promises 'spectacular views on a sunny day', plus a tarn, the perfect waterfall, peregrine falcons and red deer.

The photos do look a bit daunting though; 'spectacular' views kind of suggests being pretty high up. Which means steep. I think I might have to work up to a walk that involves hill climbing, and I might have to order some proper boots.

My body has also turned into one that belongs to somebody ten years older than me. Ash did promise that I'd really feel the aches not the day after the exercise but the one after that. So I should keep the exercise up (haha) and do lots of gentle stretches (even more haha). I don't think he meant I should spend the first day with my bum glued to the seat and only move for essential refreshments, and then spend the day after scaling a mountain. You might call them hills round here, but they are definitely mountains. I think they use the word 'fell' to lull you into a false sense of security.

Anyway, ignoring the state of my body, the app on my phone also warns of a risk of showers, which convinces me (or rather gives me the excuse I need) to plump for a

'Converses or sneakers' walk which will give us both some exercise.

It also means I've got the energy to carry a rucksack full of sketch pads and drawing stuff. I feel like I'm on a bit of a roll and don't want to stop. In fact, to be honest, I daren't stop in case I can't get going again.

The drawings I did yesterday were my best for a long time, and I'm convinced that sitting in a shady glade will be the perfect inspiration for finishing them off. I'd also quite like to do a few more sketches of Bella, if there's time. Drawing her seems to help bury the doubts, and makes me feel I still at least have some talent.

'What do you think, Bella? Waterfall, woodland, a picnic spot and squirrels?' She perks up at the word 'squirrels' and wags her tail, then leaps in the air. She's funny. It's hard to stay miserable and gloomy when she's displaying so much happiness.

I really am going to have to make a sign and pin it above my bed – be more dog.

Apart from the chasing squirrels bit.

Bearing in mind the death threats issued by Georgina, I hunt out the long lead that she told me was stashed with the rest of Bella's many belongings. I don't expect her to be able to climb the trees after squirrels, but what if there's a particularly stupid one that decides to just leg it across the countryside with the dog in hot pursuit? I think tethered but free to sniff around a bit is the best compromise for both of us.

I have discovered my own little slice of heaven. The view from the cottage is amazing, but this is a whole different world. And I would never have discovered it if I hadn't had to walk Bella. In this sheltered spot, I can't see the looming multi-coloured crags, or the vast lakes, that make the area so breath-taking. I'm tucked away from all the spectacular scenery and am surrounded by the gentle side of nature.

I take a deep breath and sigh. For all its glory, I think a quiet spot like this has to be as good as it gets when you want solitude but comfort at the same time.

I have to admit, when we'd set off, I'd been thinking about what the hell I was going to do next, if my *Mischief* ideas were laughed at. Like Teddy would do if he saw them. Then Bella pounced on an imaginary animal, before spinning in circles chasing her tail, and I had to smile. Then she shot off round a bush and it took ages to untangle her long lead, especially as I was laughing all the time.

My face ached. Probably because I haven't laughed this much for ages. In fact, I can't remember when I last had a good giggle, let alone a laugh that gives you a pain in the stomach and makes you cry.

Anyway, I was still grinning as we rounded a bend in the path, Bella tugging me along as she bounded ahead. And it was there. I stopped smiling, not because I was worrying but because it took my breath away.

The sound of the tumbling waterfall echoes from some distant place, but right here there is just the mesmeric sight of the stream meandering its way in almost respectful silence, its surface only broken by the insects and birds that plunder it, and the occasional stone that breaks its path.

Above my head there's a canopy of green, like a crocheted blanket with its holes to let in the gentle sunlight and flashes of white and blue as clouds scud over the sky.

It's too late in the year to see Wordsworth's yellow daffodils; the brash and glorious colours of early spring have long since given way to the subtler colours that May and June bring. In the garden the bright orange, red, violet and royal blue bedding are already king, but here where the sun struggles to make itself seen, the muted pinks and reds of rhododendrons and azaleas are still at their wonderful best.

There's been no sign of a red squirrel yet, but it doesn't matter. Within ten minutes of settling down on my blanket, there was a flash of coppery orange breast and iridescent turquoise and I sat motionless, willing Bella not to move as the beautiful kingfisher zipped its way up the stream.

Of course, I knew now that the turquoise was an illusion. I was devastated when I was at art college, and a particularly nasty and vindictive cow laughed like a horse at my watercolour of a beautiful kingfisher lurking in the shade.

Apparently, it's a trick of the light. The fabulous colouring. They're brown, so need to be in the light to look blue. I never forgave her and hated her even more when I saw her snogging the hunk who'd been our life model. He'd been the first male under sixty-five we'd seen in months. Apparently, it was more valuable to study bodies that demonstrated the ravages of age than the beauty of youth. They told a story. Yeah, right, a tale of saggy balls and greying skin. I mean, fine, study ravaged people with their clothes on. But naked?

Anyhow, to discover the kingfisher was as much an illusion as what I'd hoped was my irresistibility to the opposite sex (he'd raised his eyebrows and smiled at me several times as I'd wielded my paintbrush) was annoying. Until I remembered that good art is all about magic and illusions anyway, but it was too late for a smart retort.

I hoped his big cock was also an illusion, and more about positioning and perspective than real life. Or he had a splint on it, and it would flop over like a dying tulip when he wasn't posing.

'Oh heavens, that is magnificent.'

I jump at the unexpected sound of a human voice. My musings about life models are interrupted by a man togged out in those big, baggy walking shorts with lots of pockets, chunky socks, brown boots and a checked shirt. He looks so stereotypical that for a second I just stare. He is studying my picture.

'Is that Ash's little dog?'

Bloody hell, I can't get away from Ash even if I try! 'Georgina's,' I correct him with a smile. 'It's Bella, I'm looking after her.'

'Ahh.' He raises an eyebrow, then taps his lips with one finger. 'Well, it's splendid. You've really captured that cheeky look of hers, not easy with a black dog, eh?'

Bella chooses that moment to emerge from the trees behind, where she's been pottering about on her lead, and lollops up to him.

'Talk of the devil, here's the little lady herself! And how

are you, trouble?' He strokes her head, and she licks his hand before having a sniff around his pockets. When she realises there's no food on offer, she heads towards the stream.

'It is good.' He nods again.

'Thank you!' It's refreshing to have a real person say they like one of my pictures. Normally these days it's all commissions for books. I'm not saying publishers aren't 'real people' but most of it is done remotely, and nearly always includes required changes 'to fit the brief'.

To do what I want to do, just because the fancy has taken me, is nice, and to have somebody like it as well is a bonus. 'It's my job. I'm an illustrator. I do book covers, illustrate children's books, stuff like that.'

'Would I know you?'

'Maybe not, unless you read women's fiction, or books for the under sevens.' We share a smile. 'And my credits are pretty small if I get them at all.'

'You do commissions?'

'Not often, I'm pretty busy. Though I am taking it easy while I'm house- and dog-sitting for Georgina.'

'And you're here for…?'

'For a month, at least.'

'Beautiful spot, isn't it?'

'Gorgeous. It's really inspirational, it's given my creativity a bit of a kickstart.'

'I bet. I bet. Now…' He starts to delve about in his pockets, first one, then another. It goes on for a while, until he gets back to the second one and flashes something triumphantly. 'Here we go, my card! I've got a little art shop in the village, very popular with the visitors. If you had time, I'm sure your pictures would go like hot cakes! One like that one of Bella, with the stream behind, would go like that.' He clicks his fingers.

'Well, maybe.' I look at him a bit doubtfully. 'If I have time, I can't promise...'

'No pressure, no pressure. Just a thought! Wonderful to be busy, my girl. Wonderful. No worries, pop in though if you're passing and we can have a chat. Always nice to chat to an artist.' He taps my shoulder, then points at the picture. 'You must show Ashley that. Splendid, splendid.' He peers closely at the picture one more time, and with a brief wave he turns and heads back the way he came. I listen to the snapping of twigs as he goes.

'What do you think, Bella? Bella? Oh, Bella!' Bella, who has been sniffing along the bank, isn't interested in my pictures, she is interested in the water. With a plop she lands tummy-deep, then turns to look at me, her tongue hanging out as though she is laughing. I can't help myself; I laugh back. 'I'll have to video you so I've got something funny to watch when I go home, you're better than any YouTube vid!'

She wags her tail as though she approves, causing ripples.

'Oh Bella, come out you little horror! Sugar, hang on, it's my phone. Don't move, no, no...' Bella starts to splash her way up stream, then reaches the end of her long lead and turns back. Bouncing along like Tigger.

'Becky?'

'Hi!'

'Becky, can you hear me? It's Ben.'

I can hear him, but it doesn't sound like he can hear me. I stand up. Drat, the phone reception round here is really patchy. 'Ben?' If Ben needs to talk to me, then this is important. He is the senior designer for a big publisher. I trust him, I like him, and I've been relying on him to keep sending work my way. A lot of the commissions might not be exactly what I want to do, but they will pay the bills for now.

Okay, there is one hitch. A major hitch. He works for the same publisher as Teddy. And they often work together.

I try to ignore the prickle of unease.

Life would be so much easier if I could cut ALL ties with Teddy, but I can't. I have to be sensible. It would be professional suicide. I need the work.

'I can hear you now… breaking up a… that cover des…'

'Ben? I'll call you when I get in?'

'Ace, need… will email you with editor's sugges…'

I've lost him. I slip the mobile phone back into my pocket and look down at the very soggy doggy, who has jumped out of the stream and is now shaking herself all over my legs, and my blanket. From the few words that I managed to hear, I got the message. Bloody Teddy has been sticking his oar in and tweaking my covers again.

This just isn't fair. Even out here, I can't escape him.

I mean, I can take constructive criticism, I'm happy to make changes, but Teddy seems to request alterations for the sheer hell of it. My cover matched the brief, the author was happy, the editor responsible for the book was happy, the design team were happy, the marketing team were happy, and now Teddy has chipped in. But it has nothing to do with him!

Actually, now I come to think about it, he's a complete control freak. He has to stick his oar in everywhere. And he's always tried to control my career. But Ben was happy with the cover I'd done, I'm *sure* he was. And now all of a sudden there's a problem.

I can feel the throb in my temples, the start of a headache – and I've not had one of those since I got here. The feeling of panic on my chest is creeping back as well.

This isn't fair. I swallow to ease the lump in my throat, suddenly feeling tearful. I've come here to escape, get kick-started. And how can I do that, with the shadow of Teddy lurking in the background? Editing my life.

'This is what I was trying to escape!' Bella wags her tail and licks my hand, then shakes, hard, showering me with water. 'Oi!' I jump back, but she follows, shaking again. Making me smile. 'Oh Bella.'

The lump in my throat eases. It's impossible to stay wound up when you've got a playful dog.

I must not get upset about losing the type of work I'm trying to get away from. If Ben doesn't want me, then that's fine – even if it is fucking annoying that it's Teddy that has upset things.

Being here was about cutting down on the work that wasn't my first choice, spending more time on the stuff I really want to do. Taking the commissions that I want to take. *That* is what's important.

I sniff and blink away the self-pity as Bella sits in front of me, staring.

'Maybe your Mr…' I fish the card out of my pocket. 'Mr Simons is right. Maybe I need to paint you and all this.' Her tongue lolls out of her mouth, so it looks like she is smiling approval. I sigh. 'After I've fixed this cover.' To be honest, now I've stopped to think about it, let's face it, my heart isn't in it. Since I arrived here, I've been more drawn to sketching what is around me, rather than some abstract idea.

I'm now going to have to send in some totally different alternative ideas (that's what 'we love it but could you just tweak…' means) based on the same cover brief.

I'd rather paint flying fish and unicorns, or Tolkien-style creatures that live in the mountains that cradle the lake. I would, I really would. And I *am* good at them. I am.

And Mr Simons loved my picture today, so I can't be total crap, can I? Even if what I'm good at isn't ground-breaking, it's still worthwhile. It's still *art*.

As we head back home the idea grows on me – not the creatures in the mountains, the pictures for the art shop.

Bella lags behind every few yards to sniff, then charges ahead and nearly drags the leash out of my hand (and my arm out of its socket) when she spots a bird, or a rabbit, or a leaf, or something that might or might not have moved. But I hardly notice.

I really should use this month to take at least one foot off the treadmill. Be a bit pickier about the work I do. Do some stuff of my own just for the hell of it, just for me.

Or just for Mr Simons.

Some part of my brain recognised I needed a break and

brought me here. And now the rest of me needs to catch up and embrace the opportunity.

I need to stop being so bloody half-hearted about this! For heaven's sake, I've got a full month. A whole month in this amazing place, with this gorgeous puppy, and Grasmere gingerbread, Kendal mint cake, local gin and... well, hills to climb. Real hills, not just metaphorical ones.

I can't just spend the time doing the same-old, can I?

My mouth starts to twitch at the corners and my pace picks up. I'm striding along before I realise it, Bella bouncing at my heels.

Magic flying ponies are where it's at, monsters in the lakes, kingfishers (*blue* ones, very definitely blue ones), muddy dogs chomping daisies, scenery. Glorious chameleon-like scenery.

Not covers for books that fashion dictates have to be a plain colour with a blob in the middle. Because it's intriguing. Meaningful. In!

I don't need to be 'in', I don't need the pressure of trying to make my blob in the middle look slightly more eye-catching than somebody else's.

The last few years have been all about my career. Now don't get me wrong, that is how I've wanted it – but I think I've been barking up the wrong tree, or rather straying up a dead end. I've been working all hours, and for what? To please other people. People like Teddy – who could pull the plug any time anyway. Well, let's face it, he has, hasn't he?

Going freelance was supposed to be about artistic freedom, balance, making my own choices. Maybe this month should be all about reminding myself of that.

I slow my pace to a dawdle. Except I need to check my bank balance first. Not-so-artistic blobs pay a lot better than pretty illustrations – which is why I let myself be led that way.

Honestly, falling for that old chestnut, sacrificing my artistic integrity for money! Ha! But I'm not stupid; in fact, I'm pretty sensible, and I'm not cut out to live in a hovel eating baked beans out of a tin, because of some idealistic dream. I'd grown out of that by the time I graduated and realised just how competitive life was.

'Argh!' Bella suddenly starts barking and lunges forward, snapping me right out of my daydreaming, and nearly snapping my neck as I take a dive. 'Bloody hell.' I clamber back onto all fours, then slowly pull myself onto my knees and brush my hands off. 'Ouch.'

Bella shows no sympathy. I think she's forgotten I am attached to her. She is staring into the trees, wagging her tail like crazy, straining against her collar.

I peer in the same direction, hanging on tight to the lead. For a moment I swear I can see movement in the bushes. Man-size movement.

'Rubbish. I'm imagining things.' I get to my feet and look at my grass-stained knees, and then over to Bella. No way can it be Ash stalking us, can it?

They are the only drawback to this perfect little escape. Georgina and Ash. Talk about *drama*. I came here to chill, to work, to get away from all the relationship angst – and have ended up dropping headfirst into somebody else's. I could do without it. But what's the alternative?

'Come on then Bella, let's get home. I think we both need a bath!'

I also think I do need to get a bit fitter. I'm panting and I've let a little pooch pull me over, and I'll be absolutely no match for Ash if he runs off with Bella. Maybe I need to ask my SAS man for some more tips? Maybe I do need a 'how to get fit in four days', or something like that? But without doing any more of his bootcamp sessions.

It's not worth it. Not even for the opportunity to see him in tight T-shirt and shorts.

Nope, definitely not.

Well. Maybe.

Chapter Eight

Mistake number one. On a whim I send Georgina a photo of Bella so she can see her in all her soggy glory, before I dump her in the bath.

Rather a silly whim, it turns out.

'Oh my God, you can't take photos like that!' She's Skyping me while I'm still grinning at the funny picture.

'What?'

'Don't post it anywhere, tell me you've not posted it anywhere, please. Swear you've not put it on Insta.'

'Sorry?' The woman is crazy.

'If Wuff Togs, or Plush 'n' Tangle Free see something like that I'll lose my sponsorship, it's so off-brand.'

'Off-brand?' I don't mean to sound scoffing, but I'm sure there's a hint of it in my voice. Bella loves the outdoor life and is as far from a pampered pooch as you can imagine. I want to say it, but I don't.

'God, I'm sorry, I'm so, so sorry for shouting at you.' Her voice has lost its aggressive edge and she looks like she's about to burst into tears. The sudden change makes me feel a pang of guilt.

'It's okay, she's your dog, and I didn't mean…' Sugar, what have I done now? She could be in the same kind of situation as me. She needs her income from Wuff Tangle or whatever they're called, and she's scared of screwing it up. 'I'm sorry, but I didn't…'

'No, I'm sorry. Really. It's just…' She sniffs and wipes her knuckle under her eye. 'Oh shit, I didn't mean to…' She puts the palms of her hands over her face and sits for a moment obviously trying not to cry. I feel awful. 'Sorry, sorry.' When she looks up again her eyes are red and there's a wobble in her face. She takes a deep breath. 'Sorry, it's not fair to saddle you with my problems. I'm not usually like this, I… it's just everything's going wrong, with Ash, with Bella, and oh my God, oh just promise you'll keep her safe for me? Don't let him have her? Please? I couldn't cope if…'

'I promise, I promise I'll keep her safe. I'm sorry, I just thought you'd like to see her happy, I didn't mean to upset you.'

'I do, I do want to see her happy, I love seeing her happy! But you've seen my account, that's my life Becky, not, not, not…' She's waving her finger in Bella's direction. 'My life isn't supposed to be a mess!' I'm sure she is welling up again now at the sight of her perfect pooch looking all bedraggled. 'My life is supposed to be like my Insta account. It used to be; it was so perfect.' She bites down on her lip and looks so upset I want to hug her. 'Nothing like this has happened before.'

That Instagram account, that perfect representation of

her life, is as important to her as my art is to me. She loves Bella, clearly, and it must be hard to leave her with somebody else. Especially with the threat of Ash taking her. 'I promise I won't put the photo online, anywhere. It was just for me.'

'The whole Ash thing is bad enough; I can't lose Bella.' She sniffs again.

'It's okay, okay.' Oh gawd, I am getting all hot and bothered. I need to be upfront with her here though. Mistake number two coming up. 'Talking of Ash, er, he came by again yesterday.' Never mention a hated ex when a woman is already upset.

'What do you mean?' She's gone pale.

'He was in the garden when I let Bella out for a wee.'

'And?'

'Well, he, er, said she's his as well as yours.'

'What? I asked you not to let him in!' There's a hint of panic in her voice.

'I didn't let him in. He said he came through the gate.'

'What did he want?'

I feel like I need to reassure her. 'I think he just wanted to see her, to play with her?'

'I shouldn't have done this, should I? I should have brought her with me, or taken her to a dog-sitter somewhere else or something?'

'Maybe if you'd explained, and I'd known what to expect?' This is potentially a mess, but it's my turn to feel panic. I don't want to be sent home early! I love being here, I love looking after Bella. And I quite like seeing Ash.

Though something tells me I should steer clear where he's concerned, this sounds like it's messy enough already. 'Look.' I don't want to say this, but I have to. 'If you want me to take her somewhere, to lock up and go home, then that's fine.' Not that I have a home to go to, so that could be an issue.

'I'm sorry Becky, no, no I don't mean that.' Phew, thank heavens for that. 'It's just whenever anybody mentions *his* name, I get so, so… Oh Christ, you know how it is.'

I'm not sure I do. But I do know she's upset. 'Oh fuck.'

'What?'

'Nothing. Absolutely nothing.' I turn around, so that she cannot see Bella, who has just dashed back into the house at high speed.

Okay, call me stupid, but I didn't close the door behind me. I was too busy fielding the call from Georgina. So Bella, soggy Bella, slipped out. And it looks like she found a mud bath. Or made a mud bath. She is caked in the stuff. And she's now doing zoomies round the kitchen, showering the cupboards (and me) with goo, plopping her big fat hairy paws all over the cushions.

I am sure this is not on-brand behaviour.

I think she might have dug a very big hole. Like I seem to be doing. Maybe I *do* need to go home. To my own life, my depressing, terrible… no! I don't want to go home.

'I've got to go; Bella needs her paws wiping.' Wiping? That has to be the understatement of the century. Oh my God, what has she got in her mouth? It looks like a dead rat.

I hold a hand out – not that I want it, but you have to

show willing. She play-growls, shakes it and takes a step back. Then chomps.

Shit. Can dogs die of eating rats?

'I suppose at least she likes you,' Georgina says reluctantly. 'We'll see how it goes for a few days, shall we? And if you see Ash, you can tell him...'

'I thought I wasn't supposed to talk to him?' But I'm talking to a blank screen. She's gone. And so has Bella. She's dropped the rat, grabbed my flip flop and managed to dodge past me and out of the kitchen.

I can hear her trampling about upstairs. So much for clean bedsheets. I scramble up after her, narrowly missing banging my head on the low beam, and missing her as she dives through my legs and back down.

Sugar, I bump back down on my bottom and dive into the lounge just as she abandons my shoe and grabs the rodent again.

Bugger.

She drops her prey in the middle of the cream sheepskin rug and dodges past me.

Luckily, when I edge closer, I see it's not a rat. It looks more like a sock. The sock I couldn't find when I got dressed this morning. Flaming dog! She's the naughtiest, most mischievous animal I have ever known. It's a good job she's so cute and funny.

My phone beeps with a message.

Sorry, bad connection, I'm sure you're doing your best.

Hmm. I'm not sure how to take that. Do I detect a hint of

sarcasm? But I haven't got time to work out if it's nice or nasty. I dash upstairs. Bella is curled up in the middle of the bed, with my flip flop in her mouth, play-growling. There's mud spattered everywhere. Bugger. It's going to take me hours to clean the place up. Practically the *whole* house. I take a step nearer, and she jumps away, flip flop gripped firmly in her teeth.

This is *so* not what Georgina's Instagram account is about. Or Georgina's perfect life.

I think that's it though. Yes, this place is amazing, but is the life she's portraying in those photos a little bit *too* perfect? Before I came here, I'd had the impression that Georgina had it made. A polished career girl with the perfect dog, the perfect house, the perfect man. I was *so* envious of her.

And now the man is her ex and she's scared she's going to lose so much more.

Like I have been. Maybe we're not so different after all.

Okay, my life was never as perfect as hers, but everything was kind of going in the right direction.

Until somebody threw a massive spoke in the works. I've been scared that it's all crumbling around me, and maybe Georgina is too.

Bella suddenly interrupts my thoughts as she dives past me, and back down the stairs. I catch up with her in the lounge and grab the end of the sock. She growls. I mean, I know it's play fighting, but she is not going to let go. I try and prise her jaws open, but she's got a grip an alligator would be proud of.

'Give, Bella! Leave it.' I sit on the floor in front of her, determined not to give in.

Bella tugs, also determined not to give in. And with each tug there's a funny little growl or grunt as her feet slide on the wood floor.

'Please?' I'm not too proud to beg.

'You'll never win at that game, you need food!'

'Shit!' I'm so shocked at hearing a voice, I let go, fall flat on my back and Bella dives off, her nose in the air, proudly bearing off her trophy.

Luckily, she is caught before she heads off back into the garden with it.

I sit up.

Ash is standing in the open doorway and has swooped Bella off her feet and is holding her high in the air.

He's framed by the large glass doors that lead onto the patio and show off the magnificent view of the lake.

Bella drops the flip flop, right in his face – serves him right.

'Bloody hell, Bella, you're a right ragamuffin!' he chuckles, then glances at me. 'There'll be hell to pay if you let Georgina see her looking like this!'

I collapse back onto the floor. 'Unfortunately, she has. She was not impressed.'

'I bet.'

'What do you want?' He hugs Bella closer to him, not caring about the mud. They make a cute couple. 'Apart from the obvious, of course.' I scramble to my feet. 'Give her back!'

He kisses the top of Bella's head and reluctantly puts her

down, so I can grab her collar. Then he hands me my flip flop.

'It's a bit awkward.' He shifts uncomfortably. It's odd, he doesn't look the type who ever feels embarrassed. 'I bumped into David, he said you'd done an amazing picture of Bella.'

'David?'

'Simons, he saw you by the stream? In the wood?'

'Ah.'

'If he says you're good, then I know you are. It might sound daft, but I couldn't, er, commission a painting of her, could I?'

'Oh.' This is not what I expected at all. 'It was only a quick sketch, hang on.' I drag a protesting Bella off to the kitchen, and lock her in, then go and get the picture I've done and hand it over. My knuckles brush against his and it's almost a sensuous touch. An intimate touch that makes my insides clench with anticipation. Oh my God, that's weird.

I jump back, embarrassed, my face heating up, and shove my hands in my pockets.

He hasn't noticed. He's staring at the sketch.

'This is brilliant. You're really talented.' He looks up at me then, and I blush even more.

'Don't sound so bloody surprised!'

'Sorry.' He grins. 'I didn't mean it as an insult.'

'I can do you one like that but finished, of course.'

'I couldn't have…?' He waves the sketch.

'Well…'

'I'll pay.' The dimples deepen, but he's looking at me

earnestly. Then he glances back down, and his features soften. 'She was bouncing about with the rest of the litter in the daisies when I first saw her, flopping about on the mown grass, and when she got up, she had a daisy in the middle of her head.' He motions. 'Daft apeth! It sealed the deal, how could I resist a noddle like that?'

Then he looks back at me, and his lips are pressed together in a rueful smile. 'Sorry.' He shrugs.

'No need to apologise.' I know my voice is stiff, it has to be, otherwise I might give in to the urge to well up or hug him, and that would never do. Oh. My. God. He really does love this dog. 'She's a cutie. Sure, have it if you want, but it's not really finished.'

'It's perfect.' He takes a couple of strides away, then stops. 'I know a few really great viewpoints round here I could show you, that might be good for painting. You know, in return for this? If you fancy it, that is?'

'You do mean walk, not another of your bootcamp sessions?' I say, suddenly suspicious. If he thinks I'm up for an SAS-style clamber up mountains, then he's got another think coming.

'You don't fancy a bit more training? We could throw in some light weights next time.'

'Get lost!'

'Bricks in the back of your rucksack, strengthen your core?'

I scowl, and this time he laughs properly.

'I'm kidding! Honest! Though I reckon you would be up for it, given a bit of persuasion.' Nope, not even when he grins his cute grin, puts his warm hand on my waist and looks me in the eye. No. Absolutely not. 'This time though I do mean a walk with a view, a view of fells, lakes, wildlife.' He is still grinning. Does he know how motivating I found the view of his bum when I was jogging after him across the lawn? 'All good clean fun.' He winks. He does. He must know. 'Mind you, the view I had during our workout wasn't too shabby.'

Now that is flirting. I'm sure it is. This man is dangerous. I should stay away.

Oh, why the hell should I? This is the new adventurous Becky. I am experimenting with my work, my fitness routine. Everything!

What happens in Cumbria stays in Cumbria!

And a stroll has to be better and easier than the workout, doesn't it? And he is offering to show me places I might not discover on my own. Off the beaten track. 'Wow, yes, sure, that would be great.' I should say no, what about Georgina? Oh, bugger it, they're not going out. I'm single, he's single. 'Brill. Lovely!'

'I know a quiet spot where there are often young deer.'

Okay, that does it. I don't need persuading. He doesn't need to offer any extra incentive, although I'll definitely have to take some photos if we are going to see some wildlife.

'Thursday?'

'Fab!'

He salutes me, then strides off across the lawn whistling, and occasionally glancing down.

I think I am grinning. I actually feel like punching the air and then hugging myself.

Oh, Ashley James, you are far too sweet and sexy for your own good. And mine. Wheedling your way into my heart and good books, and I'm not even supposed to talk to you, let alone like you!

I'm just too soppy. Show me a man cuddling a puppy or kitten and I'm putty in their hands. Except I can't be. Georgina is my boss, and Georgina loves Bella just as much, I'm sure.

Bloody hell, this would be a lot easier if Ash was the good guy, and Georgina the evil ex I had to avoid!

I stare after him, then let my gaze take in the lake. The colours and the muted tones bring a lump to my throat.

Georgina is right. She *could* find somebody else to replace me. I could go home, avoid all this emotional hoo-ha, which I really could do without. Or I could just leave here with Bella and come back on weekends to check on the house. That way the dog would be happy, and I'd be avoiding all risks of Ash taking her or leading me astray.

Distance. That is what I need.

Except I don't have a home to go back to, because I've got my own flat-sitter in. And I don't want to go to my parents' house, do I?

Oh my God, what am I doing even thinking like this? I want to be here. I don't want to run away. I want to go off on an adventure with Ash, I want to have some fun, to challenge myself, to laugh.

The sound of something tearing snaps me out of my daydreaming and I rush to the kitchen.

Bella is chewing on something, pulling back and

ripping, and I suddenly realise it's my sock. Why didn't I put it somewhere out of reach? Like the washing machine!

'Oh Bella.' I shake my head, so she shakes hers. Hard. As though she's trying to kill the sock. I can't help myself; I smile. She's funny.

To be honest, even though she's turning my life upside down, I've had more fun here in the last few days than I've had for months. I feel like I'm unpeeling the boring layers and getting back to the old me.

I look at her. Yep, it pays to be more dog. She's all happy smiling face, wagging tail (that is putting streaks of mud along the cupboard like some random paintbrush), and – oops – muddy, muddy paws. The bit we could do without.

Nope, no way could I go to my parents. Mum would have a hissy fit if I turned up with this little mud-seeking missile. She'd refuse to let her in the house until she'd been washed down and blow-dried.

And no way can I walk away from her. It's like *The Bodyguard*: I am the Dog-guard protecting her from her obsessive stalker. Not that there are death threats for her – but there could be for me, from Georgina.

My phone bleeps and I realise I've got my fingers crossed. Please don't be Georgina, please, right now I don't think I can cope with any more drama.

It is not Georgina. It is an email from Ben. Marked urgent.

Oh my God, I'd forgotten all about him! A few days ago, I would have been refreshing my emails every twenty seconds waiting for him or another editor to get in touch, but I've forgotten all about obsessing about being shot down. I've been too busy with Bella, and Ash.

I reluctantly open the email. It's just as I thought. The 'tweaks' have got Teddy's stamp all over them. And so has the request for two more covers. Covers that do not make my heart soar, but rather make it sink with boredom.

'I think I've had enough of this, don't you Bella? Oh hell, don't swallow the damned thing.' She is gagging on my sock, but still growls possessively and tries to wrap her paws around it when I catch hold of the end. My God, she's got a firm grip, and sharp claws! Flipping heck, choking my charge to death isn't supposed to be on the agenda.

Then I remember what Ash said. Food! It's a bit tricky hanging on to the toe of a sock, and dragging a dog across the tiles, but I'm determined not to let go as I head towards the fridge. Thank goodness for slippery tiled floors, she wouldn't budge if there was a rug! Plus, bonus, her furry tummy is soaking up some of the dirt like a mop. Well, smearing it if I'm honest.

'Oomph.' I nearly bang my head on the door, as the second I open it, Bella lets go of her trophy. 'Cheese or ham, madam?' I don't think she's fussed.

My rat-like, bedraggled, holey sock goes in the bin. Then I look at my email again.

I have had enough of tailoring my life, and my work, to Teddy. Okay, it was a bit different when we were an item. I wanted to please him, I wanted to help him, and I was truly grateful that he wanted my career to flourish. But now I come to think about it, he wasn't exactly supportive, was he? And it wasn't really about *my* career. I was an extension to his.

And while I was flattered, I do know it can be hard to find decent cover designers – very few of us want to work in-house these days (and I was the closest on offer), we want the freedom of being freelance. House-sitting when (and where) the fancy takes us, haha.

But until now I've pushed my own preferences to one side, and desperately said 'yes' to everything Teddy has pushed my way.

I've got a horrible feeling he was the only one really benefiting from our relationship.

'What do you think, Bella? Do I need to stop trying to please him, and everybody else?' She licks my hand.

So I quickly type a polite but brief response to Ben, thanking him for the comments, giving him a date that I'll get the changes back by, agreeing to provide one of the new covers and regretfully declining the other (which sounds dire and dismal) due to 'other commitments'. Meeting him partway seems sensible – I'm not completely stupid, I don't intend throwing a huge chunk of my income stream away without a second thought. If I'm going to establish my new career, then I need to do it gradually.

'Got to keep us in crisps and cheese eh, Bella?' She yawns and sits down, exhausted by all the fun.

Now all I've got to do is harden my heart against the man who wants custody of my charge. He obviously loves her, but sometimes love on its own isn't enough, is it?

I have a work plan, now I need a dog-protection plan.

My natural inclination would be to go down the

conciliation and negotiation route (you can tell I come from a family of solicitors, can't you?), and give Ash supervised access, but I'm not sure Georgina's going to buy that. She seems a bit inflexible where Ash is concerned. And upset. So, what do I do?

'I think it's wine o'clock, don't you, pup?' Bella yawns. 'With Pringles and a Netflix binge?'

She follows me upstairs and watches from the bed as I pull on my comfiest baggiest T-shirt and joggers, then pads down after me waiting expectantly as I root in the giant fridge freezer.

'Oh my God Bella, salted caramel ice-cream! What do you think, ditch the Pringles idea?' My mouth is literally watering at the thought of it. So is Bella's, she is drooling all over my bare feet. I grab the tub, then notice the smaller one behind it in the freezer. It makes me laugh. 'I don't believe it. She's bought you doggy ice-cream!' Bella wags her tail harder. 'Spoon each?' She spins around in a circle as I get one large and one small spoon from the drawer and two bowls, and she bounces around as I head into the lounge and grab the TV remote. 'Bridget Jones is on! What do you think, Bella? Shall we watch Bridget?'

This feels so naughty as I sit on the floor, my back against the couch, Bella at my side.

Teddy wasn't a fan of Bridget, or really any romcom. Or sitting on the floor.

I take the lid off the tub and grab a bowl and spoon, then stop dead.

'You know what, Bella? I don't need to do it that way.' Teddy's way. 'I can ditch the bowl and be totally bad, what do you think?' Teddy definitely wasn't keen on eating ice-cream straight out of the tub. 'But he isn't here, is he? And it's not his life – it's mine!' She wags her tail in approval. 'And he'd have a fit if he saw me doing this!' I dig deep into the tub with the big spoon, then do the same with the second, smaller tub, and hold out the small spoon for Bella and giggle as she licks, spreading it all over her nose and beard.

This is like escaping back to real life after being locked up for ages not being allowed to do anything that you really, really want to.

I can actually do whatever I like.

I laugh out loud and Bella jumps. 'Sorry, pup.' I fondle her furry ears and give her another spoon of ice-cream. 'And that's your last bit! You do know dogs can only have ice-cream as a special treat, don't you? I'll get you one of your healthy chews instead, how's that?' She gives me her sad eyes look. She is not impressed.

'What the hell have I been doing the last few months?' She doesn't comment, she just lies down and rests her chin on my legs and gazes up adoringly. I know it's the ice-cream she adores, not me, but it doesn't matter. 'You know what, you're better than any therapist.' She rolls over so I can tickle her hairy tummy. 'Harder work, but better. Never a dull moment with you around, is there?'

I grin at the TV screen, then take another mouthful of ice-cream. This is where I need to be. Not just because of the amazing views and the gorgeous house.

This is about my life.

It's one thing being considerate and fitting in with

people, but it's not good to try so hard to please another person that you end up losing who you really are. What you actually want.

I'm not crap. I'm not doing it all wrong. It's time I tried to find that confident girl I used to be, the one that believed in herself. 'If I don't, nobody else is going to, are they Bella?'

Chapter Nine

'I can't just keep fending him off and running away, Abby.'

My sister rang me late last night, just as I was getting ready for bed.

Well, I say late. It wasn't late in 'city' terms, but it was in my Lake District life.

I've taken to getting up earlier, so that I don't miss the countryside waking up, and have the chance to capture the elusive quality of the light that disappears as the sun strengthens. The lake has a gentle shimmer on its surface, the mountains an almost nostalgic sepia colouring, and the dew magnifies and mirrors everything. It's amazing. And anyway, there's no point in staying up late – not even the bats do that around here.

Anyway, she caught me brushing my teeth and so I settled into bed and we had a bit of a natter. She told me about how she was sure her boyfriend, Ed, was about to propose, how she hates her new office on the first floor because they're all so competitive, and it's further from the loos (apparently there are only gents' toilets on that floor, as it used to be an old-fashioned firm and there was no demand for a ladies'), and how she's been arguing with Ed about repainting the lounge because he likes on-trend grey and she thinks it will be depressing. I told her about the kingfisher, Bella, and my real-life version of the War of the Roses. And I asked her advice, because she knows all about family law and custody battles.

'She's probably in denial. I'm only guessing, but maybe she can't accept their split because it wasn't on her terms, so she can't accept that he isn't a total bad guy and maybe should see the dog? Or she could be right, that he's telling you a load of bollocks and just wants to steal the dog back to piss her off!'

'Gee, thanks a lot, sis. That's helpful!' Hmm, she has an interesting point though. Maybe it is something to do with accepting that her perfect life isn't quite so perfect after all. I don't know Georgina very well, but I'm already getting the impression that she's used to everything going well, and right now it doesn't seem to be.

'Well I don't know them, Bec!'

I need to try another tack. 'I know, pretend *she's* our client.' Abby is used to seeing things from her client's point of view, she works best when she can relate to things – something to do with her logical brain. 'Or maybe we need to look at it from both sides—'

'Our? We? Since when was this my problem?'

I ignore her. If I carry on, she'll get drawn in; she can't help herself, she likes to interfere. 'It could be the other way around, maybe she's stopping him seeing Bella to piss him off.'

'I don't think that's seeing it from her point of view,' Abby says reasonably. She has a point. 'And why would she do that anyway?'

God, don't you hate solicitors? 'I don't know! Maybe she's jealous, well she is jealous, she said he was childish, the way he tried to win her over, be Bella's favourite. Or they could have had a nasty split and she just hates him. Or she might just be a cow.'

'Wow, he must be sexy! You fancy the pants off him, don't you?' I can hear the smile in her voice.

'Don't be ridiculous. He seems a nice enough guy, but I don't know him! Before you say another word, I am not twisting this round in his favour. I just feel sorry for him.'

'Sure.' She laughs.

'And you always say it's important to have a balanced view, see it from both sides.'

'Not really. All is not fair in love and law.'

'And she is a bit of a cow, she shouted at me earlier!'

'Had you done something daft?'

'Abby! And no, I hadn't, I just sent her a photo of the dog which was "off-brand". Honestly, you'd think it was a bloody celebrity, not a loopy mutt!'

'Off-brand?'

'Oh yeah, with Georgina everything is about being on-brand.'

'You're kidding?'

'Nope, this isn't just any dog, this is a special Instagram dog!' Abby giggles. 'So, what do I do, oh clever little sister?'

'Okay, she does sound slightly over the top.' I can tell she's trying to stop giggling. 'So why not ask him, or her, or both of them whether there's a middle way.'

'I've been banned from talking to him!'

'Banned?' That sets her off laughing again, and it's infectious. I join in. Honestly, when you say all this out loud it does sound bonkers. 'So, have you stuck to that?'

'Er, well no, not exactly.' I don't think I'm ready to tell her about the bootcamp session with Ash yet, or the planned walk. Better to keep this simple.

'You're house-sitting Becky, you're not under contract! What's the worst she can do? Send you home?'

'It has been mentioned,' I interject.

'Well, sounds like you might be well out of it! Sounds crazy to me, must be one hell of a cute dog.' My sister is not a dog person, she's a cat person. She likes polite distance, verging on indifference, and cleanliness in her pets.

I sigh. 'I do like it here.'

'I guessed that.' Her tone has softened, and I can hear the smile in her voice. 'And you did need a break.'

We both sit silent, thinking for a few minutes.

'So, now I've given you a free consultation, and the benefit of my worldly experience in dog custody, will you look at these paint colours for me and tell me what you think? I'll Skype you at the weekend, during the day when the light's good and you can have a look. We painted sample squares on the wall!'

'Sure.'

'You do sound happy Becs, happiest you've been for ages, kind of more carefree, like when we were kids.'

'I do?' I think about it. 'I think I am. I ate ice-cream out of a tub, watched *Bridget Jones* and slobbed out with Bella the other night.'

'Sounds perfect.' Her voice has a soft edge.

'It was.'

'On your own?'

We both laugh. 'Totally, well apart from Bella.' Abby is right though. I am happy, I really am. Okay, I haven't got my life or career sussed yet, but I definitely feel more positive. I don't feel dread when I wake up, just the solid weight of a dog on my stomach. And I'm happy on my own, this is not about a guy – this is me being happy about me.

'I've missed you Becs.'

'What?'

'You stopped ringing for a proper chat.'

'I did call!'

'I know you called. We talked, but we didn't *talk*.'

She's right. We've always been close, me and Abby, until I started seeing Teddy. She was even less reserved about passing an opinion on him than Mum. It made things awkward, seeing her roll her eyes when he made some derisory comment or was patronising. Except of course, I didn't think he was at the time.

'Sorry. I've missed you too.'

'Night Becs, sleep tight.'

'Don't let the bed bugs bite!' I chime back and we both blow kisses.

So, after sleeping on my brilliant sister's non-advice, I decide I was right. I cannot just avoid Ash (not that I want to). Sadly, I probably shouldn't sleep with him either (I think I might want to do that bit). I think I need to call Georgina and suggest some supervised access for Ash, during which I will promise not to listen to any lies he might tell about her, or let the dog out of my sight, and will promise not to let him shove her in his rucksack and run off. Seems reasonable, yes?

I send her a text, asking if we can have a quick chat tonight, then I get dressed so that I can let Bella out in the garden for her morning constitutional. I am not risking running into Ash without any clothes on again.

Bella dashes out onto the lawn at high speed, wees, then pauses. Nose in the air. After a brief sniff of the air, she spins around. Her nose is down and she's snuffling along at high speed, pausing every now and then and chomping on something.

When I say she's a food machine, I do mean she'll eat literally anything. I swear when we were in the woods, she was crunching squirrel poo, and now all I can think is that she's after bunny currants. Rabbit droppings, in case you're wondering – actual currants aren't good for dogs. Though I'm not sure poo is either. Never seen it on a doggy diet sheet.

I throw a doggy treat that I've brought out with me, and she totally ignores it. I watch her from the terrace, not sure whether to go after her or not. These are obviously very tasty morsels, far better than mine. It's really funny watching as she follows a zigzag trail.

Yes! That's exactly what it looks like – a trail! Oh my God, I don't believe it – Ash has laid food out for her. She's heading straight towards the dense shrubs at the side of the garden. I break into a trot after her as she speeds up. Even though she's slowing down briefly to snaffle up the snacks, she's still going at a fair pace. Bella heaven!

He must be watching me, worried I'll get to her first, because he suddenly launches himself out of a rhododendron bush. I'm sure he's judged it carefully, aware of her speed, knowing when she'll reach him.

But he dives just as I put my foot on her long lead.

Bella is yanked to a halt. 'Sorry Bella! It's for your own good!' Even from this distance the look on his face is brilliant! I wish I had my phone and could take a photo, or better still a video, I'd get so many shares on Reddit or TikTok!

I mean, how brilliant am I? I am really getting good at this dog-protection lark. After the last episode of finding him in the bushes I made two resolutions. One, to never go out in my pyjamas, and two, to clip the very, very long leash onto Bella's collar so that even if he got his hands on her, he wouldn't be able to run off without having me in tow.

It's worked out better than I could have ever hoped!

'What the fu—'

'Long lead!' I yell triumphantly, bending down to

retrieve the end of the lead that is under my foot. It is black, like Bella, hidden against her coat, buried in the grass that is overdue a mowing. And I reckon he was watching her so intently, he couldn't see anything else. 'Loser! Hahaha!' I start to reel her in quickly, and head towards her at a jog, just in case he decides to grab her anyway – and take the lead (and possibly me) with him. I'm not going to risk the humiliation of being dragged down the lawn behind him. 'Not much of an SAS man after all then, are you!'

He laughs, then laughs some more. A proper infectious belly laugh that is hard to resist. Then he sits on the grass, rubbing his large capable hand over his lightly bearded chin. I bet it feels all nice against your cheek when he snogs. Not red-rash bristly, just a tickle. Like down. Oh God, Becky. Stop!

He stops stroking his chin and drops his hand. He's got a nice chin. Firm. Clefted.

I could draw that chin. I could kiss that chin. I could…

'You are kidding?' He's grinning. 'You really do think I'm SAS, don't you?'

That stops me. I think I might be burning up. Em-bar-ass-ing. I didn't mean to say that out loud. My fantasies are supposed to stay in my head.

'No! Oh my God, no!'

'Wow, I'm flattered!' His eyes have gone all twinkly.

'Stop laughing!' I gather Bella in close to me, just out of his arms' reach. Which is a bit mean, when he obviously wants to cuddle her – but he's let me down. 'I was going to tell Georgina you weren't all bad, and you should be allowed to see her. Now you've spoiled it!' I wave a schoolmistress finger at him. Which makes me feel a bit daft.

He shrugs. 'I don't just want to see her.' His eyes widen to emphasise his words. 'I want her back... Becky Havers.'

'How do you know my name, Ash?'

We stare at each other for a long, silent moment. His name rolled off my tongue naturally. But now it seems weird that we've said each other's names out loud.

'You signed your picture. I googled you.'

I don't say that I googled him as well and found out absolutely nothing. Which kind of sadly reinforced the SAS idea. Bummer.

'Impressive CV.'

I don't know whether to be pleased or annoyed. Or whether I'm blushing out of embarrassment or pleasure. God, this man confuses me.

'Now I'm going to have to take her *everywhere* with me, to make sure you don't take her!' So much for my little planned solo trip to the art shop today. Bella will have to come with me. I can't trust him not to break in. 'I felt sorry for you, and now I'm disappointed.' I'm cross with him. I wanted to help, but what am I supposed to think now?

He smiles, not at all bothered about the telling off. 'Can't blame a guy for trying!'

'Yes, I can! Poor Georgina, she's really upset about all of this.' They need to clone Bella if she's so important to both of them. I don't know anything about the ins and outs of their relationship, but I do know I have to keep Bella safe until Georgina comes home.

'I know.' The smile fades from his face, and he looks

worried for a moment. 'But things change. Sometimes you have to let go and move on.'

He could be talking about me. I was just expected to let go of my work and move on. 'Well, maybe you need to help her a bit!' Okay, it's a bit snappy. I shouldn't be snappy, but he's hit a nerve. 'Not everybody can just forget about things they've worked hard at, things they think are important in their life.'

'It's not a failure to admit it and walk away when something is wrong.' His tone is soft, and his normally piercing gaze is looking at me in a totally different way.

I squirm a bit inside. Maybe he's right. Maybe I should have just said to Teddy, 'Hey, you know what? You're right! I'm crap at doing this weird work you made me do, I'm going to go and do what I want', but it isn't that easy, is it? I don't know if I can do anything well anymore, I don't know if I'm as crap at doing what I want to do as I am at doing the stuff he told me to.

Except lately I've begun to think that maybe I'm not that rubbish. Maybe some of my stuff is okay after all.

Maybe Georgina needs to know that it's okay if her life isn't quite as perfectly-perfect as she thought it was.

'Letting go and moving on is part of life.'

'Maybe,' I say grudgingly, it is poor Georgina we're talking about here, not me. But I can understand now why she's been so strung up, so upset when I've done things wrong. When I've talked to Ash. 'I don't think she wants to let go of you or Bella,' I say, as the thought comes into my head. His face clouds over. 'Though of course it's none of my business,' I add hurriedly. It really is none of my

122

business. I should keep my nose out. 'Sorry, I better go back in.'

'She's not trying to hang on to us because it's right, but because she doesn't want to admit it's wrong.' He sighs. 'And, yes, you're right – it is none of your business.' His face has tightened. He's shutting me out. I don't think he intended saying any of this to me, a stranger. Or to anybody.

'Huh, well yes, but I do have to do my job and right now, you're not helping by trying to steal my, I mean her, dog! She needs time!'

'My dog.'

'Whatever!' This is one argument I can't win. I don't know whose bloody dog she is.

His face lightens up a bit. It's like the clouds have cleared as quickly as they do over the Cumbrian hills. 'You're quite a little lioness, aren't you?'

'And don't you forget it – but less of the little!' Poor Georgina, cute dog, cute guy, perfect life, and it looks like it has started to crumble around her. I know what it is like to try and let go of stuff, even when in your heart you know that you need to. 'Now go away!' Sadly, I can't stop myself from smiling, so I've not got quite the authoritative effect I was aiming for.

'See you later!'

'Not if I see you first,' I mutter, tugging on Bella's lead, but feeling strangely smug. He's going to see me later!

Okay, earth to Becky. It's Bella he wants to see really, not you. 'Come on lady, breakfast time – if you're still hungry after all those treats!'

He chuckles, and I swear I hear him say 'SAS'.

'Haha, funny, isn't he, Bella? Hilarious!' Bella doesn't care, the little food machine is intent on dragging me back to the house, so she can eat something else. It's a good job she bounces round so much, or she'd be the fattest dog on the planet.

I think my to-do list might be a bit ambitious. Or I need to get up earlier and not spend the first half hour of the day trying to outwit Ash.

I know my priorities. Number one is walking Bella. A week or so in, I have learned that the more tired she is, the less destructive she is. This is important as I am on a mission to save as many of my socks from destruction as possible. Give the dog her due, she's creative.

It's not just the anti-destruction angle though; walking Bella is definitely not a chore. Well, yeah, at first it was just a job on my list, but I soon realised that it makes a difference to my *whole* day. It's good for me, I'm feeling fitter than I have for ages, and it's also given me thinking time and just being-me time. I've not put headphones on, because I need to be alert in case of animal or Ash noises, so it's just been me, Bella and the world around us.

Have you any idea how good it is to listen to silence, or the murmur of water in a stream, or the distant bleating of lambs or just the breeze in the trees?

I've not stopped and listened to the world for like, well, forever. And it is *so* hard to wallow in self-pity, or grouch about a person, or hate the world, or worry endlessly about whether the work you've just done is a pile of horse shit, when you're clambering up a hill after a dog and are out of breath, or when you've turned a corner and found a family of baby rabbits bouncing about.

So, that. Priority one on my list is important for more reasons than I could ever imagine.

Number two on the list has to be tidying up – you have no idea how much mess one dog can make. It's a bloody good job she doesn't moult as well, or I'd never keep up. In a way though, that's therapeutic as well, another major distraction from checking emails or social media.

Number three on my list is new work. Today I need to do some further sketches for *Mischief the Magic Pony* because my client said the concept sketch I sent her was 'awesome' (awesome, you hear that Teddy boy? Awesome!), and would I be interested in illustrating the series? Are you kidding me?! Interested? I did a jig round the kitchen hanging on to Bella's front paws, then picked her up and spun her round until we were both giddy (I collapsed, she did zoomies, barking her head off, note to self, do not wind the dog up). Then I rang her back and said, 'Sure, I'd be happy to discuss terms.' How cool am I?

Unfortunately, it turns out that 'terms' with this publisher aren't quite on the same scale as 'Ben' terms. Which I guessed would be the case, but I still live in hope. They have a much smaller budget, and although they'd love 'copious illustrations' it does rather depend on interest.

But it *could* be massive.

Wow, I've just realised, I've rediscovered a bit of my

optimism! I'm awesomely happy with 'It *could* be big'! And it's a cool project. And I want to do it *so* much. And if I keep doing bits of work with Ben (but be more selective about what) then I've at least got some income, and I can pay the bills, and it does give me time to branch out into stuff like this.

Isn't that what I really need to do? This could be my life changer.

So, really this should be priority one, but I have responsibilities while I'm here, and they come first.

And number four is to make the agreed cover amendments for Ben that I promised.

I also want to do some doodles for the art shop, as well as visit it.

Anyhow, bearing all this in mind, and as the village is only three miles away, I need to combine activities.

I will walk, not use the car. So that covers number one for the day, and also cuts down on dog-napping opportunities for Ash, and reduces number two, as there isn't as much time in the house to make mess. I am not going to let Bella out of my sight though. She is coming shopping with me.

I pack my small rucksack with treats for Bella, poo bags, a bottle of water and my sketch pad so David Simons can see some of my actual work – rather than just the stuff on my phone. Photos aren't the same, my artistic side needs to touch the paper, see the definition of paint and pencil, and I think Mr Simon's might be the same.

Yesterday I decided to download the Ordnance Survey app to my phone (Dad suggested it – I didn't know such a thing existed) and it means I don't just have to rely on Georgina's walk guide. It was easy to spot that there was a nice path that I could join at the bottom of the garden and follow along the edge of the lake. Then there was a short incline through fields to meet up with the road where it emerged opposite the church in the middle of the village. Perfect!

Chapter Ten

Bella snuffles her way down the lawn, checking that she didn't miss any treats that Ash might have dropped this morning, then speeds up as we near the lake and starts pulling against her harness. It's all or nothing with her, she's either steaming ahead or stopped dead because she's found something interesting that she needs to investigate.

In fact, she is so excited, and is wrenching my arm so hard, it feels mean not to let her off the lead.

But I don't. Because I'm sure I have just spotted the unmistakeable outline of Ash watching us from further up the hill. He's a hard man to miss.

He obviously didn't take my 'go away' very seriously.

'Oh no you don't, mister!' I shake my head. I'm up to this challenge. No way is he stalking us to the village, laying out treats as he goes to tempt Bella away from me. If he thinks I'm falling for that, he's got another think coming. I'm not just going to outwit Mr Sexy Pants, I am going to give him a run for his money. I am getting good at this.

I eye up the little boat that is tied to a mooring post and can feel the grin broaden on my face as the idea takes root.

'You really do love the water, don't you?'

Bella grins back at me, then does a little growly-barky thing. It's the nearest a dog can get to talking. She does it quite a lot. I glance back up the hill.

'Shall we?' The urge is getting stronger. I feel like a kid – unable to resist the impulse. Whatever else Ash is capable of, walking on water can't be one of his skills.

I glance around. Nobody else in sight. It can't do any harm, borrowing it just for a little while, can it? Nobody needs know.

'You will stay in the boat?'

She barks and starts to leap up at me trying to grab the end of the lead out of my hand. 'Okay, okay you lunatic!' Oh my God, I do feel like a giddy child again. My stomach is jumping about with anticipation as though there's a run of salmon in there leaping upstream. Years ago, when we were here, Dad took me and Abby in a rowing boat on Lake Windermere. My brother (boring even at twelve years old) sat with Mum (scared of water) on a bench, while we had the time of our lives – and I cried when Dad said we had to head back. Abby didn't, she is sensible and accepts things. I used to cry quite a lot; in fact, I admit I did quite often turn on the waterworks to get my own way. Not always. Just sometimes. I was known as 'the emotional, feely one' so why not capitalise a bit? I don't do it now. Never. Crying is for babies and the weak.

I plonk my rucksack down on the gravel that edges the lake and tug on the rope to pull the tiny rowing boat in closer, then look up the hill. Oh my God, he's heading our way! 'Bella, quick, quick, we've got to do this!' I'm giggling to myself and hopping from one foot to the other, my hands fumbling with the knot and Bella is bouncing about in excitement.

The boat looks in quite good nick, definitely sea (or lake) worthy. I can't really see Georgina splashing about, so maybe it was Ash's?

There's a yell. I'm sure he just yelled out to us to stop. Haha to you, Ashley James. I bet it is his boat. But whoever it belongs to, Bella definitely knows what it's for. She's leaping about, wagging her tail, play bowing and whining for me to hurry up. 'Okay, okay.' I try and hang on to her as I put my other hand out to steady it and she starts to bark with excitement. 'Go on then.' I laugh as she takes a flying leap and it rocks from side to side, water splashing in, then she sits down on the bench with her back to me – looking out at the water expectantly.

What can I do? I can't let the dog down, can I?

Seconds later, I'm holding the oars tentatively and try dipping one into the water experimentally. The boat wobbles its way from the shore. Bloody hell, I feel like Bilbo Baggins off on a big adventure, escaping the evil dognapper! This is way outside anything I ever did with Teddy – Mr Boundaries and Control. The most adventurous our lives got was taking a short cut in Ikea so that we didn't have to go around the entire shop.

Or asking for extra pepper on a pizza.

I pull harder and we practically zoom along, we're metres from the bank now.

I'm brilliant at this!

Bella's long lead pools around my feet, so I unclip it from her harness. 'Now you be good!' I can still grab the harness if I need to – it's got a handle, real-deal, expensive, rugged outdoor wear for the dog-explorer. Goodness knows how much the sponsor pays for her to be pictured wearing this in the lake or perched on top of a mountain.

We start off very wobbly, but I soon get the hang of it because I'm bloody determined to put some distance between us and Ash before he gets down to the shore. Soon we're kind of going in a straight line, and far enough out that not even he can wade in and grab Bella.

I snigger to myself, then put down the oars and gaze around. A smile on my face as I trail my hand in the ice-cold water and sneak a look back to see where Ash is. He looks miles away! I've won!

It feels like freedom. Time has stopped, we can sit here for hours just watching the water dimple around us as insects scud across its surface, watching the ripples spread and fade into nothingness. Looking at the brilliant blue sky and the grey-white sparkling clouds above us.

I can have a snack, do some sketching.

Bugger. For a moment I panic when I can't see my rucksack in the bottom of the boat, then realise that in my rush to get away before Ash reached us, I didn't pick it up. I twist round and can just make it out, abandoned on the gravel at the side of the lake.

The boat rocks violently as Bella spins round and barks.

'Stop it!' She ignores me and does a bit more totally boat-inappropriate bouncing. 'What the fuck…'

She's looking back towards the bank, her front feet perched on the back of the boat, jiggling about and bouncing in a way that is not a good idea. The most piercing whistle possible carries clearly across the water and Bella knows exactly who is making the noise. Ash.

She crouches slightly, her back legs tensed for the jump. 'Bella, here. Ignore him!' I lean forward and reach out, trying to grab hold of the nearest bit – her tail. If I work my way up her body, I can put my hands over her ears. What does the idiot think he's doing, getting her all excited? 'Sugar.' She's gone, her silky tail slipping through my fingertips as I make a final desperate grab for a back paw. I can't let her drown! Oh my God, Georgina will never forgive me. I'll never forgive myself. Ash will never forgive me.

Why didn't I think before I jumped in this stupid, bloody boat?

I can see the headlines now: *Dog-sitter drowns canine media star!*

I'm supposed to be keeping Bella safe.

Bloody hell, the boat is rocking. I teeter, lose my balance and lean too far over the side. I'm aware I'm flailing around desperately for something to grab, but all I find is thin air.

Then water.

Christ, it's cold.

For a second, I'm under the surface, then I come up spluttering, spitting out a mouthful of mucky lake. 'Fuck.' It is unbelievably cold, even with all my clothes on. 'Bella,

Bella.' I splash about on the spot, and she's nowhere to be seen. Oh God. Where the hell is she? I flail around in a circle, there's no sign of her! My eyes burn and I blink back the tears.

'Bella!' My throat has tightened up so much that it hurts when I bellow her name. I get a mouthful of water and splutter.

I grab onto the side of the boat. I need to get back in, I need to row around, I need to search the lake. She can't have gone far. She can't have just drowned already.

But I can't see her.

The panic gurgles about in my stomach as I thrash about wildly with my legs, trying to propel myself out of the water. But my clothes are soaked; I feel heavy, and the tiny boat just tilts alarmingly every time I try and launch myself into it, threatening to overturn.

'Shit, shit, shit.' I brush my hair back out of my eyes and squint, trying to see the dog against the glare of the water.

Oh my God, this is terrible. Where is she? I can't see Bella anywhere – I can see Ash though. He's powering through the water like an Olympic swimmer, broad shoulders and muscled forearms impressively cutting through the surface as though he was born with flippers. And he's heading straight for me.

'Not me! Find Bella!' I yell, waving madly.

He reaches me about two seconds after the words come out of my mouth, and it's like a whale has swum below me. There's a tremendous upwards force and I'm dumped unceremoniously back into the boat.

It would be funny if I wasn't on the verge of tears. 'Find Bella, you idiot!' I'm going to start crying, I must not cry.

He grins, his large hand wiping over his face and slicking his hair back. The sunlight reflecting from the water and dancing in his blue-blue eyes. For a moment I'm mesmerised then I snap out of it. 'It's not funny.' I choke the tears back. 'The dog!'

One hand on the side of the boat, he turns around slowly, taking me and the craft with him, and points with his spare hand.

She is on the bank, bouncing about and barking, and ragging my bloody rucksack as though she is trying to kill it!

I collapse back in the boat onto my back as relief surges through me, relying on the fact he'll keep a hold and not upturn me.

Actually, I don't care any longer. Tip me up. Drown me.

She's okay. She is okay.

Ash chuckles, and it's a rolling, rich, right-from-the-belly kind of chuckle that brings me out in goose bumps.

I'm still trying to process it when he looms above me, pushing himself upwards with his two hands on the side of the boat.

Bloody hell, I take it back, don't drown me yet. Let me have my own little Mr Darcy moment.

I have never, ever seen quivering pecs and a washboard stomach like this before. And believe me, I have seen a few in my time – I can practically count the muscles, and I've studied enough nudes in art school to know these are all in the right places.

It is obscene. No man should be allowed to wear a T-shirt that looks like this when it gets wet.

'Are you okay?' He sounds concerned.

'Fine,' I say weakly. *Just knocked out by the view.* 'I just feel a bit faint.' *I may need the kiss of life.*

'Budge up then.'

I blink.

'On second thoughts I'll just tow you in.'

'Quite happy to budge up,' I say pathetically, but we're already on the move, scudding across the surface of the water even faster than I was when I was rowing.

I watch, speechless, as he wades out of the water and ties the boat up. It's not just the way his T-shirt clings to him like a second skin, I am now being treated to the sight of his trousers draped over strong thighs and hugging his slim hips and positively snogging his well-defined bum cheeks, and OMG as he turns round, his groin. This isn't like a second skin, or a wetsuit, this is body-paint. With extra shadowing and shading so my eye doesn't miss the most important bits. I'd close my eyes, but I can't move. Not a muscle.

'Come on.'

I still feel faint. All I can do is stare at his outstretched hand. My brain is overloaded, it can't take in the graphic scenery *and* the invitation to move.

'Becky? Becky, are you okay?'

'I just need a moment,' I croak out. I think I must have water on the brain, it is distorting everything. Magnifying things. I thought cold water was supposed to cause shrinkage.

'Come on, I need you moving, you're starting to shiver – it's a killer, that lake, if you don't get warm straight away. This your bag?'

I nod and he scoops it up with one hand and leans closer to me. I slip my hand into his, which is gorgeously warm and capable, and let him haul me over the side of the boat and onto the gravel. The heat of his touch has just made me realise he's right – I'm freezing cold. I'm shivering and my teeth are chattering. I let go so I can wrap my arms around myself and discover rather alarmingly that my legs are all pathetic and jelly-like. I'm shaking and I'm not sure if it is from the cold, his body or relief.

He grabs my elbow about one second after I notice that the ground is tilting and trembling like there's an earthquake on its way.

'She could have drowned.'

'Shh, she hasn't, she's fine, she can swim like an otter.'

'But I didn't know. She could have…'

'I'll carry you.'

I forget about Bella for a moment when he leans in closer as though he's going to grab me. 'Oh my God, no. No!' I can just see it. He'll throw me over his shoulder and my bum will be in his face, my fingers will be tantalisingly close to his own firm buttocks and in my confused state I'll do something totally embarrassing.

'Oh my God, yes, woman!' He chuckles. He shouldn't do that. It's disorientating, and so is being swept up into his arms so that I'm snuggled with my mouth only inches from his taut, tanned throat.

Oh shit, he smells good. I close my eyes and it makes it

worse; my sense of smell is heightened if that's possible and my nose is twitching like a rabbit's. Even in my pathetic state I am so tempted to stick my tongue out for a quick lick. Thanks goodness he can't see what I'm up to under his chin.

One of his thumbs is nestled under my boob, on my rib cage, and I daren't move a muscle. He might think I'm cuddling up. Or worse. I can hardly breathe. But boy, am I wet and clammy and totally uncomfortable. It's a good job I'm icy cold, if I heat up too much I'll be steaming. Must think cold thoughts.

'Bella!' He whistles, and she lifts her head from where she's been sniffing and scampers after him.

'She never does that for me!' I say grudgingly, trying to distract myself from my situation with grumpiness.

The low laugh rumbles from his chest against my body. It's a bit like sitting on a purring cat, not that I've ever tried it, you understand.

'We've been together a while,' he says, and it doesn't sound like an admonishment. I start to forget dangerous sexual attraction and relax slightly.

'First time I saw her she was four weeks old, picked her out of the litter.' I can hear the smile in his soft, even-toned voice. He seems to like talking about her. It's nice listening to him. We're climbing steadily now, and despite lugging my heavy weight he's not huffing or puffing at all. 'Right little tinker she was, she came bobbling over with that daisy on her head, then leapt on my bootlaces and tried to race off with the end in her mouth. Went back a month later and I swear she remembered me, went straight for my boot again, she did. Didn't you, you little monster?' I realise then that she's walking at the side of us, glued to his leg, gazing up as though she loves every bone in his body. Bugger, he's making this dog-sitting – sorry dog-protection – lark harder every day. 'She was a tiny scrap of a thing, all fluff and big eyes. You okay?'

I seem to have stopped shivering. Now I just feel a bit awkward. And damp. And conscious that I am willingly pressed against his body, and he is the enemy! Just because he loves Bella, doesn't mean she's his. Or he can take her.

Though on that subject, why didn't he just leave me to my fate in the lake and run off with the dog? Or drag me to the shore, check for a pulse then run off with the dog? Maybe he's not *quite* as bad as Georgina would have me believe.

It is his fault all that happened though, so maybe he's just being nice because he feels guilty.

'You shouldn't have whistled her!'

He grins and shifts my weight in his arms. I can see his dimples properly from here. And the cleft in his chin, which I'm very tempted to touch. If I just reached out and… no! I must not. I must keep my hands to myself. 'I thought it would be funny if she jumped out, how was I to know you'd dive in after her?'

'I didn't dive. I lost my balance.'

'But you would have done.' He gazes into my eyes solemnly. No hint of mockery. 'Take your duties seriously, don't you Becky?'

'Very,' I say slightly stiffly, then his warm hand moves against my thigh and I realise it might be better not to be stroppy in case he drops me, and I roll all the way back down the hill. I'm not sure I've got the energy to crawl back up.

So, this is all about self-preservation, nothing to do with how nice it feels to be wrapped in his strong arms. Pressed against his firm chest. Shit, I'd better not get too cosy. 'It's, erm, nice how the garden goes down to the lake.'

There's a long pause, and I'm trying to think of some other pleasantry, when he starts talking again. 'There used to be a boathouse where the boat was tied up.'

'Really?' I can just imagine it. A small, wooden, painted boathouse. 'That would make a lovely picture.' For a moment I forget about his magnetism and the dog-napping danger.

'It did.' His voice has an edge. There's a pause. 'I can show you a photo if you like?' The deadness has gone, the steady tone is back.

'Great!'

'I used to play in it when I was a kid. Then when I was older, I'd fish from the jetty with a long stick and some twine.' He chuckles again, and my insides go all squishy. 'Then take the boat out. It was my hiding place.' He's smiling. I daren't look up in case I meet his eye, but I know he is.

I need to get on solid, sensible ground. Right now, my body is like that fish on the end of his twine, flipping around and being drawn closer and closer to danger. He will soon use his SAS survival techniques (I don't care if he's not actually SAS, he is in my fantasy) and eat me. 'So you've lived round here all your life?'

'Yup, most of it. Right, here we go your ladyship, home sweet home.' He loosens his grip and I slither down onto my feet, a supporting hand round my waist as I fumble for the keys and unlock the door. 'Come on Bella, in the kitchen. I'll dry you off in a sec.'

It really would be better if he left right now. 'You can leave—'

'No way. You might be able to talk through those chattering teeth, but I'm not going until I'm sure you're not going to catch hypothermia. I'll run you a hot bath.'

'No, you can't come—'

He's heading up the stairs three at a time while I'm still clutching the banisters at the bottom and wondering how I'm supposed to stop him. He really shouldn't come inside.

'I promise I won't take advantage and steal Bella while you're up here, if that's what you're worried about!' he shouts back down, his deep voice filling the space. 'I like to face my enemies properly!'

I have a feeling that he is not a man who easily takes 'no' for an answer. And I also have a feeling that a hot bath would be very, very nice. If only I had the energy to get up to it.

But I also know that it isn't just Bella I'm worried about. Though I am of course very worried about her. But oh my, being held by him has sparked so many bad thoughts and desires, well, just honest to goodness plain lust, I suppose. I've not had sex for a while. I didn't think my body really cared, but boy, have I just discovered I've been in a desert that needs water. And that sweet side to him is an extra aphrodisiac that has sparked something in my heart as well as my groin area.

I'm not surprised Georgina told me to keep him at arm's length.

Any decision-making is taken out of my hands a few minutes later, when he reappears, throws me over his shoulder, carries me up and dumps me just inside the bathroom.

'I'll be downstairs if you need anything, just shout. I'll make you a hot toddy.'

'I don't li—' I'm talking to a space. 'Like hot toddies,' I finish pathetically before eyeing the steaming water. He's chucked in some bath oil. It smells nice.

Irresistible. Not at all like that cold lake.

Peeling my damp-claggy clothes off and exposing the goose-bumpy pale skin underneath, I clamber into the water.

It. Is. Bliss.

I could stay in here forever. Except the enemy is in the house. And might kidnap Bella. But he did say he'd be downstairs if I needed anything, and he did say he wouldn't take advantage. I guess I'm just going to have to take him at his word.

Right now, if he headed off with her at a snail's pace, I wouldn't have the energy to follow.

The only thought as I look up at the ceiling and wallow is, what's he going to do about his own sodden clothes?

This actually sets my mind off on other various thoughts. Most of them rude.

Chapter Eleven

'**B**etter?'

Ash is sitting on the kitchen chair, Bella on his knee, looking very much at home. He also has clean, dry trousers on. Shame.

But this is good, very good, I tell myself, trying to be sensible and ignore my deprived body.

And his body.

The other bit, that isn't dressed.

'How did you do that?' I squawk and point. Must concentrate on the trousers, not on the bare, naked, manly, muscled, tanned, naked (sorry, did I already say that?) torso.

'Magic!' He winks, one corner of his mouth quirking up. 'Spares.' He nods towards a rucksack by the door that I hadn't noticed him carrying. 'I was going for a long hike when I spotted you—'

'Spotted me? You weren't waiting for us?' I don't know whether to be disappointed, or not believe him.

He smirks. 'Pure coincidence.'

'Really?'

'Really.' A proper smile breaks out on his tanned face, showing off startlingly white teeth between those full, sexy lips. 'I thought seeing me once in a day would be enough for you. Don't want you to get over-excited, do we?' He raises an eyebrow and it doesn't come off as at all cheesy or conceited, just cheeky. So cheeky my stomach is doing funny little quivery things. 'Have to admit, I've never known a girl to throw herself in a lake before to avoid me, though.'

'I've never known a man I've had to do it to avoid.' I can't stop looking at his chest. It is obscenely attractive.

'Anyway, I usually carry some spare clothes, just in case. My T-shirt's drying outside.'

Shame. Oh, flipping heck, my pulse rate has just soared, Bella has started lovingly licking his pecs. Oh my God, I want to be her. He's fondling her ears now, and oh no, he's just flexed a muscle. I'm staring. I can't help it. Staring. Still staring.

'So, er, the bare, sorry the boathouse, you said there was an, er, boathouse, by the lake.' Where else would the bloody thing be? Stop blabbering, Becky!

'There was.' There's humour in his tone. 'Here.' He pushes a glass towards me. 'Brandy, thought you might need warming up on the inside as well as the outside.'

My insides are fine. Warm, practically boiling over. 'Not hot—'

'You said you didn't like hot toddies.'

Ah, so he did hear.

I take a sip and it zips down my throat like molten lava, making me splutter. A burning throat is brilliant though, dampens down the sexual urges a treat. 'No, I don't,' I croak. I do some coughing and grunting, to clear my throat. 'When did it, er, the boathouse fall down?' A boathouse is safe ground. I can talk about a boathouse with no hint of desire or sexiness.

'It didn't.'

I frown at the brittle note in his voice and risk another sip of brandy which actually is quite nice. Mellow. Once you get used to the fierce heat. I think I need more. 'What happened?' I take another gulp.

'Georgina happened.' He looks quite stern.

'Oh.' Even with a good measure of brandy inside me, it's still awkward.

There's a long pause, then he fishes his phone out of his pocket and fiddles before holding it up for me to see.

His forearms are strong, muscled. Even his *fingers* are masculine. No hint of moisturiser or manicure there.

Teddy had very nice, clean nails. Smooth hands. Ash doesn't. His are slightly rough. You'd know when he touched you. You'd know you were being touched.

I need to think about something else, I need... then I see the photo and it is easy to be distracted.

I can't help but smile. The place is unbelievably cute, and not at all the simple wooden hut I'd imagined it would be. This is a magical hideaway that any young boy would want to play in.

I take the phone from him, so that I can enlarge the photo and look at it more closely. It is perched, one end firmly nestled in the land, the other hovering over the dark water of the lake. Lichen-spotted stone walls glow a golden brown in the evening sun, and the thick green-grey slates that cover the roof dip midway, giving it the look of an old man surveying the view. A rustic jetty stretches out into the lake, mirrored below its surface as though it is rooted in the depths.

It belongs, as though it has grown out of the landscape and has been there forever. Should be there forever.

'Wow, it's amazing.' I smile at him. He's looking wistfully down but glances up when I speak. 'Can I have a copy? I'd love to paint that landscape with it actually there.'

He stares at me steadily for a moment, then snaps out of his memories and nods. 'Sure. Have you got WhatsApp? Forward it on to yourself if you like.'

I hit forward, type in my number, then pass his phone back to him.

His fingertips brush against mine and there's a spark, a tingle in the base of my stomach. He's felt it as well, I'm sure he has, because he pauses instead of moving away.

Then he moves, brushing my damp hair back from my face. The touch of his fingers as they trail across my cheek makes me tremble – with anticipation, excitement? I'm not sure.

He's got deep laughter lines at the corners of his eyes. His face is tanned so they show in relief. His nose is strong, but slightly crooked as though it might have been broken, his mouth uneven, one side more used to lifting than the other. His lips are a strong, firm line. So firm. Dry.

I run my tongue over my own dry lips and realise I'm

holding my breath. I drag my gaze from his mouth and glance up, and he's staring back so intently my heart pauses for a second.

And then he kisses me.

A light, fleeting touch that I have to lean into, follow, so that I don't lose it.

'Sorry, I should go.' He pulls back.

'No. Don't.' I want to prolong this. I want more. 'Stay, I'll make you some lunch. To say thanks.' Shit, I shouldn't be doing this. Talk about forbidden fruit. 'Unless you've got stuff to do?'

'No stuff.' Our gazes are locked. 'I don't need to go. But maybe I should?' There's a question at the end. Another long pause. 'Let you get over your shock? I don't want you to think I'd take advantage.'

'You're not.' My throat is parched. Sandpaper. 'I'm fine, fine, I don't need rest, but you can go if you want.' I really, really don't want him to go.

We're adults. Why should he go just because I happen to be looking after the house where his ex, who hates him to bits, lives?

I'll come back to that one later.

'Maybe I should stay to make sure?' His voice is soft, and it is more intimate than any conversation I've had with a man before. 'Can't have you dropping dead and Bella left to starve, can we?'

I gulp, moistening my dry throat. Talk about tension; there's an undercurrent stronger than any riptide. I'm being dragged under and I don't want to do a thing about it. 'Oh, definitely not.' I try a laugh, which comes out all weak and feeble. God, I'm pathetic.

But my brain is still functioning. I have had a brill idea. He is hot, he is incredibly sexy, so maybe I can seduce him, or let him seduce me, and keep him as a sex slave (sorry, backtrack, getting carried away) or just keep him, but sexually enthralled so he doesn't want to leave (and seriously pushing the boundaries of believable here), then I can work without the worry of him nicking Bella.

If he's single. But he's acting like he is. And if he's not I'll go back to the sex slave scenario. But let's be honest, what kind of girlfriend would let him loose to stalk his ex and try and nab her dog? They'd be with him, wouldn't they?

I think the brandy has taken over my brain.

'I could make you something to eat.' He breaks away, stops looking at me and goes over to the fridge. Then he laughs, which instantly breaks the tension. 'What the hell do you eat? Wine, cheese, eggs, gin?'

'Eggs are good.'

'Indeed.' His tone is mock serious. 'Omelette it is, then.'

'Or we could just sit in the sun for a bit, have a glass of wine?' We will have wine, lots, his judgement will go out of the window. There'll be mad passion. He can stay, the dog problem will be solved, I can work in peace and be physically as well as mentally satisfied (sex helps with relaxation and is a stress reliever – fact!), and Georgina can sort the rest out when she comes home.

'You need to line your stomach, boost your energy.'

He looks at me as he says the words and my heart hammers a little bit harder.

Who knew watching a man beat eggs could be a turn-on? Who knew eating an omelette could be the best foreplay a girl could get?

Oh, to hell with wine and the rest, forget it, I just want him.

I can't stop watching his mouth move as he eats. He leans forward. 'You've got something…' Wipes his thumb over my mouth. Leaves it resting there. Hang on, who's seducing who here?

My lips part, I can't help myself. I let the tip of my tongue rest against his skin. He doesn't move. It doesn't matter who is seducing who.

I've never wanted to taste a man more in my life.

'Not hungry?'

'Not for food.' I very deliberately put my knife and fork neatly down on the plate and stare straight back at him.

This time, when he leans in, he tangles his fingers in my hair and pulls me close.

This isn't like an end-of-date, oh-we-should-have-a-quick-snog-now. Or a 'why not?' This is a want, a need. I don't care if it's shock from my soaking, or some kind of delayed reaction, or I'm just feeling sex-starved because I've not done it for months.

I just want to satisfy the craving. And this hungry kiss is just the start, the start of something amazing. He smells like the woodland I've just walked through, fresh, natural, deeply sensual and sense tingling. His touch is firm, definite, but so, so seducingly gentle.

His mouth...

Oh my God, I feel weak, light-headed, dizzy.

'Becky.' Nobody has ever said my name like that. I try and focus on him, drink in his face, his eyes, but it's hard, so hard. 'Becky.' People *have* said my name that way before. 'Becky!' It is more like my mother says it. He also seems to be prodding me with his finger, not the part of his body I'd been looking forward to meeting...

Where am I? What happened? Bugger, what flipping time is it – it's dark! I sit up abruptly, then regret it and sink back on the pillows. My pillows. In my, well, Georgina's spare, bedroom. On my own.

One thing leads to another as they say.

Except they didn't. I'm pretty sure they didn't.

For one, I am still fully clothed. I put one hand on my leg to be sure. Then the other on my chest. Yup, definitely covered up, this delicious delight has not been unwrapped.

Disappointing.

Very disappointing.

Not that I consider myself irresistible, but that kiss! There was definitely a kiss; I remember a hot kiss. Tongues and tonsils. Lip mashing. Groping.

Oh my God. I remember everything now. I was planning on seducing Ash, having my wicked way. Then an omelette intervened, and I was powerless, he took over.

Then I passed out.

Yup, I am pretty sure that was what happened. Not from

passion, or exhaustion from orgasm overload. Nope, I passed out from being plunged in icy water and ingesting half the lake.

My brain might have been panting for action, but my body copped out.

Shit. How unfair is that?

Or not. Passing out was a smart move.

What the hell was I thinking? What kind of moron would decide sleeping with the enemy was a smart move? Totally not. Totally lust-driven bad idea. I wasn't thinking straight, what kind of dog-protector am I?

Frig.

'Oh shit! Shit, shit, shit. Bella!' I sit bolt upright in a panic, my heart pounding. He's taken her, I know he's taken her.

There's a funny groan, and something kicks out at my ankle. There's a black fluffy mound at the foot of the bed, indignant at being woken up. I sink back flat again, exhausted. I reach out one hand, so that it is resting on her. 'Phew. Thank fuck for that.'

The pillow crinkles. Except it is not the pillow, it is a piece of paper at the side. A note.

You were breathing fine, checked all vital signs and thought you were safe to leave on your own! Sleep well.

PS: I do play by the rules, Bella was snoring at your side when I left – but I am going to take her back. A new day, a new dawn and all that – so watch yourself! A

I can imagine him grinning as he wrote it.

Dawn? I glance at my watch. Bugger. I have lost nearly a whole day. I haven't done the work I wanted to or been to the art shop.

I feel knackered but force myself to sit up again and swing my legs off the bed. I'll feel better when my feet are on the floor. That's what Mum always said when I tried to skive off school.

I do feel surprisingly fine. Mothers are always right.

Downstairs the place has been tidied up. No sign of soggy footsteps or omelettes. It's like it was all a (rather erotic in a weird way) dream. Except when I catch sight of myself in the kettle, my hair is a mess of ringlets and my eyeliner is smudged down nearly as far as my cheekbones.

Bella brushes against my leg and makes me jump.

'Well, at least you're still here, trouble! Good job. Bet you wanted to go after him, eh?' She looks at me, big hazel eyes questioning. 'Ash?' She wags her tail and grins. Yes – this dog can grin, as well as nearly talk. Never underestimate a cockapoo! 'Hmm, don't get ideas. You are not to get dog-napped, okay? Deal?' I hold a hand up high-five-style, jokingly, and the bloody dog high fives me back. Well, I'll be blowed! 'Is this still part of the dream?' She barks. I wince. Pretty sure I'm awake. 'Okay, I'll feed you—' she barks again '—then you've got to let me work in peace for an hour or so.'

It's not as easy to work as I thought it might be. I guess I'm still in shock from being submerged in a lake, and then manhandled by Ash.

I can't help but touch my lips, remember what it was

like to be kissed. Except it's all a bit elusive, which is frustrating. I'd quite like to be able to remember properly.

I'd also quite like to know more about the boathouse, and what happened to it. I didn't imagine Ash's reaction; he was genuinely annoyed and upset. And what was his connection to it? Did it belong to Georgina's parents, did they both play here as kids? Grow up together? There's definitely a Georgina connection.

I have been doodling, idly sketching as I think about Ash and the strange day – and I realise I've drawn a vague outline of the lake before me. And the boathouse.

With a sigh, I prop my mobile phone up in front of me, Ash's photo displayed on it. I half wish it was a photo of him, not a boathouse. I have a sudden urge to capture his amazing face, even though I'm not a portrait artist.

But instead I stare at the boathouse. And it is almost like it's still there. I can sense it, see it.

Sometimes you just have to go where your imagination wants to take you. The Magic Pony can wait until tomorrow.

Chapter Twelve

'No Dogs.' What the hell do they mean? No dogs! This is the Lake District. Every other person is a hiker with a dog. Or two.

How can they have a 'No Dogs' sign on a shop?

Well, okay, I suppose *a lot of* people are in pairs. One is on dog duty, the other goes inside. But in my case that is no help at all. I can't leave Bella outside. I've had too many close calls, and if Ash materialises and sees her tied up all alone, he'll think all his birthdays have come at once. And I'll have no defence when I explain to Georgina. She'll rip me to shreds, hang me up to dry, blacken my name on every pet-sitting site in the country. But I need my gingerbread, and this is the only place they sell it!

I could pay some kids, but there don't seem to be any loitering about. Wagging school mustn't be a thing in Cumbrian villages. Mid-week in school term-time, this place seems to be populated purely by ramblers who remember the Seventies. Or earlier.

And they don't look in need of a fiver to watch a dog that's currently barking at its own reflection in the window, and smells like it has rolled in something that's come out of another animal's bottom.

Which I think it has.

'It would help if you'd shut up, Bella.'

Maybe I should also carry air freshener so I can give her a quick spritz.

After an early night, and a very good long sleep, I woke up this morning feeling full of energy and positivity – and ready for battle.

Letting Bella out for a wee was (unfortunately) issue-free. Bor-ing.

I have to admit to feeling a bit let down, and disappointed that Ash hadn't appeared at daybreak armed and dangerous – or at least dressed in combat gear, face smeared with mud and twigs in his hair, either hiding in the bushes or wriggling his way commando-style across the lawn. Preferably semi-naked.

I was all prepared. I had a makeshift water pistol (think washing-up liquid bottle), bombs (as in bath bombs – hard but presumably would crumble on contact, I want to scare not maim), and enough chopped-up steak and smelly fish to keep Bella on my side for as long as I needed. I googled 'high value treats' before I got out of bed this morning, and I can up his dog biscuits any day. Tomorrow I am making liver cake. Yeah, I have never in my life felt the inclination to bake – until now, for a dog.

But the battlefield was bare. I even did some experimental poking with the handle end of the kitchen mop in the rhododendrons just to be sure. And I jabbed at one badly pruned collection of twigs with the other end, convinced they had to be hiding his head. Okay, some might say this was a bit unjustified, and possibly nasty, but he deserved it. It was his own fault – he left me to SLEEP when I'd been primed for a night of hanky-panky.

Well, maybe not a night. An hour or so, or minute or two? How could he be so bloody noble and considerate? I'm not saying he should have molested my unconscious body, but he could have hung around for a bit while I had forty winks. Then tried to wake me. With a hot snog.

And okay, it wasn't his fault. He probably couldn't have woken me up even if he'd stripped me naked, smeared me in chocolate, licked every inch of my body and prodded all my erogenous zones, I'm not exactly Sleeping Beauty. I've been known to sleep through thunderstorms, snoring my head off and resistant to anything but a kick in the shin.

I am pissed off though. I was *this* close to a good shag.

He probably would have been a disappointment. All his blood is probably diverted permanently to keeping those muscles in good working order, none left in reserve for the bit of his anatomy he keeps in his trousers. *And* he's probably better at finding landmarks than erogenous zones, one of those men that can't do anything without a map, GPS or full illustrated instructions.

Anyway, whatever. He didn't show up. I think he might have decided to leave us alone today.

But I'm still not going to chance it. There is a chance he'll be back and won't have given up on his one-man mission. So, the smelly treats, a strong lead and harness and a pair of binoculars I found in the bedroom are now packed about my person. He isn't going to sneak up and catch me unawares.

I eye up the woman in the woolly hat, despite the warm sun, and consider asking her to hold Bella while I go in, but she turns away as though anticipating being roped into something by a weirdo.

I could give up. Except I need that gingerbread. I promised myself that I'd get some. It is part of my Cumbrian experience. Along with Kendal mint cake, local gin, and Cumberland sausage. With the obvious exception of the gin, they are the tastes of my childhood holidays. Oh, and sticky toffee pudding. Must not forget that.

When we came here as kids, visiting this shop was a bit of a ritual. It is the only place that sells this particular homemade gingerbread, which is why I'm now so determined to go in there. When I look back now, I can see it was more like bribery, but that's parents for you.

We were told 'We're going on a good long walk, so that we can buy gingerbread!' with the underlying message that there was no way we could have the second without the first. Then there was 'Super-long walk tomorrow, up a big windy mountain where we might lose you off the edge, but we've got mint cake to keep us going. First one to the summit gets the extra bar!'

I was never first to the top, I have super-competitive siblings, who'd plan out the best route (even when they were still tiny children), so I insisted on extra categories such as 'first one to the bottom' and 'one with the cleanest boots when we get back to the car' (I was excellent at that – I'd have licked them clean if I'd had to).

Abby and Daniel used to say I was cheating; I'd rather think of it as innovation and creative thinking.

But even the thought of the spicy, amazingly scented gingerbread, and the super-sweet and mouth-tinglingly minty mint cake takes me straight back to those days when the biggest challenge in my life was how to get out of homework without actually lying.

I can almost taste the ginger now. Maybe I could shove Bella in my rucksack? If I pull the toggles tight super quick, and race in and out, she won't have time to bark or wriggle free.

'Would you do it, for me?' She's not even listening. She's gazing across the road, and then keels over. Flat out, on her side.

Oh my God!

'Bella?' I bend down and practically scream in her ear. She flaps her tail weakly, lifts her head slightly so she can lick my hand, then flops back down. 'Bella, get up.' I tug her lead slightly, no response. Bloody hell, what have I done to her? Has she eaten something poisonous?

Fuck. I don't even know where the vet is, there's a phone number at the house, but I've not got it on me. I should have. I should be prepared. Georgina will kill me. Ash will kill me.

But she was fine when we set off!

I touch her head, maybe it's heatstroke. Do dogs get heatstroke?

There's a snigger. The old woman in the woolly hat is

grinning, and just clapped her hands together! Bloody lunatic, she's probably got heatstroke as well.

Except her husband is now standing next to her and is smiling as well, and Bella has started to wag her tail with a bit more effort. She scrambles onto her feet, shakes, practically pushes me out of her way and then starts to leap around like a kangaroo. At Ash.

He catches her mid-leap. 'Clever girl!' And they have a love-in. I'm jealous. Which makes me angry – along with the fact that I was really worried.

'Can you do it again, honey?' The woolly hat smiles up at Ash, waving her camera in the air. 'My husband missed it!'

I frigging missed it! Ash puts Bella down, forms his fingers into a gun shape, 'bang!' and down she goes again, as though she's been shot.

'You stupid idiot! I thought, I thought…' My voice tails off, along with the clapping. Put on a brave face, Becs! I grin – though it is a fixed face-ache grin – and join in the '*oh how brilliant*'s. Then I stamp on his foot, jab him in the ribs when he gets close enough, and hiss. 'What are you playing at!'

'I thought you'd think it was hilarious!' He chuckles.

'About as funny as being made to jump into a lake!'

'I only said…' He does it again, raises his fingers and: 'Bang! Didn't you hear me shout?'

'Stop it! It's still not funny.' He sobers at the look on my face. It wasn't his fault. I shake my head and sigh. 'I was miles away.' Back in my innocent childhood days. I feel a bit stupid for panicking. What kind of moron can't tell a dead dog from a dog playing dead?

Bella is still bouncing. She always gets super-excited when she sees Ash.

'Sorry.' He looks a bit like a dejected puppy himself.

'It's fine.' I wrap her lead round my hand a bit tighter.

'Were you going to buy gingerbread?'

I nod. He really has got the most gorgeous mouth. It's mesmerising when you watch him talk. I've never felt the urge to watch somebody's lips before.

'I'll go and get you some, an apology for scaring you. A peace offering!'

This sounds excellent.

'Hang on then, I won't be a sec. Shall I take Bella in with me?'

'No!' It comes out as a slightly over-the-top yell; I pull her in protectively. What kind of a dastardly plan has he cooked up now? 'They don't let dogs in there. No dogs – look!' I point at the sign.

His dimples deepen. 'Oh, they know Bella, they'll let her in.'

Of course they do. Everybody knows Bella. Bloody hell, I could have been in and out before he'd got anywhere near us and started shooting randomly.

'She can stay here with me.' I mean, can you imagine if he absconded with the dog, and my gingerbread? Complete fail.

'Oh my God, that is good.' The closest I've got to an orgasm in weeks. And I'm sure I was tantalisingly close yesterday, but we'll forget that for now.

We are sitting on the small bridge, legs dangling over the edge, Bella between us and I close my eyes so that I can savour the flavours as I take a second bite of the slightly chewy, spice dusted, slice of gingerbread. It's not gingerbread like you get anywhere else in the world. It's not a thick, bouncy soft cake, or a crisp biscuit, it's a combination. I keep my eyes closed and sniff, letting the wonderful aroma take me right back to the last time I was here. We had some good times, even if sometimes I just wished I was more like Abby. Easier to be proud of, to be loved. Though I never felt *not loved*. Just not quite special. I was the unpredictable one.

Abby didn't feel special last time we were here though. It was hilarious. Poor controlled, perfect Abby (I'm not being mean; she just *was* like that as a child) was so cross she called me a stupid cow. Out loud. Not like Abby at all.

I can't help it, I can still see her standing there, all outraged. The snigger is out before I can stop it.

'What's tickled you?'

'Last time I was here?' He nods. 'I pushed my sister Abby off this bridge.'

'That's a bit naughty!' His smile is gentle, it softens his face and gives him a totally different look to the cheeky one, or the cross one, or the *I love Bella* one. He's got an expressive face. Which makes it harder to believe he really is the lying, cheating, horrible man Georgina claims he is.

Maybe she is just hurt. Maybe he hurt her. Maybe he

isn't a scumbag in the way I'd thought, he's just a heartbreaker.

That I can believe.

'And what did your poor sister do to deserve that?'

'Less of the poor! She ate the last bit of gingerbread.' I'd been waiting for that last bit, was all prepared to eat it so slowly and savour every last crumb.

'Ahh, fully justified then.'

'Definitely. Although...' I pause and look at him, his twinkly eyes dancing with laughter. 'She did actually earn it, by being the first one to name some flower in the stream or something. But it wasn't a fair competition, she knows loads more stuff than me!'

'She's older than you?'

'Nope. Younger, so it's even worse! Just a swot, she was bloody annoying actually. I suppose I should have pushed Dad in instead, for asking a question he knew I wouldn't win.'

It's funny really, I did it partly because I was annoyed at her being right *yet* again, like any sister would be, partly because I just couldn't resist the temptation.

I guess sometimes I didn't feel like we were completely equal. That other people just had to be comparing us. That my sister and brother were better than me. They were like Dad, solicitors in the making, so I guess I can understand why he leaned towards them. And me? I was always just different. Not like Dad, or Mum really. The daydreamer. The non-academic one. Bit of a bummer really. But it was just normal sibling rivalry. Until Teddy came along insinuating that things were different than they really were, when I should have been grown up enough to tell him to get lost. Instead of taking his side against my family.

As kids, I never *really* felt the need to prove that although I was different, I was just as good. We had some really great, fun family times.

It was Teddy who highlighted the differences between me and Abby. Who made a big deal of them. My parents weren't criticising my choice of him, my life, they were questioning the decisions I was letting him make for me. And I took his side, I decided they just didn't understand who he was and what he was doing for me. Teddy knew best. Not.

Ash nudges me playfully with his elbow. 'What question would you have won on? Not spot whether the dog is dead or not!'

'Watch it, or you'll be in next!'

'You wouldn't dare.' He chuckles.

I laugh back. 'Try me!' I must phone Mum and Abby more when I get back home.

'If I go, then I'm taking you with me!'

He would as well. His warm fingers dance briefly over mine, making me forget all about my family, then he pulls away again. 'Fully recovered after your dunking yesterday then?'

'I'm fine. Thanks for, er, putting me to bed.'

'On the bed.' He grins. A cheeky grin.

I concentrate on my spicy gingerbread. 'So, it was you who taught Bella to high five?'

'It was indeed. She's a clever pup.' He ruffles her head. 'The poodle side of her, smart gene. The spaniel side is all about the sniffing and the food.' He kisses the tip of her nose. 'I dropped my jacket up on the hills a while ago, I'd no idea where, but this one tracked it down.'

'Wow.'

'Helped that the pockets were full of treats!' Bella pricks her ears up at the word, then begs.

'Are they now?' I say suspiciously.

'Of course! Never go anywhere without some liver cake, you never know when and where the opportunities might arise.'

There's the hint of smile lines at the corners of his eyes, but something tells me he's serious. 'You can't have her, you know.'

'She's mine, I only want what is already mine.'

'But you'll have to sort that out when I go home. I promised…' I don't want to say her name out loud, saying it feels like it will spoil things. Although we both know who I'm talking about. 'It's between the pair of you, not me.' Maybe appealing to his better side will make him back off? He'll leave Bella until Georgina comes back. I can relax, we can relax, I can just enjoy seeing him – without the guilt. It's like seeing the last piece of cake and knowing it is somebody else's but you still can't help thinking that you have to eat it, and worry about making up some story later.

'I've waited long enough.' It sounds like a warning.

Bugger. He doesn't look like this is negotiable. I might have to go back to plan A, sex slave.

'You were right the other day when you said she needs time, but we've had time, she needs a clean break, not to be thinking any of this will change.' His jaw has tightened. 'We can't rewind the clock. That's not fair on her or me. Life isn't about living a lie, is it? However much it hurts.'

'I feel like piggy in the middle here!'

'Sorry.' There's a strained smile on his face. 'I didn't mean to make you feel bad.'

'You aren't, it's just...' I've got a feeling it doesn't matter what I say here. 'You're not going to leave me alone, are you?'

'Nope!' He lifts one eyebrow and looks very naughty indeed. 'No way could I leave you alone, Becky.'

I've turned the colour of a beetroot. I don't want him to leave me alone actually, but that sounds soooo suggestive I'm worried he's read my mind and my dirtiest fantasies about him. I need to change the subject quickly. 'Hmm, have you been following us?' If he has, I'm a bit worried. I thought I was pretty on my toes during our walk, and I didn't even get the feeling we were being tracked, let alone heard anything.

'Nope, just a coincidence.'

'Again?'

'Again! It's a small place and man cannot live on omelette alone.' He grins, fully relaxed again, and the heat rushes to my cheeks. It feels like it is just the two of us. Conspirators.

'We really should stop bumping into each other like this.'

'Why?' His question takes me by surprise. 'Okay—' he holds a hand up '—don't answer that. Let's not spoil our lunch.'

'You call this lunch?' I wave the final piece of gingerbread at him.

'Yup!' Before I can react, he swipes and it's gone from my hand.

'Don't you bloody dare. If you eat that you are *so* going in that stream!'

'I wouldn't dare. My God, you're worse than Bella when it comes to guarding food, and that's saying something!'

I put an arm round Bella and pull her closer. 'Us girls are sticking together!'

He splits the gingerbread, and we share the last piece.

'Right, I guess I'd better leave you in peace.' Swinging his legs effortlessly back over the bridge and onto the pathway, he stands up, dusts himself down then holds out his hand.

It feels natural to take it, to enjoy the touch of a strong, warm hand. To allow him to pull me to my feet so that we're practically touching.

If we were lovers, this is the point at which we'd kiss – before walking off, strolling up the street in step, still holding hands.

Boy, this is going to get tricky if I'm not careful.

Or not. He has disengaged and hooked his thumbs through his belt loops as though to point out they're out of bounds.

'Enjoy the rest of your walk around the village, or what there is of it. I can recommend the sandwiches at the café further up the river.'

'I'm going to the art shop.'

'Well, no problem with taking Bella in there.' He winks.

It spells danger. 'Take care.' He starts to stride off before I get a chance to think of a reply. Bella whines.

'Hey, I've started to do a picture of the boathouse, would you like to see it when it's done?' I shout after him on impulse, wanting to let him see Bella again, wanting to see him myself again if I'm honest – but by arrangement.

He half turns. 'Love to! And don't forget our date.' That word makes me blush. 'Walking day tomorrow!'

'How could I forget an offer like that? It isn't going to be too adventurous though is it? Just a walk? Stroll?' I say hopefully.

'Well, a bit of a clamber.' The corner of his mouth twitches. 'Not up for the challenge?'

'Of course I am!' Damn. I'm doing it again. Why can I never admit to not being up for a challenge? I think I need to be at least a little bit honest. 'Though these hills are a lot steeper than I'm used to, I've got a bit knackered following Bella up them. Just a bit—' a lot '—out of condition!'

'I can always put you through your paces again, give you some more of my special SAS training, another bootcamp session if you fancy, then we can see if you'll survive the walk! Up for it?'

'No way!'

Inside, he's laughing at me, I know he is. He's not going to let me off the hook for the SAS comment the other day in the garden. Well, I might have told Bella I needed a fast track to fitness, but this is not what I'm after.

'You can give me some tips, but that's all!'

'Sure! See you tomorrow morning then! Six o'clock okay, before it gets warm?'

'Ace.' Six o'clock? Is he mad?

'And you can let me know how the painting is going.' He gives me a thumbs-up and blows Bella a kiss. 'See you later, babe.' I'm not sure if that is directed at the dog or me (the dog I think), and whether it's a promise or a warning (I'm going with the second).

Or it could just be an innocent reference to the fact that he's looking forward to seeing my painting.

'I'll message you!' I know I should probably add 'no need to pop by without an invite' but I wouldn't mean it.

Chapter Thirteen

The village is smaller than I remember. I suppose most places are when you grow up. When I was a child, it seemed massive. A maze of narrow, winding streets flanked by old cottages and gardens overflowing with heavily scented honeysuckle and riotous colour. A stream meandered around the village, cutting between the fields before it emerged at the foot of the hills – the starting point of many of our long (competitive) walks.

It's prettier than I remember though. Grey stone cottages adorned with rambling roses, smart houses and B&Bs mingling with more modern, white-painted buildings adorned with bright hanging baskets, the stark white softened by fading wisteria and ivy that creeps up, fanning out as it reaches the slate roofs.

The narrow roads widen out intermittently into green-grassed spaces that are studded with benches and bordered with bright flowers. Stone walls, just the right height to sit on, flank the buildings, protect them from the road and busy pavements.

The art shop is easy to find. I'm fairly sure it was an old-fashioned newsagent's and general shop last time I came here. It nestles between a busy café with outdoor seating, and an ice-cream shop that is positively shouting my name. It seems to be a Bella favourite as well; she's straining at her leash and I'm quite sure if I tied her up outside, she'd happily sit begging and trying to accost people coming out all day.

Not that I'd tie her up and leave her. Not for one second.

'Art first, ice-cream after, Bella. You've got to earn it before you spend it you know!' She doesn't look convinced. Bloody hell, I'm beginning to sound like my parents. I reckon I rolled my eyes at them in the same way she's now doing at me.

'Well, well, if it isn't our brilliant artist and my favourite dog!' David Simons appears the moment we walk through the door. He gives Bella a biscuit from the jar by the till, and links his hand through my arm, all within a couple of minutes. 'I was wondering if you'd come!'

'I would never miss the chance of looking round an art gallery, Mr Simons!'

'Call me David, call me David. Now I wouldn't label my humble little shop an art gallery, I'm sure it's nowhere near as grand as the shops you're used to, but I know what I like, and I know what sells in our neck of the woods, or should I say lakes, haha?'

I smile back at him as he leads me through the front of the shop. It's surprising how big it is once you get inside – it widens out and must run along the back of some of the other, smaller shop fronts.

'Now, Becky, what do you think? I would rather value your opinion, as a proper artist.'

'Wow, these are beautiful!' The big open space flooded with natural light is the Lake District encapsulated on canvas. There are watercolours, sketches, graphite and oil. Large canvases, small ones, mountain vistas, lakes and individual portraits of the animals and birds that inhabit the area. From woolly sheep to curious cows, from predatory falcons swooping in for the kill to timid red squirrels in their glorious colours. Expensive originals sit side by side with limited-edition prints and mass-produced prints, something for every price range but all carefully selected by somebody who knew what they were doing.

David beams at me. 'I know each and every artist, you know. Many of them are local, some just regular visitors, but I do think that if you truly love a place then it shines through, don't you?' I nod. 'The best pictures come from the heart, created with love, or for love. Passion, love, joy, it's all there, isn't it?' He walks closer to one picture, his head on one side as he studies it.

'It is. It's such an inspiring place, it's the colours, the light is just different here.'

'The view is different every day, even though you're looking through the same window.'

'Exactly!'

He beams at me. 'Oh I just knew we'd be on the same page, talking of which, have you thought...?' He leaves the question hanging.

All of a sudden, I know. Before, I was still dithering a bit, but now I know I have to follow my heart, my instincts.

I want to do some pictures for his shop, just like I want to do the Magic Pony illustrations for the whole series of books.

I will take back control of my career. Because I know which path I want to take. And if it proves to be the wrong one, then I'll double back and try again.

I don't need somebody like Teddy telling me which choices are best, I need to believe in myself – because if I don't, then nobody else is going to, are they?

'I'd love to see my pictures hanging here, if you think they're good enough, that is.'

Teddy used to get cross at me for what he saw as false modesty. But it isn't that, I've just been brought up thinking art is fine, as a hobby. But as a career? Even now, with a steady income and a list of contributions I'm proud of, it doesn't feel quite real.

Imposter syndrome looms large every time I'm asked what I do.

'Oh, I'd be delighted at anything you'd push our way. That picture of little Bella was delightful, they sell very well, pictures like that, you know. Very in demand. I have to admit to a little bit of googling, and your animal portraits are extraordinary. You capture something, even with your line drawings. Top notch!'

I blush and smile, then reach for my rucksack. 'I've had a few ideas, I thought you could look through, see if any appealed.'

'Oh wonderful, splendid! I think we need a coffee, don't you? Then we can have a proper chat. Come through and make yourself comfortable in my coffee corner! Bella knows where to find the water bowl and there's a bell on the door, we'll hear if anybody comes in.'

———

'Oh goodness.' David puts his cup down, and I glance up with alarm when the saucer clatters and I realise his hand is shaking. He wipes one finger under his eye. 'Excuse a silly old man.'

'You're not, I mean… I hope… I'm sorry. Are you alright?'

His smile is slightly strained. 'I'm fine dear, don't worry.' He pats my knee, then props up the picture he'd been looking at, leans in for a closer look while he gathers himself and then moves back to arm's length. When he speaks again his voice crackles with emotion. 'This is so wonderful, it just, I'm sorry…' He takes a deep breath, swallows, then continues with a stronger voice. 'It brought back memories. I really didn't think anything would have the power to hit me like that these days.' The half-smile is wistful. It makes me want to reach out, hold his hand. 'It took me quite by surprise.'

I glance down at the picture. I don't think I have ever made a grown man well up before, well, not with my art.

The dreamy watercolour that he's staring at is of a glade on the banks of the stream, not far from the spot where I originally bumped into him a few days ago.

'This—' he taps the picture '—is the exact spot where I proposed to my wife.'

'Oh, wow.' I don't quite know what to say. I can't even begin to imagine a man falling for me so completely that he'd propose, let alone get so emotional about the memory of it afterwards.

'I always think good art is like a good book, the artist forms the structure, makes it real enough for the reader or viewer to want to be a part of it. Pictures can mean so much to us, can't they? They speak to us, give back what we put into them as artist and simple admirer. You imbue the picture with a part of yourself, the part that needs to be satisfied; familiarity, or hope.' He pauses, and I find myself blinking back my own emotions. 'Memories. I have many good memories of my beautiful wife, but they've not risen to the surface quite so abruptly for months. My goodness me, my dear, what have you done to me!' He squeezes my hand, but his gaze is fixed on the picture. 'During that first year after she died, they were there every day, but they fade, you know. They fade, however much you want to hang on to them. But this is splendid!' Luckily, he has brightened up. I never know quite what to say when somebody is upset, grieving. There don't seem to be any right words, do there? As much as I want to express sympathy, I'm totally relieved he's cheered up. 'This, my dear girl, is spot on!' He glances up at me. 'You are talented enough to create the window people can look through. Well now, what else have we got here?'

David slowly slides the picture to one side and stares at the next one.

The kingfisher (blue not brown!) had come alive in my bright oil pastels and I have to say that even though it is more a first outline than a finished product, I'm really chuffed with it. 'Incredible.' He taps the edge of the paper with a fingertip. 'Such amazing little birds.'

'They are, I love them. I was so excited to actually see one!'

'My wife loved them too, she had just the same reaction as you! She was a real nature lover, but this little chap was by far her favourite. You've captured it so beautifully, Becky. It's a shame she's not here, she'd love it.' We sit in companionable silence as he looks through my drawings and paintings before pausing and pulling another one out so he can study it properly.

'Ahh, little Bella! Little Bella makes me happy because she comes as part of the parcel with dear Ash. Lovely pair, aren't they? Wonderful.'

Oops. Awkward. David seems to think Bella and Ash come as a package. You've got one, you've got both. Although he has got a point – wherever I go, Ash seems to pop up, intent on taking advantage of any opportunity to take the dog.

Strangely enough though, David has not mentioned Georgina at all.

'He was a rock for me when my wife passed, a veritable rock. I'm not quite sure what path I would have headed down if he hadn't been there. A strong man, but he understands.' He nods. 'He doesn't always open up much, which isn't surprising, is it dear?' Fortunately, he doesn't seem to expect an answer to any of his questions about Ash, all I have to do is nod. 'But he knows the right things to say when he does. He knew who to turn to when he needed somebody, right?' We share a smile, but I'm a bit confused. I suppose he must mean Georgina – and assume he knows more about their relationship than I do. So, I just nod back and finish my coffee.

'Well well, I won't keep you. I'm sure you're busy and have got much more important things to do than listen to me blithering on!'

'You don't blither!' I'm not quite sure what that means. 'It's been fab to chat to you, and I love the shop so much. But I have got rather a lot of work on, and Bella is dying to have a dip in the stream.'

'I'm sure the little ragamuffin is! Well, I can't tell you how much I'd love to add some of your works to my modest display.'

We spend a happy few minutes talking terms and I promise to complete a picture of the glade for him to buy, plus do a couple more for display in the shop.

'Give my regards to young Ash when you see him! Off you go young lady, get painting!'

'I will!' I grin back at him as he stands waving in the doorway. 'Come on then Bella. You heard the man! We've got work to do.'

And I need an early night in preparation for my walk tomorrow with Ash.

Now I'm here, back at my desk, and Bella has been fed. I'm looking out of the window but not really seeing the view as it is now. I can only see the boathouse.

I glance down at where I've recreated it on canvas. I'm actually really pleased and quite proud with how the painting is going. It's nearly finished, and it gives me the warm and fuzzies. Which is excellent. David was spot on when he talked about emotional investment.

Create with love, or for love, he'd said. But I'm not quite sure what the hell my heart was playing at when it led my hand on this one.

Maybe part of the reason it makes me feel so good is because, deep down, I've been doing it for Ash.

Responding to the raw emotion that showed in his face, his voice, his whole body, when he talked about it.

Intense, moving, a hint of the real man that lies beneath the teasing exterior. I've never been one to write down words, describe with metaphors. I've always wanted to translate feelings into brush strokes, always aspired to painting some kind of artwork that speaks to people – whether it's a Magic Pony that transports you in your head to somewhere wonderful and mystical, or a grounding landscape with the depth of memories. I sometimes wish I could do portraits justice, really show a person's life in their features, their skin, the sparkle in their eyes. But I can't. Not yet.

I lost that for a while, I realise now. But it's coming back.

David could see something in my pictures, Ash could. And I think I'm starting to again.

It's early evening, dusk will be rolling in soon and the view is hauntingly beautiful. The long-gone boathouse is a bit of a mystery – like Ash. Slightly brooding, full of secrets.

I feel like I want to know more about it – not just that he once loved the boathouse and is annoyed it isn't there anymore. In the same way he's annoyed he can't get his hands on Bella.

Pictures mean things to people, David said, and I guess this view – the boathouse – means something to Ash, but I don't know why yet. And the more I look, the more I want to know.

I've tried to paint it through his eyes, tried to put his emotions into it.

Which is ridiculous. I hardly know anything about him or his life. All I know is that he's been hurt, that Georgina doesn't want to let go of him, that he's funny, sexy, that he plays by the rules.

Luckily my phone bleeps with an incoming email and I'm distracted from my thoughts.

Unluckily it is from Teddy.

B,

Spoke to Ben. Am frankly horrified – think there has been confusion, mixed messages.

No mixed messages, mate.

Teddy always writes emails and texts, and sometimes

speaks, like this. He's an editor who never uses complete sentences. Or words sometimes. He's also quite often 'horrified' and things are 'appalling' and 'outrageous'. Jerk.

Haha, I just thought of him as a jerk! Why hasn't that occurred to me earlier?

You can't seriously turn down commissions I rec'd you for.

Yup, I can!

This is an act of pure selfish abandon and reflects on my own judgement.

Pompous prick! I am not selfish; this has always been more about him than me and he's just proved it.

Will tell him you've reconsidered.

Don't you bloody dare!

It carries on in much the same vein, high profile, blah, blah, portfolio, blah, blah, damaging my rep as well, blah, blah, need to get back to London and reality, blah, blah, see a therapist to put you back on track.

Argh! That last bit really annoys me. And I mean really. I can feel myself bristling. I'll give him therapist!

Bloody hell, how did I ever fancy him, let alone sleep with him? Eurghh!!

Draft email below for you to fwd to Ben, cc me in.

Rgds. T

Draft email? See, this is what I was blind to before. He moved from being just a bit bossy to become totally domineering and controlling. Right down to telling me when, to whom, and how I should apologise and backtrack! What a total pretentious plonker. What right does he think he has to tell me what I should and shouldn't do?

Especially now.

What do they say? Never mix business with pleasure. And he's not even pleasure anymore! Was he ever though? Actually, now I think about it, it was never actually *fun*. I've had as much, no, *more* fun with my dog-protection plan than I ever did with him.

I am not letting him spoil my evening. I'm going to finish my painting.

Except he has spoiled it. He's wound me up, taken the enjoyment away. Tried to reignite my doubts.

No way am I going to finish my beautiful picture with anger at him in my head.

This picture isn't about hate, anger, regrets, bad decisions. And I'm not going to let his influence seep into it.

I type out a quick reply to the email because I need to get it out of my system, so I don't waste even more time thinking about it. I don't care if it's rushed and not carefully worded. I just need to say what I think – just tell the truth.

Be more me! Oh my God, this place has a lot to answer for – in a good way.

T.

No confusion or mixed messages. Ben and I have agreed terms.
No need for your intervention.

Becky.

Wow, I'm really chuffed with myself. Business-like, polite and to the point.

I did initially type 'Thanks, Becky' which is my normal way of signing off, then decided I wanted to make it unambiguous. I am not thanking him for anything. So I tried 'best wishes', then 'best', then 'regards', then decided that life was too short to faff about wasting time ending an email I shouldn't even have to send and settled for my name.

Bella nudges my knee, then squeezes onto my lap so that I have to stretch around her to reach the keyboard. 'Oh Bella, you are a funny one!' She lifts her head so that she can lick my nose and makes me laugh. 'You want me to stop work?'

I swear she nods her head.

With a smile on my face I add a final line to the email:

PS already got a therapist, called Bella.

Then hit send.

Bella is definitely as good as a therapist, any day. She's made sure I get my daily dose of exercise and fresh air, forced me to get up early in the mornings, got me out of the house, given me the opportunity to talk to David, a complete stranger who I reckon would have passed by with barely a 'hello' if it hadn't been for her, and now she's making sure that I don't let things (as in Teddy) get to me. No way will I be allowed to work too many hours or obsess about anything with Bella about.

She jumps down as I close the lid of my laptop, as though she knows it signals the end of work. I push the chair away from the table. I'm going to have a glass of wine, watch the bats and chill.

Tomorrow I will finish the work for Ben and tick that off my list. And I'll block any correspondence from Teddy, who quite frankly has already taken up too much of my life and thoughts.

And as I am feeling on my toes, I think I will call Georgina tonight and give her an update. I also want to try out my 'supervised access' for Bella and Ash line, as I did ask him if he'd like to see the boathouse picture when I finish it. And I don't like lying to Georgina, so think I need to come clean, or at least fudge the issue, about talking to him. And letting him in the house. And letting him touch Bella.

And kissing him.

I think maybe I have stepped over some of my house- and pet-sitting boundaries. Well, demolished rather than stepped over.

Maybe Teddy was right in at least one way. I have been selfish. I've put my own lust ahead of Georgina's wishes, and been far too busy thinking about my own career and possible new avenues, rather than concentrating on my primary reason for being here.

Nope, it's not working. Lecturing myself is not making

me feel guilty. Just frustrated. Does it really matter what Ash gets up to? He's her ex! And if Bella is happy – and I promise, promise, promise on my life not to put her at risk or have the slightest chance of her being dog-napped – then surely that's fine?

It's funny, the more I think about Georgina, the more I start to think there are similarities between us. I mean she is way more successful and polished than I am, a real career woman from the looks of her Insta account, and I'd love to be like that. Being honest, I know I'm never going to be. I mean, I can't be bothered to constantly put the effort into looking my best or keeping my house super tidy. I just need to slob out a fair bit of the time. But it would be kind of cool to be that successful, that fab at what I do, and I was thinking I'd like to be that confident. But I'm starting to realise that maybe she isn't all she appears to be, and maybe she has the same kind of worries as I do.

I guess she feels like she's got more to lose, she doesn't want to admit that she and Ash aren't made for each other. She hasn't been able to let go of him. She hates him because she still wants him. I more or less spotted that bit from day one. I mean if you break up with somebody that you're not that keen on, you only hurl abuse for a few hours, don't you? Whereas if you thought they were for keeps, that's a whole different thing. That's when you get into 'slashing their suits and sticking prawns in their curtain rails before you go' territory, isn't it?

Ash hinted at it the other day. For Georgina, admitting it's not working is like admitting she's wrong, that her perfect life isn't quite perfect. That she's hit a glitch that she can't fix.

Like I did.

Letting go of Teddy hasn't been my problem since our breakup. Maybe I'm not the passionate kind that will ever fall that hard and feel like that. Oh my God, what if I'm not? What if I'm never going to fancy somebody so much that I need revenge? That's a bit scary, and sad.

No, I mustn't go down that route. I've just not found the right person yet. Teddy definitely wasn't that person. The being dumped didn't make me feel shit.

It's been letting go of the idea I could design the cover of some *Sunday Times* bestselling book. Why has it taken me so long to admit that I've been hanging on to something that isn't right for me? Teddy sacking me doesn't reflect on the rest of my work, or on me. Teddy has done me a favour. He's set me free, let me reset my clock and start remembering who the real me is. And Bella has helped. And so have Ash and Georgina. Everything about being here has helped.

I feel like I need to help Ash and Georgina.

I'll keep it simple though. No need to go into all the why's and wherefore's. I will just make a case for him having access.

Just as I pick up my mobile, it rings.

Abby.

'Oh my God, Bec, he did it!'

Abby never shrieks, or sounds totally excited, or shouts out before she's even said hello. She has just done all those things.

'Did what? Who?'

'Ed, you noddle! Oh my God!' She also doesn't say that. 'He proposed! Even though I kind of thought he might soon, it was still totally, like, unexpected! I welled up, I nearly cried, can you imagine?'

'Not really.' I laugh. Abby is not a crier. I am. 'Oh wow, Abs, that's brill! Congratulations.' I am genuinely pleased for her. Even though this is yet another thing she has proved better at than I am. Surely, as older sister, I was supposed to get married first? 'Er, you did say yes?'

'Of course, I did!'

'Because if you're not sure, there's some *really* hot guys out on the hills here…'

'Becky!' She giggles, and she's all out of breath. She knows I'm kidding, but right now probably wouldn't notice if I wasn't.

'I saw some of them fell running yesterday! I mean actually running up the bloody hill, I find it hard enough walking!' Will I be able to do that after Ash has put me through my paces again tomorrow? Shit, it's tomorrow. I should be in bed, or eating carbs for energy, or resting or something. Does wine count? I'm sure there are loads of carbs in wine.

Actually, thinking about wine, I'd much rather share a bottle of that with him than stomp up a hill. I must be mad for saying I'd go.

She laughs. 'You should try it, you used to be ace at running, you were so fit! Go get them guys!'

I've not told her about Ash and my workout yet. How he nearly killed me.

'That was when I was fifteen!' I should at least tell her about our planned 'stroll'. 'But Ash has said he'll put me through my paces tomorrow. Get me fell-ready!'

She squeals. 'Put you through your paces!'

'It's not like that, sadly!' I can't help laughing along with her though.

'I bet it is! I knew it!'

'It's in return for me doing a picture for him, which he's paying for as well, before you call him a cheapskate.'

'Would I heck!' she says indignantly.

'Yes, you would!'

'Okay I would. But it sounds good.' I can hear the smile in her voice.

'Certainly does, and I do want to be fit enough to clamber over—' she sniggers, I ignore her '—some of these hills before I have to leave. Anyway, just let me know if you want me to throw a fell runner your way, you know, before you dash up the aisle, if you're not one hundred per cent...'

She laughs again. 'Oh my God, it doesn't feel real!'

We talk about weddings, and when it might happen, and all stuff like that.

'Mum's insisting we have some kind of engagement party. I mean, I don't know why, we're not bothered, but you know what she's like.'

'I do.' I shake my head affectionately. 'She's happy for you, just promise you won't let her take over with the wedding – you'll end up with his'n'hers thrones or something.'

'Promise.' She laughs again, I've never heard her so happy. 'You will come if we have a party?'

'Course I will.' How can she think I wouldn't?

'It wouldn't be the same if you didn't.'

'I will! How could I miss your engagement party?' I actually feel quite upset that we've got to the stage that she thinks I might miss something as important to her as this.

'So we'll do it when you get back, what's that, in two or three weeks? Oh my God, I can't believe this is actually happening!'

Oh gawd, it feels like I've only been here a few days. I don't even want to start thinking about the fact that at some point my dog-sitting duties will end and I'll have to go home. That makes me feel sad. I'm nowhere near ready to leave this place yet. But I mustn't feel sad, my little sis has just got engaged.

'Sounds amazing, can't wait to see you and celebrate in person!'

'Me too! Better go Bec, I've got to ring Dan and tell him, I just wanted to make sure you were the first! Speak soon, love you.'

'Abby?' I stop her before she has a chance to put the phone down.

'Yeah?'

I need to start making this right. 'I'm happy for you, really happy, you know. He's a good guy, you'll make the dream team.'

'Aww, thanks Becs, I'm happy too. In case you hadn't guessed!' She giggles. 'And hey, I'm happy for you, you know. The old adventurous Bec is back, you used to be up for anything! I always envied you for doing what you really wanted to do and ignoring the easy way.'

'Envied me?' This is news.

'Yeah, but it was cool to have a big sis like you when I was at school.'

I like that. Cool. I was cool. I still can be cool.

'I mean, sometimes you were a bit weird, but most of the time you were cool.'

'Watch it, pipsqueak!'

'I'd better go I suppose.'

'So had I, I've got to be up and ready for 6 a.m.'

'Six a.m.? Bloody hell, he must be hot, you're keen!'

'It's before it gets too sunny!' I say a bit huffily.

'Yeah, yeah, heard it all before. Speak soon?' Then she blows a kiss and is gone.

'So...' I look at Bella. 'We'd better talk to your mum, I suppose?' She lies down, puts her chin on her paws, and I swear, she groans. 'Or we could leave it and see how things go, and maybe mention it next time she calls?'

She wags her tail lazily.

'I could message her?'

That's the answer, if she's anything like me she won't want to be put on the spot, she'll need time to think it over, cooling-down time after an initial reaction that is bound to be angry.

Hi Georgina, I was wondering if it would be good for Bella to see Ash just for an hour or so? She misses you and it might be nice for her? Becky x

A text pings back almost instantaneously.

No, he's not having her G x

That's a no then. 'Hmm, that sounds pretty definite, doesn't it eh, Bella? She said no, we thought she would, didn't we?'

I put my phone down with a sigh. Talking to Georgina is never easy. 'She hasn't taken this well, has she? I think you need to give her plenty of cuddles when she comes home.' Bella wags her tail and barks, then runs off and comes back with a ball for me. She drops it at my feet and waits.

I've only just thrown it when my phone rings again.

Teddy. Really? I honestly can't be arsed. 'Sod off!' I cancel the call and switch my phone off and throw the ball again.

Then I turn some music on very, very loud, let Bella do zoomies over the couch, and top up my glass of wine.

Honestly, why the hell did I think this would be an 'escape from it all'?

Chapter Fourteen

'Good morning!'

Morning? This isn't morning, this is the middle of the night. I don't think there is anything good about it, and I don't think I should have had that last glass of wine.

'Let's get this party started!' Ash is as perky as a puppy; he's bouncing about on his toes like a boxer warming up for a fight, and he looks like he has been awake for *hours*.

'I don't call getting up at this time a party.' I wipe the sleep out of the corner of my eye. I must be mad. What did he say, he was doing this in return for the painting? This is for *my* benefit? 'Remind me why you've got me out of bed at this time again?'

He grins, which helps a bit. 'Well, well, who's a grump in the mornings? I would never have guessed!'

'I need three cups of coffee and no small talk for at least an hour before I become human.'

His chuckle makes me revise that to two cups of coffee and half an hour.

'Good job I've come with peace offerings then.'

'Gingerbread!'

'No!' He really does laugh then. 'You're addicted to it girl, that's your Christmas and birthday presents sorted then.'

Oooh, I'm down to one coffee and fifteen minutes now. It might have been a careless comment, but I quite like the idea of him sending me a gingerbread box for my birthday.

'But I have got a new antler for Bella to keep her busy while we're out.'

'We're not taking her?' This surprises me.

'Nope, not really safe for her where we're going.'

'Safe?' Oh my God, I am definitely going back to bed. If he's planning on going somewhere that is dangerous for the dog, then no way am I tagging along. 'I think I'm going off you.'

'Good to hear you were on me.' His eyes are twinkling.

I groan and blush. I am on him, but really? Okay, honesty, I'd much rather have a night in with a bottle of wine and the opportunity to climb all over him, than an early morning *dangerous* outing.

'I'm kidding, it's just we'd have to keep her on the lead a lot of the time which she hates, because of the livestock and the steep drop.'

Steep drop? I think I've gone even paler than my normal early-morning shade.

'You'll be safe, I'll make sure. Promise! Trust me.' He's giving me that intense look that grabs at my insides and does strange things to me.

'Okay,' I say weakly.

'She's got no sense; she'd just jump off a cliff if you let her, but do what I say, and you'll be fine.'

I'm really not sure again. One minute I feel up for anything, and the next I'm wondering who will miss me if I die on the Cumbrian fells.

'Come on, I'm winding you up! I wouldn't take you anywhere I thought you couldn't cope with. Young kids go up there!'

'I break more easily than young kids, my legs aren't as bendy.'

'You're funny.' For a moment he looks serious, his voice softens. 'I think you'll love it, it's an amazing place. But if you don't...' He straightens up and backs off slightly as though he's overstepped that mark.

Now I feel like I *have* to go. This sounds like it's a special place, somewhere he wants to share with me. If he thinks I'm worth showing it to, then I want to. I need to.

'Sure! I want to, I really appreciate you taking time out to show me places I wouldn't find on my own.' Wow, that sounds a bit stilted and formal. But I'm taken aback and feel a bit awkward.

'Great!' His smile is back. I don't feel awkward at all. 'Anyway, this is for her—' he fishes a chew out of one pocket '—and this is for you.' He holds out a flask. Wow, how did he know? The man is a genius. 'We'll stop for a drink before we start the ascent.'

'Ascent?' I squeak. Don't they use the word ascent when they're talking about climbing Mount Everest and big, *proper* mountains like that?

'You are so easy to wind up! Come on, let's go, let's see what you're made of, Becky Havers.'

That sounds ominous.

I think I would rather run around the garden with Bella, drink a gallon of coffee and work.

But I can't say no, can I? That would be wimpy, and I am not wimpy. I am a girl who is going to stand up for herself, who is not going to say no to anything, unless it's illegal or very, very dangerous.

I also want to see this place. If it's important to Ash, then in a strange way I feel like it's important to me.

Weird.

It is a good job I have revised my view of Ash and no longer suspect him of being an axe murderer, because his Land Rover left the road some time ago, and we've been bouncing across the countryside for what feels like miles with not a soul in sight.

'This route's a bit inaccessible, but it keeps the tourists away.' He grins at me as we bounce over a rock, then turns his attention forwards again. 'There is a car park over that way.' He waves and I want to squeak 'Keep both hands on the steering wheel' but I manage not to. 'But I've got access up here, so it's better. Quieter.' He lifts an eyebrow in a way that makes me blush. Again. 'Not far now and you can have your coffee!'

He expertly steers the vehicle over the bumpy track, his tanned hands holding the steering wheel lightly – if I was driving, I'd be hanging on for dear life, my knuckles white, but I guess he's used to doing this. Well, he definitely is, given the mud-spattered state of the four-wheel drive.

Then he pulls to a stop by a stone wall and turns the engine off.

There are only sheep for company, and not many of them. Where the hell are we?

'Here we go. You pour the coffee, while I get the gear out.'

'Gear?' I don't like the sound of that.

'Paraglider.'

My fingers falter on the flask. My throat has gone very dry. 'Paraglider?'

'I didn't think you'd want to walk all the way down, it's a long way.'

'I'd love to walk all the way down,' I croak. No way are my feet going to leave the ground. Is he mad? I've seen YouTube videos of people jumping off fells and swooping down over lakes. I feel ill.

'Oh.' He pauses and frowns. 'Ropes then? We could abseil?' He's out of the driver's seat and has opened the back door before I can object.

I feel sick.

I'm acutely aware of his presence behind me, the hairs prickling on the back of my neck as he rummages around.

'I can't abseil,' I squeak out, turning.

He looks up and chuckles. 'I was kidding! I think we'll need a few more bootcamp sessions before we start leaping off cliffs together. This is a different kind of gear. Come on then, if you've had your coffee, get your arse into gear!'

He slams the door shut and the whole vehicle shakes, in much the same way as my knees are doing as I clamber out and watch him put a large rucksack on.

'I hope that's full of gingerbread!'

He grins, then taps the side of his nose. 'You'll soon find out. Ready?'

For the first time I look around properly. We are surrounded by vast open moors, not steep fells. I stop panicking. I can do this, whatever it is. I am a bit confused though. 'Where's the steep hill?'

'It's more of a down than an up, come on, you'll see.'

'Steep down?'

'I've done it tons of times, it's safe, I promise.' His gaze meets mine and this time he's not smiling, he's totally serious. 'It'll be worth it. I wouldn't have brought you here if I didn't know you could do it.' His certainty, his belief, wins me over.

'O-kay, let's do this then.'

I shut the heavy door with a clunk and straighten my top. Something tells me that Ash *will* look after me.

To be honest, I'm beginning to wonder what lies ahead as we saunter across the moors. Because it is like a saunter. This seems far too easy. I glance over at Ash a time or two, but he is walking steadily, keeping his pace to one that suits me and looking completely chilled.

I have absolutely no idea what is in his rucksack, but it doesn't look like it's weighing him down so I'm hoping it's a pile of well-wrapped bacon sandwiches and a good slab of gingerbread. And more coffee.

His steady pace settles me after a while. It's addictive. It's impossible to stay wound up and nervous. So after a while I forget to worry about what challenge lurks round the next corner and allow myself to breathe in the air and appreciate the wide-open space, the stillness, and the fact that there isn't another living soul to spoil the feeling that we're in an untouched place.

My ears are tuned in to the sounds of birds, the distant bleating of sheep. The soft sun is warming my face and I realise I'm smiling.

No way would I have ever imagined a few months ago that I'd be striding across the moors with a fit man at my side and only the wildlife for company. It's like my world has been reinvented. Everything is different. Even I'm beginning to feel different – how can I not?

'Look!' Ash comes to a halt and pulls me in to his side, startling me out of my daydreams.

I hear the sound first: the unmistakable sound of splashing water. And then he has me close, is drawing me forward.

'Wow!' I stare. This is totally unexpected. I lean forward a bit more, even though we're dangerously close to the edge. But I know Ash will hold me and I need to see this properly.

There's a dark pool below, but it's not that which really catches my eye. A waterfall cascades down at one end where the rocks drop down abruptly. This isn't pretty, it's wild and spectacular. In places the drop is sheer, the rockface hard and unforgiving, in other parts the slope is dotted with greenery and looks steep but accessible and there even looks to be a shale beach. 'What is this place?' I look round at him and he's smiling. Not his cheeky grin, but an expectant smile that tells me he likes my reaction.

'It's a quarry, Tranearth quarry.'

'It's amazing!'

'I told you it was worth the walk,' he says softly, turning to look back down at the quarry, and we stand in silence for a moment. I'm aware of the warmth of his arm around my waist, the closeness of his body against mine. Even more aware when he pulls away.

He swings his rucksack to the floor and starts to pull things out. 'Here you go!'

Not bacon sandwiches.

'What the heck?' I can feel the frown form on my face. Talk about disappointing! It looks like he's brought clothes not food.

'Wetsuit for you, I've already got mine on!'

'What?' As I look at him, realisation hits. 'We're not?'

'We certainly are! This is one of the best places for cliff jumping that I know, I reckoned you might be a wild swimming kind of girl?'

His grin is cheeky, definitely cheeky. 'You seem to like the water!'

I look at the wetsuit, then look back at him.

I shoot another glance down at the pool. Gulp. 'How do we get back?'

'Scramble up the rocks on the other side! Come on, I dare you!'

He really should not say that! Oh, what the hell? You only live once. He's already stripping off his outer layers and a blaze of excitement shoots through me as I pick up the suit. I think adrenalin is to blame. No way am I going to let him go without me though. 'Last one in is a cissy!'

'Are you ready?' He hasn't made it a race. He has waited for me to undress and put the suit on with fumbling fingers.

I'm not sure I'll ever be completely ready for this, but I bite my lip and nod as Ash takes my hand in his large, capable one.

'On the count of three?' He squeezes my hand. His eyes are shining, and his enthusiasm is infectious. I've got butterflies in my stomach and my heart is pounding, but I suddenly really want to do this.

We leap together, soaring through the air. For a moment we seem suspended and then it is over so fast I can hardly believe we've fallen so far. The water hits me, icy cold even with the wetsuit. I'm under the surface then bobbing up, brushing the wet hair out of my eyes and spinning around in the water looking for Ash, feeling so totally alive. I think that is the definition of exhilaration!

He's right behind me. His face only inches from mine, slicking his own wet hair back. 'I want to do it again!' I splutter out.

He laughs a loud, full laugh as he moves even closer. 'You've got to climb all the way up there first!' He points back to where we've come from, the sheer rockface looming over us. 'Though Bella has managed to bounce up those rocks, so I'm sure you will make it!'

'I don't care! I will. That was amazing! Thank you!' I can't help myself; I throw my arms around his neck and lean in to kiss his cheek.

Somehow my lips don't meet his cheek, they land on his mouth. For a moment neither of us moves.

His hands are on my waist. I can feel every inch of his fingers even through the wetsuit. His intense blue eyes are staring into mine, framed by amazing thick dark lashes that the water emphasises.

I feel him pulling me in closer. I feel his body against mine. And then he pulls back slightly. Ever so slightly. But I don't want him to. I can't help myself; I wrap my own arms around him on impulse, close that gap between us and press my lips to his.

I never intended to do it. For a split second I wonder if it's wrong, but then his hold tightens, and I am being well and truly kissed.

I can't feel the cold water, all I can feel is the heat of his body against mine, the warmth of his hand on my neck, the taste of him, the need to get closer, to have more.

It is Ash who breaks it off and pulls away, breathing as heavily as I am.

He blinks, looking as stunned as I feel. That kiss might have only lasted a few seconds, but it was one hell of a hot snog.

We both stare. I know I'm flushed with the excitement of it all. He brushes back the hair from my eyes.

'Wow.' His pulls a funny face, breaks the spell and stops

me feeling embarrassed. Then he takes my hand in his. 'Again?'

I nod and let him help me clamber out of the water.

We scramble up the path together, which is far, far harder work than the coming down was and leaves me feeling breathless and my legs wobbly. Although I was breathless before I started – from the jump, and from the kiss.

The second time, after we leap, there is no kiss. Just his warm hand to tow me to the side. But it feels natural, good. I feel on a high, pumped full of energy.

'Had enough?' Laughter dances in his face. He's so alive, he makes me feel alive as well. A no-boundaries type of guy who dares me to push myself, to feel the same highs that he does.

'Definitely!' I suddenly realise that I might feel pumped, but my limbs haven't got the message. I need to sit down. 'I need to recover!'

He laughs, that rich gorgeous laugh that makes the world seem a happier place, and leads me towards the tiny shingle beach. We sit down, side by side. 'It's beautiful here.'

'I thought you'd like it.' He smiles. 'I used to come here a lot as a kid, but I've not been for ages, it's not really Georgie's scene.' A brief frown flits across his face, but it scuds on as fast as a summer cloud on a breezy day. 'I did bring Bella once and she loved it, but I thought it would be nice just the two of us, without me having to worry about keeping an eye on her.'

It's a bit odd without Bella. I've never really been with

Ash on my own, she's always been there. A buffer. It feels strangely intimate without her. Would we have kissed if she'd been here? Or would I have been looking for her, checking she was okay?

'Here.' He reaches behind a rock and pulls out a rucksack.

'Bloody hell.' I laugh. 'Are you always this prepared?'

'A good soldier never lets his troops down.' He grins back and opens it up.

'Oh my God, you've got gingerbread! And another flask of coffee!'

He's watching me closely when I glance up, amusement in his eyes, a gentle smile tugging at his lips. 'I love a girl who's easy to please.'

I'm not sure why, but that sends a fizz of pleasure through me, makes me want to hug myself – or him. Instead I tuck into the surprise picnic as we sit and look at the water, my knee occasionally brushing against his. Our shoulders are touching.

'We'd better get back; you'll start to get cold.' He brushes the crumbs off his hands and stands up.

Disappointment hits me. I'd like to stay longer, I'm not sure I'm ready to go back and work, but I know he's talking sense. And he might need to work, even if I'm flexible.

I climb to my feet and somehow slip on a rock – before I know it I'm going down, grabbing the first thing I can to try and stop myself.

It is his thigh. I am hanging on to his thigh. It's remarkably solid.

'Here.' He's grinning, looking down at me with his hand

out, but all I can really see is that firm tightly clad leg and that tightly clad bulge a bit further up.

He peels me off and sets me back on my feet.

Embarrassing.

It's hard to stay embarrassed for long though as he leads the way back to the top, always ready to help me when the going gets steep.

He steadies me, his hands on my waist when we finally get to the top and I have to stop to draw breath.

'Okay?'

'Amazing.' I do actually feel amazing. I've not done anything remotely like this for so long I'd forgotten how much of a buzz I get from pushing myself, from daring myself. I can do what I like, I really can. The laugh bubbles up inside me and is out before I can stop it.

Ash doesn't say anything. He just grins, but I've got a feeling he knows exactly how I feel.

He jogs around to where he left his other rucksack then slips his hand into mine and we make our way slowly back to where we parked up.

We drive back home in silence – comfortable silence.

It hadn't hit me until I'd leapt through the air just how stuffy life with Teddy had been. How much I'd compromised. Let him mould me into a person I'm not.

And it hadn't hit me until that snog just how superficial kisses with Teddy had been. No lip-mashing there, no teeth clashing or tonsil-sucking. And even when we were naked, his touch hadn't left me feeling goose-bumpy or melt-in-the-middle.

Unlike the kiss and grope with a neoprene-coated Ash.

I've got to stop thinking about that.

We're pulling up outside the house far too quickly.

'Today was fantastic. Thanks for taking me there.'

'You're welcome. I'm glad you liked it, really.' His dark gaze is intent, and then he turns, roots about in the rucksack and holds something out. 'I saved the last bit for you!'

The smell of ginger tantalises my tastebuds, I can't stop my mouth watering.

'I'd say keep it, but that wouldn't be me!' I take the packet, letting my fingertips brush against his. Then I clamber out of the Land Rover and wave as he pulls off.

I put my hand to my lips as I walk inside. Oh my God, I groped his thighs, practically glued myself to them, and to his mouth. I snogged him, totally snogged his face off after jumping off a cliff!

Maybe I'm more of a passionate type than I realised.

Chapter Fifteen

O h, bloody hell, why do I feel so nervous?

I have just plumped the cushions up for the umpteenth time and I'm not a cushion-plumping kind of person. I don't do it. It's ridiculous. Why make cushions look perky when all you're going to do is flatten them again?

Georgina softened (slightly) a couple of days after her 'no' message, and got in touch to say that maybe she'd consider letting Ash see Bella, on common ground, with me holding the leash. She'd think about it and let me know. Which left me feeling so much more positive, and less guilty. I have taken this as a green light. I have been given permission to converse with the enemy. Yay!

Though it's not just conversing I'm interested in. I mean, I'm an adult, we're both adults. We're single and we fancy each other. Or at least I fancy his arse off, and he wouldn't have kissed me *like that* if he'd found me repulsive, would he?

I've not seen Ash since our clamber and hot snog, so it will be a bit awkward, but that doesn't explain why I feel like a teenager on a first date. It's not a date.

It is a picture viewing.

With possibilities.

I sent him a text this morning.

I've finished the boathouse picture, would you like a private viewing?

Well, that was the first attempt, which I decided sounded a bit wink-wink flirty. So, I took out the 'private', and that made it old-womanly formal, which I am not. So, I changed it to 'would you like to see it?' Which seemed a bit flat. And let's be honest here, I *am* actually flirting, so I went with the original.

Well, okay, I have harboured some 'maybe after a glass of wine there'll be some more lip contact' thoughts. I mean, you don't just invite a sexy man, whose thighs you have groped, round to look at a picture, do you? However good you think it is. And however much you really, really hope he likes it.

So, I've made sure I've got wine in. No falling at the first hurdle! And it is breathing – more freely than me at the moment.

My only real worry is that he is actually not at all how he appears to me, and Georgina is right. I have kidded myself he is nice and likes me, because I lust after his body and we seem to have some kind of chemistry going on.

And we all know how good I am at kidding myself. I

kidded myself that Teddy and I could make a go of it, even though he was a reptilian control freak who should be cast in a weird episode of *Dr Who* where he will be zapped and get his just rewards.

I am also feeling anxious about the upcoming engagement party for Abby. Oh God, I want her to be happy, I love her, I want to share in her happiness. But I mean, I just feel so desperate not to be the one at the next family party whose most recent relationship ended after everybody had more or less told me that Teddy was a loser. I want them to be proud of me, I want to be leaving here with a plan for the rest of my life. I want to be able to say quite truthfully that I've got commissions, that I'm happy with what I'm doing and I have a fab new direction. And I don't know if I'm going to have all that in time.

I promised Abs I'd go though, and I will go. She's my sister. But really?

Maybe I need to get Ash into bed, be a complete sex-bomb with no inhibitions who he can't resist, and persuade him to accompany me to the party, in return for the performance of any sexual acts he desires? That way everybody will be shocked into silence and not ask me what's going on.

Maybe not.

I mean, let's face it. He could be a step ahead of me here. All along the snogging could be part of his evil plan to lull me into a false sense of security (or a state of being so shagged out I can't move) so that he can grab Bella back.

Oh, and I do have another worry. The painting of the boathouse.

Actually, if I'm honest, I'm sure I can put my nerves down to the painting. It's got nothing to do with my family, or snogging, or my future. It's this painting. When I put the last touches to it, I stepped back and welled up. There was an actual lump in my throat. I felt like a proud parent.

It speaks to me, even though I've never actually seen the boathouse in real life.

And I want to know it speaks to him. I want to see the look on his face and know I've got it right.

Which is making me nervous.

I feel sick.

What if he hates it?

What if it's like Teddy all over again; he thinks my work is crap and just like that, any attraction between us is knocked on the head as well? Double rejection.

I feel like I'm setting myself up to be knocked down.

Except I have to, don't I? I did this for him. It's good, I'm sure in my heart that it is. Which would make it even worse if he doesn't agree – because I've just realised, his opinion really matters to me. It is more important than any opinion of Teddy's, because that was just linked to cash and my career. This picture is personal.

I'll just move the picture to a slightly better angle, for the twentieth time, but the light does keep changing at this time of day and—

'Hi, I'm not too early, am I?'

'Shit!' I nearly drop the painting on the floor, and then fumble like mad with shaking hands to prop it back up again safely. 'You made me jump!' I fold my arms to hide the fact that my hands are trembling.

'Sorry.' He grins, and one side of his mouth is lifted, dimples deeper than ever. He is standing at the open window and he's not looking sorry at all, but sexy and chilled. Unlike me. I am a hot mess.

I wish he wouldn't grin like that; it makes me think dirty thoughts.

'You don't look sorry!' He doesn't. He looks fit. Totally fit, he is the dishiest man I have ever known. Not to put too fine a point on it, but I want to jump him in a totally indecent way.

His hair, which is normally all messy (like Bella's) has been tamed, which makes me really, really want to run my fingers through it and make it scruffy again. Its dishevelled texture is calling out to me. Just the thought is making me all dry-mouthed and hot and bothered. 'What are you doing there?'

'The front door was locked.'

See? I can follow *some* of Georgina's instructions.

I open the patio doors and Bella, who has been bouncing about barking, shoots out. A bundle of frantically wagging tail, flopping ears and lolling tongue, as she winds round his legs, jumps in the air up to chest height and then sets off on zoomies round the garden, crashing through the borders and flattening flowers as she goes.

She is excited.

That makes two of us. I am trying to contain mine though. Boy, it would be much easier if I was a dog. A joyous, happy dog. Though to be honest, I think I am catching a bit of her loopiness. Life somehow seems much better than it used to. I used to be a glass-half-full type of person. I'm not quite sure when I switched to half-empty mode, but it's impossible to stay that way when you're around a dog like Bella.

'I brought wine?' He holds a bottle up. 'Is that okay?'

'Great, fine!' Brilliant. Although, is it friendliness, foreplay or part of a dastardly plan? And do I care either way?

'So, this is it.' He takes a step inside, passes me the bottle then folds his arms and stands, legs wide, staring.

The silence lengthens. It goes on. And on.

Forever.

My chest starts to constrict uncomfortably, and I realise I'm holding my breath. I let it out as quietly as I can, so I don't disturb him, and bite my bottom lip instead.

He finally takes a step back, hands on hips now. The muscles in his forearms ripple, then he lifts one hand to his chin, his forefinger resting on his bottom lip.

He really is quite beautiful in profile.

Beautiful as in full of character.

And he has this stillness about him. A solid stillness that makes my heart constrict and my fingers twitch. If I was a portrait painter, I'd have to capture him.

I'm not, but I want to anyway.

'Well.' His lips thin, then relax back, the corner lifting in that now-familiar quirk.

My God, this is like the most terrifying interview ever.

'Do you, er…' I clear my throat. 'Do you think it's okay? Is it like, well, like it was?'

'Becky.' He closes his eyes briefly, then opens them, and half turns so he is looking straight at me. And I mean *straight*. It's like he's interrogating my soul and it's exciting, not scary. I've gone all trembly inside. Again. 'This is bloody brilliant.' There's a gruff edge to his voice. I register the smallest shake of his head, but his gaze is still holding mine. 'I don't know how the hell you did it, from one crappy picture, but it's spot on. You're a genius.'

I think I feel like Bella does when he's cuddling her, tickling her tummy and telling her she's the best. If I was a cat I'd be purring. I'm glowing inside and out.

This is why I paint.

Right now, at this moment, I know I've got it right. I've proved I can do it. Even if 'it' isn't what Teddy thought it should be. I want to punch the air, or hug Ash.

But I settle for grinning inanely.

Ash turns back to the picture, leaning in to study it more closely, and the moment for hugs has gone.

'I'll get some glasses for the wine.'

I don't think he hears. All his attention has been diverted.

When I return, he is standing in the open doorway, leaning against the door jamb, one hand in his jeans pocket. Looking out at the lake.

'Sorry, didn't mean to be rude, it just kind of blew my brain a bit.' He runs his fingers through his hair, then grins sheepishly and takes the glass of wine from me. The touch of his fingertips makes my heart race even faster than it did the first time. 'Who knew looking at a picture could be that intense? Cheers.' We clink glasses, and all words appear to have been evicted from my brain. He is *so* intense, so deep. 'Shall we sit down?' He motions towards the chairs and table on the patio, and all I can do is nod mutely and follow him.

Bella crashes out at his feet, one of her paws on his trainer as though she wants to be sure he can't sneak off unnoticed.

'It's amazing here, isn't it? Timeless.' Okay, as first words go, they aren't very impressive, but it's the best I can do. I just want to stare at him. But my brain does seem to be kicking up a gear, closer to normal. The silence isn't uncomfortable, but I feel the need to fill it, maybe to stop myself from grabbing him. 'I feel like we're just visitors, here briefly, passing through leaving only the tiniest of marks.' I'm starting to ramble, so I let myself pause. Try to copy his stillness, something I'm normally brilliant at. 'We're an unwelcome blip on nature's perfection.'

He smiles broadly, showing white teeth. They're not perfect, one is chipped. But they're bright white against his tanned features. 'I like that.' He chuckles, and it comes straight from the centre of him. 'You're a constant surprise, you know?'

'Me?'

'Yeah, you.' He settles back more comfortable in the chair. 'Who'd have thought you were such a brilliant artist and an incredible rock climber.'

'Haha.' I know the climbing comment is a joke, but I'll take the artist bit. 'Incredible?'

'Maybe incredibly bad.' He laughs again, but his eyes meet mine and it dies away. We're both thinking about that moment. His hands on my waist, his body pressed against mine.

'Incredibly.' I clear my throat once more.

'I had you down as one of Georgina's groupies.'

'I'm not a groupie!'

'I know that now. Sorry, no offence intended.' He shrugs, broad shoulders barely moving, but his shirt tightens over his chest, making me even more aware of his maleness.

'None taken. How were you to know? I'm a house-sitter, not a follower.'

'No.' He studies me more intently again, but this time I don't feel uncomfortable, or want to squirm away. 'You're not, are you? As individual as they come.'

I've never thought of myself as individual. 'Is that an insult or a compliment?'

'Interesting how you said insult first.' His voice is a low drawl. I'm beginning to think he's one of those people who is measured in every way, actions, words, all thought through. All there for a reason.

I shrug. 'I guess criticism is thrown out more often than praise, isn't it? It's more "don't do that" than "do more".' I try to keep my voice steady. This is teasing, tempting, it's an ebb and flow, one moment almost seductive, the next teasing, then almost dinner party conversation. The anticipation being ramped up slowly, notch by small notch.

Is this what attraction is really about? Because I've never felt like this with a man before.

'True.' He nods. 'Very true. We're all quick to judge, aren't we?' There's a long pause as we both drink our wine, then he sits up straighter and leans in, his forearms on his knees, and I resist the urge to creep in closer. His eyes are bright and there's humour lurking in his face. 'So what made you think I was SAS?'

Oops. Embarrassing. Except, with one warming glass of wine in my stomach and emotion churning in my veins, I'm beginning not to care quite so much.

'Sorry.' I meet his gaze. 'It was just I saw this picture of you on Georgina's Insta account, in your combats, looking like, well, like you were in the SAS or something.'

A shadow crosses his face.

'You follow her Insta account?' There's a defensive edge to his question.

Oh no, I knew this was too good to be true.

'You're into all that, are you? For your pictures.' He adds the last bit as though to justify his slightly interrogatory tone.

Well, bang, there go my chances of a good, well, bang. He's managed to drop a bomb into the cosy camaraderie like an expert.

'I don't really follow her account, it was just to find out about the house, who she was, where I was coming. But, yes, I do post stuff on Insta.' He's giving me a slightly hostile look. 'That's a bit judgy, most people do!'

'Most?' His look and tone hold a big 'most people like you' side to them. He doesn't need to know that most of my research, for house-sitting, work and lots of other things, is done via Instagram. And Google Images. And Pinterest.

'Most!'

'Doesn't anybody have a private life these days, then?'

'Well yes, stuff online is just an image, a pimped-up

snap, it's not real, you know. It's pretend, make-believe. My best life, all that crap!'

'It is real when somebody else starts to post photos of you, your home, everything.' He sounds genuinely upset. I have a feeling this has been brewing. 'And you don't have a say.'

Ahh. 'That photo of you that Georgina posted…'

'She shouldn't have done. And—' he looks at me intently '—the old Georgina, the one I used to know, wouldn't have done that. It wouldn't have been about "my best life" and fuck what anybody else thinks.' Bella jumps on his lap and nuzzles in close. It seems to make him take a breath, pulls him away from his anger. He strokes her head, steadily, evenly. She looks up at him adoringly for a moment, and the artist in me wishes I could capture it.

Talk about man's best friend.

'Some things aren't meant to be plastered over the internet. Our privacy, our safety, is more important than a fifteen-second moment of admiration that you've got a boyfriend on a tour of duty.' His tone is more measured again, but I hardly notice. Tour of duty!

'Wow! So you are SAS!' I can't help myself, it just comes out. But all of a sudden, the tension is broken. He half smiles, relaxing slightly. Then he unexpectedly shakes his head and grins.

'You're not? Really?'

'Afraid not.'

'You bugger!' I thump him none too gently and he pretends to flinch. 'You did that keep fit thing with me, had me climbing stuff and wriggling under things and getting mucky because I thought you were! You pretended—'

'You thought I was, and I just let you! Not the same thing at all!'

'You… you fraud! You had me doing all kinds that you said would test me out, and that wasn't a proper workout!'

'Nope.' He chuckles. 'Hadn't a clue what I was doing, I just wanted to see you wriggle about in your tight top and shorts.' Laughter lines fan out from his eyes.

'Bugger. So I'm not going to be fit and ready for anything in five days? You could have broken me!' I knew a five-day fitness plan had to be too good to be true.

'I'd say you're already fit.' I've never seen such gorgeous eyes, I can't stop gazing into them, and as for that low husky voice, it's making parts of my body tingle. 'And as for ready for anything, I reckon you always have been, Becky Havers.'

I'm not quite sure what to say to that. I lick my dry lips. 'I had you down as SAS or at least the gardener.' Not a good seduction line, but it stops me climbing onto his lap.

'I know you did!' He throws his head back and laughs. Bella puts her paws on his chest and licks his chin, then jumps off his knee and curls back up at his feet.

'Okay, okay, stop laughing at me! If you're going to dress like a soldier one minute, but then lurk in the bushes the next, I reckon that's reasonable!'

'True.' He's stopped laughing, but he's still grinning. Cute. 'Sorry to be a let-down.'

I'm not sure he's that. 'So you really aren't in the SAS?' I think there is a wistful edge to my voice. Up until now he'd laughed at me saying he was, but not actually denied it, which is what somebody in the SAS would do, isn't it? Or kill you. So I secretly still hoped he might be. He's now blown my fantasies right out of the water. Well not all my fantasies. That body of his is seriously hot. 'You're not even in the TA?'

'You're funny, come here.'

To hell with it. With an invite like that, why am I resisting? I scoot my chair in closer to his.

'Closer.' His voice is soft as he drapes his arm round my shoulders and pulls me in. 'You're good for me, you know, I've not laughed with anybody like this for ages.'

Nobody has ever said I'm good for them. 'Nor have I.' Maybe we're good for each other.

His chin rests on my head, his words gently vibrating through my body.

'Georgie and I were happy once, but it seems a long time ago now. Way before she started posting pictures she shouldn't. I guess I should have been more understanding, it was just her way of making it seem like we still had a chance.' He sighs. 'Bella was a bit of a sticking plaster to be honest, that's partly why she wants to hang on to her. Why am I telling you all this?'

I glance up.

He gazes at me so intently that the world shrinks down to him and me. His eyes narrow slightly, blood pounds in my ears.

I swallow.

'I was in the Royal Marines.' His warm hand has dropped from my shoulders, leaving a cold gap.

'The Royal Marines?' But… wow! Close enough for me!

'I don't talk about it.' He shifts back slightly.

Ahh. Right. I bite back my 'why?' and wrack my brain trying to think of something sensible to say. 'So, you're not my fantasy woodchopper. Disappointing!' I'm not sure that's sensible.

'Always happy to oblige and get my chopper out for you if you'd like me to.' His tone is dry, but his eyes have darkened and there is definitely a new kind of tension in the air. 'If you promise not to post pictures on Instagram.' The corner of his mouth quirks up.

Oh. My. God. This man is gorgeous. I need him.

This is heating up again. There is so much deep undertone that it makes me feel like I could spontaneously combust. Instead I take a good mouthful of wine.

Talking to Ash, being with Ash, is a bit of an emotional rollercoaster. I'm not sure it's good for my blood pressure.

But boy, is it making me feel alive in a way nobody has before! I feel a bit light-headed. And fizzy. And giddy with anticipation. Maybe I need to invest in a fan, because I better not bloody faint again. If I do, I will *never* forgive myself.

'My Insta account is purely for works of art.' My throat is parched, raspy, so I glug back the wine, empty my glass. I reach blindly for the bottle, to top my glass up.

'It's empty.' His deep voice and the way he's studying me so intently is bringing goose bumps up on my arms and some totally different sensation in my pelvic region. I've not felt this tense since a particularly sadistic yoga instructor told me I needed to work on my pelvic floor, when she'd caught me joking to my best mate Kate that I had wet knickers.

She'd got the wrong end of the stick completely – all that squeezing, relaxing and wobbling about, while thinking about Chris Hemsworth in *Extraction* (sorry, I can't do the 'empty head' thing during yoga, I need something to occupy my mind) had made me wish I was in a darkened room alone. *That's* what I was referring to, not incontinence.

Ash puts his own glass down, very slowly, very deliberately and I forget yoga and can practically hear the thump, thump of my heart.

'Shall I open another one?' I squeak.

'I don't think so, do you?'

He's moved back in closer, he's within touching distance. Groping distance. I shake my head and stare at the nutmeg-brown skin at his throat.

'Well?' His finger is under my chin, drawing it gently but firmly up so that I am gazing straight into his eyes – eyes that have darkened.

I can smell the fruity wine on his breath, smell the earthy-woodiness that is him.

'We could do something else?'

He half smiles. 'We could. Except last time we were at home and I kissed you, I seem to remember you passed out.' He's near enough to kiss. But it isn't his mouth I want to taste first; it's his neck. I want to breathe in his smell, taste his skin.

'That was after you'd tried to drown me. I was in shock.' I match his soft, low tone, but can't quite keep the quiver out of my voice. 'I don't think it will happen again, but we could test that out.'

'We could.'

Oh God, this is intimate. And we've got all our clothes on, and the only contact between us is his hand on my chin.

I think I'm in shock now, he's just moved his hand, but stripped off his shirt! But I'm not going to pass out this time. I don't think. I bloody hope not.

His chest is perfectly tanned, and perfectly toned, and heck I want to check out if the rest of him is as well.

I reach out a finger to touch his sculptured abs, trace them down as they taper towards his belt, and his sharp intake of breath makes me smile.

Then I stop. His lips search out my neck, before I get the chance to taste his.

His mouth is hot, damp, thigh-clenchingly teasing. Oh my, his tongue, his tongue is circling in a way it shouldn't. I'm throbbing in places that shouldn't even know this has started yet. Normally I'm not awake down there until we've got to the totally naked stage.

'You sure about this?' He pulls back and I can see the effort, the want in his face and I'm sure mine mirrors it.

'Kiss me. Anywhere.' I arch up towards him, wanting him to kiss my neck again. Such a desperate hussy.

'Becky?'

He doesn't move closer and kiss me again. He's waiting for an answer, he's not going to... Oh my...

'Ye-e-e-e-s.'

How can he ask a question like that, when he's just put his hand between my legs?

Chapter Sixteen

I can't believe it; this hasn't happened after sex before. I'm awake, and he's asleep. I think my lady parts have become turbocharged. That hasn't happened before either. They've been pulsating like strobe lights at a rave and I feel totally drained. In a very nice way.

I am still more than capable of admiring his physique though. It might only be half-light, but I can see every muscle etched out as though on canvas. The gentle light makes him even more perfect. He's kicked one leg free of the sheet, which drapes over the other, his groin, his hips. His chest is bare and I watch him breathing for a moment, resisting the urge to touch him. To feel the beat of his heart. To kiss his exposed throat. Run my fingers through his hair.

Oh hell! Bella! I never locked her up. I was going to lock her up in the other en-suite. I should in case he wakes up when I'm asleep, grabs her, sneaks out... he won't find her there... wow, feel a bit tired... later... will find her in a bit...

When I wake up again, he's shifted onto his side and is

facing me. But he's still asleep. I have done it. Slept with the enemy. And done other stuff with. Lots of other stuff. Everywhere.

This man has got stamina and moves I have never been introduced to before.

'What are you doing?' he says without opening his eyes.

'Just looking, not touching.'

He opens one eye. 'Ahh, touching, I like the sound of that.'

And he demonstrates a few more things I didn't think were possible.

———————

The light is peeping through the curtains as I roll over lazily for one more cuddle before I have to get up and let Bella out for a wee. I think it's the only thing I've got the energy for. Cuddles. I've been bad, very bad, but in my current sleepy, satiated state of mind I don't think I care.

My fingertips meet cool sheets. I reach a bit further, up towards the pillow. The empty pillow. I pat the space with the palm of my hand, then open my eyes.

There is nobody there.

Shit, this is bad. I am awake, wide awake now and about to panic.

That bit about not caring that I've been bad? Wrong. I've just realised I do care. It matters. I have slept with Georgina's ex, in her bed. Well, not in her actual bed, in the spare room. But in her house. And now he's gone!

But she didn't say don't have sex, she said not to talk to him, or let him touch Bella.

Oh bugger, Bella.

Has he taken her? I sit bolt upright, fully awake and feeling slightly queasy.

Did I lock her up safely? I know I put a pile of tasty treats in the bathroom before Ash arrived. I do remember that bit. I don't think I put her in though. I'm pretty sure I didn't. I don't remember doing anything when I woke up though. Just falling asleep again.

And I don't remember locking her up in the kitchen before we came up or letting her out for a wee before she went to bed. Bloody hell!

'What are you stressing about now?' Ash is standing in the bedroom doorway. Naked.

'Nothing. Not stressing at all.' I can't drag my eyes away from his groin area. 'Er, Bella, I was just wondering... Eurgh.'

At the sound of her name, Bella apparently leapt in the air and has landed slap bang in the middle of my stomach, knocking me back onto the bed. Talk about passion killers.

'Eurgh, stop it.' She was licking my face, and has managed – the moment I opened my mouth to talk – to stick her tongue in. 'That's horrible! Stop it! She doesn't sleep in here!'

'Does when I'm here, don't you babe?' He gets back into bed, pulling her into his arms so he can hug her close and kiss the top of her head. Cuteness overload. 'I just let her out for a wee, and now I'm all yours again!' He grins, mischief all over his face.

I pull the sheet over my head. 'I can't, I can't, I need rest. I think I need you to gooooo…'

His chuckle reaches right down to the spot between my thighs where his fingers are dancing, and my traitorous body says otherwise.

'Why are there dog treats in the main en-suite?'

'Er, no reason. Why have you been in there?' I squeak, trying to ignore what he's doing to me.

'No reason.'

I want to object and interrogate him further, but I can't. His fingers are on my thighs, his mouth is on my neck and I am powerless.

Until he stops. 'She is mine. I've never lied to you.' He strokes my inner thigh. 'I picked her, bought her, registered her. But whatever, she means a lot to me.'

'Mmm.' I can't think straight.

'She means an awful lot. You have the most gorgeous body, you know.' He slides down the bed, his mouth replaces his fingers, and off he goes again…

We both doze off for a while, but I can't sleep properly. Because my mind won't stop whirring. In the end I slip out from his embrace and leave him and Bella snoring away on the bed.

They look so cute together. So happy. And he's never changed his story, always insisted that she really is his.

I pad down the stairs barefoot, knowing where the

squeaky floorboards are, and go into the study. I sit down on my chair and try the drawers.

They're not locked.

No reason to be, I suppose. I've not even thought to snoop around since I've been here. Why would I?

Except…

The first drawer is full of stationery stuff, the odd screwdriver, things like that. The next one has more of the same, and I move on. I'm trying not to be nosey and look at things that are nothing to do with me. All I'm looking for is a file with 'Bella' at the top of it.

If she's his, then any paperwork will back him up, won't it?

I don't find a file in the next drawer, or the first one when I look on the other side of the footwell. But I do find a dog vaccination certificate, pet passport and puppy information pack.

I look through them and my breath catches in my throat.

Every single piece of paper relating to Bella has Ash's name on it.

Every. Single. Item.

'Looking for something?' It's a low drawl, and I jump guiltily, drop the vaccination certificate and swing round.

'I don't er, normally, snoop, I was just…' My voice tails off as he stoops down, picks up the paperwork and wordlessly hands it back. 'I wanted to know.' *She means a lot to me*, he'd said. And it's obvious, she does.

'You couldn't take my word for it?' The disappointment on his face makes something catch in my throat.

'I did, I believe you, Ash. But I just thought…' What did

I think? That if I knew for sure, I could talk to Georgina about it? Even though it is none of my business. 'Ash, she just needs time to get used to the idea.' I take a deep breath and say what's really on my mind. 'I feel guilty even having you here, let alone...' I wave a hand in the air.

'I know, I get it, I'm going.'

'I didn't mean that, not right now.' A pang of alarm hits. Does he think I'm throwing him out? I don't want him to go!

'No, you're right. This shouldn't have happened. It was fun, but...' His voice has an edge that makes me feel uncomfortable.

'Ash!'

He looks me straight in the eye for a second, then glances down. 'I wouldn't want you to think that I, that we...'

'I'm not here to start a relationship!' I'm not, I don't know what I want. I do know that right now I need independence, because the last thing I need in my life is another Teddy. Not that Ash is anything like Teddy. But I got that so wrong, so I'm not exactly ready to start again, am I?

'I'd better go.'

'I'm not daft Ash. I do know Bella means a lot to you.' I want to grab hold of him, but I don't. 'And I do believe you, and I thought maybe with proof I could talk to Georgina, persuade her she should let you see Bella, negotiate and...'

His laugh is short and harsh and makes my skin tingle for all the wrong reasons. I feel cold all over. 'Negotiate?' He shakes his head. 'You are kidding?'

'But—'

He stares at me. 'Don't you think I've tried to talk to her? Oh yeah, yeah, I know.' There's a grim smile on his lips. 'I'm the evil one, trying to ruin her life, take everything. What else did she say?'

I open my mouth, but he lifts a hand to stop me. 'Forget it. Don't tell me, I don't want to hear it. I've got stuff to do, you should work.' He sounds resigned. Switched off.

It is horrible. It makes my heart sink. I feel sick. I don't want him to walk away like this. We had fun last night; we could have more fun. Well, not right now, but later. But I know he's doing it because he's hurt. And I know that this goes deeper than a fight over custody of a dog.

I never wanted to get involved in the war between Georgina and Ash, I wanted to come here to escape drama. But it seems I'm my own worst enemy.

Just being here means I'm involved.

Sleeping with Ash means I care about what he thinks, what he feels. And I know that the truest reaction I've seen from him, apart from with Bella, was when he arrived here last night. When he saw my painting.

If I never have the chance to ask him anything else, I need to know about that.

'Ash?'

'Yes?' He pulls the T-shirt that he's holding over his head.

'What did happen to the boathouse?'

'It was knocked down.' His lips tighten, then he sighs and shakes his head. 'It spoiled the view apparently.'

'Spoiled?' I stare at him, slightly speechless.

'Don't get me started.'

'Please.' I drop the paperwork and stand up and face him.

'She had it knocked down.' He draws himself up to his full height, as though getting ready for battle. There is real anger in his face – jaw tight, eyes narrowed, his hands are tight fists and he's talking through clenched teeth. 'I came back to a pile of stones and shattered timber.' The way he's staring ahead and looking straight through me, makes me think he's seeing it all over again. As vividly as the first time. 'Destroyed. All gone. Guess that's what happens when you're away for a while. On tour.'

'She? You mean Georgina?'

'She reckoned it spoiled the view, and Instagram is king.' He laughs, then focuses on me properly as though he's remembered where he is and sinks down onto a chair. His head is in his hands. 'Sorry. Sorry, that's a complete overreaction. It's just it's complicated, me and Georgina.'

It must be. I mean, even if it was hers to knock down, surely she knew how much it meant to Ash? Surely, if she loved him at all, she would have at least warned him?

He sighs, and his whole body softens. 'Sorry, I'm being unfair. It's not her fault.' He shakes his head slowly. 'It was a difficult time, I overreacted back then, like I am now. Sorry.'

'You don't need to apologise.'

'Oh, I do.' His smile isn't humorous, it is lopsided, rueful. 'It did need work doing on it, it was tumbling down, a bit like our relationship. She thought it was a good thing to do, but it was a shock.' He looks me in the eye. 'I guess it showed just how far apart we'd drifted that we didn't really get what the other person wanted at all by then.' He sighs and grimaces. 'My fault, I completely fucked up with Georgie. Dragged her out here, changed her life, then came back from the Marines a different guy. None of this is her fault. But it's not something I'd want to do to somebody again.' He looks me in the eye. Again.

'Ash, I enjoyed last night, it was fun. But I'm not in the right place to start something again, either.'

'Fine. Great.'

'And anyhow, somebody else beat you to it and tried to fuck up my life!'

His laugh is short, but there is a tiny trace of the fun-loving funny Ash in there.

'I'm not going to be fucked up twice!'

He laughs properly and shakes his head. 'You're funny. Very funny.' Then he taps the end of my nose.

'Mates still?'

'Mates still.' The upturn of his mouth is slight, but it's there.

'I mean, I don't want you to think I'd do that with anybody, I don't normally…'

'Me neither.'

'Cool.' It's not cool, this feels awkward.

'So…' He puts his hands in his pockets and stands up straighter, as though he feels he should end on a 'mates' note and is trying to think what to say. 'I hear you've agreed to do some pictures for David?'

'Yeah!' I grin; he's said exactly the right thing. I can't help but feel good when I start thinking about work these days. Wow, I hadn't stopped to think about that before. When did that creep up on me? I'm actually enjoying work again! 'I decided it's time for a change. I want to do more of the stuff I want to do, you know, stop doing all the boring stuff that somebody else wants me to. A new start, kind of!' Saying it out loud to somebody suddenly makes it feel all the more real, but the feeling is good. It hits me, I don't feel scared and uncertain now.

'Are you doing any more of Bella?' He's back on his feet again, ready to go.

'Maybe! I'm surprised you've heard about it though. I've only just agreed!'

'Word travels fast in these parts.' He smiles, then takes a step closer to me and drops a kiss on my head. 'You're brilliant, you know, kind and clever – Bella has definitely landed on her feet! I'm glad you came.'

Now that has a note of finality about it.

I watch from the door, hanging onto Bella's collar, as he walks down the driveway. I don't know about her landing on her feet with me, I think it's more the other way around. Bella is so much more than a dog; she's listened to me, got me motivated again, and in a strange way seems to have given me the confidence to be me.

She whines. 'Yeah, I know. I don't want him to go either.' She's also been a lovely fluffy bundle of fun to curl up with when I've needed a hug – something I feel I do, we both do, now.

You know the worst thing about brilliant sex? The comedown when it all goes wrong.

That feels shit. I want to call him back, talk a bit more.

I feel flat and empty. Because this makes it feel like a massive mistake. The sex. And at the time it didn't feel like that at all.

It felt incredible.

Like he knew me inside out, and we fitted together perfectly.

But we don't. And right now, it feels wrong on so many levels. Doing this in Georgina's house. Whatever the rights and wrongs about the Bella thing.

Guilt is gnawing away at me. This feels like some kind of betrayal. Maybe it did to him as well, which is why he shot off so quickly.

But he was right. I snooped around in her study, because I wanted to know. And I guess I wanted some kind of justification for doing what I'd done. I could just tell myself that what happened was fine, because Bella is his after all. Definitely. Georgina is unreasonable.

Except she isn't. I know in my heart she isn't. She's hurt. She's successful, she had a great life and for all I know an amazing relationship, and it all went wrong. And when things go wrong it can be bloody hard to admit you've failed; I know that better than anybody.

Why couldn't I have just plain kept my nose out of it instead of souring what had been an amazing evening and night?

Gah. I hold my head in my hands.

'Not sure that was good, Bella. Well, not a good idea… it was good.' It was definitely good.

Ash is a bit of the strong, silent type. I guess I'm not

used to that. I'm used to people like Teddy who have everything out on display.

And yet I'm a bit like that myself and would love people to take me as they find me. Let me decide when to reveal things. Not rummage into my life like some kind of crazy stalker. Oh my God, I'm turning into a crazy stalker woman!

I mean this was fun, no way do I want it to be anything else, but it makes me feel empty and slightly sick inside to have a morning-after like this.

My phone beeps and my heart lurches – it's him!

It is not. It is Georgina.

I have thought about it. I don't want Ash anywhere near Bella, I can't risk it. Please tell me you'll keep away from him?

Oops.

Chapter Seventeen

I'm brilliant! I think I need to add 'peacemaker' or 'negotiation skills' onto my CV. I decided not to take no for an answer. After much persuasion, and many swapped messages, Georgina has agreed to at least talk to me about 'supervised visits' between Ash and Bella.

I did feel pretty shit this morning when Ash left, but after a walk with Bella I ended up feeling strangely positive. I think it must have been the fresh air and exercise, but I stopped feeling slightly sick about his brush-off. I mean, oh my God I can't believe it, I had a one-night stand! I've never done that before! Never, ever. Is that sad or what?

It was amazing. The best sex I have ever, ever had and I was totally uninhibited.

I laughed out loud and Bella came back all excited to see what had got into me, and we had a mad game of hide and seek in the trees. Okay, I'm not saying people, well, I, should sleep around, but it was just so un-stage-managed. It just happened! This is how my life should be: impulsive, doing what I want, in the moment.

After I got back and stopped grinning like a loon though, I couldn't stop thinking about him. Even though I've managed to royally cock things up between me and Ash, before anything really started.

He might not want a relationship with a girl, or me in particular, but I do know that there's something primal about his need for Bella, some deep hurt in him. This isn't just about getting his own back on Georgina, there's something more meaningful to it, and I feel sick at the idea of not trying to help him.

I also think that however little I know him I can't have completely got him wrong. Georgina might say he's evil and a smooth talker, but he's had the opportunity to take the dog – and not taken her. He could have easily grabbed her after the lake incident, when I literally fainted at his feet, and he could have agreed to cracking open another bottle of wine, got me legless, tied me to the bed and hopped it with her.

But he didn't.

So he can't be all bad.

And I think Georgina knows that. Which is why she's so upset.

With this in mind, I suggested to her that stopping Ash seeing Bella altogether seemed to be making him even more determined, and letting him see her could reduce the risk of him dog-napping?

She messaged straight back agreeing to discuss it, yay result! So I sat down, finished the work for Ben (while trying not to keep looking at the boathouse picture) and put *Mischief the Magic Pony* (who has been left out at pasture and sadly neglected recently) back on my desk.

I'm just wondering about whether a plate of nachos for lunch is a teeny bit greedy, or necessary fuel for a long dog walk (dogs are a brilliant excuse for a bad diet) when my phone rings. Georgina!

For the first time since I got here, I answer her call with a smile on my face.

My master plan is going to work! Ash will be happy, Bella will be happy and I will be happy – and able to get more work done!

'I can't do it!' Georgina blurts the words out the second I pick up. 'I'm sorry, I just can't.' She sounds close to tears; the quaver in her voice brings a lump to my throat. 'I can't just let her go, let it all go.'

My smile slides off and a boulder drops into the bottom of my stomach. 'I'm sorry, it's just Ash seems upset as well and…'

'You don't understand, it was so good, you don't know what it's like.' She sniffs.

'I don't,' I say softly.

'Bella is all I've got left. He's never going to come back if he's got her, is he?'

'You wouldn't want him back just for Bella, would you? Georgina, you can tell me to sod off and it's none of my business, and I don't know what it's been like for you, but I do know what it's like to be in a relationship that isn't right anymore.'

'You do?'

233

I take a deep breath. 'Yes, I do. I was with somebody and trying to be who he wanted me to be and I wasn't being me, and it has taken me ages, months to realise what a mistake that was.'

Wow, what made me say that? I mean, I've admitted it to myself, in my head, but I've not felt ready to tell the world. It felt really strange saying it out loud – and to a complete stranger – but strangely liberating. I don't feel like crying, I don't feel stupid. It's almost like I've realised inside that I've got to the point when I'm no longer just trying to *persuade* myself that I'd got it wrong, that I'm right to come here and try to change. I actually *believe* it now.

I'm not usually the over-sharing type though. It seems like this trip is bringing out a whole new side of me, maybe it's all those late-night chats with Bella.

'We split up months ago, ages, as well.' Georgina sounds dejected, but at least she's listening, and I'm pleased that I told her, that I was honest.

'But it does take ages to get over stuff like that Georgina, it takes ages to work out what you really want, why sometimes what you thought you wanted isn't the right thing for you at all. I mean, I thought it meant I was crap and I was in the wrong, but I'm finally beginning to realise that maybe I wasn't. Not that I'm saying that you think you're crap, because of course you don't, but,' I take a deep breath and slow down. 'Hey, what I'm trying to say is that splitting up doesn't reflect on you at all, you know. Honestly. You're so successful, your Insta is amazing, you can make it even more amazing even if you've not got Ash or Bella. You can do it on your own, Georgie!'

'You think?' she says grudgingly.

'Definitely.'

'I don't know.' She sounds doubtful more than tearful now. 'I'm not sure. I mean Bella is important to me.'

'I know.'

There's a long silence. 'Look after her for me until I come home.'

'I will, and Ash?'

'I don't want him to have her.'

'She is his though, isn't she?' Even as I say it, I know I shouldn't. It doesn't matter who bought her. She belonged to them both. She was part of *their* family.

'No, she isn't!' It comes out part yell, part wail and it makes me flinch.

Why was I so stupid? She's upset. I've told Ash myself that she needs time and now I'm basically doing what I told him he shouldn't. I feel bad enough upsetting her, but what if she's now so upset she wants to get rid of me? I don't want to be turfed out and branded a bad house-sitter. I like house-sitting!

'You do know he's been trained in actual lying and getting his own way, don't you? It's his special skill!'

I would quite like to point out that IMHO his special skill involves his tongue, thumb and a featherlight touch on the inner thigh. But that might not be appropriate, and I don't think it would go down well right now.

It also brings back the feelings of guilt. I just got a bit miffed that she was accusing him of lying, when it's her that is actually telling a fib.

'I didn't, no.'

'She was ours, not his!' Well, that's fair enough. 'Please don't talk to him, don't let him take her!'

I don't even know if he's coming back, though I'm pretty sure he will keep an eye on Bella even if he's not keen on being near me. And I'm also pretty sure he won't want sex again. Though if he did (being optimistic here) maybe silent sex would mean I'm getting satisfaction, but staying within her guidelines? Not sure he'd agree on that one, especially if I have to hide Bella first.

There is a silence apart from what I think is the tapping of her fingernails. 'This is so stressing me out. I'm getting a migraine; I need to go and lie down. Can you give Bella a hug from me please?'

'Of course.' I press the end call button. I came here for a quiet life and a few dog walks, not to act as peacekeeper in a war zone.

Or to have wild sex.

I slump down on the sofa. 'Oh God, Bella. My head hurts. I'm knackered.' She wags her tail and rests her head on my knee.

Unluckily I am not the peacemaker I was hoping I was, so no Nobel Prize nomination there then, but luckily the rest of the day passes in perfect peace. Well, not quite perfect, because I have to admit to half hoping Ash will climb over the wall with a pocketful of treats, or just come and pick up the hoodie he forgot when he left in such a hurry. He doesn't.

I fear that my intentions might have been dishonourable, and I might have been hoping to offer puppy visitation rights for my own ends – so that I can see him again.

And I fear that his intentions might have been to work out a grand master plan to take Bella.

But it doesn't matter, eh? It was just a shag. Well, not just any shag, it was amazing. A grown-up expression of lust and sexual compatibility that went on for several hours.

Phew, I'm getting hot and bothered. I think I need a long walk or a cold shower. Or both.

Chapter Eighteen

'Party time!'

'Sorry?' I have been up since 6 a.m. adding glittery highlights to *Mischief the Magic Pony*, have had at least six cups of coffee, one slice of toast and think I might be hallucinating.

There is a giant dog and a man with a camera on the doorstep.

I know I'm staring, but they must be used to it.

My gate buzzer went two minutes ago, and I practically leapt out of my seat, grinning like a loon, sure that it was Ash.

Then I tripped up over Bella's strategically placed bone, recovered temporarily then skidded on her rope (she's cross that I've been working not playing so has booby-trapped the place), then went flying after putting one foot on her ball.

Ignoring my elbow, which I'd banged fairly and squarely on my funny bone, I scrambled towards the intercom desperate to stop him from leaving before I answered and hit the 'entry' rather than the 'answer' button by mistake.

It isn't until I saw Fido and photographer at the door that I remember Ash has never rung the gate buzzer. He just comes in and lurks in the shrubbery, or peers through a window, or appears at the patio doors.

I rub my painful elbow. It hurts so much this can't be anything other than reality.

'Party for Georgina and Bella,' says the dog, who seems to be in charge. Then she lifts her fluffy head up and underneath it is a blonde-haired girl in her late teens who looks a bit hot and sweaty. She brushes strands of hair off her forehead and mock-smiles. I know it's not real, she's scowling at the same time. Impressive. 'You got a text?' she sighs, world-weary before her time.

I look at my phone. Shit. I have missed so many calls and messages! I'd put my phone on silent and left it in the kitchen while I worked – partly because I was pissed off with all the messages from Teddy, which I was trying to ignore, and partly because of the absence of calls from Ash, which I kept pathetically checking for.

Teddy is at the top of the hit parade, with a total number of texts in the teens, plus an impressive number of WhatsApp messages and two missed Skype calls. Ben comes in with one, just losing out to Georgina who has sent two. Big fat zero from Ash.

I open the first one from Georgina.

Be in this afternoon, it is Bella's birthday and I have stuff ordered for her. Do NOT give her any breakfast or she'll be sick.

Whoopsie.

Do NOT take photos, I've sent a professional. Geo.

The second one is to the point:

Confirmed for 2 p.m.

Shit, is it that time already? No wonder I'm starving.

I glance up. The dog and photographer are waiting. 'Oh, right fine. Er, you've brought stuff? A cake?'

'She's got the full package,' says the dog with another sigh, before jamming her head back on. 'You have shut the gate?' I nod dumbly. 'Right, I'll get the rest out to let off steam before I set up if that's okay?' I nod again. 'You can help if you want?'

'I'm just here to take photos.' The photographer waves his camera in the air to excuse himself, and the dog folds its arms and stamps its foot. I think underneath the cute exterior it is glaring at us.

The photographer winks. 'Jake.' He shoves a hand my way and we shake. 'Beer would be good if you've got one?'

'Er beer, right, I'll look.'

'Georgina usually has some stashed away. All have our good points, eh?' He winks again. 'Known her long?'

'I don't really know her at all, I'm just house-sitting, and looking after Bella.'

'Come on then, I'll help myself. Might be better to be out of the way for five minutes. You okay, Fluffy? Won't be long!'

I don't think Fluffy is impressed. She starts throwing things out of the van as though she wishes she was dropping them on his head.

'Ignore her,' he says. I probably look alarmed. 'I've worked with her a few times, she's good with dogs.'

'Oh, right.'

'Crap with people, but can't have everything, can you?'

'I suppose not.'

'She brought five.'

'Five? Cakes?'

'Dogs. Haha.'

It is at this point that 'Fluffy' opens the rear door of her van and all hell seems to break loose. There are dogs everywhere, of every shape and size, and colour. They are jumping up at me, running circles round Jake, rolling on the lawn, barking at each other.

'There looks to be more than five.'

'Haha, I'd let Bella out if I was you. Sooner we start, sooner they'll calm down.' And with that he barges his way into the house, lets Bella out of the kitchen and ploughs on in search of refreshment. 'Don't worry, she's met them before, at her last party,' he yells back at me.

It gets worse. Now the dogs have spread out I can separate them into individuals. There is another cockapoo, the brown version of Bella, and she heads straight for it. If I thought zoomies were dangerous with one cockapoo, it takes on a whole new side when there are two. I've never seen dogs run so fast. There's also a border collie who seems to be stalking an invisible herd of sheep, a Great Dane who is sitting watching what's going on like a spectator at a tennis match, he's tilting his head from one side to the other, then turning from left to right. Then there's a fat Labrador wandering round sniffing the shrubs (I hope Ash isn't in one of them) and cocking its leg up at regular intervals, and a Chihuahua who is in hot pursuit of the cockapoos barking its head off angrily, getting regularly jumped over (and occasionally bowled over) and generally seems to be trying to stir things up. The Labrador ignores it when it rushes up and bites his ankles, and the Great Dane has decided to lie down and try to flatten it with one giant paw.

I don't blame Jake for going inside, it's dangerous out here.

'Enough!' Fluffy hasn't even shouted particularly loudly, but all of the dogs grind to a halt. Apart from the Great Dane which is already immobile.

It slowly gets to its feet, and the others amble over, tongues hanging out.

Fluffy hands out treats and points to the low trestle table she has set up while I've been transfixed by the chaos.

Weirdly the dogs seem to know exactly what is required, and head for specific places around the table, before sitting down… on little (or big in the case of the Great Dane) raised mats… like primary school kids in assembly.

'Awesome sauce,' says Jake, ambling over, beer in one hand, camera in the other. 'Hold this, sweets.' I have never been called 'sweets' before but I am in a state of shock and unable to respond. I meekly take the beer. 'Bonus that Miss Fancy Pants isn't here.' I think he means Georgina. 'It's stand here, stand there, crouch down, lower, lower. As though I don't know what I'm doing.' He sits down at the end of the table, waiting as Fluffy goes around and puts a party hat on each dog. Bella gets a crown and a sash that says 'Birthday Girl' in very small letters. I guess it's the thought that counts.

'Cats!' shouts Jake and they all perk up for a moment as he snaps away. 'Last time I did one of these gigs, I shouted *squirrels* and the party boy shot out of the garden and we didn't see him again.' He laughs, shoves a hand out for his beer and takes another swig.

Fluffy meanwhile is placing sandwiches and sausage rolls on plates. 'They're fake, they're grain-free, organic baked goods,' she says, as though it's a script she has to read off. Jake is right, she's brilliant with the dogs – not exactly people-friendly though. I think she hates me.

Jake takes more pictures. I act as beer trolley.

'Now Monty, don't you dare!' shouts Fluffy, before distributing cakes all round.

Six pairs of doggy eyes are fixed on their plates. I'm holding my breath; I can't quite believe that Bella is leaving food – normally she grabs anything if I'm too far away to stop her. Jake snaps away.

'Okay Bella!' Bella looks at Fluffy and she nods, then she wolfs it down. The peanut butter coating is smeared over her nose and whiskers.

'Perfect shot!' yells Jake, very pleased with himself.

'Sometimes have to have two or three goes at that, the buggers swallow them down so bloody quick.'

While he's busy studying his photo with delight though, all hell has broken out again.

The Labrador is trying to hoover all the other cakes up, and has already scoffed his own, and the one that was in front of the border collie (who is busy preparing to pounce on the flower in the middle of the table). The Chihuahua has launched itself onto the table and is heading down the middle like a missile, before jumping on the Labrador's head and going ape.

'Believes in fair play, that one,' says Jake, chuckling.

The Great Dane meanwhile has bored of the whole thing and crashes onto the table, which collapses.

I'm not sure if this counts as successful or not.

'Musical chairs now. Video time.' Jake is standing up.

'There's more? You're kidding me?'

'No joke!' This is a new voice, in my ear. Warm breath fanning my neck. I whirl around and come nose to nose with Ash. Oh my God, Ash!

All I can do is grin at him like a loon. I'm just wondering if I can get away with a kiss when something black and furry wedges itself between us. Wriggling away like a ferret.

'Oh man, ace to see you, thought you were persona non-grata.'

'I am, mate.' Ash holds Bella at arm's length so that she can't French-kiss him, and grins back at Jake, before they high five. 'Keep schtum. Not a word that I've been here.'

'Keep me in beer and not a word will pass my lips. Though to be fair, this one's been doing a good enough job.' He winks at me. It is a bad habit. Almost a nervous twitch.

'What are you doing here?'

Ash waits until Jake has moved away to take more photos, then whispers in my ear. 'I brought Bella a birthday present, of course! Keep it to yourself until the rabble have gone!' He's got the hint of an embarrassed blush along his cheekbones. It's cute. We share a conspiratorial smile. 'Where is it?' I whisper back.

He puts a finger to his lips. 'After the party is over. She emailed me last night.'

'Oh?' I look at him hopefully.

He shakes his head. 'I gather you must have said something? Thanks for trying, but it's fine. I'll sort it with her. I don't want to mess this—' he waves a hand to encompass the house and garden '—up for you. And...' There's a long pause, during which he gazes into my eyes, which makes me feel all gooey inside. 'Sorry I stormed off the other day.'

'No problem,' I squeak.

'I was wound up. But it's not your problem.' He sighs, watching Bella as she runs around with the other dogs. Musical chairs for dogs is something special. There are special chairs, appropriate music (at this particular moment we have 'Who Let the Dogs Out' blaring out) and when it stops, they all dash to a chair and put their front paws up. Apart from the Chihuahua who is small enough to fit on the chair. And then growl at anybody else that comes near.

I don't know whether this is ridiculous and totally crazy, or cool.

Either way, it feels even more fun now that Ash is here.

'But...' Ash is not looking at me. 'It doesn't change anything. I still need Bella back, I guess I just hadn't thought properly about how long was long enough for Georgie until you said something.' There's another lingering look, which this time sends a tingle right down to the base of my spine. 'Thank you.'

He touches my hand lightly and I feel faint. It's probably lust, a conditioned response after the sex.

'Go Bella!' His laugh is even hotter than his looks. Bella has just collided with the border collie, who decided it wasn't interested in the game anyway, and bounced away before cocking its leg up – showering the other cockapoo.

'Can't we have a truce until Georgina comes back? You see Bella but promise not to nab her?' I can hear a wistful note in my voice. It would be nice to see him and know I can drop my guard.

We both watch the dogs, and not each other.

'Where's the fun in that?' I can sense he is grinning. 'And it'll be harder for me when she's back!'

'Are you calling me a pushover?'

He chuckles in reply and warms me up inside. Oh boy, the challenge is on, nobody calls me a pushover!

He doesn't answer, he merely frowns. 'I think I heard the gate. Are you expecting anybody?'

I shake my head. 'Nope. I don't know anybody round here apart from you and David.'

'I'll get it.' I watch as he strides purposefully down the driveway.

Oh my God he is so masculine. And sexy.

I'm glad he's come back, even if it is only for Bella's birthday. For Bella. Not me.

Fluffy now has the dogs playing catch. I cannot believe anybody has gone to all this trouble for a dog's birthday. I mean what's wrong with a few treats and a new toy?

Although I suspect this is more about the photo opportunity than anything else. I haven't missed the fact that there is branding on absolutely everything, including the party hats and the little chairs that they used for musical chairs. Which I hope Fluffy is going to hose down and disinfect.

'Last game!' shouts Fluffy, before lining up all the dogs, side by side, and laying out a load of (branded) cushions a few yards away.

'Hang on, just getting another beer, but I need to vid this,' says Jake, with one foot already inside the house. 'And take a photo. Turn that tartan bed round thirty degrees, can't see the label properly.'

'You need to move!' shouts Fluffy at me.

'What?'

'You're in the way! We're having a race from where they are, to the beds! Basil, sit!' She's quite assertive actually, however young and ditsy she appears. I nearly sit, until I realise she's talking to a dog.

The dogs love her. Basil the Chihuahua sits. Then the moment she takes her eyes off him, he creeps forward and lies down a bit closer. 'Back!' He crawls back, commando-style. 'More!' He wriggles back a couple of millimetres. It's hilarious.

I move over to the other side, where I can watch in

safety. The border collie, who has been crawling forward, suddenly can't hold itself back a moment longer and dives round in a big circle, intent on herding the naughty Basil back into place.

Fluffy folds her arms. 'Thank you, Charlie. Bella?' Bella who had been about to stand up, hears the note of warning and sits down abruptly, with a 'who me?' look on her face.

'Okay, ready, steady, bed!'

'Go Bella, go!' I can't help myself, this might be totally loopy, but I've been drawn into the excitement. And what can I say? I'm a competitive mum. I realise I'm leaping up and down. If Teddy could see me now, he'd die of embarrassment.

You should see those dogs fly towards the finishing line though. They are awesome.

Somebody unfortunately doesn't. Somebody marches straight across the line of fire.

For a moment I think it must be Ash, then I realise it definitely isn't.

Because Ash is standing across from me, legs apart, hands on hips, looking very action-man like.

'Fuck, what the, gerroff me, get off you nasty—'

The yelling stops, I think that is because Bella has done her tongue down the throat trick.

'Stoooooop!' As the figure thrashes around under the sea of dogs, I realise I recognise the shoes.

It is Teddy.

Teddy has never been much of an animal lover – another reason why our relationship would never have gone to the next level. He flings his arms around wildly. The Great

Dane starts to bark and bounce up and down like a dinosaur.

'Stop thrashing you idiot, you're winding them up!' yells Fluffy.

I try not to snigger.

Teddy rolls over and Basil jumps on his head, snapping at his hair. Bella crawls under his protective arm determined to kiss him, and the other cockapoo zooms in and grabs the trilby hat I hadn't noticed.

'Help me, you morons!'

We all stare at Teddy, under a pile of dogs.

Jake snorts and moves in closer; I suspect he might be videoing.

I look at Ash, who is grinning. I look over at Fluffy. She has taken her head off. She is now very hot and sweaty underneath, and her mascara has run. She looks like a big dog even without the fluffy head. In fact, she looks like she's been crying. She wipes her cheek with the back of her hand. 'Sorry.' She stifles a sob. 'Sorry.' She hiccups. Then I realise she is trying not to laugh. 'Mouse, come back!' I think Mouse must be the cockapoo, but as Fluffy has lost her normal assertive tone, due to hiccups, Mouse ignores her and runs around ragging the hat as though it is a dead rat.

'Come back with that!' He is out of the rugby scrum, and on his hands and knees, pursuing Mouse, who has come back and keeps teasing him by running close, until Teddy thinks he can get his hat back, and then leaping back as he makes a grab.

Finally, he gets a hand on it. Mouse growls, thinking this

is a great game of tug. I've seen Bella do this. It is not going to end well.

Fluffy finally sobers up enough to yell, 'Leave it' and Mouse lets go abruptly and sits down. Teddy falls over backwards.

I try not to laugh.

Very, very slowly he gets to his feet and wipes the grass off his legs. He straightens his hat out as best he can – it is not good; it will never look the same again – and puts it on his head. This last bit is a mistake. We all want to laugh.

Fluffy sticks her head back on quick, I put my fist in my mouth, Jake studies his camera intently, biting his lip, and Ash… well, Ash laughs.

Then he pulls himself together and looks at me.

'This guy says you're expecting him?'

'I'm not,' I mouth back. 'Teddy, what the hell are you doing here?'

Teddy adjusts the crotch of his trousers and winces. Then stalks past me towards the house, his legs bowed cowboy-style. Which nearly sets us all off again.

'I need a word with you, inside,' he says stiffly.

Ash raises an eyebrow. 'Been a naughty girl?' He's right, Teddy does sound a bit of a dick.

'It would be nice if you'd let me and my girlfriend talk in private,' Teddy adds, still hobbling, but doing his best to look debonair.

'Ex,' I mouth in Ash's direction.

It's quite startling the contrast between Teddy and Ash. If Teddy hadn't been trampled by dogs he'd look his

250

normal, well-groomed, immaculate self. One could quite picture him with Pimm's, playing croquet on the lawn.

But right now, with his foppish hair sticking out in all directions, clothes crumpled and what looks like grass stains down his shirt, he looks totally out of place. Trying too hard.

Whereas Ash would look good if he'd waded through a swamp and been trampled by a wildebeest.

Ash, who is tanned nutmeg-brown, every sinew of his body delicately defined. Ash, with his genuine, open face, and startlingly intense pretence-stripping gaze. Ash, with his just-there beard which emphasises a strong, square jaw rather than tries to disguise a weak one.

Ash, with his large capable hands.

A shiver runs through my body. I really need to stop thinking about him in this way.

But what the hell did I ever see in Teddy?

'I'll, er, pack up, shall I?' Fluffy brings me back down to earth. Her voice has a quaver of laughter in it and her head is trembling. I stop swooning and try to hold my grin behind pursed lips.

'Sure, fine, great... er... party. Georgina will be thrilled!' I say.

'Want me to hang around for a bit?' Ash raises a questioning eyebrow. 'I can look after Bella?' She leaps up at him at the sound of her name.

I'd love him to hang around, so would Bella, but I'm not sure it's a good idea. I don't know how long this is going to take. And however much I dislike Teddy, it wouldn't be fair on him. 'Maybe not.'

I call Bella over, and snap her lead on to her collar, throwing him an apologetic look. Awkward. 'I need to stop her chasing the other dogs into the van!' He just looks and doesn't comment.

It makes me sad. He could have put her lead on for me, kept an eye on her. Given her birthday cuddles.

I know if he took Bella with him, he'd look after her. But I don't even know where he lives.

Trouble is I do trust him, take him at his word. And his word as far as Bella goes is that he's going to get her back. Whatever it takes.

So now I'm doubly sad, following Teddy dejectedly, dragging my feet like a child who knows they're about to get a bollocking and wants to put the inevitable off for as long as possible. And dragging Bella, who isn't happy that the party is over. And that her favourite person is going.

Talk about the low after the high.

Teddy beats me to the house and has nosed round and found the study within seconds. He is standing in front of my boathouse painting.

'What are you playing at, Becky?' He doesn't even turn to look at me.

'Sorry?' Fuck, how does he know that I'm supposed to keep Ash at arm's length, well actually on the other side of the gate? How does he know we've had rampant sex?

'With Ben?' Phew, this is about work. Thank heavens for that! 'What are you playing at? Has somebody pressed your career self-destruct button? Spending too much time with the locals?' Snap, snap, snap of the alligator jaws, and he's getting closer as he does it.

I try not to flinch or back off. I am gobsmacked. I'd forgotten Teddy could be like this. Because he was never usually like this with me. With his authors, agents, publishers even. But not me.

'What?' I am pretty much speechless, shocked he's here, astounded he still thinks he has a say in what I do.

'I've driven a long way; I'd appreciate it if you could stop keeping saying "what?" and answer the questions.'

I laugh. I can't help myself. If the dog party was a bit surreal, this is taking it a step further. I feel like Alice in Wonderland. I've fallen through a hole and haven't a clue what is going on. 'Why are you here, why have you driven a long way, Teddy?'

'Because you wouldn't answer my calls!' he says stiffly.

'And how did you know where I was?'

He doesn't answer my question. He stares at me. Why have I never noticed how lifeless and pale his eyes are before? There's no emotion there at all. They also dart from side to side; he doesn't actually meet my gaze and hold it. It's more of a peppering of short looks, an assault. 'Are you mad, Becky? Have you completely lost your mind?'

'For not answering your calls?'

'Oh, don't be ridiculous. The commission! For not taking the commission with Ben. What on earth does your father think?' He puts his hands in his pockets, his ridiculous hat still perched on his head. But any traces of humour that were lingering inside me dissipate. 'Or haven't you told him?'

I could punch him. I really could. 'What on earth has my dad got to do with this?'

'Oh, come on Becky, don't be disingenuous. Working with Ben is the closest you'll ever get to a proper career.'

Out of all the boyfriends I've had, my dad did quite seem to like, or rather approve of Teddy. He might be in the 'creative industry', but he has the trappings. The flash car, nice house, connections. Dad warmed to him initially. He thought he had a 'proper job' and approved of his attempts to guide me. Initially.

It hasn't clicked properly until now, but suddenly it is crystal clear. I've got to admit, since coming out here and actually having some time and space to think, I have realised that Teddy had reinforced my feelings of being a disappointment to my family, feelings that I hadn't met their expectations.

It was *him* who always undermined who I really am, what I really want, not them. It was Teddy who was controlling, not my parents. It hits me properly now. They might not have always thought I was doing the right thing, but they've never been manipulative. Never tried to actually mould me to suit what they've wanted and hoped for. But Teddy has. And I've let him. And Teddy has tried to make me think all along that I've been letting them down. Which is rubbish. I let him create a distance between me and my family. I joined in. No wonder they weren't keen on him.

'I have got a proper career, thank you!' I can feel the anger bubble up inside me. I clench my fists, livid. 'What the fu—'

He takes a step over to my desk. 'Let's face it, this stuff is a bit shit, isn't it?' He pokes a finger at my sketches of

Mischief. It's like waving a red rag at a bull and I can feel my eyes mist over. 'Like that terrible last cover Ben made you rework.'

'What? What?' I am almost speechless. 'It was you who told me to do it like that, it was your fault!'

He ignores me.

'But it's nothing to do with you now, none of your business, you had no right!'

I realise now Teddy was never one to admit his mistakes. I can't ever remember him saying sorry, or saying he was wrong. He is back looking at the boathouse now. His short laugh is full of scorn and derision. 'I mean, look at this crap.' He moves in closer to peer at my painting again, then waves a dismissive hand. 'Pah, chocolate box pictures, what's happened to your artistic integrity, your creativity? This is crap!'

'*You* happened to my artistic integrity, Teddy!' I think I may have stamped my foot. 'You did! This isn't about my integrity and my creativity, it's about your fucking bank balance.'

His neck is red. It's a sure sign. He also keeps looking shiftily over at my Mischief pictures. He can't help himself. Those are what this is about.

'Ha! I'm getting close, aren't I?'

'You need to come back and be sensible.' He ignores my question. 'Don't let our personal lives interfere with business.'

And suddenly I know. I totally get it. This is totally about Teddy. It always has been. This is about *his* business connections and *his* career.

Normally I'd let it go. But I can't. 'You promised Ben I'd do this, didn't you? What for, Teddy? What does he give you in exchange? Take on one of your *new brilliant* cover designers?' The anger bubbles up inside me and my voice has got an edge, but I can't help myself. He's using me even now, even after he's told me he doesn't need me. Doesn't want me. Even after he's told me I'm rubbish at my job, he's still using me. It would be laughable if it wasn't so bloody annoying.

His cheekbones are red-tinged, his pale complexion blotchy. He still can't stop glancing down at Mischief.

All of a sudden, I realise this isn't about my art, or my replacement. It is more than that. My anger fades and I just feel sad that I didn't spot what a fake he was earlier. I've been such an idiot. 'Hang on, no hang on. This is about these books, isn't it? Am I getting warm?'

Teddy definitely is. 'Rubbish.' He sneaks another sideways look, it's as though he can't help himself.

'Well, whatever. You know what? I don't care! But I do care that you used me Teddy!' He stares coldly back at me, just a hint of colour tinging his cheekbones. 'You used me!'

'Well, that's life!'

'It's not my life!'

'Oh, we can't all be fluffy-headed idealists Becky. Open your eyes, look at your family! Think about them for once.'

That does it. 'I have opened my eyes now, at last!'

'Don't be ridiculous. You could have talent—'

'I do have talent!'

'If you'd let yourself be directed. You can do cutting

edge, you *were* doing, and not this, this!' He's spluttering. 'This is like a bloody school project.'

'Well, Ash likes it!' Shit. Why did I say that?

'Ash?' He frowns. 'Ah, I get it, the musclebound goon outside!' He's got a glint in his eye, the one that says he's ready to move in for the kill. 'And there was I thinking he was just the hired help.' His gaze wanders again, then stops. Bugger, Ash's hoodie. I'd forgotten about that! He put it down when he was looking at the picture. 'Good God, Becky, you have let your standards slip. Though I always suspected you liked a bit of rough. A rugged hero, like all the ones in those mind-numbing films you insist on watching.' He's got a nasty sneer lurking at the side of his mouth.

It is my turn to splutter. And blush.

'He is not musclebound, he's just fit!' Boy is it hot in here. 'Which you wouldn't know anything about!' Teddy did join a gym once, but he's more the measured type. Lightly toned to maintain the sleek, long lines that look good in his Mediterranean-style, incredibly slim-fit trousers. They wouldn't get past Ash's ankles.

His eyes narrow. 'And he seemed more interested in that bloody silly dog than he was in you, you fool!' He stops talking, half smiles and bestows upon me his best patronising look. 'Your new boyfriend likes rubbish like this —' he gestures lazily with a hand, thinking he's on a winning streak '—because he is not sophisticated, not clever, not refined. He has simple tastes, he really isn't smart enough for somebody like you, Becky. You need a man of the world, a man with vision so you can make the best of yourself.'

How dare he call Ash thick!

'Get out.'

'Pardon?' He looks at me blankly.

'Out!' I stamp one foot forward and he actually jumps. 'Out, out, out.' I'm getting into this, and so is Bella, who leaps up and starts to bark. I don't think she's quite sure what we're doing, but she's on my side. Teddy steps nervously towards the patio doors. It makes me feel brilliant, power crazy, slightly mad! I grab the nearest thing to hand and wave it, and he scoots – straight out of the doors.

'You're mad! Call me when you've calmed down, you'll regret this.' His voice is shaky, and he's backing away as he talks.

'I am never going to call you!' I bellow. Calling him, even if this all goes wrong and my Mischief illustrations come to nothing, would be the coward's way out. The easy option. I'm better than that. I've told Georgina she should be brave and walk away from her old life – well, that's exactly what I need to do.

And it's not just Ash who thinks I have the ability, it's David, it's the people who thought my draft sketches of Mischief were 'awesome'. And, most importantly, *I* think I do.

Teddy stumbles across the lawn and I stare at what I've picked up to wave at him. Bloody hell, I've been brandishing a fire poker! No wonder he ran for it.

But wow, that felt good. Standing up for myself.

Reaction hits as I drop the poker and sink down on the floor, and Bella clambers on me, licks my hand then curls up half on and half off my legs.

There is something very worrying about my reaction. Not the fire poker – he deserved that, he's had it coming for a while.

What worries me is that I didn't throw him out when he criticised me, or my work... No, I threw him out when he criticised Ash.

Shit.

I bury my face in Bella's fur and feel like crying. 'Oh Bella, I'm screwed, aren't I?' She licks my nose. 'And so are you, you can't have him either.' I lean back against the chair and stroke her. It is quite therapeutic. Calming. It drags me out of my self-pity party.

Oh, I really do need to stop thinking about Ash though. I'll be going home soon. All this will be over. I'll never see him again.

I will see Teddy though, unless I actually move away from my flat for good. I live far too close to him for comfort.

Why did he come all this way?

This is about him, his career. It has to be. Everything always is about Teddy.

I glance over at the Mischief pictures. I'm sure my instincts are right, I'm sure the pictures are what has really annoyed him. He couldn't stop looking at them.

The answer will be on the internet, it always is. The screen of my mobile phone lights up and I start to type.

And I find Rosie.

And then I know.

I can't help but smile as I lean my head back and stare up at the ceiling.

This is Teddy all over. Talk about a woman scorned, they've got nothing on Teddy – who always has to come out on top. I remember him talking, or should that be ranting, about Rosie. And giving her the cold shoulder at parties.

Rosie was once his wonderchild, his protégée. And his lover for a while – I'd say girlfriend, but I think it was looser than that. Looser than even we had been. Teddy is a user, not a boyfriend.

Then Rosie left the publisher they worked for and went somewhere else – as an agent. She signed some MEGA books and made some MEGA connections. People love her.

I guess, like me, she realised that Teddy was too much of a driving force, that he wasn't letting her make her own decisions. Even though her instinct was good. So, she went out and proved him wrong.

She also signed the author of the *Mischief* books – with a rival publisher that Teddy had aspired to but had never managed to crack. He particularly hated the commissioning editor who had climbed the ladder way quicker than he had.

This isn't about me not doing the work for Ben (although I'm sure he has some deal going on there); no, it's about a rival, about his pride, and let's face it, about the bottom line financially. Every deal somebody else gets means a deal he's lost. In his eyes at least.

And I, his pawn, have betrayed him. I've signed up for the other side.

The publishing world is small, and he'd heard, and it

had wound him up so much he had to track me down and check whether it was true for himself.

Fucking hell, it must be exhausting living like that.

'Fancy a stroll, Bella?'

She wags her tail feebly. 'Ah, too much party fun? Bloody hell, I've just remembered. Ash never gave you your present!' He also never picked up his hoodie.

I dither for a bit, then decide to text him.

Fun party – didn't know dog parties were a thing! Wondered if you wanted to pop by with Bella's present? B x

I dither even more about adding the kiss. Is one too many, or not enough? We've shared *real* lip action – but never on a text. In fact, we've hardly shared any texts at all. And he just let my ex in, then I told him to go home. Help. What will he think? Should I have added more kisses? Or should I call him?

I call him. There's no answer, and leaving a message seems desperate and clingy, when I've just texted. I have to leave it.

It is then that I remember all the messages from Teddy and Ben. I delete the ones from Teddy without reading them.

Ben's is in his usual style, simple, to the point. He said I'd aced the amendments (I send Teddy a two-fingered salute in my head), would love to work with me in the future if I was willing (not sure on that one, but wow, he still likes my stuff!) and said we could chat, and warned me that Teddy was on the warpath and heading my way. And apologised that he might have let slip where I was.

Shit, if it hadn't been for the dog party, I'd have read that. I'd have been warned, been ready.

Except, would it really have made any difference?

Probably not.

I feel exhausted, but relieved that at least that is one mystery solved. I know how Teddy found me.

I text him back, promising to get in touch once my backlog has cleared.

I like Ben. I just need to be working with him independently – not with Teddy bleating in the background.

Then I sit down at my desk, finish off the *Mischief* cover and email the publisher.

And pour a very large gin and tonic.

And try not to be bothered that Ash hasn't responded to my text.

Chapter Nineteen

'We'll go for a long walk soon, okay?' The cover art I'd finished for the *Mischief* books the day of the party was given an immediate thumbs-up, and I'm now trying to get ahead of the game with the illustrations. I'd forgotten how much I love doing the kind of line drawings they've asked for. It's the simplicity, the artistic lines that allow me to get into the rhythm in a way I never can with paint. Once I start it's hard to break away – but Bella does need a walk.

The patio doors are wide open and there's a gentle breeze blowing in today. It's much more refreshing than the last few days when we've had wall-to-wall sunshine, and heavy stifling air which has left her dozing in the shade.

It's been perfect for work though. I've even let go of all my inhibitions about feeling silly and clichéd and made a jug of Pimm's and sat on the patio sipping an ice-cold drink and sketching.

I'm sure Bella will enjoy a potter and sniff in the woods

today though, and we both need a break and good walk. I, for one, have to lay off the Pimm's. It's addictive and telling myself it's just a fruity drink can only work for so long when I'm downing it by the jugful and feeling so tipsy I'm giggling at the TV each evening. Even when there's only a period drama or the news on.

'I might even let you have a dip in the lake if you're good!'

I sit up straighter and stretch my back, then lean forward, chin on my hands, and look out at the incredible view.

I'm going to miss this place so much. I've already absent-mindedly searched through the local estate agent websites though, and the prices are way outside my current budget. But I could do another house-sit. I'm sure there must be other places in the area, even holiday homes that people would like to have occupied out of season.

Except it is still season, so I'd have to wait a while.

'Oh, come on, Bella. I've got lots of time to do these, let's go!' It's not too hot for her, and why am I wasting the opportunity to get out? I can work this evening. I can work all hours when I have to pack my bags and go back to my old boring life and street views. The forecast says that the weather could break tomorrow, and if it's cloudy the views will be nowhere near as spectacular. 'We'll go on one of those long walks in a couple of days, when it isn't so hot.' Bella wags her tail and trots into the kitchen, waiting for me to catch up, before she heads to where her lead and harness are kept.

She's good company. I can see why Ash misses her. At

first, I have to admit, I did find her hard work, but she's a creature of habit. She likes her routine, and we just had to work one out that would suit both of us. And we have.

Or rather, she's trained me so that I stick to hers. And made sure I provide enough treats and chews so that she doesn't have to steal socks to make her point. She is still exceedingly bossy, and has to have the last word, but it's quite cute. As long as you don't try and beat her at her own game.

In return she's been a better best friend and more patient co-worker than any person has ever been. She never, okay hardly ever, wanders off when I'm talking to her and never judges. Even when I jump into bed with the man of her heart. The man of her dreams might have four legs, but Ash has her heart.

My phone rings, just as I'm pulling my shoes on, and I end up on my hands and knees as I scrabble in my back pocket to get it before whoever it is rings off.

Just in case 'whoever' is the person Bella and I are pining for.

I roll over onto my back, Bella peering down her nose at me. She looks funny, all big nose and eyebrows.

It is Mum.

'You sound quite chirpy, dear!'

'I'm laughing at Bella!'

'See, I told you a dog was a better idea than a man! I know how much you love them. But you just sound more your old self!'

I think I am, sorry I *know* I am. Since I arrived here, I have been shedding my old skin, like a snake does but more slowly. I have cast off Teddy and *his* aspirations for me and I'm sure that's why I feel so much lighter when I start work each day. I actually *want* to do it.

There's not been a single morning lately when I've woken up and just wanted to stay in bed, and thought 'fuck, I've got to work'.

I don't say all that though, she'd think I was going bonkers and insist on sending a rescue party. 'I love it here, it's even better than I thought it would be.'

'We used to love taking you and the other two there.' There's a comfortable silence while we both think about those trips. Bella shuffles a bit closer so that she's practically breathing the same air that I am.

'Bleurgh!' I push her away a bit, and she leans against my hand.

'It wasn't bleurgh!'

'No, I know!' I laugh, and Mum chuckles back. 'It's Bella, she's practically kissing me, the daft dog.' It's nice to hear my mum's laughter. When I was little, we laughed together a lot; we seem to have lost that. It's sad, but I guess that's what growing up is about. You push your parents away a bit, want to be independent, but then reach a stage in your life when you want them back. Maybe it means I actually am more content. I do know what I want and I'm realising she can't threaten that.

When I go home, I should go and see her more. Do girl stuff together.

'I wonder if that gingerbread is as wonderful as we remember?' She sounds wistful. It's nice sharing memories.

'Oh, it is, it's amazing! Even better than I thought.'

'I do need to try it again sometime. Actually, I've just had a thought.' Sounds dangerous. 'We can come and see you! A day out would be lovely, your dad and I hardly ever do that these days. Yes, yes, we will.'

'Er...' I was thinking I'd work up to 'girl stuff' gradually.

'That's a brilliant idea, why didn't I think of it sooner! We'll all come.'

'All?' I stare at Bella, mild panic setting in. She stares back, tries to lick my nose.

'I'll ask Abby.'

'Abby? Why would—'

'And Ed! It can be like an engagement party, but in Cumbria! That's a much better idea than waiting until you come home. Oh, doesn't that sound perfect? We can picnic on your lawn. I'll ask Daniel as well, though you know how busy he gets. This is fabulous! I can bring the food, you've no need to worry about that.'

Oh. My. God. No. I look at Bella in horror and she pulls back, alarmed on my behalf. 'But Mum—'

'Wonderful! How about Saturday?' Saturday? Saturday! What's got into the woman. 'I'll check with the others, and the forecast. Oh, before I go, did I tell you Teddy got in touch? He was being sneaky, trying to find out where you were. I told him to email you and you could tell him yourself if you wanted him to know! Honestly, the cheek. He did *block me* on Facebook, you know!' I don't think she's going to forgive and forget that one for a while. My mother can bear a grudge splendidly.

Am I angry? I suddenly realise I'm not. I don't care

about Teddy and his underhand ways. I don't care about Teddy full stop. He is irrelevant.

'Right, I'll let you get on. I'll call Abby and ring you back tonight. Isn't this lovely?'

Absolutely.

'Oh, and she's got more news to share! It was a bit of a shock, but I'm sure we'll all get used to it in time.'

Let her be pregnant, please let her be pregnant. I have my fingers crossed, which is mean. But Abby is so bloody perfect. If she cocked up just once, just one time, then it would be the perfect time to slip in my new career plans.

'Ed has been promoted and of course Abby has—' of course she has '—so they're moving. It is a move up, I mean it's a lovely house, but we won't be able to just pop in like we can now!' I wonder if this is why they're moving?

'Are they going far?'

'Only to Tappleton, they're buying one of those wonderful cottages on the green. Isn't that amazing? You always liked those, didn't you?'

'Yup.' Of course they are. They are moving to one of those idyllic cottages that I spent my early years lusting after but will never be able to afford.

For me, living in Tappleton is as unlikely as getting a place here.

Now is maybe not the time to come clean about the fact that I have stepped away from my links with a major publisher and practically guaranteed bestsellers, and instead am putting all my efforts into a Magic Pony who might, or might not, be the next big thing. And a Cumbrian village art shop.

Telling Mum might feel impossible right now, but I have to believe this is the right thing to do. For me.

_____

It is much cooler in the dappled shade of the trees down by the lake, in the spot next to where the boathouse used to be.

There is nobody else in sight, which is amazing considering I'm in Cumbria in the middle of summer. But that's the wonderful thing about this house. It's within walking distance of the village, but you could just as well be in the middle of nowhere.

I've forgotten Bella's long lead, but she's quite happy pottering around at my feet, especially when she discovers I've got a makeshift picnic.

For a couple of hours I am not going to work, I am not going to look at my phone (apart from to take photos), I am not going to think about my entire family gate-crashing this idyll (difficult), I am not going to think about Georgina (tricky), or Ash (trickier still), I am not even going to sketch. I am not going to do anything but chill and eat my picnic and drink my can of ready mixed gin and tonic.

'Don't you dare!' Bella is eyeing up the food as I unpack it.

This isn't a posh picnic; this is a last-minute raid-the-fridge type of picnic. I really do need to go shopping – the trouble is when I'm in full flow workwise I tend to forget stuff like that. Which is fine when you've got an open-all-hours shop two minutes away, less fine when you're a few miles from a very basic store and lots of miles from a proper supermarket. Still, I call this a success. I have dips, some carrot sticks cut from carrots that were going slightly floppy but not at all mouldy, some rolled-up slices of ham, a chunk of cheese (that was going mouldy, but I cut the green bits off), and two sausage rolls that I have cut into mini slices so that they look daintier and the drying pastry isn't quite as noticeable.

'Good, eh?'

Bella drools all over the edge of the picnic rug, so I throw her one of her high-quality, totally natural chews (she eats far more healthily than I do) and snap open the can.

It is amazing. The best G&T ever. The cool liquid slips down my throat and I groan and close my eyes.

When I open them, it is to see Bella grab at least three slices of sausage roll in her mouth at once and back off.

'No!' She takes another step. 'Bella, drop it!' She growls; it's only a play growl, but doesn't help the situation at all. I stand up, and she's off! This is when it's a mistake not having her on a leash.

It is also a mistake thinking I can catch her. She's gulping down food as she goes, the best game ever. Running past me and back to the blanket where she scoops up some ham and keeps running. At least she can't get my gin, that's in my hand!

We're on our fourth lap, and are down to carrot sticks, dips and a couple of slices of ham with teeth marks at the corner, when it dawns on me that I have to play clever here. I change direction, and head her off before she gets to the rug again.

She woofs and wags her tail even harder. Cheese spills

out from her mouth as she shoots straight between my legs, along the top of the bank and then leaps into the water.

Side by side with another dog that has appeared from nowhere.

They both come out of the water, shake then zoom back up the bank again. I dive, trying to grab her, but it is too late.

They both soar over the top of me, showering me with droplets of water which becomes ten times worse when they hit the lake and I get well and truly splashed.

I'm still game. I'm going to grab her when she comes out this time.

Except she doesn't.

Both dogs start to swim away from me.

Bugger. Double bugger – I've just crushed my can of gin!

'Bella!' I yell as loud and authoritatively as I can, but my voice is completely drowned out by a much louder bellow.

'Bella! Sam!'

Then I notice the rowing boat that seems to have materialised from nowhere.

Ash. Who else?

He is whirling what looks to be a dead rat on a rope round his head, and whistling. The dogs are both doing doggy paddle as fast as they can towards him, which is away from me.

I can hear his chuckle from here as he hauls both dogs into the boat.

'Git! You aren't going to win!' Of all the underhand ways to carry on. He's now given up on luring her away with food and sent a dog in to do his dirty work! 'I'm coming, Bella!' Sugar, no way am I going to swim after her.

I scramble down the slope, mainly on my bum as I'm in such a hurry, then run over to where I found the rowing boat last time. It is still there!

It is so much easier rowing without a bouncy dog in the boat as well, but I'm slightly shocked that Ash is still in sight – mainly, I think, because he hasn't got much choice. The dogs keep trying to chase each other around him, despite him telling them quite firmly to 'sit'. His boat is rocking so much that it sets me off giggling, which makes it even harder to row so it probably looks like my boat has hiccups.

I'm determined though, even though my ribs ache from trying not to laugh and I'm literally crying. But I am *so* close.

He seems to be spinning on the spot now, and whoops, he's lost a dog!

I drop my oar, and grab the side of his boat, just as he leans over the other side to grab the lost dog and haul it back aboard. 'Haha, got you!'

The look on his face is comical when he turns in surprise to look at me. Both the dogs sit down.

Bella barks and wags her tail furiously. The other one copies. Their tongues are lolling out and they look so funny and cute I can't help but grin.

'Ah, I forgot about Ginny!' He gives a rueful smile and it's like a little bubble of happy has burst inside of me and is rippling its way outwards. I'm like a newly poured glass of fizz.

'Ginny?' I am smiling like a loon.

The last few days, I've not seen him or heard from him, and for an awful moment it felt like he'd disappeared. Gone for good. Which I guess is why I let my guard down.

I mean, I know after the shag he'd been pretty pointed about not being up for a relationship, but even the 'mates' side of it seems to have died a death after Teddy had popped up at the dog party.

'The boat.'

'The boat's called Ginny?' I take my squashed can of drink out from between my knees and take a welcome swig. This rowing is hot work, and I'd been so determined to reach him I'd not realised quite how knackered I was until now.

'Did you bring me a beer?' Light twinkles in his eyes, one dimple deepens.

'Sod off!'

'Not seen you around for a few days.'

'I've been busy working.' I smile. 'Miss me?'

'Oh yeah…' He pauses. 'No opportunities to grab Bella at all.'

'Ha! You can go off people, you know.'

'I know.' There's a long pause. 'This is Sam by the way.' Sam wags his tail so vigorously at the sound of his name I'm surprised he doesn't fall over. He's cute and golden-brown, his colour getting lighter by the second as it dries in the sun.

'He's a spaniel?'

'Yup.'

'He looks smaller than the one we had as a kid, bouncier, lighter.'

'He's a working one, yours was probably the show type.'

'You didn't text back,' I blurt out. Aware that we're just skirting around what we should be saying.

'I didn't want to get in the way with your boyfriend.'

'He's an ex and was my kind-of boss, well he recommended me for commissions, until he found somebody better.' What on earth made me say that? I haven't said that to anybody! 'A proper cover designer.'

'You're a proper cover designer!'

I have to smile. 'He was here about work, cross that I hadn't done this stuff he wanted and...' I blab on then stop when he doesn't say anything, and shrug instead. 'I chased him off with the fire poker.'

'Resourceful.'

We sit for a moment, our boats rocking gently, me still hanging on to the rope at the end of his with one hand, and my can with the other.

'What's with the dog bait then?'

'Ah, yes, well Sam here belongs to a mate of mine. She's broken her leg, so I'm helping her out. I used to walk him sometimes with Bella before me and Georgina...' He doesn't finish the sentence. 'Bella is besotted, aren't you girl?' She grins at him and lifts a paw so he can stroke her chest. 'He was her birthday present, I brought him for a play date and I didn't realise it was party time.'

'I didn't organise that.'

'I guessed not.' He gives a wry smile.

'I can't believe she actually arranged a birthday party for a dog!'

'That's Georgie for you, even the dog has to be leading her best life. Preferably in public and filtered.'

'Are those dogs even her friends?'

He puts his head back and laughs, a full belly laugh that makes my thighs tingle, and makes me want to laugh with him. 'You're kidding me? You're really asking?'

'Well…'

'It's all fake, fake friends, hired help. Like the rest of the stuff on her Insta account.'

'She's posted lots of party pics on Instagram.'

'I bet.' He shakes his head but doesn't seem too angry. 'She's obsessed. It's her whole life and to hell with reality.'

'It *is* her whole life,' I say seriously, holding his gaze. 'That's why she can't bear to let it go.'

'I know.' His tone is soft.

Georgina posted several photos over the day of the party and the couple that followed, all with brand names prominently displayed, and all tagged.

'Bella looks happy in the photos!' It's a bit of an inane thing to say, but he is in love with the dog, and I do need to break the silence between us.

'High five to that eh?' They high five each other, which makes me laugh.

'It was fun, you have to admit it!'

He grins, a broad genuine grin, that makes me feel carefree. 'You really enjoyed yourself, didn't you?'

'I did!'

'Mrs Competitive, eh? I can't believe you were actually racing alongside her to make sure she'd go faster!'

'Are you laughing at me?'

'It was cool! I loved it.' His gaze is still for a moment. 'You're pretty cool.'

'It was the best dog party I've ever been to.'

His dimples deepen. 'Best as in only?'

I grin back. 'Yeah, well, maybe. The bar has been set high now!'

He chuckles and seriously disrupts my insides. 'I love the way you threw yourself into it, Georgie would never have done that. She was all about the organising, not the taking part.'

We share a look.

So, like Teddy then. Not a lot of letting their hair down.

'Everybody is different, I guess.'

'I guess.' He's watching me, in a slightly assessing way, which is making me shivery with anticipation.

He lowers his hands, and rather unexpectedly Bella makes a leap towards me and lands slap bang between my legs, interrupting the moment and leaving me with a totally different feeling of anticipation. One of getting wet.

'Bloody hell.' I grab both sides of the boat in alarm, dropping my nearly empty can, which lands on Bella. She leaps up and spins around, then jumps straight back into Ash's boat – just as Sam jumps into mine. He's wagging his tail ten to the dozen in my face, which makes me laugh, which sets Bella off barking and before I know it, she's back over here as well. Sam play-bows and bounces then takes a massive leap straight over Bella, the side of my boat, and over the top of Ash's and lands with a massive splash in the water.

It's funny. So funny that one look at Ash's face sets me off laughing even more. He chuckles as Sam tries to get back in his boat. He hauls him in, and the dog shakes himself dramatically – showering us both.

My sides ache. I feel helpless, weak. And then I catch Ash's eye. His look is intent, even though he's smiling. And suddenly I feel even weaker.

I hardly notice that miraculously the rocking of the boat has stopped.

Ash has his hand on it. He speaks, breaking the spell. 'Okay?'

'Sure.' I hope this isn't going to turn into musical boats, with the dogs carrying on leaping from one to the other. At least I am now back in possession of a dog, the right dog. I right myself and try and act casual, as though I haven't just screamed, laughed or stared like some lovelorn teenager. 'You've taught her loads of tricks.'

'I have.' He's still holding my boat, but his face is serious as he gazes straight into my eyes. It's not an 'about to kiss you' look now though. This is more, far more. It brings a lump to my throat. 'I had plenty of time.' He strokes Sam's head with his spare hand and gazes out over the lake. 'When I came home.' He reaches forward into his rucksack then and pulls out a beer – holds it out to me. 'Some of us came prepared,' he says with a wry smile, then roots around for another one.

We crack them open in silence and take a swig.

Both dogs settle down in the bottom of the boats.

'When I quit the Marines and came home, I wasn't in a particularly good place.' He turns the can of beer in his hand. 'I'd lost somebody close, and…' He gazes upwards at the sky. 'I'd lost my whole purpose. I felt useless, out of place.'

I can't imagine Ash without purpose. He strikes me as the kind of guy that always knows what he's doing and where he's going.

'I'd gone from full on, never stopping, having an end goal, having people at my side, to nothing. Zilch.' I watch his Adam's apple as he gulps down the beer. 'I can't blame Georgie for being upset, she didn't know what to do. Didn't know how to cope with me. I was a total pain in the arse.' He gives a wry chuckle. 'In her eyes I'd gone from never-at-home hero one day, to angry loafer the next.' His boat rocks gently and nudges mine, as Sam settles into a more comfortable position. 'I wasn't the action man she'd fallen for; I was difficult to live with. I guess I was a bit of an unexploded bomb, and after a bit she kept lighting the touch paper to see what would happen. Just to get a reaction from me, to try and get me to communicate. Like she did with the boathouse.' He shakes his head as though to clear it, then glances my way again. 'I got Bella and—' his eyes narrow as he frowns '—it might sound dramatic, but she saved me. Didn't you, girl?' She flops her tail at the sound of her name, knowing he's talking about her. 'Life just seemed better. She was a reason to get up in the morning, a reason to eat because if I didn't, she wouldn't.'

I nod, swallowing down the lump in my throat. This man gets my knickers in a twist and sends my emotions haywire. 'I get that.' If Bella hadn't been here, I would have moped, worked less, lost even more confidence in myself. The doubts might have just deepened, except having Bella meant I couldn't be like that.

'She gave me a reason to walk and run because otherwise she'd wreck the house and give me and Georgie something else to row about. And what can I say? She just likes doing tricks. I soon found out that she was as tuned in to my body, my hands, as my voice so it was easy.' He leans back slightly in the boat, stretches his long legs out. 'She's clever, she knew when I was wound up, knew when I wanted to cry, knew when I wanted the comfort of a warm body.' He looks me straight in the eye. 'It had got awkward with me and Georgie. She didn't know what to do. Emotional outbursts from a man who'd promised to protect her, be strong, were way outside her comfort zone.'

'You shouldn't feel so guilty. Shit happens, life happens, Ash, and people change.' I get it now; this has never been a nasty battle between him and Georgie. It's been guilt and determination on his side and hurt and a desire to put the clock back on hers. I can't blame Georgina for not wanting to let go of this dream.

He shrugs. 'I do feel guilty; I brought her here, promised her one life and gave her another. She was so desperate to escape me she turned to the internet!' Bella perches on the edge of my boat and leans in towards him so she can lick his nose. He strokes her ears. 'That was her safe place, because *I* wasn't anymore, I'd failed her. And the more time she spent, the more obsessed she got and the bigger the gap between us. She built up the perfect picture of her life on there that wasn't real. There was no way we could match that.'

'She doesn't want to let go of that, Ash. It's hard to just walk away when you *think* it's right.' And don't I know it. 'The time has to be right.'

'I know.'

'And you had Bella.'

'And I had Bella.' His tone has lost the edginess and intensity of a moment ago. Bella seems to have that effect on him. 'Georgie hadn't even been that keen on having a dog at first, until she'd seen how popular puppies were on Instagram.' He laughs. 'Strange world, eh?' He shakes his head slowly. 'But I guess I used Bella to keep my distance as well, I told her things I couldn't tell Georgie.'

'Sometimes it's easier to talk to a dog than a person, I've done a lot of that lately!'

We're in separate boats. We're not touching. And I guess Ash would find it hard to say all this if we were any closer. Maybe this is why he's chosen this moment to tell me. Or the moment has chosen him. Life can be like that. Offering the perfect space to do things – and all you have to do is be brave enough to take them.

This feels so intimate. I feel closer to him than I ever have in any embrace. The real him, beneath the laughter and kisses, beneath the hard, physical presence that has been all I've known of him until now.

His voice is soft and steady, almost like a gentle caress. A hug of words.

'You have a closeness to people when you're serving.' A

smile plays at the corners of his mouth as he strokes Sam. 'You're one of a litter of puppies.' I grin back.

'Bloody big puppies.'

'Massive.' The smile fades. 'But they're family, close family. Reliable. They understand.'

'Why did you come back, Ash?'

He props his elbows on his knees and looks out over the water, not answering for a long time. 'Another time, long story.'

Another time. It warms me up inside, knowing he doesn't intend walking away from me just yet.

Our boats don't drift far apart. They occasionally rock, and bump as we drink our beer and the dogs snooze.

Bella rolls onto her back, exposing her pink belly for me to rub.

'She likes you.' We've been silent for so long that the sound of his voice surprises me.

'Hope so.'

He pauses. 'I didn't text you back because I didn't want you to think, I didn't want…'

'Any misunderstandings?' He looks awkward. 'Like me thinking you were after anything but Bella?'

'Well, I…'

'No problem.' I am tensing up, my voice is coming out all sharp and staccato. 'Just another tactic, eh?'

'I didn't mean that Becky.' He looks miserable. 'I wasn't using you, it wasn't a… tactic.'

'So, what was it?' It felt like pretty hot sex to me, and it might be irrational, after all it could have *just* been a mind-blowing shag between two practical strangers, but it's making me angry being dismissed like this.

'It was fantastic.' He sighs. 'Totally unexpected and totally fantastic.' Oh! 'But…' He breaks the eye contact. 'We live in different worlds, Becky. I just didn't want you to think…'

This seems to be going downhill rapidly and I'm feeling a prickle of unease. 'Oh yeah sure, different boats.' I try and lift the atmosphere.

'I live here, you live in London… I dragged Georgie out here and look what happened!'

'Oh God, it was just fun, Ash! I don't want anything.' Or at least that's what it was at the time. But boy, have I missed him. I've been moping about waiting for a text or call; I've not been able to get him out of my head. 'I like being on my own, doing my own thing.' I do, I'm getting used to it. 'I don't want some heavy relationship; I want to have some fun.' But even if I do, he obviously doesn't so that's fine. I'll cry into my pinot grigio and head back to 'my world' soon. But another shag before I go would be quite nice. I might never get the chance again, and boy, was it good. Too much to ask?

'Oh. Fine.' He looks a bit taken aback. 'I just…'

'I'm not Georgina, Ash. And even if I did want this to be more and I came back here—' which I won't, or will I? I do love it here, thinking about leaving is horrible '—I wouldn't expect you to be responsible for me being happy. I'd be doing it for me.'

He blinks. 'Woah, say it like it is!'

'But one person shouldn't be held responsible for the

other one being happy! Don't you get that, Ash?' I don't know why I'm suddenly so definite about this, it's only just occurred to me. But it's true. Ending things with Teddy, stopping relying on him is letting me finally move on. 'I'm happier without Teddy, I just had to let go, and that's what Georgina will do when she's ready. No way do I ever intend repeating my mistake with Teddy, and whatever happened between you and Georgie doesn't have to happen again!'

'So, this was just…' He waves a hand in the air. I think he's referring to the snogs and sex.

'Fun!'

'Oh.' There's a long pause. Silence apart from the sound of water splashing against the side of the boat. 'I wish Georgie was more like you, independent, brave. It would make it easier for her.'

I'm independent and brave? I am!

So why doesn't he want me? Uh-uh, I am not going to go down that road. 'She will be, in her own way, in time.'

'I don't think she knows what she wants.'

'Maybe not, but she'll figure it out. It took me ages to realise I could be me, not the people-pleasing arse-licking idiot I've been the past few years, because of people like bloody Teddy!'

'I can't believe you were ever one of those!' He finishes off his beer and puts the empty down. Having Ash around makes me feel better, makes me surer that I'm going in the right direction. I will be really, really sorry to say goodbye to him. I'll miss him like crazy.

'Ash, change isn't always bad. Maybe coming here for Georgie was actually good for her in some way, she just doesn't know how yet. If I hadn't done the work I did with Teddy, if we hadn't split, if I hadn't come here…' I shrug my shoulders. 'For a start I would never have had the joy of a dog party!' Or met a man like you.

'How the hell did this convo get so heavy! I told you I could be a moody git!'

'The black clouds of Cumbria suit you!' I grin and stroke Bella on the head, knowing they will blow over. 'Look, I'm not in the market for happy ever afters right now, Ash. But I do like being with you, so…' I leave it open. 'I should get back.'

'Sure. Sorry Becky, I, er…'

'You should have Bella.' I am so tempted to just hand her over to him. It seems wrong to keep her, she seems so much *his*, and it's irrelevant what any ownership papers say. And then I could just row away, out of all this mess, and go back to my own mess.

But I can't. I still feel responsible, and I haven't seen her really with Georgina.

And much as I'd love to be, I'm not one of those people that can just walk away without a second glance if there are any doubts at all.

What if she's as much *hers* as well?

'I will have her,' he pauses, 'when the time's right. And hey, I like you too. It'd be good to show you more of the sights, or…' The wrinkles settle round his eyes. 'Put you through your paces again!'

'Oh no! I am not going there again!'

'Let me know if you change your mind.'

He gives my boat a gentle shove, and when I've

gathered my oars and look back, he's already rowing away in the opposite direction. Sam stares back at us, wagging his tail.

'Never!'

He waves a hand lazily. 'Never say never!'

My boat drifts gently back to the shore, and the second we reach it Bella leaps out and runs to the picnic blanket to polish off the rest of the food. I haven't got the energy to shout at her.

Chapter Twenty

*Had confirmation that HappyDogzDinnerzzz will be there at 10
a.m. G*

How I love waking up to messages from Georgina.
Especially weird mind-boggling ones that make no
sense at all.

I also now know better than to ignore them until after
my first coffee, when my brain cells might kick into action.
That tactic leads to repeated messages culminating in a
video call.

I don't want anybody to see me before I get out of bed.
Not even my family, and definitely not IG-ready Georgina.
Video calls require preparation.

Sorry? Confirmation?

I can almost hear her sigh.

*Can you **please** check the diary? It is booked in. On Saturday.*

I have to remember that this is important to Georgina, her way of controlling her life. Focusing on work has definitely helped me, it's just a shame that focusing on Bella probably isn't the long-term solution for her. Maybe I need to help her find something different to concentrate on?

Sure, thanks!

Phew, thank heavens for that. For a moment I thought there would be somebody knocking on the door before I'd even had time to brush my teeth and hair. I've got until Saturday.

My God, this dog has got a better social life than me. Is this normal? I'm sure when we've had dogs before they've only expected daily walks, feeding and the exciting annual highlight of a vet visit for a vaccination or squeeze of their anal glands.

They never had their own diary or personal appointments.

Not even a birthday sausage, let alone a birthday party. With fake friends.

Do I need to do anything?

Make her presentable, if it isn't too much trouble.

Do I detect a hint of sarcasm?

You've got all day. A bath, fluff her up properly, and trim her eyes – I could hardly see them on her birthday. G

Saturday does ring a bell though, I'm sure there's something going on. Maybe I did know about this after all, subconsciously.

Oh flip, no. Saturday is when my parents are coming. No, correction. MY WHOLE FAMILY is descending for an engagement party.

I am now fully awake.

Shock does that to a person.

What does she mean, I've got all day? Buggering hell, it is Friday! How did Friday creep up on me like that? It's tomorrow. Saturday is tomorrow, it follows Friday.

And what does she mean 'trim her eyes'? My phone beeps again.

Email.

Dear Becky,

Hope this finds you well? Our author is thrilled with your interpretation of Mischief! You'll be thrilled to know that pre-sales are exceeding expectation with international interest being shown, and so publication of ARCs is being brought forward pre book fair. It would be enormously helpful if we could agree to bring your deadline forward by two weeks.

Hope this works for you!

Regards.

Works for me? How can this work for me?

I have a dog diary to maintain, eyes to trim and a bloody family party!

It's all well and good Mum saying she'll bring the food, but I have to tidy up, wash my hair, pluck my eyebrows (Abby will look perfect) and provide nibbles. And booze. Plenty of booze. I need bubbly, do they sell champagne in the little shop, or do I need to go into town? Have I got time to go into the nearest town, which isn't near at all?

Sugar! I want to show them me at my best, I want to be at my best. I mean yeah, I know they love me as I am, but I want them to be proud, and happy for me. Because things definitely are on the up, people LOVE my work!

Fantastic news! No problem at all. Thrilled to be a part of this!

I hit send.

Did I actually say, 'no problem at all'? I am doomed.

But book fair. Concentrate on book fair, international interest. My name in the book. Great pre-sales. This was what my gamble was all about. Doing what I really want to do, following my path. I should be over the moon it's panning out.

Argh. It's just the timing though! Why now?

And breathe. Breathe…

I can do this. It is easy. I just need to be organised. I need a schedule.

I will get up early tomorrow to prepare Bella and tidy.

I will ring Ash and beg him to source some champagne and wine and give him extra visiting rights. No, no, I won't.

I will do late-night shopping this evening. I've got a whole day ahead of me. Then I will work all day Sunday on the illustrations. Then I will work in the evenings on the paintings I'm doing for David.

Easy peasy. Piece of piss.

I will pluck my eyebrows now, after I've had a gallon of coffee. Then shop. Then walk Bella and 'trim eyes'. Going to have to google that one.

Who do I bathe first in the morning? Bella, as that will make me hot and sweaty, but the later I can do her the better, or she'll be all un-fluffy and possibly muddy by the time her visitor arrives.

I might have to have my own shower after Bella's visitors have gone. Before I get stuff ready for my family.

I google HappyDogzDinnerzzz to discover they are organic, grain-free, additive-free, cruelty-free, full of vitamins and practically guarantee fresh breath, zing and sweet-smelling poos. I think I might be a convert.

I might serve their food as nibbles to my family.

Meantime, I might need to hide away all the crap-filled treats I have bought for Bella and for me.

They are definitely not on-brand.

I'm exhausted just thinking about it. So I sit down and drink coffee.

My email pings again.

Hi Becky,

Bad news I'm afraid, marketing team have decided may need complete rebrand so have a new cover brief to market test. Will get back to you ASAP. May have to shelve this one.

Ben

Great. I think my head might explode.

It's going to be like Piccadilly Circus here tomorrow with Bella's visitors and my parents, and I've now got an extra piece of work. Or not.

Maybe I've blown it. This could mean that Teddy was right. I have got it completely wrong and have now lost my one big client.

Has Ben just realised that I didn't smash the changes, well, not in a good way? Shit, is *he* going to dump me now as well?

I do some short sharp yoga breaths out.

Calm, must be calm.

I can do this. I have made my decision; I am going to stick to my guns even if it kills me. Which it might. And even if it doesn't, I might still be skint. And if I'm living on the street, how do I work? I don't buy the whole penniless artist thing, you need a laptop, internet connection and expensive software, plus all the other 'artistic paraphernalia' as Teddy used to term it.

I must be brave. I am brave. Ash said so. I have told Teddy to piss off, and now I can draw a line under my relationship with Ben and move on.

Wow, I've just realised! Bella is Georgie's Ben! Yes, that's it! We're both hanging on to a link with our past that we really shouldn't.

But argh. Oh God, when I leave here, where am I going to live if I can't afford the rent on my flat? My situation is loads worse than hers, at least she's got a lovely home.

I am NOT going to go and stay with Mum, and Abby is far too busy getting married, and buying a new, posh, proper couples house in Tappleton, and living with my brother Daniel would be like living with an alien being, who doesn't approve of me. And Kate's place is even smaller than mine.

I'd always known Abby was a step or two ahead of me, but the gap is widening by the minute. She's got the life, got it all. Soon she'll have adorable toddlers (mine would be screaming banshees, hers will be adorable) and well-behaved Labradors pottering around the garden – and not digging up the shrubs, or peeing on them, or pulling the lawn out by the roots. A career. A husband with a career.

Am I as mad as Teddy told me, trying to be an idealist and throwing away the real things? The things I could actually succeed at. 'Not many people can afford ideals, Becky,' he'd sniped at me (in one form or another) many times, before grabbing his red pen and setting out to destroy the dreams of yet another of his authors.

But if we've not got ideals, not got dreams, what have we got? Ten hours a day of drudgery so that we can afford a nice kitchen, sexy high heels, the latest lippy, but no joy?

Much as I love my lippy, I don't think it's the path to total fulfilment.

Bugger, bugger, bugger. I was relying on Ben to be my

backstop. Enough work to mean I could survive, with anything else being a bonus.

I need *Mischief* to turn out to be totally magical. Like, the next *Harry Potter*. But more quickly.

Bella plonks her paw on my knee, so I move the chair slightly away from the table and she jumps up and licks my nose, gazing adoringly into my eyes. 'Oh Bella, you're right.' I give her a hug. 'We can do this, can't we?' She barks. Talk about positivity, it is practically oozing out of her as she wags her tail with enthusiasm. 'You know what I think?' She blows up my nose, then leans her head against me under my chin. 'I think we need a good long walk to clear our heads.' One thing that Bella has taught me, is that you can't beat a good run. A good run (and squirrel chase and pee by a tree – not that I'm going to do these last two) is guaranteed to clear my head and solve any situation. 'How about that one that promises *"spectacular views on a sunny day, a tarn, the perfect waterfall, peregrine falcons and red deer"*?' She barks, jumps down and takes a step back, waiting for me to get up. 'I'll have to get changed, put some decent shoes on.'

Sometimes you need to take a moment. Recharge.

This is easy! I don't know why all these hiking websites and books make such a fuss about walking, I think they just want to put normal people off and keep the best bits for themselves.

It's the perfect antidote to all the stress and hassle

though. My head already feels lighter, and I actually feel free. Like nothing else matters. I am striding out into my new life!

I've brought my mobile phone (fully charged of course – but also on mute). I took a photo of the walk instructions, plus I've got the Ordnance Survey app thingy so I know exactly where I am. I've also got a rucksack with water for Bella and me, a supply of Kendal mint cake (any excuse), lots of dog treats, a long-sleeved top and waterproof in case the weather suddenly changes (haha, how likely is that?) and some plasters. I packed all this before I realised that conditions were massively exaggerated. I'm bloody glad I didn't go all the way and pack a compass, tent and emergency flares.

'Isn't it fab, Bella?' She gives a tug on her lead, as though to say, 'Well, it would be if you'd let go!', so I do. I unclip her lead. I mean, what's the harm? We've just walked across a very photogenic bridge that straddles a small beck and are plodding up a slightly inclined stony path that slices across fields of rough grass.

Not even Ash could stalk us here without me spotting him miles away. Not even he can hide on open ground like this. Unless he disguises himself as a sheep.

We come to an old, wooden wobbly stile, but Bella leaps over it easily and waits on the other side as I start to clamber over trying not to catch a foot and fall flat on my face.

Sitting on top of the stile I can see for miles.

Talk about inspiration! A lump forms in my throat, I am going to miss this place *so* much when it's time to go home.

Whatever happens, I'm going to find time to come back and visit.

The sky is startlingly clear, apart from the hint of thin white clouds that lurks along the sharp edges of the mountains, blending and softening.

Below my feet, the muted greys of the stone path lead my eye across the brown-green of sunburned grass, to the patchwork walls that criss-cross the landscape, disappearing into the distance.

If I'd brought my sketch pad I could just stay here for a couple of hours, but instead I make do with taking photos.

I wish I could stay here forever. Is that running away, or just starting over? Is it just the scenery, the space or the man who has taken up such an important part of it? The man who is always on the horizon, the one I'm always looking out for, the one who is in more dreams than any man should be.

Shaking my head, I turn away. I don't know where that thought came from. Except he always does seem to be in my head. And it isn't just the fact that I fancy him like mad, he's a bit like Bella, he makes me feel good about life, about myself. He makes me feel like I can do anything, try anything – and it doesn't matter if it doesn't work out.

Bella barks and I glance up at her, and the long, rough track that stretches over the other side. For miles. Getting steeper. 'Come on then Bella, this had better be bloody worth it!'

Cotton-wool clouds bubble over the summits of the crags ahead, but above them the sky is a glorious clear blue that would look false if I tried to recreate it on a canvas.

The track narrows to become a bridleway, the stones slipping under my feet as I plod on. Bella hares off after a rabbit, then comes lolloping back when I whistle. She's panting, her tongue hanging out, but she is still bouncing about full of energy, which is more than I am. I am staggering, one foot in front of the other, but determined to do it.

Maybe this hiking lark isn't quite as easy as I thought.

Ahead looms a fell, gloomy in the dramatic shadow of the cloud, and behind me the pale green carpet of grass falls away, drawing my eye down to the beck we crossed, which now seems small and insignificant.

It literally takes my breath away. I wobble, feeling slightly dizzy as I look down. Boy, we really are high up. Once I get used to it and stabilise, I pull out my mobile and take a few photos, turning in a circle to take in the view in all directions.

I can see why people do this. Walk. Get addicted to it.

Behind me is the forbidding fell, to my right the dark stillness of a lake nestling between the cleft of mountains as though they are cradling it. Caring for it.

Nature looking after itself.

In all directions, every hue of brown and gold from tawny orange to russet, of grey and steel, every shade of green binding them all together as it runs from freshness to burned ochre. And above the brightest purest of blue, bumping into the whites, greys and black of clouds and emerging pale and watered down on the other side.

I can see for miles.

I really do feel like I'm on top of the world. Alone. But not lonely alone, free-alone.

There is the cry of a bird and I look up and laugh. I spin around to glance back at the path ahead, its steep, treacherous surface scarred with the rocks and stones that hold it together. It snakes around the jagged broken edge of the hillside ahead, disappearing from view, tempting me on.

Bella does a little play bow as though to say, 'Come on', wagging her tail furiously.

'Okay Bella.'

She scampers ahead, barking, and disappears around the corner.

That corner is a corner too far.

One minute I am thinking it might be a tad steep, but doable. The next I'm on a narrow path clinging to the side of a mountain with a steep drop on one side, the wind is blowing a gale and I'm staggering like a drunkard chucked out at closing time.

I am going to die. I can't breathe and my legs are all wobbly and heavy. I might have been a tiny bit over-ambitious. I also now realise that Georgina's walking guide has likely been written by either a sadist, fitness freak, or possibly ex-Royal Marine. Not by a girl who spends most of her time building an Instagram platform around her dog.

My lungs are empty.

If I sweat any more, I will be a mere dehydrated husk of myself.

It is so bloody steep my muscles are trembling like I've run a marathon – well, how I imagine they'd feel if I ran a marathon, the furthest I've run is to the bus stop.

My heel hurts, I think I'm getting a blister.

Okay, facing the facts here: I'm more an ambling kind of girl, than a walking one, but I just felt like I needed a challenge. I felt that some strenuous exercise would clear my head and give me the answer to all my problems. You know, highlight some brilliant plan I'd completely missed, or just create a miracle. And I really did want to do this walk before it's time for me to leave Lake View Cottage, and that time is approaching scarily fast. Even faster now I've discovered that I could soon be penniless and homeless if I lose the work with Ben.

I have to do this though. I have to get to the top. This is my metaphorical mountain to climb, before I have to face the real-world one. If I don't do this, I am doomed. If I make it, if I meet the challenge and win, then it is a sign.

Boy, this is harder than my bootcamp session with Ash was. Harder than our walk. And Ash was proud of me. I can't let him down, or myself. One way or another I can do this.

Would it look bad if I crawl the rest of the way? I mean, it's the doing it that counts, not the how, isn't it?

It can't be much further, can it?

I round the next corner and dare to glance up, while clinging to the tufts of grass with one hand. I'm not keen on heights – well, only if I'm behind glass, or maybe if there's an extremely sturdy handrail. Here I am exposed. Totally.

Oh hell. I am not there yet; the path goes up *even more steeply* if that is possible. Have they never heard of steps in this part of the world?

Or escalators.

I've gone off the great outdoors.

It is hard work and scary.

Maybe if I imagine that Ash is here, just ahead, holding out his hand to help me.

Yeah, that helps. His strong grip, strong arms, strong thighs... no, maybe not. This is taking me to an altogether different place.

A sheep bleats and I close my eyes.

A lamb can do this, a dog can do this, Bella was practically *scampering*, so surely a grown woman can?

It is then, sitting on my bum, trying not to look down that I realise I've not seen her for a while.

'Bella?' She bounded ahead of me. I'd expected to see her when I rounded the corner, all wagging tail and bounce before she took off again.

'Bella!' I yell loudly. My words disappear into the vastness.

Complete silence apart from the odd baa of a sheep, and a bird flying over.

This is weird. She never goes far. She's always waited for me to catch up. She even put off diving in the beck until I was on the bridge and gave her the okay.

A tiny, hard lump forms in my chest. It's silly. I'm being daft. I'm just tired, yeah that's it, tired and overreacting. No need to panic, she's only been out of sight for a few minutes. 'Come on Bella, come and see what I've got! Crisps!' What if she's fallen? They have disused mines on these hills. I know they do, I read about them online. There were warnings about not letting your dogs near them.

Stop Becky, take a breath. You checked. There is no mine here. None.

But there will be rabbit holes, and badger setts, and well, just holes. Massive holes. Steep cliffs.

She's got no sense, Ash said. She'd jump off a cliff if you let her.

Oh God, what have I done? Why didn't I keep her on her lead?

I yell again, and again until my throat is hoarse. Dry and raspy.

There's an emptiness in my stomach and my pulse pounding my ears.

If I keep going higher, what if she's gone down? But if I go down, I'll forget exactly where I last saw her.

I scramble down on my bum, sending shale in all directions, to where the path widens, and look upwards, cupping my hands round my mouth to try and magnify my shout. But it's hopeless. The vast space swallows up my feeble voice.

That lovely vast nothingness is now scarily big and empty. I'm alone, miles from anywhere. Nobody in sight. I haven't seen a soul for the last half an hour. Only sheep.

What do I tell Georgina? She'll kill me! And Ash, oh my God, Ash will be devastated if I've lost her. I know he will.

I'm supposed to be keeping her safe. I had one job, just one job.

She means everything to Ash. Why has it taken so long for me to realise that to Georgina she's just a bargaining tool, an asset, a life she's hanging on to? But Ash loves her with all his heart.

I am even more panicky now. I mustn't overreact. It will be fine. I'll find her. I have to.

'Everything okay?'

I jump and slip on the loose stones at the sound of a voice. Somebody puts a hand on my elbow and steadies me.

'Becky?' It is David, looking worried.

'I've lost Bella, I can't find Bella!'

'Hang on, hang on, she'll be around somewhere, I'm sure. I'll help you call her.' He pats my shoulder. 'She won't have gone far, probably chased a rabbit, the little tinker. How long since you saw her?'

'Not long.' I feel a bit stupid now. 'Just since I was around that corner, but she never goes far.'

'No, no, I know. But once they get a scent, whoosh, they're gone, and when they stop, they haven't a clue which direction they came from.'

'Really?' I feel slightly reassured. I was being silly.

'Certainly.' He smiles. 'She's probably carried on pottering the wrong way and can't hear you. The wind up here doesn't help. Let's try this.' He digs into one pocket and pulls out a whistle.

It's piercing.

She has to have heard that.

I hold my breath, expecting a black fluffy dog to bound into view, waiting to tell her that she's naughty but I love her.

She doesn't appear.

He whistles again. And again.

The sudden lightness of hope I'd felt in my chest

disappears and I'm scared. Something terrible has happened to her.

'Let's walk on a bit and try again.'

We try again, and again, and again.

Each time the expectation is less, and the weight of the let-down is heavier.

She's not coming back.

Even David's smile is more strained.

It's harder to speak, harder to walk. We plod on in silence. My legs feel leaden, but I can't stop pushing David to try one more time.

The sun has gone in, the clouds that were so cotton-wool cute are now threatening.

I feel cold, and I don't know whether it's the weather, or dread.

'Well, she must have really lost her bearings, not like little Bella to stay away from food.' The optimism that's been in his voice from the start has been replaced with concern.

'Oh God, I know.' I feel even worse when David says that. I want to bawl. I wipe my forearm across my eyes.

'Time to call out the cavalry, I think, and go and get you something to eat. You look terrible.'

I feel terrible. Losing Bella is about more than just letting people down, I love her. And it feels like I've lost far more. Bella has helped me confront my issues, helped me believe in myself. Helped me be me. 'But we can't stop, what if—'

'You'll be no good to her if you keel over,' he says gently. 'She's tougher than you are, she'll be fine.' He gives me a quick hug that makes me want to sob like a baby and fishes out his mobile phone. 'No signal, but I know where there is.'

I look at my own phone. I haven't got any kind of signal either.

'Come on.' He motions down the path. 'It's fine when we get from under the shadow of these peaks.'

'Who are you ringing?' I scramble after him, my feet slipping and sliding, while he strides on, looking at his phone, as though this is a walk in the park.

I feel *so* hopeless and pathetic but moving faster (and downhill) somehow makes me feel slightly more positive. I think it's the adrenalin, the change in direction.

'Search and Mountain Rescue.'

I'm so shocked, my feet forget to move, then I have to hurry after him to catch up again. I've got visions of helicopters, search lights, people in hiking boots.

Which makes me think of... 'Ash!' I didn't mean to shout his name out.

'Exactly.' David glances back reassuringly. 'He's one of their best dog handlers.'

'Oh.' I feel a bit faint again. 'I didn't mean, I didn't know he was... I just thought he'd be able to help.' It was the image of a capable man, and big hiking boots that had made me think of the obvious. Bella would come to Ash. Ash is her favourite person in the whole world, and even if he's not exactly talking to me right now, it doesn't matter – she needs him. 'He does search and rescue?'

'Yep.' He gives me a quizzical look. 'I thought you knew; he's part of the team, it fits in well alongside his guided walks and orienteering work.'

'Sorry.' I'm slightly breathless as I hurry after him. 'I just thought she'd come to him.'

David grinds to a halt, and I nearly slip into him, taking us both down.

He neatly sidesteps with a hand out to steady me, then holds his phone up. 'Reception! Wonderful. I'll call.'

There is no answer, so David leaves a message. Then he glances back at the mountains and shakes his head.

'What?'

'You need to get home, and I'll go and see if he's at his place.'

'But, but… I can't go down, I can't leave her up here on her own!' This is so, so much worse than if Ash had stolen her. I wish he had. At least I'd know she was safe.

'Weather's changing.'

'But the forecast…' My voice tails off. I had checked before we set off, it was supposed to be okay, I'm sure it was.

'I can feel it, the rain is coming in. That's what happens here I'm afraid, catches folk out.' He shrugs. 'You get back and grab yourself a torch and a decent coat. It'll go cold up here and if you freeze to death you aren't helping anybody, are you?'

'But—'

'No, Becky. People get hurt up there, and no offence, but you're not exactly a hardened walker, are you?'

I shake my head, and he pats my shoulder.

'You get sorted, and I'll see you back here in an hour. Okay?'

I can feel my face crumpling, but I try and nod with

confidence. David squeezes my shoulder, and the kindness brings the rush of sadness brimming over. I turn away so that he doesn't see.

'Sure,' I shout back as I stumble away. 'Thanks for helping me.'

'Least I can do.' When I glance back, he's striding away up the beck with a measured pace. 'Oh and grab a spare collar in case she's lost hers, happens a lot!'

What was I thinking? I've been living a complete fantasy since I got here, dreaming of a different career, imagining I was the type of person who could look after a dog and go hiking up the peaks. Without even checking the flaming weather forecast properly.

I can't trust my own judgement.

I've fucked up my career, and I've lost Bella, and right now, the thought of that is making me feel ill.

I start to jog, my thighs burning, heart pounding as though it wants to burst out of my chest, my calves tight with every step.

What have I done?

Chapter Twenty-One

'What?' For a moment I think I must be completely losing my mind. I stare at the hooks. Bella's spare harness has gone.

I rummage in the baskets and drawers where Georgina keeps her coats and toys, throwing things in all directions.

Then I tip the contents out completely and push them to the side one item at a time.

Just to be sure.

The harness is missing, and so is the long lead that I've taken her out on when I was worried about losing her. Or having her dog-napped.

My stomach hollows out. Oh my God. It can't be. Ash can't have come and taken them. This can't be his grand plan to steal Bella. He wouldn't. Surely he wouldn't steal her away off the hills and leave me in a panic. He's not that cruel, I know he's not.

Her favourite squeaky ball isn't there.

I'd have seen him on the fells. I would. And he didn't

even know we were going there; I didn't know until about five minutes before we set off.

There has to be a sensible explanation.

I feel like bursting into tears, the lump in my throat is stopping me from breathing and my whole head feels like it's going to burst.

My phone vibrates in my pocket and I pull it out, still sorting through Bella's stuff. One last check.

'Becky.'

'Ash!' My legs feel strangely wobbly and I sink down onto the cold tiled floor. 'Where is she, what ha—'

'Where've you been? I've been calling.' There's an edge to his voice. 'Where are you?'

I gulp. 'My phone was on mute. I'm at home, I mean the cottage. I came back for Bella's harness and—'

'I've got it.' Relief whooshes out of me. He has been here. 'I came to get some of her stuff in case...' There's a painful silence.

The dread returns. 'You've not got her?'

'No.' The one word is flat. 'I got a message from David, I'm on my way out there.'

'David made me come back to get a jacket and torch, and spare collar.' I quell the sob that rises up in my throat. 'I'm coming back. Oh God, Ash, what if...'

'Shh.' His voice is soothing. I can tell he's worried, but he's being nice. He'll blame me later. I'll blame me. 'I've got Sam with me; don't panic, he'll track her down if she's up there.'

'But what if—'

'She's smart, Becky. I'm sure she's fine.'

I look out of the window and it has started to rain. With the heavy drops there's a darkness that makes me shiver. Every trace of blue sky has disappeared behind the heavy veil of clouds, the quiet stillness of the lake is pockmarked with angry punctuation, and along the shore it swirls and churns as anxiously as my stomach.

Poor little Bella will be drenched and bedraggled. She loves water, but she hates rain. She'll be cold and think I've abandoned her.

I grab my jacket and tug the hood up, then take the car keys from the tray by the front door. I'm going to drive into the village and park at the start of the footpath to save time – and because I feel so knackered. I've been running on adrenalin, but now that I've taken a few minutes to stop and collect stuff from the cottage, I've lost all my impetus. I just want to cry now.

Which is pathetic.

The narrow lanes are already awash with water running in streams down the sides, and my boots splash in the puddles when I get out and start to make my way up the gently sloping rough track.

Ash is there, a soggy Sam at his side, his tail and ears bedraggled and dripping. He's got a red jacket on, the same as Ash.

Ash lets him smell Bella's favourite toy and then gives the word, and he's off. He zigzags his way up the path, his tail going, his nose down. 'He'll bark if he finds her,' is all Ash says, before setting off after Sam.

I want to say I'm sorry, I want to say so many things, but this isn't the right time.

We're soon at the point where the path narrows and turns before rising steeply. 'Wait here.'

'But I want—'

'Becky.' A little bit of the sternness leaves his face, and he must sense the hot tears pricking at the back of my eyes, because his voice thaws and he rests his hand briefly on my arm, and squeezes. 'I'm sorry but you're more of a hindrance up there than a help, you'll slow us down.' He pauses and looks me straight in the eye. 'And I'll be worried you'll fall and hurt yourself.'

It's the caring look that does me in – unleashes all the pent-up feelings of panic, fear. Failure. 'This is all my fault!' I wail. He puts his arm round my shoulders and pulls me in and I blub. 'And I thought, when her lead had gone, I thought, you, and…' I am aware I am hiccupping and not making any sense.

'Shh.' He pulls me in tighter, until my feet lift off the ground, and kisses the top of my head. Then he very firmly plants me on my own two feet.

With the gentlest of touches he wipes my cheek with his thumb, and I catch hold of his wrist.

'You will find her, Ash?'

'Promise.'

I watch man and dog as they work their way up the path, until they disappear from view and I just hear the occasional whistle.

Then silence.

For ages.

I'm getting stiff, the water is seeping through my cheap jacket at the seams and dripping off the hood down my face and into my eyes but I daren't move from the spot.

I daren't do anything. I just stand and shiver, and hug myself, and promise I'll be a better person and try harder if only he finds her.

I'm concentrating so hard on the path he took, that at first the sound of his whistle is disorientating.

I turn, blinking. Off to my right there's a tall figure heading towards me, and it has to be Ash. A spaniel is casting round in large circles, heading down the bank and being whistled back.

He's done a circle, is coming back at me from a different direction.

Ash shakes his head in frustration when they get back to me, and he clips Sam's leash on. 'Bloody dog wants to head down there—' he points '—and head back up the beck, he must have picked up an old scent or something.'

'Are you sure?' I try not to, but I can't help the shiver.

He glances up at the dark skies. 'Maybe we need a break anyway.' His sigh is so heavy it breaks something inside me, I feel like I'm crumbling, falling apart. He runs his fingers through his hair. Dirty hands, caked with mud from where he's climbed. Spattered boots and legs. 'He's only young, they make mistakes, but he's tried hard, haven't you mate? Can't blame him.' He ruffles the hair on the top of Sam's head.

'You can't give up! We can't—'

'I'm not giving up.'

'You are!' I'm biting back the tears and begging him to

carry on, but a part of me wants to reach out, touch him, tell him it will be okay. Wipe the smear from his cheek. But I can't. I can't, because what if it isn't okay?

'I'd never give up. But you need a break, Becky, we all do. Even Sam, it's not fair on him. It's just too dark and he's not much more than a pup. Come on, I'll get you home. We'll come out first thing in the morning, I promise.'

'I can't leave her out all night.'

'And you can't find her either. It's too dangerous in the dark, Becky. You know I love her. Trust me. Please?' He ruffles the wispy hairs on Sam's head, then the dog jumps up and he catches him, holding him close. 'Let's at least get back and give this one some food, then make a plan?'

Bella is licking my face, and Ash is holding me, cuddling me, leaning in and kissing me.

He's so warm, the bed is so cosy, I snuggle in deeper.

'Beck?'

I open my eyes.

He's not in bed with me, he's fully dressed and leaning over me, shaking my shoulder. Ash isn't in bed with me because he doesn't want that. Ever. I'm not his kind of girl.

Another lick stops me feeling sorry for myself. It isn't Bella – it is Sam nudging and licking at my face. Which makes me want to cry again. I wanted it to be Bella so much it hurts.

'Come on, it's getting light. I've made some bacon sandwiches and packed a thermos.'

'What?' It takes a second, then yesterday floods back and I roll out of bed and look round in panic for my clothes.

'Your stuff is at the bottom of the bed, I put it in the drier for you.'

'Anybody ever tell you you'd make a brilliant wife?' I yell back, trying to sound brighter than I feel.

Bella has been out all night. All night, while I've been curled up in bed and Ash has warmed my cold damp clothes up.

She'll be freezing and damp, and dirty.

I should have trusted my instincts, gone with my heart, not some stupid agreement with Georgina. I should have let him have her. He'd have kept her safe.

But Georgina needs her as well. Georgina needs to find her own kind of closure – which she can't if we don't find Bella.

Ash is already in the car, engine running when I get out there.

It's a stunning morning. Even in my current state I can appreciate that, stop for a second to take a deep breath.

Daybreak has to be one of the nicest hours of the day. It's so still and quiet, with a perfect soft glow of light that holds so much promise. Yesterday's rainstorm is a distant memory, this morning there is only the dampness of dew.

Yesterday's nightmare isn't distant though. I stare out of the window and blink back the threatening tears, trying to concentrate on the beauty and not the nightmare scenarios that are dancing around in my head.

'You know what, I'm not sure,' Ash says as we park up and climb out, Sam poised at the foot of the track.

'What?' I blink at him.

'You asked last night if I was sure, about Sam following an old scent? But look at him.'

I look at Sam, who's pointing in the same way the stream flows, his tail wagging crazily.

Ash gives him the word to go, and we follow him up the track, over the bridge. He pauses again at the beck, then looks back, as though asking permission.

'Maybe you should trust him. I know I don't know anything about dogs, Ash. But doing it your way isn't working.'

He studies me, assessing eyes travelling slowly over every inch of my face. Then he nods decisively.

'Okay. We'll follow Sam. At least we can grab a drink where he's heading.'

'Out here?'

'Out here.' He nods, a grim hint of a smile on his face.

We walk along the bank of the stream for what feels like miles. Mainly because I have several rather painful blisters on my feet. There is no big-enough, soft-enough plaster in the world to make them feel better.

Sam never lifts his nose; he just zigzags along making little 'wiffle' sounds. 'He's taking in the scent,' says Ash, when I throw him a look.

He resists the pull of the water and keeps on at his job, and soon the path, muddy from yesterday's downpour, widens and becomes stonier.

It's a relief not to be slipping and sliding about as much, as I jog to keep up with Ash's long purposeful stride. Sam seems to be happier as well as he speeds up and is soon galloping along.

'Oh hell.' I have visions of losing a second dog. But Ash puts a steadying hand on my arm before I can shout at Sam.

'It's okay, I know where he's going.'

'You do?'

He nods. A small smile plays at the corners of his mouth. 'I do. You were right, I should have trusted him.' The path snakes away from the stream, drying out under the shelter of the trees, becomes a proper track and then opens out into a glade.

I slow, letting my eyes accustom to the softer light, and am just picking up pace again when there's a yelp. Sam suddenly zooms back past us at high speed, leaping over fallen logs, his tail between his legs, and nearly cannoning into Ash. He circles, and I take my gaze off him for a second and realise he's being chased.

There's a bark, a loud ecstatic bark and it dawns on me. It's Bella!

'Oh my God!' My sight blurs with tears, and I put my hands over my mouth as she leaps up at Ash, then fawns at his feet, wriggling and squirming and rolling in the leaf mould.

Sam jumps up at me, his tail wagging as though he's telling me he's clever. 'You are clever, you did it, Sam, good boy. You're so clever!' I grab him, kiss him and leap around as madly as he is. I realise that I'm crying, that my hands on his ears are wet because my face is damp. But I don't care.

Ash is grinning. He's standing up, Bella in his arms, and the smile on his face is the biggest I've ever seen. He buries his face in her fur. She turns to lick his face, nibble his nose, then wriggles to be put down again. So that she can dash round with Sam.

She's dirty and bedraggled but looks unbelievably happy that we've found her.

She can't stay still. She leaps over Sam, then she's in front of Ash again, she's squirming onto her back, then back on her front. She leaps up at me, then dashes off, running around and around the opening in the trees with Sam, and then nearly bowling both of us over.

'I think she's pleased to see us.'

'That is the understatement of the century,' I say, crouching down. 'Oh Bella.' My voice is croaky, hoarse with emotion, but I couldn't care less. 'I am so pleased to see you too. You can't believe how pleased.' I look up at Ash and wipe the tears off my face with my forearm. 'You found her; Sam found her.'

'Teamwork.' He smiles. 'You told me to trust Sam so how could I not?' His gaze holds mine, his voice soft. 'I reckon we make quite a good team, the four of us. Right, coffee?' He rests his hand briefly on my shoulder, warm, strong.

'What do you mean, coffee? We drank it!'

He grins, takes a step further into the clearing and holds his hand out for me to slip mine into.

There is a camper van, a bright orange old-fashioned VW camper van. To one side there's what looks like a fire, with a pot hung over it. Either side of the doorway are pots filled with herbs.

'This is where she came?' I laugh weakly, relief and exhaustion mingle together.

'Yup, this is where she came. She probably slept underneath it, and—' he gives a wry grin and points '—emptied the bin of scraps.' He shakes his head. 'I don't expect any cockapoo ever died of starvation.'

'What is this place?' I'm dying to look inside. It is unbelievably cute.

'This, Becky, is the place I call home at the moment.' His face is serious.

'You live in a camper van? But...' I look him up and down, and grin. He just looks too big to live in a tiny van like this!

'It's temporary.' He smiles back. 'My secret hideaway.' His eyes twinkle.

'Ahh, this is where David came to find you yesterday!'

'It is, he's one of the few in the know. Shame Bella hadn't already got here, would have saved us a sleepless night.'

'You didn't sleep?' I ask guiltily. I slept – for those few hours between crashing out and being woken up at daybreak. I was totally knackered.

I want to hug him.

'I'm used to it. Some of us are tough, you know.' Laughter dances in his beautiful face. I never thought I'd call a man's face beautiful, but right now, his is.

'How long are you here for?' I blab on, trying not to give in to temptation and grab him for a kiss.

'Until the stuff going on at my place is sorted.'

Which doesn't tell me anything. I wonder where his place is. I wonder if I'll get a chance to see it before I have to go home.

If I knew where it was, maybe it would be okay for him to have Bella there with him. I don't think there's room for a dog in the camper as well as him!

'Sometimes I prefer it here though! I might just stay.'

'What?' I'm so surprised my hold on Bella slackens and she wriggles free from me, dashes past him and waits at the door, barking. Laughter bubbles up inside me. 'Stay?' Oh my God, he's a real-life Crocodile Dundee or Robinson Crusoe – but with a camper.

'It's a long story.' He wags a finger at me. 'I hope you're not laughing!'

'Never.' I grin back. 'I think you need to tell me.'

'Another time.' He motions towards one of the chairs, and I sit down, Bella leaping onto my knee, and I don't care if she's dirty and smelly, or is trying to French kiss me. He strides over and gently strokes her head. 'I've not brought her here before though, she must have picked up my scent, or Sam's.'

'Yours. It's you she was looking for,' I say. 'Definitely.' She knew she'd be safe if she followed Ash's scent. The thought brings a lump to my throat, and hot tears prick at my eyelids.

I'm overtired. Emotional. That must be what it is.

The morning sunlight edges through the tree canopy and I put my head back and close my eyes.

I'm knackered. With mental relief as much as anything physical.

Bella snores softly, Ash clatters about in the van and Sam is lying on my feet.

The amazing aroma of coffee drifts from the van, along with the even more amazing smell of bacon.

'Here you go, don't say I never give you anything!'

I inhale. It smells heavenly. 'Oh my God, Ash. I love you!'

I didn't mean it like that. He knows it, but when I open my eyes, he's staring straight at me. We hold eye contact for a second, and then he winks and passes me a mug of coffee.

'A girl with simple needs?' He's studying me intently; it is a bit unnerving.

'Too true.' He smiles and breaks off the look. I wrap my mouth around the bacon sandwich. 'Now shut up and let me eat.'

He does shut up, watching in silence as I take a bite. I can't drag my gaze away from his face, his eyes. He's got the gentlest smile on his face, a hint of tiredness around his eyes, a stillness I've grown to love. It should be unnerving, being watched so intently, but it isn't. It is like the moment you see in the movies, that shared moment in bed when you wake in the morning. Face to face.

Not like any moment I've ever believed existed away from the big screen.

'That brown sauce on your nose is incredibly sexy, you know.' He breaks the spell.

'Tip I picked up online, how to catch a man.'

He chuckles, sending ripples of want swirling round in my stomach. 'Winner!'

'I know, now will you be quiet so I can eat this?'

'Didn't anybody ever tell you not to talk with your mouth full?'

'Not really. Oh my God, this is bliss.' I talk through the crumbs, and push Bella away gently with my foot. 'As good as sex, orgasmic, the best thing you've ever done.'

He chuckles. 'Guess I need to try harder in some areas then!'

Normally I'd blush, but right now I'm too busy wiping sauce off my chin and licking my fingers. Then wondering exactly what he means.

'Haha.' I knock back the rest of the coffee and sigh with contentment. Even with all the looks and suggestive comments, all I really want to do is curl up and go to sleep right now. Is that wrong?

'Come on, we should get you and the ragamuffin home.'

'You've read my mind.'

'Or the fact you're struggling to keep your eyes open!' He hauls me out of my seat. 'There's a shortcut back to the car. Can you make it, or do you need carrying?'

I'd love to be carried, but to be honest I reckon he must be at least as knackered as me. And I am totally and utterly knackered. I could sleep for a week. After I've bathed Bella and taken a long shower.

'You don't need to come.'

'I do. I want to check you're safe.'

We walk in companionable silence. Sam casting ahead then running back, his tail wagging all the time. Bella staying at our heels, between the two of us – occasionally glancing up, never straying far, and at some point along the way our swinging hands meet and our fingers entwine. And it feels right. Normal.

I'm almost sad when we turn a corner and I can see my little car.

'I can drive, if that's okay with you?' Ash's voice breaks the silence. 'Don't want you falling asleep and ending up in a ditch.'

I nod as I clamber into the passenger seat. Bella jumps onto my knee, rests her head on my chest and gazes up at me. Totally relaxed.

It was nice to see Ash's camper van; it feels like a shared secret. Our place.

I ruffle Bella's ears and gaze back into her gorgeous eyes. She's watching me steadily, knowingly and it makes me smile as I draw her warm body in closer.

'Did you plan this?' I whisper into her soft fur. 'Did you take us there on purpose?' She wriggles and licks my nose.

Okay, I'm being fanciful. Bella has no interest in bringing us together. She's just a dog.

She groans and sinks down on my lap.

'Okay?' Ash leans in and ruffles the fur on the top of her head, and I don't know if he's asking me or her. But I nod, share a smile with him. 'Ready to go?'

'Sure!' I think I'll just have forty winks on the way.

Chapter Twenty-Two

'**S**urprise!'

Oh hell. It is Saturday. How did I forget it was Saturday?

I don't know whether to laugh or cry. Whatever I expected when we got back with Bella, it wasn't a welcome party.

I stare and laugh slightly hysterically, clinging on to Ash's hand. And then I burst into tears.

'Oh, Becky, what's happened?' Mum rushes up, ignoring the very muddy Bella and wraps me in a big hug – which makes me blub even more.

I can't stop the steady stream. I wipe my face with the back of a very dirty hand and sniffle.

'Darling, are you okay?' She alternates between holding me at arm's length to study my face and wrapping me up in her arms.

'They're happy tears.' I hiccup.

'Happy? But you look…'

'The dog got lost,' says Ash, the master of understatement. 'We've been out looking for her.'

'Since dawn!' I hiccup.

'Oh no, oh, you do love your animals, don't you, Becky? She was so upset when she was little if anything happened to one of the dogs, a thorn in a paw and she'd be distraught, bandaging it up and calling the emergency services.'

'I did not!' I discover I am capable of stopping the tears. 'You exaggerate so much!'

'No, she doesn't,' says Abby. 'You can be so drippy.' But when I glance at her she's got the daftest of smiles on her face, which nearly sets me off again. Instead I disentangle myself from Mum and go to hug her.

'Eurgh no!' she yells, backing off. 'The state of you, honestly Becs, have you been mud wrestling or something?' Then she looks over my shoulder. Ash chuckles and my cheeks burn.

'No, I haven't!'

She grins. 'Would quite understand if you had.' Then she mouths the word 'buff' at me and does a tiny thumbs-up. Ed, who is standing next to her, laughs. I've never heard him laugh like that before, he's usually pretty stuffy and doesn't say much. I only love him because Abby does, and I trust her judgement.

'Shut up Abby! This is Ash by the way.'

'Ahh, I thought it must be. The dog-napper!'

'Abby!' I need a hole to open up so that I can fall into it.

'Really? You've told your family I'm a dog-napper?' Ash drawls.

'Only Abby, although they do all know now.'

He raises an eyebrow but doesn't look cross. 'Ash, this is my mum, dad, Abby, her fiancé Ed, and, oh, and Daniel.' My jaw drops at the sight of my brother, who I really wasn't expecting at all. 'You came!'

'How could I miss something like this?' He chuckles, and it reminds me of chubby baby brother Daniel. Before he became serious over-achiever hot-shot Daniel, the barrister who I never saw because he was too busy and important.

Maybe he never has been too busy and important. Maybe that bit has been in my head.

I grin at him. We've never been big on hugging each other. He gives me a thumbs-up too. 'This family would be so boring without you, Becs!'

'Daniel!' shouts Mum, and Dad just chuckles.

I look from one to the other of them. 'But you're all early! Way early. You aren't supposed to be here for hours.'

'I know, isn't it, er, fabulous?' says Mum. 'We thought we'd set off early and beat the traffic.'

Abby sniggers. Dad grins. But it is Daniel who actually laughs properly.

'Only you, Becs, only you could invite us over for a party and arrive last, caked in mud.'

'Well, actually I didn't invite any of you, Mum did.'

'And a jolly good thing I did, or we'd all miss out on seeing this fabulous place, and your lovely boyfriend and ador—' She stops herself, staring at Bella, who is now trying to jump up at her. 'And the dog.'

'Do you want me to hose it down?'

'Yes, Daniel, I'd love you to hose her down, but she likes warm water and soap suds.'

'Bit of a princess eh? Not like you at all then!'

'And you'll need to blow dry her.'

'I've changed my mind.'

'Oh no, you offered!'

'I'll help,' Ed unexpectedly chips in. 'As long as there's a beer in it.'

'And *we* can talk about the wedding!' Mum chips in, which explains why Ed and Daniel are so keen to wash dogs. They saw this coming, In fact, from the look on their faces, they heard it all the way over in the car.

'Cooeee, is anybody in?'

We all turn around. A vision in pink and black is walking up the driveway, followed by a man staggering along under a big box, with what looks like a camera bag slung over his shoulder.

'Oh shit.'

'Don't swear, Becky!'

'Expecting somebody else?' Ash asks, raising an eyebrow, humour in his voice.

'I thought I heard voices,' says the girl, smiling broadly at each of us in turn. 'Sorry we're a bit late!'

I glance at my watch. It is 11 a.m. How can it be that time already?

'HappyDogzDinnerzzz, I presume?' I feel a bit light-headed. I want to scream 'Go away!' but I am remarkably restrained. I smile.

'Spot on!' the woman says, pointing at her chest. The name is emblazoned across her T-shirt in gold. How did I miss that?

'I don't think we're in a fit state.'

She suddenly spots Bella and beams, then starts to laugh. 'Well, we do like natural! No additives.'

'No, no way, no, no, no – Georgina will kill me if you take a single picture of her baby looking like this!' I grab Bella, cover her head with one hand and hang on as she starts to wriggle like mad, splattering me with even more mud, if that's possible. 'I need to bath her first!'

I look down at her, and she gazes straight back at me with her gorgeous big round tawny-brown eyes. She's happy, but she's tired. She's been out all night, on her own, scared and hungry. I know exactly what I need to do.

'Look, I don't know how far you've come, but you really will have to go.' Georgina will sack me. But right now, I don't care. I am a bit shocked to find I have a firm edge to my tone, rather than an apologetic or embarrassed one though. Maybe I'm getting better at this 'doing things my way' thing. 'She's had a traumatic night, and she needs food and a good sleep.' I think she might have had food. Ash reckoned there was half a pack of ham, a rabbit stew and a good portion of carrots missing. 'You'll have to come back another day.'

'Stop for a canape and some bubbly though if you like!' Mum says.

'I'll go, if everything's in hand?' Ash's voice is soft in my ear, but somehow bat-ears Mum hears.

'Oh no, *you* have got to stay! He's got to stay, hasn't he Abby? You sound so interesting. I need to get to the bottom of this dog-napping thing!'

I look at him. 'You don't have to; I wouldn't inflict my mum and her interrogation techniques on anybody.'

He shrugs and grins. His dimples deepen. He really does suit the mud-splattered, not-shaved-for-a-few-days look. 'I've suffered worse.'

'You think?'

His chuckle sends a tremor straight between my thighs.

'Now go on you two, go and get a shower while the boys bath the dogs, and I'll get the food out of the car. I think we should crack the champagne open at twelve, don't you?'

It's a bit embarrassing, 'going to get a shower' with Ash, on my mother's instructions. But we decide to do it anyway.

———————

'My goodness, this place is idyllic, Becky. Aren't you clever, finding it?' Mum is happy. She has laid her food out on the table on the terrace, picked some flowers from the garden for the vase, supervised the baths for the dogs, and 'organised Dad'. I think that means she sent him on an errand into the pantry to find the few bits she'd 'forgotten'. Mum doesn't forget anything, but she's very good at finding things for people to do. 'Busy hands make happy hearts' was one of her sayings when we were younger, which made me and Abby snigger and wriggle our fingers about suggestively when we got to a certain age. 'You two have got filthy minds' was always Daniel's retort, before he'd stick his head back in a boring book.

'Isn't she clever?' she asks Ash.

He smiles. 'Very, it's wonderful.' He sits back, quiet, but totally relaxed with my family.

'Such an amazing view! And it has inspired you, hasn't it, Becky?'

'Sorry?'

'Oh, those pictures are adorable! That flying unicorn!'

'Pony. You've been looking in my study?'

'Of course I have! You don't often give me the opportunity; very secretive, she is,' she says as an aside to Ash. 'Has she shown you them?' She doesn't give him time to reply. 'So much better than that dry stuff you did when you were with that Teddy boy. He drained you, didn't he?' I nod, speechless. 'He was so possessive—' she directs that at Ash '—couldn't cope with the competition of family, could he?' She smiles back at me, squeezing my hand. I'd never thought about it like that. 'And that painting of the lake! Oh, my goodness me, Becky you are a clever girl. The way you did the water, and that lovely little boat place. Your grandfather would have been over the moon.'

'Grandad?' My grandparents died when I was young. Daniel, Abby and I never really knew them that well. We had hazy memories of sitting on the beach with them, of being served tinned potatoes and peas, of special lemonade, and of ice-creams and donkeys. But how many of the memories were real, and how many we re-imagined as we looked at photographs, I'm not sure.

'Oh yes, pour the bubbly, dear!' Dad uncorks the bottle on command and smiles at me. 'Oh, your grandad was quite the artist, wasn't he?'

Dad nods. 'He was very keen, sad when his eyesight went like it did.'

'He always said he wished he'd followed his heart earlier and done more, too late when you're dead he used to say.' She pauses for a moment. 'He was one of a kind, was Dad.' She studies me, strangely silent for a moment. Mum isn't one for silences. 'You're like him, you know. He would have been so proud of you, love, over the moon.' She sighs. 'He did love this part of the world. We used to bring him here for the day, and he'd set up a little easel down by the water. He'll be looking down on you and overjoyed that you followed your heart and did that art degree. He told me to encourage all of you to do what you really wanted, he said it was braver to follow your gut, than follow the money. Although he did also say that an empty bank account meant an empty gut and sometimes a broken heart, so who was he to say?'

'I didn't think anybody in our family painted!'

'Well, not seriously, Becky. Not like you have as a career. Try that couscous, I put some mint in it.' She fusses around for a moment, then settles back in her chair. 'Have you seen that picture of the lake she's done, Ash?'

He nods. 'It's very good.'

'I knew you'd appreciate it, not like that silly boy she went out with before. He was all modern stuff, straight lines and deep meaning.' She says 'meaning' as though it's a dirty word, and it makes me smile. 'Honestly, talk about the emperor's new clothes, who on earth wants to look at pictures they don't understand? I think you should have put a boat in it though Becky, not that I'm interfering or anything, but people like boats. Don't you think? It might sell better.'

'Oh Mum.' Abby laughs. 'Have another drink and shut up.'

'I don't want to sell it,' I say softly.

But Ash is studying me silently and his look says it all. People *do* like boats. Sitting on the lake with him in the middle of nowhere – our own little island – had been the place he'd finally decided he could show me a deeper part of the real him.

'She's right,' says Daniel. 'The one thing I really remember about coming here, is the boats. These sausage rolls are weird, Mum.'

'You just remember the boats, not the gingerbread?' asks Abby.

I grin, and so does Ash.

'Oh, you sod! You told him about pushing me in the river!'

'That's enough, children! And they are not weird Daniel, it's a recipe I got from the TV, though I hadn't got smoked paprika so I put chilli powder and turmeric in – they're the same colour if you mix them together.'

He rolls his eyes. 'It's about taste, not colour!'

'Says the boy who grew up putting tomato ketchup on absolutely everything!'

Abby slips her arm through mine, leans her head on my shoulder like she did when we were younger and shared secrets. 'I like him,' she whispers.

'So do I,' I whisper back.

'I've always been jealous of you, big sis. I wanted to be

the creative, daring one instead of the predictable boring sister, but you've really done it this time!'

'I have?'

'Phew, yes, I mean look at him!' She spells it out slowly, word by word. 'And all this, the pictures... dog... this place. It is so you.'

'I'm going home soon!'

'Yeah? You sure that's what you want?'

For a moment our gazes lock, and I know she's searching my face for an honest answer. I don't respond, because I can't. I'm not sure I want to go home. Where is home? I've had the best time ever since I've been here. It's an amazing place, better than I could ever have imagined when I hit submit on that house-sitting site. I've never for one single second felt out of place, like I don't belong here.

And I've met a man who makes my pulse race in a way nobody else has ever done. A man who believes in me, a man who makes me feel safe.

I thought I belonged in the city, in my cramped flat, with my hectic lifestyle.

I thought all I wanted from Ash was a fling and some fun.

'Sausage roll? They're disgusting by the way!' Dan, a sausage roll in each hand, plonks himself between us, just like he used to do when we were kids.

'Oh, you are cheeky!' Mum lobs one at him, scoring a direct hit on his nose. Not at all what she used to do when we were children. Or ever.

This place has a *very* funny effect on people.

Chapter Twenty-Three

It is late by the time everybody goes. I wander back round to the terrace, stand and take in a deep breath of pure air, then smile at Ash.

Abby's question pops back into my head. *Am* I sure about what I want?

'I spotted a nice red wine in the utility room. Fancy a glass?' He pads into the house in his bare feet and Bella follows close behind. He comes back with glasses and a bottle. 'I've left her in her basket to chill, she's worn out.' Then we wander down the lawn without even discussing it and settle on the grassy bank where you get the best view of where the boathouse used to be.

Our shoulders are touching.

I feel like he's a buddy, somebody who I can rely on, a man who'll always have my back. It's the most comfortable I've felt with anybody ever, apart from with Mum, that is – when I was young, and she'd fold me into her arms, read

331

me a story and tell me that yes, I could be that princess, I could be anybody I wanted to be.

'Thanks, for everything. For finding Bella, for staying.'

'I told you, it was teamwork! They're nice, your family. I didn't expect them to be quite that chilled to be honest.'

'Nor did I. To be honest.' I smile back at him. 'It must be this place.' I take a sip of my wine. It's warm and fruity. 'They're always hyper busy doing important stuff. Abby's a solicitor like Dad, and Daniel's a barrister.'

'Smart family.'

'And I'm the odd one out.' I pull a goofy face.

'Definitely odd.' He chuckles, that sound that never fails to make me feel happy inside. His arm has somehow found its way over my shoulder. He squeezes.

I'm beginning to wonder if a lot of being the misfit is in my head though. Today has been good. Today, here, in this wonderful place it was like back when we were kids. Competitive, but in a healthy, not destructive, way. It has reminded me how much I love them. All of them.

'Hey.' He's put his wine down and reaches over, placing his hand over mine. I freeze, not quite sure if this is good or bad. 'You're different, not odd, you know. Different is good.'

'You reckon?'

'I know.' He kisses the top of my head, then rests his chin there.

This seems very good. I think. I clear my throat and try not to think about just how close he is, and what it could mean. 'Mum never told me that Grandad used to paint.'

'They're proud of you.'

I play with the blades of grass. 'I know. But they've never said so before.'

He shifts sideways slightly, so I can see his gorgeous face. His serious, steady gaze. 'People don't always. Do they? Say, I mean.'

'But sometimes you need them to. I was sometimes a bit jealous of Daniel and Abby, the perfect children.'

'Unlike you, the little tearaway?' He grins, but it's not his normal full-bodied, cheeky grin, there's a gentleness in it.

'You know what I mean. They met all the expectations.'

'You've done what you truly wanted, what you believed in, not what you thought other people wanted you to.'

'Not entirely, I've gone off-piste a bit now and then, trying to please other people and believing they know best.' Like bloody Teddy. Honestly, I feel more of an idiot for not realising he was controlling me like he was, than I do about the fact that he didn't really fancy me at all.

'But not for fame and glory?'

'Oh no.' I laugh. 'I've always felt I was the one who couldn't even get a proper job, let alone a house or a husband.'

'Do you want any of those?' His voice is soft.

'I'd like a house, a home, like this.' I gaze over the still water. 'I bet you miss this place. I mean, I know you've got your camper van, and it's lovely and...' He must have felt like he was living in a different world when he was here with Georgina.

'Small, and hidden in a glade?'

'Yeah. But it is cute. But...' I wave a hand. 'All this.'

'I do miss it.' His half smile is wry and he settles back, propping himself up on one elbow. 'More than you can possibly imagine.'

'Tell me about the boathouse. If you want to, that is.'

'You know how you laughed when I told you that boat you borrowed was called Ginny?'

He's changing the subject. Fair enough, if he doesn't want to talk to me about the boathouse. 'I do.'

'She's actually called Virginia, after my grandmother.' He pours more wine, somehow settling in closer to me afterwards.

We're lying side by side on the grass, and his fingers are practically touching mine. He traces a circle in the grass with his finger, so close to touching the back of my hand that the blades of grass tickle it. 'My grandparents lived in the Lakes all their lives. They lived and breathed it; they didn't want anything else. And…' His gaze locks onto mine, his startlingly clear blue eyes deeper than the colour of any ocean. Better than the colour of any sky. 'I spent as much time with them as I did my parents. More, probably. They were abroad a lot, Mum and Dad, foreign service, and I was in boarding school here. My grandparents visited, I stayed with them in the holidays.'

'That's lovely, I hardly knew mine. I wish I did.' Is it a memory, or imagination, the feel of Grandad's hand over mine as I draw? A shiver runs through me, and it's a physical ache. Wishing his touch was real. 'I can only remember tiny snippets, and I don't even know if they're real or feelings I've made up from what I've been told. I don't even know how much I loved them, or if I really did inherit my love of art from Grandad.'

He squeezes my hand. 'I can't imagine. I know you can't get them back, but maybe you should talk to your mum more about them?' He lets go and lies back on the grass; his wine glass cradled in one hand. 'That boathouse you painted was theirs.'

'Your grandparents? They had a boathouse here? By this house?' This is weird.

He smiles, but his lips are thin. 'I loved that place, it was my childhood, my adventures, my growing up, my grandparents, all wrapped up in one.'

I don't know what to say. He sounds so sad. He wraps one arm round my waist, holding me there. 'Georgie didn't think, she didn't realise what she was destroying. She certainly snapped me out of my brooding though! We should have talked properly earlier before it got to that, but I'd just retreated, wanted privacy, and so she went after fame and recognition. She wanted the likes, the admiration, everything I'd stopped giving her. I suppose I should have seen it was getting out of hand earlier, I should have done something. Talked to her more, like when she posted that photo of me.'

'Ah, that photo.'

He sighs. 'I didn't even know she'd taken it; I didn't know it was on her account for the world to see until days after when somebody joked about it in the pub.' He stares straight into my eyes. 'I was in uniform, I was identifiable, this place was. I have a rule; I never used to bring work home.' He waves a hand in the vague direction of the house. 'That's why there are the fences, the gate.'

'So, she at least did do that for you?'

'Did what?'

'Had it all fenced, the gate, everything.'

He levers himself up on his elbow again, then cups my chin in his hand. 'Oh Becky.' The tone of his voice starts up a swirl of unease in my stomach. 'I thought you'd guessed, this place is mine, not hers.' My heart blips and my lips part as his words form in my head, as everything I knew about him and Georgina splinters and reforms. 'Lake View Cottage belonged to my grandparents and I inherited it.'

'Yours?' I squeak. I don't know what else to say.

'It was my refuge, my place to hide away when I came home, to regroup, get my head back together again.'

'But, but, the camper van, the… I'm house-sitting, I… I saw Georgina.' I take a big gulp of wine. I think I'm in shock. I think I'm blinking like an owl. 'I didn't know! How could you let me think…?'

'I couldn't just tell her it was over and turf her out, could I? We had an agreement. I said she could stay until July, when she'd had time to get something sorted out. I said I'd give her space. I've got somewhere else to stay. She hasn't, and this place—' he waves a hand '—is her livelihood, she needed to find somewhere else where she could do what she does.'

'But she said…'

'I hurt her. It was my fault, Becky. That's why she couldn't just let me have Bella, it's her way of hurting me back. I let her down, I know I did. I changed as well, I wasn't this action man she'd bought into. I came home and wanted to shut everybody out. It was me and Bella against the world.' He gives a wry smile.

'Why didn't you tell me?' I say quietly.

'I could have.' He shrugs. 'And what? You had an arrangement with her, not me. It wouldn't have been fair on you to muddy the water. And I did say she could stay here for a few months.'

'With Bella?'

'With Bella. She was in bits about losing Bella as well as this place.'

'And in bits about losing you,' I say quietly. 'That could be why she's so upset.'

'I let her down, I'll let anybody down in the end.'

'No way.' I shake my head. 'You'd never let people down.' I reach out, let my fingers touch his, and he lifts his hands slightly, so our fingers intertwine.

I'm very afraid I've fallen hard for this man. This man who is big in more than just a physical way.

'In her eyes I did. We're only as important as the view other people have of us.'

'Where will she go?'

'We had a place in the village, where we lived before I got this place. It's rented out now, but I've told her she can have it cheap if she wants for as long as she needs. And anyway, I prefer to be in the camper. It's quiet, I've got some head space.'

I grin. 'Not much.' I hold my hand over my head; he's far too tall to live in a camper van.

He chuckles. 'I'm outside most of the time.'

'And you do search and rescue?'

'Yeah, that's how I met Sam's owner. She broke her leg on the fell and asked if I'd look after him for a bit and keep him working. So, why does your mum think so little of Teddy?'

'Long story.' I smile.

He smiles back. 'I've got all night.'

'Well, I bloody haven't, I was up nearly all last night!'

'Never make a soldier of you, will I?'

I shake my head. 'Teddy was just a jerk; it was my fault for listening to him so much. I thought he knew best. But he's just a snob really, he called my paintings "chocolate box".'

'Ah, an intellectual snob, worst of the lot.'

'True. I mean he's welcome to his own opinion, but he can't just expect me to share it, can he?'

'Nope. I hate any kind of snobbery and one-upmanship. As my grandad used to say, don't diss somebody for trying – they could be the one that saves your life with an organ, or pushes you out of the path of a bus, or talks you down from the cliff edge.'

'Have you ever been on the cliff edge?' I ask softly.

'Not for a long time. But he was, my grandad – he lived with depression, that's partly why he loved it so much here. He said it mirrors your moods, you know that after every black day the clouds will eventually lift, and it will be beautiful again.'

'He was right.' I gaze over the lake. In the morning it will be bright and beautiful again. 'I'll really miss this place.' Talking about Georgina coming back, about her deadline at the cottage has brought it home to me how little time I've got left. I take a deep breath. 'I'll miss Bella, and…' I pause, 'I'll miss you.'

A smile lifts the corner of his mouth, and he leans in, so my head is cradled under his chin.

'I'll miss you too.' There's a long silence. 'I really will miss you, so will Bella.'

'I was looking at other places round here. Wondering if I could do another house-sit, come back.'

'After all the trouble you've had?' He chuckles and it reverberates through my body.

'Sometimes things are worth the trouble. Maybe if I did,' I carry on, slightly tentatively, 'we could meet up. Dog walk?'

'Sounds good to me. Or I could come and see you in your natural state?'

It's my turn to grin. 'You mean crummy flat, as opposed to you the caveman living in a camper in the woods?'

'Cheeky!'

I yawn. He strokes my hair gently. It's nice.

'You're knackered. I should go.'

'Back to your little camper in the woods?' I move away slightly, so I can look at him.

'Back to my little camper in the woods.'

'You don't have to, you could stay.'

'I could, but I won't.' Here we go again, except something deep in the base of my stomach tells me I shouldn't panic. It's okay. 'You need some rest.' He grins. 'And you need to clear up the bloody mess your family left! Fine way to look after somebody else's house!'

He pulls me in against his body, his arm round my shoulders, so that I can snuggle in and rest my head on his chest.

'It's not just your parents who are proud of you, you know. I am. It takes guts to pull the plug on something that's kind of working and get real, do what you were always meant to.' He hugs me tighter and I don't reply. I know I don't need to.

We stay there as the sun sets, as the bats swoop past us and out over the lake, as the sky above darkens to purple-black and the pinpricks of light break through the canopy and sprinkle the world with stardust.

Then hand in hand we walk up to the house, and he kisses the tip of my nose. And he leaves.

Chapter Twenty-Four

I know I shouldn't, but it is an addiction. Resistance is futile – like ignoring the last square in a bar of chocolate, or the last Pringle in a tube. I am hooked. Well, it's not like chocolate actually, it's a kind of morbid fascination. I know I'm not going to like what I see, but I have to look anyway.

Maybe it's just FOMO. Her life is better than mine and I'm hoping some of it will rub off on me.

Or maybe it's just something I like to beat myself over the head with. Maybe I have masochistic tendencies that I need to feed.

Well, whatever the maybe's, I am drawn to Georgina's Instagram page like a moth to the flame.

I mean, yeah, I know it's shallow and meaningless, and not the truth. You'd have to be a bloody good actor to look in pain like Ash did when he talked about her, if she is all sweetness, light and hard done by as she claims, and I don't think he is an actor.

Plus, Bella loves him, and I've always found dogs to be good judges of character. They have no need of artifice, no hidden motives to drive the way they react. But I still don't know how she does it.

Not the flash pictures, I do know about Photoshop and filters. I don't know how she has so many followers, so many likes, so many comments.

I am calling it research. Not stalking.

After all, if I could pin down just a fraction of her marketing capability it would help my own career no end. Especially if *Mischief* doesn't canter into the bestseller lists internationally.

I woke up yesterday morning expecting a barrage of messages from her asking me to explain why I'd turned away HappyDogzDinnerzzz, which would have given me a major headache.

There was so much that needed explaining.

Like how I'd managed to lose Bella, why I'd called in Ash, why we'd found her at his van, why my whole family were here having an engagement party on her, sorry Ash's (I have to keep reminding myself of that weird point) lawn a few hours later.

Luckily the girl from HappyDogz had enjoyed our champagne and entertainment tremendously, so much that she'd told Georgina it was all her fault and that they'd be back another day with extra freebies (she must have worked with Georgina before).

I don't think she mentioned the state of Bella. Or me.

Or Ash.

I therefore woke up to one brief (thank God) message

from Georgina with a rearranged appointment. At first, I couldn't see the urgency to cram pack her diary now, why not wait until she got back and could handle it herself? But I'm beginning to wonder if she's 'making hay while the sun shines' as they say, knowing that her days here and possibly with Bella are numbered.

Anyway, I read the message, replied with a 'great, thanks for letting me know' and then had an amazingly successful morning working.

Ash rang to check I was okay, that Bella wasn't suffering any ill effects from her escapades, and to say he had paperwork to do and so 'How about lunch tomorrow?' Lunch tomorrow sounded good to me.

So Bella and I had a gentle stroll along the edge of the lake, and I worked late into the night, because all of a sudden I found it hard *not* to work. And despite the late night, I woke this morning feeling fully refreshed.

And now I am on Instagram for my daily dose of torture.

#puppylove #adorable #mynewcrush #newaddition #bestfriend #cutenessoverload

What?! I am confused.

These hashtags (there are actually over twenty of them, and lots of hearts and dogs) are not accompanying a photo of Bella.

This is a puppy, a very tiny practically edible puppy. With big ears, ginormous round eyes and a cute squished nose. A puppy with a heart-shaped blob of white on its silver-grey chest. OMG, this puppy is photogenic.

Definitely not Bella. Not that Bella is not photogenic, I

didn't mean that. I meant everything else – size, colour, ears.

I double check. This is definitely Georgina's account.

I blink and read the description again. This is #romanticRomeo and he's being collected by Georgina as soon as she gets home #OMGcannotwait #myheart.

Her last hashtags are #babymakesfour! #HappyFamilies!

Baby makes four? What does she mean, four? Four?

Happy family?

Four as in her, Bella, baby four paws, and who? Not Ash, surely not Ash? But she's not mentioned another man to me. My throat is dry. Not that she would tell me a thing, it's none of my business.

I don't care that it is none of my business. I need to know it isn't Ash! I feel sick.

He said she wanted to try again. Is she going to make a play for him, try and win him back?

The photo has masses of likes and comments. Puppies it seems are worth lots of sponsorship and publicity.

#puppiesruleokay!

Not bloody okay. Puppies do not rule.

What about Bella? What about Ash?

They were in love once though, and if Georgina turns the clock back, shows a bit of the old caring her, will he fall head over heels again?

After all I'm only the house-stroke-dog-sitter who will soon be going back to her own home. Out of sight, out of mind.

Did he simply think I was part of the fixtures and fittings?! Fresh sheets?

No. No, I'm being silly. I refuse to believe that.

There has been nothing, absolutely nothing to suggest he'd consider getting back with Georgina. And nothing to suggest he's been having me on. He's seemed so genuine.

So kind. Like he cared.

Okay, it was a shag (well several) and a snog or two. But we had a *totally* intimate evening of practically no touching.

And she hurt him, she really hurt him. I didn't imagine that look on his face, or the tell-tale crackle in his voice.

But four? Have I missed something?

I am being totally silly. Overreacting. I need to give myself a slap, take a deep breath and calm down.

It is obvious. Georgina is just moving on. She's taken a break to get her shit together and plan her future. She has found a new dog to replace Bella, because she has forgiven Ash, no, she has seen she is being mean and Bella is his, and she has a found a new man for her new life. Away from here and Ash.

But she said four!

My head hurts. Probably because I just thumped my palm against it. And because I seem to have forgotten how to keep breathing.

And my hand hurts. I suddenly realise I am clutching my mobile phone with rigid fingers, so I force myself to relax my grip.

It's odd that she's even managed to buy a puppy while she's been away though. She didn't tell me where she was going, but she's not a difficult person to track.

Her whole life is spread out on social media for the world to see. I can understand why Ash found it difficult living that way.

Who wants every aspect of their life on show? Especially if you're a private person, like Ash is. Like I am. I mean, apart from the risk of some weirdo stalking me (unlikely, but possible) then posting where I am, it isn't that much of a risk for me, is it? Not like for Ash, who has always counted this house as his safe place. Where he's hidden from danger.

But you could monitor Georgina's every move from your couch. She's been in New York most of the time (#NYC #Diner #Newforkcity) – so how did she find Romeo? Pick-a-pet-online?

OMG, my brain freezes along with my wandering fingers – she's in London now! She's getting close. She's just posted a picture of Covent Garden (#lovelondon).

Something curdles in the base of my stomach. Anticipation. I know it's irrational. It's her house, she's due back soon, but it feels, I don't know – threatening?

Somebody has set the timer, we're on a countdown to when I have to go, and all of a sudden, I really don't want to.

I'm not ready.

I want to do that walk up to the tarn. I want to spend more time with Bella. I want to find more beautiful spots to take pictures. I want to see the kingfisher again, watch the bats at dusk, hear the birds in the morning. Draw Mischief in the wonderful magical setting. Paint.

But if I'm honest, the thing I really hear the clock

clicking towards its final fateful chime about is me and Ash. I want to get to know Ash better.

I need to spend more time with him. Talk again about coming back.

I don't know what we have, or what we don't.

I only know that he makes me feel like I'm doing okay. That I'm who I should be, where I should be.

I'm not ready to say goodbye yet.

I am staring at the photo when I hear a noise at the front door.

'In here! I need to show you something!' Ash will love this. I don't get the whole 'four' thing, but maybe that's just Georgina and her make-believe perfect life that she can't let go of? Surely the puppy will help with his battle to get Bella back? Georgina will have Romeo, so Ash will feel less guilty for a start. All he has to do is be patient until she comes back, then everything will work out.

'What?' The voice at the door makes me spin around in my seat. It is not Ash arriving early for our lunch date; it is not a male voice.

Georgina looks like she's just stepped out of an Instagram picture herself. She has sun-kissed, golden-brown skin, designer sunglasses, sleek, caramel, highlighted hair and statement earrings that just shout out 'you'll rip your ear lobes off' to me.

I've not actually seen her in real life before, but this is

everything and more than I expected. She looks confident, polished, sophisticated. I stare, open-mouthed.

Bella barks, so she takes the sunglasses off. 'God, shut up, you daft animal! What is it about you and sunglasses? It's me!' She sighs melodramatically.

Bella, confident now that it actually is her mistress, and she's not been taken over by goggle-eyed aliens, bounds over and sits at her feet. For a moment Georgina ignores her, then relents and bends down to pat the dog on her head.

It is at this moment that I know. Some things, some people are wrong. Georgina doesn't truly love this little dog; Bella really would be so much better off with Ash – who would move (or at least climb) mountains for her if necessary.

I have, kind of, come to like Georgina. I've felt some kind of kinship, in my head. I'd thought maybe I could help her move on – because I understand. Reality has hit though. The Georgina in front of me is not the one in my head, or the one on the Zoom call. She looks unstoppable. And a bit mean. How can she ignore Bella?

'What do you need to show me?' She gazes around. 'It looks tidy enough in here. Have you kept on top of the garden?' I nod. 'Oh, you're a fan!' Georgina spies her account on my phone, puppy photo on display, and is at my side in an instant, the garden forgotten. 'You've seen him! Isn't my little baby just adorable? I saw him on Facebook and just could *not* walk away, know what I mean? Look at that heart on his little chest! He will absolutely kill Valentine's Day.'

She pulls her own phone out and starts to flick through photos to show me. She has hundreds. 'They're delivering him in a couple of days, that's why I came home early! Oh my God, I can't tell you how much all the marketing people love him. Bella's lost that puppy appeal, I mean she's still quite pretty, but I could just see numbers were going down.'

She pauses to take a breath and glances at Bella, who is sitting, her head tilted to one side as though she's taking every word in, then starts again. My heart is going to break. I want to pick Bella up and hug her, tell her we still all love her. She's the best.

'It's sad, but hey ho, that's life I suppose. While I was away, I had loads more time so I really studied the stats, and talked to the people that know, and, you know, the influencers, and I just knew it was time to change direction. I was going to get one of those teacup puppies, yah? The teeny ones?'

I nod, wondering where Bella fits into all this, wondering how the hell you take a 'teacup puppy' for a walk round here. You'd lose it down rabbit holes, it would drown in the shallowest of becks. You'd have to keep it on one of those extendable leads so you could yank it up like a yo-yo at regular intervals.

I suppose it would fit in a rucksack though. Or a pocket. *'Ooh, look what I've got,'* you could say, fishing one out of each pocket of your shorts, as if by magic! I'm starting to see the appeal.

Bella whines and paws my knee, so I fondle her ears, imitating the way Ash does it, and try and tell her telepathically that she's not been replaced in anybody's affections. Well, not mine, or Ash's. I'm withholding judgement on Georgina.

'But when I thought about it, they're a bit limiting, aren't they?'

'They are?'

'Well, there are so many products they can't be ambassadors for.'

I hadn't realised it was all about being an ambassador. I thought it was about cuddles and fun and being woken up by having your toes licked.

'Like Bella, now she's older. There's a mega market we're missing out on. Even the party was a bit of a let-down, I had much better feedback for her first birthday, and apparently pugs are more photogenic.'

'They aren't!' I cover her ears.

'Oh, don't be sentimental, of course they are. Or dogs with three legs or some other issue, you know a cute disability.'

Did she just say cute disability? I want to slap her, I really, really want to slap her, or shout at her. I have never slapped anybody in my life, and probably never will, but right now I cannot believe the self-serving drivel that is coming out of her mouth.

It is hard, no impossible, to get my head round what Ash told me. That she was nice once, was kind.

I should pack right now. I should get out.

But I can't. I can't leave Bella with her.

And being practical, I don't know where I'd go.

Georgina has come back early. Why is she early? Why couldn't she wait a few more days for her puppy delivery?

I'm supposed to be staying here a few more days. It's not fair!

'And the market is totally flooded, flooded with cockapoos. They're everywhere! And black isn't that great for photos if I'm totes honest. That was a mistake.' She rolls her eyes, and I know exactly who she is blaming for that. 'Multi-coloured ones are much better. So then it was like fate, I found this puppy, or it found me! That photographer told me this is just what I need! How frigging cute is he? Totally adorbs! I mean those ears, oh God, to die for! I've already got all kinds of doggy bling lined up. French bulldogs are the thing in the States you know? And look.' She jabs at the picture. 'All smooth and silky and gorgeous, tiny little feet, less mess!'

'He's adorable.' He is. I look. I smile. I stroke Bella apologetically, feeling like I am betraying her.

'Ash is so bloody in love with him!'

'Ash is?' I am gobsmacked. How has Ash seen him?

'Oh God, yah. He's like totes dog mad, one was never enough.' She laughs; is it me, or does it sound totally false?

I think I'm turning into Queen Bitch. Which isn't really me at all. But I think I hate her. Bella clambers up onto my knee, licks my chin then leans her warm body against my chest. Some part inside me calms down as I hug her close. I realise I don't hate Georgina. I don't need to hate anybody.

'Oh God, he won't have told you? I only just like sorted this, like yesterday.' Yesterday? When he was busy doing paperwork? 'I mean, I do know he's been here, oh shit, don't feel guilty.' I wasn't feeling guilty, I'm past that. I was wondering if this is a new stage of grief for

Georgina. I vaguely remember there being anger (we had that at the start when I arrived *very* late), and denial (is this super-denial?), and depression (she was so upset), then I'm pretty sure bargaining is in there. Is this another level up of that? I'm not sure, all I do know is that acceptance doesn't seem to be on the agenda yet. 'I get that, you know he could never keep away from me and Bells, and it made me like sad.' Denial. We're definitely still stuck in denial. She pulls a sad face, the corners of her mouth downturned. 'I had time to think, like with him not in my face, and I get it!' She finishes on a triumphant high. 'He's been feeling neglected cos of all the time I spend on Insta with my fans, and it must be difficult cos he had all those men looking up at him for so long and now, like nothing.'

I nod, dumbfounded, not quite sure what to say.

I want to say that maybe it's a bit of guilt on his part too, that he felt bad he couldn't give her what she needed. But I don't think she'd get it. And let's be brutally honest here – a little bit of me is being selfish. I don't want to be matchmaker, peacemaker. I fancy the pants off him. But he's not mine to keep, is he? This is just a fun interlude for both of us. Neither of us are ready to move on. Are we?

'So I thought, you know what, maybe he's a little bit right, so I got him Romeo!' Georgina is chatting on regardless.

'You got the dog for him? Not for your Insta?'

'Haha, you're so funny! Yah well, for my Insta as well, but he does both. He's brought us together already, look! I was just about to load this, when you shouted!'

It is a close-up of Ash. You wouldn't know who it was, if you didn't know him. But I do – know him, know who it is.

I've lost myself in those gorgeous blue eyes, gazed at that very slightly crooked nose, studied every single line on his face until I know them better than any map.

Okay, this is weird.

Half the photo is of baby Romeo, cradled in his big safe hands at chin height, masking his lips, his smile, his heart-clenching dimples. The cleft in his chin.

But I can see the hint of laughter lines fanning from the corners of his mouth, sense the happiness in his gaze.

My throat constricts… Shit. I feel like crying. I can't say a word, if I open my mouth I might sob or puke up. All over her. Maybe not a bad idea.

'I've not even got Romeo yet and we're already so much closer. Ash can train him and stuff, he loves doing things like that, it makes him feel useful. Oh God, enough talk, I need a drink. Oh shit.' She grabs my upper arms in a talon-like grip. 'What the fuck was I thinking? I've been going on about my fab life, and you've been standing there thinking I'm about to throw you out! Oh shit, no, stop looking so worried, girl. Look, it's up to you if you like: go tomorrow or stay.' That is not the bit that's upset me, but I can't 'fess up, can I? 'You've saved my life, being here, giving me headspace. I totes get it if it's a bit awks with Ash, you know, with him and me and you being the gooseberry! Haha!' I think I am being warned off. 'But let's sort that tomorrow eh? I so need a drink, and somebody to, you know, like chat to, proper girlie talk?' She rolls her eyes. 'It's been all like marketing speak, and work, and like I need to be just chilled and stuff! You will stay at least tonight? I've brought more wine!'

A girlie night in was not what I was imagining tonight.

A girlie night in with Georgina was not something I was imagining would happen ever, or should I say *evah*.

'Oh, er, sure, that would be…' What? Not lovely, or fab. 'Nice! I'd planned on doing a bit of work, then taking Bella for a walk. If that's okay? Unless you'd rather?'

'Oh God, no. I'll have a shower, I must absolutely stink after that drive, and I've got to check messages and stuff. Feel free, have some Bella time before you have to go! Catch up with you later, just carry on as normal. Pretend I'm not here!'

That is easier said than done.

She goes upstairs, dragging her case behind her. A clunk, clunk, clunk up the stairs that makes Bella flinch and me cringe. She switches the shower on and starts to sing. Loudly.

Bugger. Bugger. Bugger.

Bella goes under the table; I half expect her to put her paws over her ears.

No way can I stay and compete with that. It will be like trying to work in the middle of a rock concert, where you hate the band.

Right.

Put a positive spin on this.

This could be my last chance to capture the beauty of this place. I throw things into my rucksack in a kind of silent tantrum, which makes me even more annoyed. As does the fact that Ash seems to have gone AWOL. I check my phone again. He's now late for lunch and he's not replied to my earlier messages, and I've got no missed calls. Although I suppose if he'd called or dropped in at the time Georgina arrived, it would have been more than embarrassing. Things are bad enough as they are. Maybe my best bet is to slip quietly away first thing in the morning, and it will be just like it was a dream – nobody, including me, will remember I have ever been here.

I slip Bella's harness on and she licks my hand, as though she understands. It's more nightmare than dream. It hurts. I mean, really? Really? He's been puppy cuddling and I didn't know?

'Oh Bella, I never am going to get to see those red deer with you.'

She wags her tail and barks, tugging me along as we head down the garden. As my feet hit the crunch of the path, it's like something flicks a switch in my chest, my heart.

I come to a standstill and stare at the place where the boathouse once stood. I'm not going to run away. I'm worth more than that.

I am going to enjoy these last few days. I am going to sketch out the paintings I've got in mind for David and his art shop, and take a ton of photos, mix some sample colours, fix this place in my head.

I can no more run away in the night, than I can give up on my new career path.

Or give up Ash, unless I know that he means it, and this is not all a figment of Georgina's imagination.

Obviously, if Georgina and Ash start going at it hammer

and tongs in the bedroom, then I might revise this decision. But it will still be my decision.

Bella paws my leg, so I sink down onto the lush grass where she squeezes between my legs and rests her chin on my chest.

'Is it a bit weird, or is it me?' Her tail thumps on the grass. 'She said she just got the puppy, didn't she? She's been away. So how come there's a picture of it with Ash?' She licks my chin. 'And I chatted to him yesterday. He was his normal self. We arranged to see each other today, didn't we?' I swear Bella is smiling at me, then she rolls onto her back for me to tickle her tummy. I stroke her idly. Then it hits me, and I stare out at the lake without really seeing it. My fingers still.

I don't want to run away, and I don't want to believe Georgina, because I like Ash. I more than like him.

I don't want to leave here and go back to my old life – partly because of work, but mainly because of Ash.

I can't imagine spending days on end and not seeing him. Never seeing him again. How the hell did that happen?

I felt sorry for Georgina when she was at a distance, but now she's here and still determined not to let go of her perfect life, I feel something different altogether. I think it's jealousy.

That is scary. I'm not a jealous person.

My phone pings and I scramble to pull it out of my pocket. It's a text.

Sorry can't make lunch, emergency, somebody stuck on fells. See you later? Supper? Reception crap around here, will text you when I'm heading back Ash xxx

I rest my fingertip on the kisses, a stupid grin settling on my face. He hasn't forgotten, he hasn't stood me up.

'Oh God, Bella, what am I going to do? I think this is way more than sex.'

Bella flips over and leaps on me, her paws hitting me smack in the middle of my chest and sending me sprawling back onto the lawn.

She leans forward, hot, doggy breath fanning my face, her tail wagging ten to the dozen. 'Don't you dare say I told you so!'

I am sure she's done it on purpose. Georgina has laid out her bottle of wine, two glasses and some snacks on the table on the terrace – in exactly the same spot I sat with Ash after the party. God forbid she wants to end up gazing up at the stars with me later!

I mean, yeah, this is probably where she has sat with him before – but if she suspects we did anything at all (and I'm sure she does, from all the pointed comments) then she'll have a good idea we've sat here together.

She's been fishing; it's all been a bit strained and my gut is telling me that I'm not here for 'girl-time'. No, I'm here because she wants to know if anything has gone on between us before she sends me on my way.

She's ladling on the 'Romeo and Ash' bit to see if I react.

It's amazing how quickly the first bottle of wine goes down. It all starts off a bit awkward and stilted, especially when I say, 'So you liked New York then?'

'New York?'

'And London?'

She frowns.

'Where you've just been? All the hashtags, the breakfast, you know, New York Diner?'

It's like we're at complete cross purposes, and I've imagined everything, house-sitting, her trip, Ash…

'Oh fuck!' She laughs so hard she puts her hand over her mouth to stop herself tipping forward off her chair. 'Christ, you're funny! I've not been to New York. I went to a mate's in Cornwall!'

'Cornwall? But the airport, the hashtags…'

'Shit, you should see your face! I need a photo!'

'But on your Insta, your Facebook page?'

'But that's Insta! It's not real. You don't honestly believe what you read on there?' Well, at least I suppose she recognises it's not real. 'I just needed to get some space, give Ash some space so he could see what a dick he's being! Why would I go to New York?'

There are many answers to that question, but at the moment they escape me. So, I glug down wine, feel slightly stupid and naïve, and wish I was somewhere else. Anywhere else.

I don't think I like her.

I do not belong in Georgie's world. It is an alternative

reality and I don't think even she knows which bits are the truth and which she's made up.

Three glasses in and Georgina is on top form, all giggly and girly and full of funny stories about strange DMs she's had on Instagram – men who wanted to stroke her puppies were a dominant feature. Apparently, hashtags have to be chosen with care.

'Ash hated it; he is just so jealous, you know. He said it was so false, I mean, can you believe him? He didn't used to be like that. He says I've changed, but it was him.'

'I know. He said.'

'Oh.' That slows her for a moment, then she crashes on with what is beginning to sound like a prepared speech. 'I bet you haven't seen him in a temper, have you? Here, have some more wine.' She moves in closer to pour, then stays where she is, her voice lowering to a more confidential level.

I want to stop her, right now, I want to move away, but I can't. And where would I go anyway?

'He was just away, like so much of the time, and I was supposed to look after everything and be happy on my own. You know what that's like?' I nod, but she's not taking any notice. At the moment, this is about her, not me. 'I put so much fucking effort into this place then he'd just come home after three months and would he say thank you? Would he fuck! He'd fucking moan about me moving a clock or posting a photo of his precious place.'

She's already downed her wine and poured another, topping my glass up even though I've not had time to drink barely a mouthful. I take a gulp. I need to keep up, block her out a bit. 'He was worse after he left the Marines and was here all the bloody time, getting in moods and going for long fucking walks all the time to *clear his head*.' She laughs mockingly. 'Then he'd expect attention. He was jealous of me doing my own stuff, I was just supposed to drop everything, and he was so bloody selfish, taking Bella off for walks when he knew I needed her for some photos. He went fucking ballistic if I changed anything, but this place needs modernising, it's like living in a bloody museum.' She finally runs out of steam and pauses.

'But you're planning on getting back together again?' Hashtag happy families.

'Oh shit, yah.' She smiles, wraps her hands round her glass and tips her head on one side. When she speaks again it's back to the soft tone. 'We never actually split really. I mean I know I dissed him, but he annoyed me so fucking much. But it was just a misunderstanding, you know, things getting to a head and poof, exploding.' She throws her hands in the air as though she's throwing confetti. 'He didn't mean any of it, so I had to give him time to cool down, you know? Oh God, babe, he's not tried it on with you, has he?' Quite unexpectedly she pats my arm. 'He can be a real user, you know, to get his way, like with Bella. He's been here, hasn't he? Telling you what a baddie I am?' She chuckles. 'What a dick!' It's said with what sounds like affection. I guess some people do call each other names like that. 'Just ignore him. I reckon he actually thought it would be funny to nick her and get me all wound up!'

This is not the upset Georgina on Zoom. She's not come to terms with things at all while she's been away, she's been preparing herself to win him back. Set the clock back. Try again. Oh God, he's always been nice about her and I put it down to guilt, and the fact that he's so sorry, but did I get it wrong? Are they really meant for each other?

'He went to pick the puppy then, when you were in Cornwall, like he picked Bella?' I can hear a slight wobble in my voice. I'm trying to be reasonable about this, but really I want to yell at her.

'He told you he picked Bella?' She hasn't answered the question. I nod. 'Sounds like you two were quite cosy, seeing as I asked you to keep him out of the house,' she says, carelessly flicking something off her knee. 'It's getting a bit chilly out here actually, shall we go in?'

I suppose now is the time I should point out that it's his house, that he is (or at least I thought he was) a free agent and so am I. So what if he told me stuff? But I'm not going to let her draw me in, because even though I feel drunk, a bit light-headed, I'm sure she's baiting me.

First with her taunts about them getting back together. Now with her comments fishing about what's happened while she's been away. In Cornwall. Another lie. Another fabrication, part of her make-believe life. She even went to the airport so that she could take photographs and add them to her Insta account!

I don't know what is real, and what isn't. I do know that it's him I need to talk to, not her.

She doesn't wait for an answer. She stands up, leaving the empty bottles on the table and wanders up the side of the terrace casually, stopping by the patio doors that lead into the room I've used as a study.

'So...' She pauses, and it is almost like she's rehearsed the moment. It's all too casual. It is as though all the drink and chat, all the girlie camaraderie, has actually been leading up to this moment.

She pushes the door wider open, takes a step inside, and it's a bit like watching the picture break up on Zoom when the WiFi throws a wobbler. 'I wonder what else he's told you?' She gradually freezes, the last couple of words dripping off her tongue in slow motion. 'What. The. Actual. Fuck. Is. That?' She's got a pointy finger out, and it is shaking. I glance at her face again – big mistake. If you could bottle pure nastiness, this is how it would come out.

This is staged. She's been working up to it.

She is looking at my boathouse picture which is still propped up at the side of the desk, where the evening light catches it perfectly.

I don't know why I've left it there. No, I do. It makes me happy; it gives me pleasure. And it reminds me of Ash. It lets me imagine him as a boy – unscarred, innocent, full of hope and mischief.

There's a certain purity, a certain magic about it that I am proud of.

I don't think Georgina shares my feelings.

'It's the boathouse.' I try to keep the edge out of my voice and talk matter-of-factly, but I can hear the tremor. We're both wound up, the air is practically fizzing. 'The one that used to be here.' No judgement, I must not judge. It is none of my business. 'I saw a photo, and it just seemed to finish the picture off.'

'Why have you painted that?'

'Well, I'm an artist, it's an amazing view.'

'No. Why *that*?' She fixes me with a cat-like stare. Her eyes narrowed. 'Just how much time have you spent with him? He's been here, in the fucking house with you! I knew it!'

I wonder when she spotted the picture. How long she's been simmering inside. Since she got home? Since I went out with Bella? But I am pretty sure she's been working up to this.

Oh help, I hope she hasn't poisoned the wine! She could weigh me down and drop me in the lake and my body would never be found.

I have turned beetroot-red; I know I have. My guilt and embarrassment are overriding my fear of being murdered. I feel totally guilty and in the wrong. I agreed to look after her house, her dog. Stick to her rules. Okay it isn't actually hers, any of it, but I didn't know that at the time, did I? Does it count as a broken promise if it was all based on untruths?

I dare to look at her, and I'm shaking. But what I see isn't the Georgina who has been needling me since she got back. This isn't the Georgina who is full of bravado, acting out the way she'd like her life to be. She looks like she might crumble any moment and I calm down, the panic fades away and all I feel is desperately sorry. For her. 'Yes, he's been here.' She knows the truth; it is pointless pretending otherwise. I swallow hard and force the words out. 'I didn't know you two had got back...' Nope, good try, but I can't actually finish the sentence.

'That doesn't matter! I trusted you, and you sided with

him!' She looks more nervous and wound up than I feel. 'You shouldn't have talked to him!' There's a crackle in her voice.

'He really wanted to see Bella, he needed to,' I say softly. 'You know he did.'

'I needed her as well.' There's a stubborn edge to her voice.

I get it now; she was disparaging about Bella as a way of coping. She needs her, because letting go of Bella means admitting the relationship is over. She's failed.

'Romeo's cute, he'll be great on Insta.' He will. He can be part of her new start. 'It's so amazing, your account, it can be brilliant even if you haven't got Bella.' I pause, then say it because I can't not. 'Or Ash.' I just cannot believe he wouldn't have told me if they were trying again. I can't believe he'd say goodbye and wave me off, and minutes later welcome her back home. He's not some kind of confidence trickster who was just having a laugh with me. He told me about the boathouse. He told me about his grandparents.

Unless she just asked him to go and get the puppy, and he did it to appease her. Because he still feels bad.

'I need Ash.'

I glance down at Bella, who is lying down patiently. She's always ecstatic to see Ash, he's always chuffed to bits to see her. But Georgina? I don't think Georgina really loves the little dog at all. She's already lining up a new, more marketable upgrade. Not that any dog could be an upgrade on Bella.

'You don't need Ash.' We both turn to the door at the

sound of the deep voice, and Bella leaps up and launches herself at him. He catches her in his arms and looks at Georgina over her head as she licks his chin.

It is so obvious whose dog she is. It wouldn't matter one jot who had their name on the paperwork. There's one person in this room who loves her far more than the other. 'I didn't expect to see you here, Georgie.' His tone is mild.

'Why the fuck not? I live here! I…' She pauses. 'I didn't expect to see you here.' Georgina has gone pale.

'I wanted to make sure Bella was okay.' His voice is strangely detached. Not the tone of a guy who's just made it up with his ex after not seeing her for weeks.

'Oh, bloody Bella! You care more about that dog than you ever cared about me. Bella this, Bella that.' This does not sound like a woman who has bought another puppy as part of a 'getting back together' pact. She knows. In her heart she knows.

'That's not fair, Georgina. I cared about you.'

This is uncomfortable. 'Maybe I should er, go… pack?' Pack, haha. Even if I did have somewhere to go, I have been drinking. I've had far too much wine to even think about getting in the car. 'Go to my, er, room.' Now I sound like a child.

Although I'm not sure they'd notice at all if I disappeared into thin air. Which would be a better idea – Georgina is blocking access to all my work (and I am NOT going without that) and Ash is blocking the doorway. I jiggle about on the spot, not sure who it is safest to push past first.

'You didn't care enough to find out where I've been!'

'Georgie.' He sighs. 'We split up; you know it stopped working a long time ago. Me and this "dive" bore you to tears.' The way she flinches suggests that is one insult she has actually thrown at him. 'You're entitled to go away for a break while you decide what to do. Look.' He puts Bella on the floor. 'It was amazing while it lasted.' Eurgh, amazing. I can taste the bile catch at the back of my throat. I need to get away, crawl through his legs if necessary. I think I may have squeaked. 'But we're two different people now. I can't give you what you want. I need peace, quiet, I don't want my life on show.'

'But what about Romeo?' I look from one to the another, and instantly realise that I shouldn't have spoken. Ash is staring at me like I've lost my marbles.

His brow is furrowed into a frown. 'I don't think it's bad enough for suicide, unless you're my Juliet?' I swear there's a grin teasing at his lovely lips, and something inside me soars. Or it could be the effect of the wine. But either way it's very hard not to grin back.

'Oh God, I knew it.' Georgina is pale. I feel awful. 'I knew it. You didn't just invite him in here to talk about your... paintings.' She spins on her heel to face him, and staggers slightly. We really shouldn't have opened that third bottle. 'It's not enough to throw me out of my home—'

'Georgie, I have never thrown—'

'—take my dog, try your best to ruin my career, oh no. You want fucking everything, don't you, Ashley James? You have to win at any cost.' She laughs. 'Everything.'

'What the hell are you going on about?'

She taps her long, polished acrylic nails on my painting,

and I cringe. I want to snatch it off her, but I'm frightened of the reaction I'll get.

'You even have to *have* my house-sitter.' The way she stresses the 'have' makes me want to heave.

I really should have crawled between his legs and gone while I had the chance. This is horrible.

'Well, you know what? You can have *her*. Though from what I've heard she sucks at relationships even more than she sucks at painting!'

'Georgina!' He thunders her name so loudly we all jump. Bella yelps and dives out of the door, looking for cover, Georgina blanches so pale she looks like she hasn't seen the sun *ever*, and I shake but am still thinking about what she's just said. Where did she get that from? 'I googled you! Did you think I'd take you on without checking you out?' I blink. 'I knew he'd come sniffing around, and you don't think I wanted some kind of sex goddess waiting for him, did you? I was going to come back.' A sob lurks at the edge of her voice. Just as quickly as the bravado came, it dies away, leaving an awkward silence.

'I thought you were perfect. A little bit feisty, very distrusting and not much of a catch, and you had lost your job. You upset your ex so much you know, he said on Facebook how you wouldn't listen, however much he tried to help you, and how he'd found somebody who wasn't so selfish, who wanted to support him and who wanted to settle down, who'd actually commit to him!'

I think I am opening and closing my mouth goldfish-fashion. I finally find my voice; it comes out all small and strangled. 'He didn't want to settle down!' That had never been on the cards, never mentioned.

'Whatever, you betrayed him by stealing his ideas and…'

This time Ash doesn't bellow, he takes a step towards her. 'Georgie…'

'But I realise now that I don't want you after all, Ashley, you really are the sad, stupid man I thought. I've had time to think while I've been away, and I wouldn't take you back, not even if you begged. You can have her; you can have each other…'

'Georgina, it's not like that.' I shake my head. 'We're not about to run off together or anything, it's just… oh Georgina, I know what it's like to be in a relationship that isn't really working. I stuck with my ex Teddy for all the wrong reasons, and I couldn't see it for ages. I mean, I know, I'm not saying you and Ash were the same, but…' This is hard. Facing up to the truth always is. I know now that I need to break every tie with Teddy and even Ben, and I'm ready to. And Georgina needs to face up to the truth in her own life. 'You don't need Ash, splitting up doesn't make you look bad, you're brilliant, you're doing ace at what you do.' I shake my head. 'You don't need him, Georgina. Really. I'm sorry if we, well, you know, but I thought it was over between the two of you.'

'It is,' Ash says softly.

'You know what? You're right. I don't need either of you, I'm better off on my own. I'm happy!' It's obvious she isn't; her mouth is trembling and her eyes are glistening. But I don't know her, she's not a friend, I can't wrap my arms around her and tell her it will all work out. For a start she might hit me.

'I'm moving somewhere civilised where you don't get bloody ramblers and all this frigging water.' She takes a step back. 'With Romeo!' She glares at Ash. 'You said I could have this place for two more weeks. To myself! Don't you dare shag her while I'm here!'

'Georgie.' He sighs.

'Oh, I am so over you, so over this place.' Georgina pushes past. 'I'm going to bed!'

'Night,' I say weakly. I feel awful.

We listen to her stomping her way up the stairs. Her door slams shut. The silence seems bigger than ever after all the noise, the shouting, the bad feeling. I finally dare look Ash's way, and we share a guilty look.

'Oh God, I'm so sorry you had to hear all that, I was really trying to avoid a scene like this. I had no idea she'd turn up.' He runs his fingers through his hair looking agitated. 'If I'd have got here at lunchtime like I was supposed to, before she'd hit the wine...' Our gazes meet. 'I never apologised, somebody lost their dog up on the fells and we wanted to find it before it got dark. Then I never thought to phone ahead, I just wanted to get here. See you.'

'Did you find the dog?' I ask softly. It's easier to ask about that, than to ask if he really means he rushed back because he missed me.

Ash nods. 'Don't feel you have to go.' He rests his hand on my arm.

How can I not feel that I have to go?

'Did you really not know about Romeo?'

369

He stares at me blankly. 'Romeo?'

'You know.' I reach for my phone. 'On Instagram.'

We both stare at the picture. She's not uploaded the one of him cuddling it yet.

'Don't see many of them on the Cumbrian fells,' he says.

'True.' We swap a smile, but I feel sad. 'I'll go tomorrow.'

'One last walk with me and Bella in the morning?'

'I'd like that. Ash?'

'Mm?'

I frown. 'She's got a photo of you, holding Romeo. I saw it. I don't get it.'

'Ever heard of Photoshop?' He takes my hand, leads me back onto the terrace and pulls me onto his lap, then takes his own mobile phone out.

We sit in silence as he scrolls through. The light upstairs clicks off, and there's only the moon left to streak across the lake, a searchlight in the dark.

'Was the photo like this?' He's got a quirky grin on his face.

'Like that.' It looks just the same, but there's a baby Bella cupped in his hands. He looks so happy that it brings a lump to my chest.

This was why she hadn't uploaded the photo. It wasn't for the wider world, for her Insta audience – it was for me. She'd been warning me off.

'She said you were angry when you came back home for good, demanding, asked me if I'd seen you in a temper.'

'I was lots of things when I came back. Mainly frustrated and unhappy, angry at myself, but I've never really had much of a temper. Did she actually say I did?'

I close my eyes, rest my head against his chest and think. 'She said she bet I hadn't seen you in one.'

'She's clever.' I can feel his smile against my hair. 'She always did have a way of saying things that makes you jump to the wrong conclusion. She was nice once, is nice, really, you know. Lovely. We worked for a while. Don't think she's all bad. She's just angry at the world, at me, she's used to things going her own way.' He sighs. 'We just weren't good for each other anymore and somebody had to say it.'

'It's hard sometimes to actually do it.'

'It is. It's hard sometimes to see it. But we all just do our best, don't we?'

'She'll probably thank you one day.'

He laughs, a short laugh, but it isn't harsh, just slightly disbelieving. 'I don't think we'll hold our breaths on that one, eh? I suppose I better go, it's not fair on her, knowing I'm here.'

'I guess so.' I struggle to my feet. 'Where's Bella? Are you going to take her?'

'I might as well, before Georgina changes her mind! Bella!' he calls softly.

There's no answering bark, or bundle of black fluff hurtling out of the house.

'Strange.' Bella always comes the moment he calls.

He frowns. 'She's not been outside with us at all, now I come to think of it.'

'I've not actually seen her since she hid under the table.' I've not seen her since he yelled at Georgina. Bella doesn't like conflict, upset. She's sensitive.

'I'll check she's not locked in the kitchen or something.'

'I'll check upstairs, she might have gone to bed.' I'm running up the stairs as I speak, trying to be as quiet as I can so I don't disturb Georgina. I couldn't stand another outburst.

I'm slightly worried, but sure she'll be curled up on the pillow with one of her toys as a comfort blanket. Or hiding curled up in a corner.

She isn't. I check everywhere, and as Georgie's bedroom door is ajar I even risk peering round it as I hold my breath.

I scramble down the stairs just as Ash comes in through the back door. 'Ash.' I grab his arm, can feel my heart pounding in my chest and that creeping feeling of panic. 'Georgina isn't in her room!'

His lips are pursed in a smile that is the opposite of funny. 'Her car's gone.' He strides past me, to the bowl where we throw our keys. 'She's gone.'

Chapter Twenty-Five

I can't believe it. I've spent the last few weeks guarding Bella against a dog-napping from Ash, and now that we've finally sorted things out – Georgina has taken her! This is like some madcap movie where you don't realise you've mistaken the bad guy (or girl) for the good one all along.

'What are we going to do, Ash?' I'm all fidgety and can't stand still. He looks at me blankly for a moment, it's his thinking face. Then he focuses back on me.

'She's mad.'

'You're telling me!'

'She's drunk. She was totally wasted, and she's gone off in her car.' He rubs his eyes with the heels of his hands. 'I can't believe even Georgie would be that stupid, I mean there's winning and there's being fucking stupid. She'll kill herself, or somebody else.'

'You think we should go after her? But we don't know how long—'

373

'I'll try calling her.' He fishes his phone out of his pocket. 'She'll answer, just so she can gloat.' He starts to press keys, when the mobile springs into life. 'Georgie! What the hell do you think you're playing at?'

There's a strangled wailing sound, that stops him short. Then sobs.

They carry clearly.

'Ash, Ash come and help me.' He holds the phone away from his ear, so I can hear. Though it's hard not to, the way she's yelling and blubbing. 'I couldn't stay there, I just couldn't, I… you… I ran into the hedge.'

'Are you okay?'

'My fucking car's all scratched, I just got it washed.' The sobs seem to be mixed with hiccups.

'Well, at least she's alright,' I stage-whisper.

'I'm not alright!' she wails. 'I just got this frigging car valeted! What will Romeo's people think if I turn up with a scratched, muddy car? What will they fucking think of me? I'm some sort of, sort of…' Her voice is getting louder, and this time Ash holds it even further away from his ear to save his hearing – not for my benefit. 'They might not let me have him!'

'Georgina, listen to me. Just listen to me.' His voice is so calm and even, I want to listen to him even if she doesn't. It's soothing. 'It will all be okay, we can get the car pulled out of the ditch and washed, okay?'

'By lunchtime?' There's a smaller sob.

'By lunchtime.'

There are a few sniffles. 'Will you come Ash?' It's a plaintive little-girl voice.

'You aren't hurt?'

'No.' A bigger sniff. 'I snapped a nail though and I only just got them done.'

He shakes his head. 'Oh Georgie, what were you thinking driving off like that? Where were you going?'

'To a hotel. I needed to get away.' She snuffles.

'Right, tell me exactly where you are, and I'll get you a taxi.'

She mentions a junction with a lane a couple of miles away. 'I want you.' There's a simper and a lot of feeling sorry for herself in her voice. 'Pwease Ashley.' Oh God, baby talk.

He rolls his eyes, but his voice is still soft. 'I've been drinking Georgie, I can't drive.' There's a long pause. 'Is Bella okay as well?'

'How do I know if Bella is okay? All you care about is that—'

He puts his phone down on the table, and lets her rant on, then when she runs out of steam, he very gently presses the end-call button.

'I'll call her a taxi, then I'll go and get Sam. He'll find Bella.' He meets my gaze. 'I think all the upset and shouting must have scared her, she might be a bit of a hooligan at times, but she's sensitive.'

I nod. Feeling empty and sad.

'Dogs are a hell of a lot easier to get on with than people though, aren't they?' He's got a funny, quirked smile. He's a bit sad as well.

'That's what I decided, it's why I came here to house- and pet-sit. It was Bella I was after!'

'And you walked into this.' He shrugs. 'Sorry.'

It is time for me to go home. I'll go on one last walk with Ash in the morning, like I promised. Then I need to sort out what to do next.

Coming here wasn't a mistake. I met Ash and it was lovely while it lasted, and he made me believe I can do this. And I met lovely little Bella. And I realised that there is no wrong path, just different routes. And I've finally mapped a new one out for myself. A new adventure.

It will be horrible without them at first, but I will survive. And maybe I can even survive at my parents' house until my own place is empty again.

Maybe not. I need to get back on my house-sitting site. Or borrow Ash's camper van.

'Come on then, boots on!'

'What?' I blink at him.

'You are coming with me, aren't you?' He holds out his hand and I just gawp, then slip my own in.

His is warm, big, safe.

'We'll find her. Promise.' I nod, blinking away the tears. 'We will.' He hugs me then. I'll tell him later that I'm not crying sad tears because I think we've lost Bella (though that would be horrendous), I'm crying happy tears because he said he wanted me to go with him. That he doesn't want to do *everything* on his own.

'Hang on.'

I'm locking the door when Ash holds his hand up.

'Shh.'

I freeze, as though moving a single muscle will make a noise.

'Come on.' He strides off, and I scurry after him.

'Where?' I pant out, this man can move fast when he wants to.

'I heard a noise, it could be squirrels, or rats, but—'

'Rats!' I grind to a halt, trying to grab his arm to stop him doing whatever he intends to. 'You can count me out if this involves rats!'

He chuckles and I grin, despite the threat of rats. Then he throws the shed door open, and a black bullet bolts out and nearly knocks me off my feet.

'Bella!' She belts around the garden at top speed, narrowly missing plant pots and us, then leaps – all four paws off the ground – at Ash, leaving sooty pawprints, and is off again before he can catch hold of her.

He grins, his dimples back. Oh boy, I'll miss those dimples. 'It's the coal shed.' He chuckles. 'The silly bugger must have somehow got in, and the door shut behind her! She used to do stuff like that all the time. Oh Bella, you loony!'

The loony is still racing around.

I didn't think it was possible for a black dog to be any blacker, but this one is.

The white patch on her chest is smeared with dirt and you can practically see the dust in her coat as she shakes, and then throws herself on the grass. Her once pink tummy is grey as she wriggles around rubbing her back into the soft green carpet.

I can't help it. I start to laugh. Ash joins in. We both sink to the ground and Bella leaps up and pounces on us.

Rubbing her grimy coat on our faces and hands.

Making me laugh even more.

So much that my ribs hurt.

I finally run out of giggles and we stare at each other. Bella has collapsed across Ash's knee, her tongue lolling out.

'I think we might need to go for a soak in the tub.' There's a naughty glimmer in Ash's eye.

He reaches out, strokes the back of his hand over my cheek and sets a tingle of want to the bits of my body that thought the party was over.

'Do you want me to stay?'

'That is the daftest question you have ever asked me.' My voice has a wobble, nothing to do with upset or tiredness, everything to do with lust and want.

'You're not too tired?' The corner of his mouth quirks up. 'Or drunk?'

I'm not tired. I want to kiss his dimples, lick the cleft in his chin, smells his skin.

He pulls me to my feet and we slowly saunter inside. I can't help myself; I keep sneaking glances his way and feel all awkward and bashful when I catch him doing the same.

I want to rush, not saunter. It is excruciatingly tantalising.

He pushes open the door.

Bella pushes past me.

The trail of footprints is startlingly black and smudgy against the floor, and there's a smear of black on the wall at dog height.

We can ignore it, can't we? Please, can't we?

She wags her tail and it's like the final brush strokes on a Turner seascape in the smog. A pollution special.

We can't leave her. She will paint the house black. Literally.

Ash twists his mouth in apology. 'I'll have to bath Bella first.'

I nod.

'And I need to pop back and get the bits from the camper so we can get off on our walk first thing tomorrow. Before you go?'

There's a question in his voice.

I don't want this conversation now. But I just can't afford to stay, I haven't got any money, I can't just rent somewhere in the village, or camp in the woods – I need space, light, internet... food. To stay and work.

'Talk about it later?' I try not to sound pleading.

'Sure.'

'I'll bath Bella, while you go and get your bits?'

He chuckles. 'From that comment, I take it you've never tried to bath this dog? Believe me, you need help.'

'How bad can it be?'

Very bad, it turns out. Bella loves water if it's in a stream, a beck, a river, a lake, even coming out of the flaming hosepipe – but not if it's in a bath or coming out of a showerhead.

Uh-huh. No way José.

I never knew a dog could wriggle so much or would be prepared to make a lunge over a person's shoulder or shake their coat vigorously so many times.

We are drenched by the time the water is running clear, no black dust in it.

'Maybe we just call it a day and I go to the camper first thing for the stuff?'

I think my eyes are shining. 'Yes!'

'Oh hell, just remembered, I've got Sam for the night.'

'You go and get him. I'll get ready!' I think I have a slightly dirty (and not in a coal way) smile on my face.

'Sure.' He grins back and kisses the tip of my nose. 'I'll be as quick as I can! Don't forget to wash behind your ears.'

'It's not my ears I'm thinking about.'

I cannot believe it. Totally CANNOT. For the second time in my all-too-brief stay here I have passed out before I have a chance to have sex with Ash.

It must have been the lovely warm water in the bath. Or the fact I'd polished off a lot of wine with Georgina. Or that I was far more tired and stressed by the day than I'd realised. But the moment I reclined back on the bed, perfecting my sexy pose in preparation, my eyes started to prickle. I reckoned I could rest them for five minutes then I'd be raring to go – bouncier than ever.

Didn't happen.

Ash somehow managed to get back, undress, climb into bed, check that Georgie was safe in an hotel, have a snog with Bella and wrap his arm round me without me even breaking out of my snore (according to him – but I don't snore, so I don't know if I believe all the rest).

I mean, how? Why? It shouldn't be possible to just *fall asleep* when you feel that randy. Should it?

'Come on, lazy bones, I've made coffee, we need to get going!'

Oh yes, and he got up and made coffee.

'But I want sex!'

'Later. Come on or I'll unleash the hounds!'

I prop myself up on my elbows and look at where he's motioned, towards the foot of the bed.

Bella and Sam are sat side by side, bolt upright, wagging their tails in anticipation.

'Oh God, you are kidding me?' I sink back on the pillows. 'You wouldn't dare.'

I swear all he does is raise an eyebrow, but they both launch themselves up and are on top of me. Bella lands fair and square on my stomach, Sam on my boobs.

'You sod!' It is a mistake opening my mouth to talk, Bella's tongue is straight in there. Or it would have been if I hadn't shut up quick.

He chuckles, reminding me of what I missed out on last night. 'I know you love me really!'

He's heading back downstairs before I get a chance to answer. But as I shoo the dogs off the bed and clamber out, I know it was just a glib jokey comment, but it makes me smile. It makes me sing (badly) in the shower and makes me think that today is going to be okay.

Chapter Twenty-Six

'Is this what being on top of the world means?' I glance out of the corner of my eye at Ash. We are sitting on the rough grass, elbows on our knees, staring at the scenery that stretches out below us.

'It does.' He grins. 'So, does Angletarn Pikes live up to your expectations? I know you were disappointed about not making it up here with Bella, and I wanted you to see it.' He doesn't add 'before you go'. It hangs unspoken in the air between us.

It is too good a moment to spoil with thoughts like that though.

'It's one of my favourite places, you can't beat the view from up here.' He scoots closer to me, drapes one arm over my shoulder, points out landmarks with his free hand. I try to pay attention, but I'm just enjoying the sound of his voice, the weight of his arm, the warmth of his body against mine.

I want to smell him, feel him, make the most of what I've got before I lose it.

Sam and Bella are stretched out in the sun side by side. Sam's gold coat is lit up by the sun so that it gleams, Bella's black coat as dark as the coal she rolled in yesterday – but highlighted by the streaks of light.

We share the flask of coffee he's got in his rucksack, as well as the silence, until the wind picks up a bit and my bum starts to go numb. He notices I've started to wriggle a bit.

'Come on, I've got to show you Angle Tarn. The best bit! We can eat our picnic down there.' He grabs my hand, hauls me to my feet and whistles the dogs so we can set off. This time it's easier. Downhill, not up.

I can't believe it though as the ground levels out, and we get closer to the tarn.

'There's a tent!' I point, slightly disappointed. 'I thought we'd have the place to ourselves.' After that bloody slog of a walk, I was certainly hoping we were actually 'getting away from it', I wasn't expecting rambler company. I was expecting a romantic picnic for two. Why is life never quite as perfect as it is in the movies?

He smiles, his eyes all twinkly and wrinkled at the corners. 'It's not just any tent!'

'What?'

He winks, takes my hand in his and draws me towards it.

'You can't just gate-crash somebody else's tent, they might be, er, busy in there!'

'I can gate-crash my own tent. I was thinking maybe it

was us that could get busy in there.' His grin broadens. 'Seeing as you went to sleep on me again! Bloody hell woman, you're giving me a complex, all this fainting and sleeping stuff to avoid actually snogging me!'

'Your tent?' He nods. 'You've lugged a flaming heavy tent all the way up here, just for a snog!' Oh my God, there are some things this man does that make me love him more than I thought possible.

'Well, I was hoping my manliness might earn more than just a snog.' He looks boyishly endearing. 'And I have to admit to having a bit of help from friends to get this kit up here.'

'Chancer.' I shake my head but can't keep a straight face.

The smile fades from his face. 'I thought maybe we could stay the night here.' He pulls the flap of the tent back.

'Two dogs and a tiny tent.' I shake my head and laugh. 'You really do believe in testing things out, don't you?'

'The accommodation might be a bit crap, but I can promise you it will be amazing.' He's studying me intently. 'Spectacular stars, a dawn you'll never forget. Red deer and maybe the odd falcon, if you're quiet.'

'The being quiet bit might be a challenge.'

We share a smile. 'I wanted it to be different. Special. Like you.'

I reach out, touch his face and he lifts his own hand up to cover mine. He kisses my knuckles. He turns my hand over, kisses the palm, the warmth of his mouth sending a shiver through my body.

Then he puts his other hand on my waist and draws me close, pressing his body against mine.

This time I understand what 'making love' means. This isn't a quick shag, or mad passion. Or uncontainable lust.

This is slow, languorous, so teasing and touching that it leaves me trembling with want – but I don't want to urge him on faster because I want to savour every single second.

His mouth is hot, but his lips soft and gentle as he kisses his way down my body, peeling my top over my head. He kisses my chest, between my breasts, leaving a trail down my stomach until he is kneeling in front of me, holding my waist, his thumbs rubbing tantalising circles that make me gasp.

I tangle my fingers in his hair. Close my eyes. Feel the need build as he kisses my inner thighs, as his hands move lower.

'Ash.' My voice sounds strange to my ears, seems to blend with the wind as I press against him. Nothing else seems to exist. Nothing else is important. All I can feel is his touch, his warm body. All I can see are his eyes as he lays me down beneath him.

'Oh, Beck.' One hand holds my wrists, the weight of his body presses against me. For a moment, time stands still as our gazes lock.

'Please.'

His mouth joins with mine at the same time as he enters me.

His groan mingles with my gasp as I arch up.

I'm unfurling inside, scared but unable to stop. Losing myself to him. Giving a part of myself away that I didn't know I had.

Afterwards I cling to him, waiting for the world to come back.

———————

When the sky darkens, he pulls a blanket onto the grass and takes a bottle of wine and glasses from the corner of the tent.

'Flipping heck, you've planned everything!'

'With military precision.' He pours us a drink each and settles down beside me. 'Including the bit where we make love under the stars, in—' he looks at his watch '—two hours and thirteen minutes' time.'

I mock punch his arm. 'You have to be kidding, you're trying to finish me off!' He chuckles and I grin back. I think actually it's me that's doing the kidding. If he touches me again, I won't be able to say no, and he knows it.

Bella crawls onto the rug, feeling left out, and I fondle her ears.

'Ash?'

'Sounds ominous when you say my name like that!'

'Why did you leave the Marines?'

'Ahh, that one. Complicated.'

'Try me. I'm smarter than I look!' I pull a goofy face.

He chuckles. 'Complicated for me to get it out, not for you to understand.' He sits up, his forearms propped on his knees. 'There were loads of factors I guess; I'd been thinking about it for a while. Leaving.' I nod. 'It's not something I wanted to do into old age.' The corner of his mouth quirks up into the semblance of a smile. 'And I missed this place. I bought the place in the village so I could be near my grandparents really, keep an eye on them, then I realised if I didn't do something it would be too late. My nan had Alzheimer's. In the early days I'd come home and put the changes down to old age, the things she'd forgotten, the way she'd tell me the same thing over and over.' I sit up, so we're thigh to thigh, and he puts his hand on my knee.

'Then the next time I came home it was more noticeable. She started getting confused, doing things she wouldn't normally, forgetting things I'd just told her as well as things she'd told me. It was like losing her, cell by cell. Memory by memory as though it was draining her, her whole life was drifting away bit by bit. It's like a horror movie you know, the way a person is wiped away and you can't do a damned thing about it. Then she'd have days when she was really low.' He carries on talking, monotone, and I let him.

'He knew of course, Gramps, he'd known for ages but didn't want to upset me.' The smile lifts and drops again, like my heart. I link my arm round his broad back and hug in close. 'Funny, old people, aren't they? How they try and protect us, even when shit like that is going down?'

'I guess they always feel like they're the ones protecting us. They don't want to burden us, it's supposed to be the other way round in their heads.'

'They'd gone to doctors, hospitals, they had support and he kept telling me they'd be fine, not to screw up my career and come home, but I had to. I had to come back for them.'

His gaze meets mine. His sea-blue eyes are like a young boy's, hurt and helpless. I guess for somebody like Ash, used to talking control and putting things right, it must have been a total nightmare. I wrap my other arm round him, hug hard, rest my head against his arm.

'I was too late.' His voice is expressionless. 'The day before I was due home, I got a call; there'd been an accident. They'd both been killed.'

'Oh Ash.' I hug tighter.

'Dodgy brakes on the car they said, old car, not been serviced for ages.' There's a wobble in his voice. 'Gramps never had dodgy brakes, he used to be a mechanical engineer, he serviced it himself. He always told me that if you find the right person, you'll never want to spend another second of your life without them, and Nan was his other person.' He gazes straight into my eyes again then.

'He'd left all his papers in order, even put clean sheets on the bed that morning. Shut every window, even though they usually left a couple open to air the place.' He smiles, a gentle smile. 'He'd left a bottle of good wine and a glass on the desk by the window. He told me to take it down to the lake, row Ginny out and remember that there's a right time for everything and that the hardest winters clear out the old and make way for the rest to flourish.'

I bite my bottom lip hard and try to hold back the tears. 'We used to go down to the boathouse together, he loved the view from there. When I was a kid, he'd plonk me on his knee and point out all the peaks to me one by one, tell me which order we had to climb them in together. We never did manage to do the last two.'

'You should climb them, for him.'

'I should.' He squeezes my hand and it is like he's

squeezing my heart. A lump blocks my throat and my eyelids tingle. I just want to hug him hard, and never let go.

How could Georgina have knocked that boathouse down?

Bella wanders over, licks my hand, then his, then settles again as though she's reassured that everything is okay.

'This was never just about getting a dog back because your name was on the papers, was it?'

'Hell no.' His voice is rough-edged in my ear. 'She's always been more than just a dog. I love her to bits, it was about love, and loyalty and doing the right thing. Always.'

'But I don't get why you left Bella with Georgina in the first place, let her have her.'

'I didn't. I said she could honour her commitments, do a few shoots. That's all it was supposed to be. And we never agreed she could stay here while Georgie swanned off, that was just her having a go at me, taking advantage. I'd come to pick her up the day you arrived.'

'Then you got here, to find me.'

He grins. 'I didn't expect that! A gorgeous woman, all English rose complexion, pink cheeks and beautiful eyes fighting like a she-cat protecting her kittens!'

'I'm not like a she-cat!'

'As protective as one.' He chuckles, then kisses my lips gently. He tastes of the rich, ruby-red wine. Warm and delicious. 'That's one of the things I love about you.'

'Just one?' I feel warm, content. Safe. I feel for the first time in my life that I don't have to question what sounds like a compliment. I can take it and cherish it.

He said he loved something about me.

'That and the way you'll try anything, the way you never give up, the way you're just you.' He kisses me again. 'You were a bit of a shock to be honest, and I wasn't going to launch into a full-blown row with Georgie when you'd only just arrived. She was counting on that, I reckon.'

I smile.

'Then it got even worse when I found you all sexy in your pyjamas and slippers rolling around on the damp grass! Irresistible.'

'I was not rolling around!' I punch him gently. 'Take that back.'

'Not the bit about you being irresistible.' He shakes his head ruefully. 'It was all downhill from there.'

'What does that mean?'

'I rang her up and agreed she could keep Bella until she got home.'

'Why?'

'It was a way of seeing you. I couldn't stay away... even if you did think I was just being sneaky to get Bella.'

'It was a way of seeing me?'

'Yeah. And I didn't want to upset you, when you came all this way to dog-sit. Wouldn't be the same without a dog, would it? You'd have been a bit redundant!'

'Hang on. Can we go back a bit, just so I can check. You didn't insist on having Bella back, because you wanted to see *me*?'

'I couldn't help myself. I think you're some kind of witch who has risen out of the lake to bewitch me!'

'So all the time I was trying to protect Bella from you, you weren't going to steal her anyway?'

He chuckles, his dimples deep. 'Something like that.'

'You sod!'

'So you came here to change, a new start?' His voice suddenly has a serious edge.

'Well no, I came here to clear my head. I'd got a bit stuck and a change of scene always inspires me, though I did think there'd be less drama here!'

'Didn't want you getting bored!'

'Haha. Seriously, I didn't come here thinking I *could* change, but this place has got under my skin. And so has Bella.' We share a smile. He definitely gets that bit. 'I got up every morning wanting to work, and I realised just how far I'd drifted from what I really wanted to do. You know what?' I'm a bit surprised how suddenly it is so *clear*, so obvious, in my head. 'I wasn't allowing myself to be me, I'd got so caught up trying to fit other people's expectations, trying to please other people like Teddy, trying to be closer to what I thought my family wanted me to be. How shit is that?'

'But?' His voice is soft.

'I realised when they all came over, that they only want me to be happy.' I grin. 'That, and self-sufficient. Mum obviously doesn't want me and my dirty washing, and a mucky dog gate-crashing her tidy house! But mainly she wants me to be happy.' I shrug. 'They are proud of me.'

'They are, I am. I was such a stupid twat though. When I saw him, I just saw red, a different you. I'd kind of fallen for the you that had dropped into my life.' I love hearing him say he fell for me, I could get used to that. 'And here you were saying you wanted to reinvent yourself, not be the real you.' He sighs. 'I'm such a stupid twat, of course people can change for the better as well as the worse.' He strokes his hand with the lightest of touches down my side, pausing at my waist and sending little shivers of anticipation through me. 'Although, it's just about finding out who you are, isn't it?'

I try and ignore the squirmy feeling of need building up inside me.

'Come here, woman. I want to learn more about the real Becky, and not the one who talks a lot.'

It is the soft early morning light that wakes me, as it filters its way in through the open flap of the tent. I open my mouth to call Ash, and a shadow falls across the opening.

He puts his finger to his lips, motions me to come closer.

There are deer only a few yards away, near the edge of the tarn.

I don't want to reach for my phone to capture them, to risk startling them and changing everything, it doesn't matter. It's just beautiful to see them. To lie here, with only the sound of our breathing breaking the silence.

One of the deer lifts its head, half turns, alert. It watches us for a moment, then casually retreats through the bracken, moving gracefully up the hillside, the others following behind. When I glance up, a broad smile on my face, Ash is watching me, which makes me blush.

'Shouldn't you be watching the wildlife?'

'I've seen it lots of times, I'm more interested in the great crested Becs!'

'Oh gawd, is my hair sticking up that badly?'

He laughs as I pat it down, then ruffles it back up with his big hand.

'Thanks for bringing me here.' I break our gaze for a moment and look out again at the scene in front of me. Rough and rugged, but wonderful. There's still a morning dampness in the air, touching the ground with dew, skimming the tarn with the lightest of mists.

Magical. I breath it in, trying to capture something of the place inside me, hoping I can hold the image in my head. There's something wild about it, untamed. Like the man in front of me. He blends in here; I could never imagine him anywhere else.

'You're welcome. Coffee?'

There's a lot to be said for having your own Bear Grylls at hand. 'Wow, how did you do that? And wow, I can smell bacon sandwiches! Tell me you've got bacon and I'm not imagining it! Where's the fire?'

'I've got bacon. Afraid I settled for a camping stove and meat from the corner shop in the village. Thought I'd keep my stick lighting, rabbit hunting surprises for next time.'

'There's going to be a next time?'

He crouches down. 'If you fancy it? I thought we could tackle those two crags I never did with Gramps.'

I take the sandwich. 'I'd love to come back. I'll be sad to leave this place.' I study him, his cheekbones, clefted strong chin, unfairly thick and dark eyelashes. 'And you.' Is it bad to voice it? Too soon, or just the right time? But it doesn't matter, does it? He can brush me off, but I'll be leaving anyway. I might as well be brave.

'I'll miss you too.' He smiles and touches my cheek with the back of his hand gently. Not a dog-napper at all, or a scary ex who will murder me in my bed. 'You could always stay you know. No pressure.'

'I can't afford—'

'I know of a nice camper van that's empty right now.'

'Hot and cold running water? High speed broadband? Proper toilet?'

'Not quite.' He hunkers down beside me, takes a sip of coffee, smiles. 'Just trees, the sound of running water, birds…'

'Sounds perfect.' I pause. 'Apart from the toilet. I'm a bit of a proper-bathroom kind of girl if I'm honest. Talking of which…' I look around and grimace.

Even paradise isn't perfect.

Chapter Twenty-Seven

'Thanks.' His deep voice oozes over the distance and for a moment I just let myself listen. I've only been gone a couple of hours, but it feels like much longer. It feels like I'm driving in the wrong direction. I shouldn't be leaving.

'Thanks for what?' I think I know, but I want to be sure.

'For the painting.'

I smile. 'I painted it for you.' I love that painting; I really had painted it from the heart. But at the time, I hadn't realised that the heart of it was Ash. So, I'd wrapped it up and added a note.

I can't give you the boathouse back, but I can give you this, Becky x

'Where are you now?'

'About sixty miles up the road from you!'

'Where will you head, Becs?'

'Daniel's, my brother's.' Before the party I'd thought that idea was completely alien, but you know what? He's okay. He's my brother, not some fancy-pants barrister. He doesn't think he's better than me, he knows we're just different.

It's weird how things work out, isn't it? I came to Cumbria to escape, and for inspiration. And I've realised that inspiration doesn't come from moving into other people's (often messy) lives, it's about finding my own perfect place. Finding a me I'm happy with.

'It's not so bad, but just for now, and then when my house-sitter goes I guess I'll go home. Or…' I pause. 'You probably think I'm crazy, but I might just go for it again.'

'What?'

'House-sitting!'

'You don't have to, you know.'

'I like house-sitting!' I pull over into a layby so that I can unclip the phone from my hand-free set and hold him closer.

'I meant you don't have to leave this place. If you didn't want to…'

Oh I don't, I really don't. 'I know. But it's so bloody expensive, Ash. I'd never be able to afford a place there.'

There's a long pause. 'I know you dissed my camper…'

'I did not diss it! It's gorgeous.'

'But lacking in facilities! But anyway, forgetting that, I've heard there's a nice flat for rent, above the art shop, kind of fitting? It's reasonable rates. I know the landlord, he's a good sort.'

'Short term?'

'He prefers long, but he'd settle for anything.'

'Desperate then?'

'Pretty much.'

It suddenly dawns on me. 'Is this landlord an ex-Marine?'

'Maybe.'

'We're talking about you here?'

'We could be.' He sounds uncertain, the first time I've ever heard a note of hesitancy in his voice. 'You can have it really cheap, if you want, that is, I don't want to pressure you… no strings, but…'

'Oh, I was hoping there might be strings.'

'Strings there if you want them.' There's a long pause. 'I'd like to see you; I'd like you to be here. I want more than just seeing you for a day trip.'

'I'd like to be there, Ash. Very cheap?'

'Very, if you agree to dog walk now and then.'

'Well…'

'With the owner. He likes company.'

'He does?'

'He does. If it's the right company.'

The happy feeling bubbles up inside me, breaks out into a grin on my face. I stare out of the windscreen, smiling, then realise he can't see me. Doesn't know what I'm thinking.

I love the place, it's the first place I've truly felt at home. And I like Ash. A lot.

I wanted to spend more time together, and not the kind of time where you're counting the minutes away until you need to go.

'I wouldn't want to pressure you coming back here if it isn't your kind of place. I wouldn't want you to do it just because…'

'It is my kind of place, Ash.' I take a deep breath. 'You know what? I like the sound of that!' In for a penny, in for a pound, as Mum has been known to say. 'I'll need to go back, pack the rest of my art gear.'

'There's more?' He chuckles.

'Lots more!' I want to spin the car around right now. Well, why not? What's stopping me? I'm free – I can do whatever I want to do! 'I could come back now, sort terms with my new landlord, then go back and clear my flat out when the sitter moves out? Oh hang on a sec, I've got a call coming in – can I ring you back in a sec?'

I don't normally answer when I don't recognise a number, but something in my gut tells me to pick up on this one. Well, my gut and the fact it's a London number.

'Becky? I hope you don't mind me ringing, it's Rosie Histon, I'm—'

'Oh hi!' Oh my God, it's Rosie Histon. She's not about to tell me that her lovely author, of the *Mischief* books, has had a change of mind? Gone into early retirement, or something? 'Is, er, everything…?'

'I'm sure you know what a massive fan of yours I am, those illustrations you've done are so perfect they made me cry!'

'Oh. Er. Thank you.' Wow!

'They're totally amazing, you're just so talented! I bet your ears were burning yesterday, you were the hot topic of convo over lunch because one of my other authors loves your work so much we decided to ask her publisher if they'd approach you.'

'Wow, that's lovely, thanks! You've no idea how happy —' A tractor goes by, sending a shower of straw through my open car window, but this time I hardly notice it. I'm much more used to country smells now.

'Anyway, long story short, they said they'd been after you for ages, but Teddy had always told them that you weren't available?'

Bloody Teddy!

'But I'd heard on the grapevine that you and he...' She leaves that hanging. 'So I wondered if things had changed, if you could squeeze us in?'

'Oh my God I'd love to! Well, love to talk, yes, I mean I do have some free time, but I am quite picky about only doing stuff that suits my style.'

'I totally get that! Cool! Okay if I pass that on and they get in touch? I'll message you my details and the publisher's then, if you want a chat, or if you'd like to meet the author. She is so in awe of you, she'd be totally made up if you could do it!'

A text pings in seconds after she hangs up.

I could kill Teddy. This is a publisher I adore. A major publisher with a catalogue of books with the most stunning covers and illustrations.

And Teddy told them I was unavailable. What right did he have? Except it doesn't matter now. I'm not going to let him have even one more second of my life.

They wanted me before. They thought I was good enough. And I am.

I smile as I redial Ash.

The flat is perfect, and like Ash said, it's kind of fitting living above the art shop. I get to have an occasional coffee and chat with David and check out the new artists he's discovered.

I stayed with Ash for a week in Lake View Cottage, and then headed home to my flat. I'd thought I might feel sad clearing out the place, the first place that had been 'mine'. But I wasn't at all. It had never really been home. It was too close to Teddy, and too full of memories of doing the wrong things for the wrong reasons. The negative side of my life.

Abby helped me move stuff. She insisted. And we promised to see more of each other. Like sisters should. Well, let's face it, she is now SO jealous of me dating the sexiest man on the planet, and living in the most beautiful place in the world, so we kind of feel on more of a level footing. Not that we need to be, that bit is a joke. I know now, deep inside me, that I'm doing the right thing – and because I believe in me a little bit more, I can see that everybody else does as well. They always did.

I pick up my mobile phone as it pings with an incoming message, and it opens on the Insta account I'd been looking at earlier. Georgina's. Somebody else who I think is now doing the right thing.

Her latest photo is a real family pic, though there are three of them, not the four she'd been posting about the last time I saw her. But this, for once, seems to be reality. There's a man (in fact he's in lots, practically all, of the recent photos) and this definitely isn't a snatched, secret shot – he's a willing participant. He's got the tiny puppy under one arm, and his other is draped around Georgie's shoulder. He's smiling at the camera, a proper relaxed smile, and Georgie is glancing up at him. She looks genuinely happy. Besotted, if I'm honest.

You could almost take it for a candid, spur of the moment, shot. Though of course the logo of a well-known clothing brand is prominently displayed on her boob (framed by his fingers so that it can't be missed), and the puppy has a designer collar on, and there are six trillion hashtags. But hey, so what, she's happy. It's what she does, and I'm pleased for her. She's found her own real best-life, with hopefully the right guy for her this time.

But I am dating the sexiest man *evah*. And I totally love my little flat, and the way I can sit on the balcony and people watch for hours as all the tourists and locals mingle in the narrow street below. Not that I'm at the flat that much. When I'm not at my desk I'm out on the fells with Ash and Bella, or sometimes just with Bella, or sometimes there's just me and my sketch pad for company.

And quite a lot of the rest of the time I'm here, at Lake View Cottage, admiring Ash and his stone-walling mate as they build the new boathouse at the bottom of the garden.

It's going to be amazing.

Author's Note

This is the first of my stories that has been set in the Lake District, and I don't know why it has taken me so long! Like Becky, my lovely heroine, I enjoyed lots of fabulous holidays in Cumbria as a child and have returned as an adult (in a campervan and with my husband and Harry the dog by my side) to rediscover it again.

The location of the cottage that Becky stays in, and the village, are fictional but based upon some of the wonderful places I've spent happy times in – Grasmere, Coniston and Lake Windermere to name just three. The steep climbs and wonderful views were inspired by a walk (or should that be stagger?) up the Old Man of Coniston, the gingerbread and spot where Becky sits to savour hers are inspired by the lovely village of Grasmere, the woodland walk where she sees the kingfisher is inspired by Aira Force near Ullswater, and the spot where Becky camps under the stars is indeed the real place named in the book!

If you're familiar with the area, you may realise that I

have taken liberties with the amazing Grasmere Gingerbread and made it available in my fictional setting, it can actually only be bought at The Grasmere Gingerbread Shop, and a limited number of shops, or online at www.grasmeregingerbread.co.uk. If you find yourself near Grasmere, and like ginger (as I do!), then I strongly recommend you pop into the cute little shop and buy some – it's like no gingerbread you have ever tasted before, and is amazing!

I hope you enjoyed Becky's adventures!

Acknowledgments

My thanks as always to the inspirational Charlotte Ledger. Your ideas, enthusiasm, support, instinct for a good story and ability to be encouraging and yet critical in the best possible way make you one of a kind. Thank you so much for working with me – I find it hard to believe this is our fifteenth book together!

To my fabulous editor Emily Ruston, thank you once again for helping me make this book so much better than it was at the start. I couldn't hope for anyone better to guide me along that rocky road of turning a rough draft into the final version.

And Amanda Preston, my agent, you answer every cry for help, make me smile, laugh, inspire me and always give the best advice and support.

My thanks too to the rest of the amazing OMC team, and to the fabulous cover designer. I fell in love with the design the moment I saw it!

I'd also like to thank the lovely Heather Gibbs, a

fabulous dog trainer and friend, whose amazing little dog Sam sneaks into the story to save the day.

Big thanks as well to you. Whether you're one of the people I chat to on social media, a reviewer, somebody who has read all my books, or whether this is the first one you have picked up – thank you, I hope you enjoyed the story!

ONE MORE CHAPTER

One More Chapter is an award-winning global division of HarperCollins.

Sign up to our newsletter to get our latest eBook deals and stay up to date with our weekly Book Club! <u>Subscribe here.</u>

Meet the team at <u>www.onemorechapter.com</u>

Follow us!

 <u>@OneMoreChapter_</u>

 <u>@OneMoreChapter</u>

🄾 <u>@onemorechapterhc</u>

Do you write unputdownable fiction? We love to hear from new voices. Find out how to submit your novel at <u>www.onemorechapter.com/submissions</u>